CW00712981

Praise for *The Violet Hour*

'James Cahill gets better and better. I really loved *The Violet Hour*, trying, and failing, to ration myself rather than reading in a greedy rush. Its evocation of the wonders of art and the dehumanising horrors of the art industry are spot on, of course, but as a novelist what I really admired was his narrative structure and sly choreography of his principal characters. On one level it functions as a highbrow whodunnit, and grippingly so, but it's much more than that, building into a meditation on mortality and the unreliable consolations of art, love and materialism. I can't wait to see what he does next'

Patrick Gale, author of *A Place Called Winter*

'James Cahill has done it again. *The Violet Hour* is a thrilling story told in seductive, shimmering prose. Beauty, money, power, seduction, betrayal. It's all here in this bewitching and all too often troubling backstage pass to the commercial art world'

Chloë Ashby, author of *Wet Paint*

'Cahill allows us a private view of the art world in all its rancid glamour. The artist Thomas Haller – like Wilde's Dorian Gray – has sold his soul. As painters, gallerists and collectors move between New York and the Venice Biennale, auction houses and apartments hung with Mapplethorpes or Picassos, a reckoning is coming. Pulsing with violence and longing, this is a sumptuous, sinister morality tale'

Clare Pollard, author of *Delphi*

'A hugely enjoyable yarn by an author hitting his literary stride'

Sarah Lucas

'As sensuous and glimmering as it is dark and unsettling, *The Violet Hour* depicts the art world's many troubling facets . . . a pure delight'

Jenny Mustard, author of *Okay Days*

Praise for *Tiepolo Blue*

Shortlisted for the Authors' Club First Novel Award

'Divine . . . the smart, sexy read you need'
Evening Standard

'A novel that combines formal elegance with gripping story-telling . . . wildly enjoyable'
Financial Times

'Delicious unease and pervasive threat give this assured first novel great singularity and a kind of gothic edge . . . an electric new novel'
Guardian

'Standout . . . a coming-of-age tale set in London in the 1990s that deftly explores what it is like to suffer a very public fall from grace'
Independent

'*Tiepolo Blue* is about a buttoned-up art historian in Cambridge in 1994 who messes up and gets a job managing a London gallery just as the Young British Artists enter their glory. One of them initiates his unbuttoning which is dizzying and exciting and unsettling, and beautifully told'
Reverend Richard Coles, *Daily Mail*

'Arresting . . . a masterly attention to (especially visual) detail and an irresistibly propulsive, almost swaggering style'
Literary Review

'What starts off as a campus novel soon shades into something weirder and much more mesmerising . . . It's a measure of Cahill's sleight of hand that he manages to inject his plot with such page-turning momentum'
Times Literary Supplement

'Already a compelling psychosexual story about beauty, desire and art, *Tiepolo Blue* is all the more interesting because it hits notes of such strangeness'

Prospect, Fiction Books of the Year

'Startlingly impressive . . . A heavily perfumed, sexually tender, psychologically acute novel . . . as full of light and colour as Tiepolo's incandescent skies'

Daily Mail

'With touches of Alan Hollinghurst, the musings of the book's protagonist on the radical power of art to act as a catalyst for personal change make it an exhilarating, erudite read'

Vogue

'Interrogating beauty and meaning in art, *Tiepolo Blue* rewards rereading . . . a stylish tale of love and long-game revenge'

RA Magazine

'This is the best novel I have read for ages . . . it's just masterly . . . There is so much to enjoy, to contemplate, to wonder at, and to be lost in'

Stephen Fry

'The spirit of E. M. Forster is alive and well in James Cahill. The same palpating of damaged moral tissue, the same psychological canniness, the same gently invoked erudition, the same exactitude and eloquence – except Cahill is able to explore forbidden themes that Forster feared to touch on except posthumously'

Edmund White, author of *A Boy's Own Story*

James Cahill has worked in the art world and academia for fifteen years. His debut novel, *Tiepolo Blue*, was shortlisted for the Authors' Club Best First Novel Award, and his writing has been published in *Artforum*, the *Los Angeles Review of Books*, the *London Review of Books*, the *Spectator*, the *Times Literary Supplement* and the *Daily Telegraph*, among others. James divides his time between London and Los Angeles.

Also by James Cahill

Tiepolo Blue

James Cahill

The Violet Hour

Sceptre

First published in Great Britain in 2025 by Sceptre
An imprint of Hodder & Stoughton Limited
An Hachette UK company

1

Copyright © James Cahill 2025

The right of James Cahill to be identified as the
Author of the Work has been asserted by him in accordance
with the Copyright, Designs and Patents Act 1988.

All rights reserved. No part of this publication may be reproduced,
stored in a retrieval system, or transmitted, in any form or by any means
without the prior written permission of the publisher, nor be otherwise
circulated in any form of binding or cover other than that in which
it is published and without a similar condition being imposed
on the subsequent purchaser.

All characters in this publication are fictitious and any resemblance
to real persons, living or dead, is purely coincidental.

A CIP catalogue record for this title is available from the British Library

Hardback ISBN 9781399716185
Trade Paperback ISBN 9781399716192
ebook ISBN 9781399716215

Typeset in Sabon MT by
Palimpsest Book Production Ltd, Falkirk, Stirlingshire

Printed and bound in Great Britain by Clays Ltd, Elcograf S.p.A.

Hodder & Stoughton policy is to use papers that are natural, renewable
and recyclable products and made from wood grown in sustainable
forests. The logging and manufacturing processes are expected to
conform to the environmental regulations of the country of origin.

The authorised representative in the EEA is Hachette Ireland,
8 Castlecourt Centre, Dublin 15, D15 XTP3, Ireland
(email: info@hbgi.ie)

Hodder & Stoughton Limited
Carmelite House
50 Victoria Embankment
London EC4Y 0DZ

www.sceptrebooks.co.uk

For Maggi Hambling

PART I

I

5 September, 19.39. London

The evening was so still that it could have been a picture. If anyone had been watching from the neighbouring tower block, the scene might have resembled a panoramic painting. A modern-day Bruegel, only without the people. Or the final shot of a film – the deserted road below, the treetops and roofs, the dome of the Imperial War Museum, the sky turning lilac. Evening sunlight was catching the edges of things. A terrace of 1970s houses receded along one side of the road, meeting the vertical form of a Victorian water tower. Close to the top was a steel balcony, its outer corner a triangle of light.

A young man appeared on the balcony, disturbing the illusion. His lips motioned a phrase, as though he were addressing someone through the door. Stepping back, he glanced at the sky. Then he spread his hands on the railings and drew his body upwards, sitting on the ledge. Sunlight struck his face and the blank of his T-shirt. Everything was still again, without even a breeze to animate the plane trees on the road. Then, abruptly, he toppled back – his body separating from the building. His trainers scissored above him.

The sunlight had retreated from the patch of ground where he landed. His body lay motionless. Face down, with his arms outspread, he seemed to be floating on grey water. Only the fingertips of one hand reached into the light.

6 September, 06.52. New York

The toes of Leo J. Goffman tightened around the edge of the swimming pool. Contact with the water sent warning signals to his brain. At eighty-five, his nervous system was still in working order, he figured. The water was cold – so what was new?

As he braced himself for immersion, his eyes passed over the dark oblongs reflected on the surface – the doubles of the paintings hanging on either wall.

He lifted his gaze to the glass at the far end. On this Wednesday morning, the city was medieval-modern. The easterly facets promised a beautiful day. All of it lay ahead of him like an invitation, as if he might swim through Midtown, past the spires of the Chrysler and the Empire State, grazing the ziggurats of the 1930s.

His toes uncurled. He stepped into the water and coldness closed around his ankles. At his age, you had to break the shock of immersion into increments. He'd asked his architect for a tiered descent.

He took another step. Water clothed his legs, skimmed his testicles. He threw himself forward and the pool engulfed him. Eyes closed, he plunged into the deep, submitting to the familiar sensation. He surfaced with a gasp. The Thomas Haller paintings – tall abstractions in metallic grey – rose around him, a row of three on each side.

At the end of the pool, he planted both hands on the ceramic lip. New York lay below, overhung by the droplet of water beading at the end of his nose. His eyes tracked to the glass-plated towers of Hudson Yards, one of which – he squinted to extract it from the jostling pinnacles – was his.

*

Wrapped in a bathrobe, he took the elevator to the second floor of the apartment, which was the highest habitable floor of the

Pegasus Tower. He walked down the passageway towards the drawing room, calling as he went:

'Bonita! *Coffee.*'

Before he had crossed the threshold, he could see – across the room and through the glass – the park in all its late-summer magnificence, clumped with trees and enamelled by the reservoir. He paused in the doorway and attended to the nearer magnificence of the room: double-height, eighty feet by thirty, curtained by glass on three sides.

He trod in his slippers across the shagpile and conducted a survey of everything he knew was there. Sculptures stood in a grid formation; some on cherrywood plinths, others planted on the ground. Metal constructions, stone forms. *Unique forms* – that was the title of one of them, a cyborg cast from bronze.

At the centre of the room were three couches, islands of silver upholstery stationed around the walnut altar of a coffee table.

'Coffee!'

With chlorine still burning behind his eyeballs, he felt his strength redoubling. There was a gentle fire in his limbs. His eyesight was clear – as clear as the sky around him – and his brain, well, perhaps it was slower in its cogitations, but those additional microseconds could be useful. He was more judicious these days.

This last reflection brought with it the awareness of a blade of light at the periphery of his vision. It was as if the tip of a scalpel had been pulled across his retina. He held his legs stiff, not daring to move his eyes in case the fissure should tear open. Then he stepped back and the apparition vanished. The light had been the reflection of the sun on *Bird in Space* by Constantin Brancusi. The crescent of polished bronze stood endways on its plinth, appearing miraculously balanced.

Leo's focus jolted and he saw, reflected in the bronze, his housekeeper Bonita as she bent over the coffee table.

'What is it?'

'You asked for coffee, Mr Goffman.'

He turned and watched as she left the room, a small woman in a pinafore. Her hair was black and ringleted, belying her sixty years. Untying and retying the cord of his robe, he scanned the contents of the tray: chromium pot, porcelain cup, porcelain pitcher. Beside the tray was a copy of *Artforum*.

Sitting at the edge of a couch, he took the magazine between the tips of his fingers. He felt the smooth spine and the grooves of the pages. On the cover was something he couldn't compute, a mass of gold shavings. He began to flick through.

The magazine consisted mostly of adverts placed by commercial galleries, which was why he liked it. Not too much bullshit editorial.

Anselm Kiefer: New Paintings
Gagosian, 522 West 21st Street

'Well, that'll be the same arrant crap,' he said, as if someone were there and listening.

Donald Judd: Sculptures in Plywood
Carl Ammann, Zürich

'Boxes. Did that guy ever have more than one idea?'

As he flicked on, the back portion of his brain registered Bonita's return. She was at his side, pouring coffee. He reached for the cup, still turning over.

'Beautiful,' he said, and took a sip – the coffee was hot and strong – 'but getting repetitive . . . Bonita, where are my Gerhard Richters?'

'In Montauk,' she said from close behind him. 'Fritz moved them there two years ago.'

'Did he?' Leo stopped turning. 'Well, he knows what he's doing, my curator.' He gave sly emphasis to this last word.

Returning to the magazine, he sensed the needling motions of a comb.

'Not so hard. I have little enough as it is.'

He had come to the Previews for commercial galleries, a double-page spread divided into columns. Moving from left to right, he saw a video-still of a face contorted into a scream, an installation of helter-skelter wooden planks, a crimson love heart in polished steel . . .

'Same old—' he muttered, then stalled. The next image (although possibly he'd seen it before the others, and only now was his brain catching up) was both familiar and bewildering.

He knew, before the text confirmed it, that the painting was by Thomas Haller, and yet the colour was unlike that of any Haller he had seen. A soft purple, pulsing and uneven. *Like silk*, he thought. Or the sky at nightfall. There was a touch of silver, too – a haze that intensified and dispersed in alternation. Close to the centre, the purple hardened into a dark fissure.

Leo glanced at the text – *Haller's first exhibition in six years* – before refocusing on the picture. He brought his head close, trying to imagine the true proportions.

'Can you sit up, Mr Goffman?'

The comb was agitating the back of his head, persistent as a mosquito. He flung his arms up, swiping with both hands. The comb flew from Bonita's grip.

'Give me my phone,' he said, watching as she knelt to retrieve it.

He dabbed the screen with a tremoring finger until he found the name he wanted.

'Lorna Bedford Gallery,' said a practised voice down the line.

'Get me Lorna.'

'I'm afraid Ms Bedford is out of the gallery.'

'This is Leo Goffman.'

'Can you hold the line, please?'

A guitar struck up a sequence of chords – one of those old Spanish tunes. Rising from the couch, Leo counted to ten, fifteen, twenty. The guitar snapped into silence.

'Leo?'

'Lorna.' He gave the cord of his bathrobe a tug.

'What's up?'

There was something neutral about her British accent – unsuperior. He liked the way she sounded.

'What's up is, I just opened *Artforum*. The new issue with gold chippings all over the cover.'

'They're sweets, actually. Candy. Félix González-Torres.'

'Whatever. There's a preview here for a Thomas Haller show. Where the hell has that guy been? And how did I not *know* about this?'

'Right, yeah. It opens tomorrow night. Leo—'

'That *picture*. The lilac painting. I *love* it. The depth, the iridescence' – he groped again for the cord and his hand fumbled at damp flesh – 'the *texture*, Lorna. Those tonal shifts. Is he using some new technique? Silkscreen? Airbrush?'

'No, but Leo—'

'I want it. Don't try telling me it's sold. You can unsell it. Don't say it's not for sale. I'll pay. You know me – you know who I am.'

And who was he, other than Leopold Julius Goffman? One of the biggest names in real estate in this city, which meant the world. Rich beyond anything that mattered. But what counted, more than any of that, was his profile. His reputation. Benefactor, collector, man of deep culture . . . He felt a surge of furious longing.

'Leo, I can't sell you that painting. The exhibition isn't at my gallery. Thomas is doing a show with Claude Berlins in London. It has nothing to do with me.' She gave a bitter laugh. 'I wish it did.'

'*Berlins*? I don't get it.' Leo stared down at the words on the page – *Galerie Claude Berlins, London* – so blatant now. 'You are Haller's dealer. Always have been.'

'I know. But Thomas does what he wants, and let's face it, there's no such thing as a contract in the art world.'

'Since when did Berlins have a gallery in London? He's German, right?'

'French, actually. But his gallery's always been in Düsseldorf.'

'So, what is this? He needs a new place to launder money?'

'Claude's a global dealer. Or he intends to be. He already has outposts in Geneva and Madrid. The space in London is new. He wants to be as big as Gagosian. Bigger.'

'Let him try. That man will never be satisfied. Not if he opens a gallery in every city on the planet. Are you going to this show in London?'

'I'm flying out tonight.' Her voice was quieter – less assured.

Leo held the phone hard to his ear. 'Will you secure this picture for me? Will you do that, Lorna? Say you have a client, but don't give my name.'

'I'm not sure that'll work. You know, you could just go to Claude yourself.'

'No, no, no, *no*.' Leo reared upright, off the couch, hearing his voice turn hoarse. 'I need you to do this. Keep my name out of it. Not a word about me to Berlins. Say it's for a Saudi, or a Russian, or whatever you have to do. I want that painting. It has to be *that* one, no question. The one with the purple scar.' He felt desire rising in him like sweet bile.

'I'll do what I can, Leo. But it may not be much.'

'You'll do it, I know you will. I have faith.'

'I have to go. I'll call you when I get back.'

He tightened his grip on the phone. A gust from the air conditioning stirred around his midriff.

'You'll do whatever it takes,' he said, his voice husking into a whisper.

The line had died. He clenched his teeth and opened his hand. The phone fell into the shagpile without a sound. He stood perfectly still, feeling the heat of the sun glancing across his body.

2

Lorna chucked her phone onto the couch. It landed on a cushion a few inches from Justine's feet.

From her horizontal position, Justine glanced at the phone, then at Lorna, before returning to the proof copy of her book. The title was printed in utilitarian letters on a blank cover. *How to Take Control.*

Lorna watched her, thinking that Justine looked odd with glasses, vaguely unfamiliar, and younger than her thirty-three years.

'Remember me when I am gone away,' she said, mock-serious in her recitation. 'Only you're the one going, and I'll be left here with the dog.'

Justine kept reading. 'No one's dying. I won't be gone for ever. You *do* like to be dramatic.'

'I really don't. I'm pretty stoical, actually.'

'And anyway, you're going to come and visit, right? Hong Kong Island has the most incredible beaches.' Justine peered over the top of her book. 'When did you last put on a swimsuit?'

'At the same time as running a gallery, sure, I'll hop over for the day.' Lorna rested a knee on the arm of the sofa and smiled down at Justine. 'I'm guessing there are no nudist beaches in Hong Kong.'

'You old hippie. No one goes in for that any more.' Justine reached to the floor for a pen. 'Who was on the phone?'

'Leo Goffman.' Lorna turned away as she answered. Beyond

the desk, through the shutters, the morning was bright. Tompkins Square Park was a mesh of green shade.

She looked back. Justine had placed *How to Take Control* on the same cushion as the phone. Her expression was inquisitive and sceptical, just what Lorna might have expected.

'I was up at Columbia yesterday,' Justine said, as if she meant to embark on a story. 'To use the library. I took a walk at lunch – and, you know, it's incredible how Harlem has changed. All those salvage warehouses and projects – gone. Razed. Companies like Goffman Associates are replacing the old fabric with condos. Or retrofitting from within, like some horrible virus.' She looked hard at Lorna. 'Galleries, too. They're moving in. Gentrifying the place. Squeezing out the communities – people of colour, mostly – who lived there. If I had more time I'd write a piece on it.'

'I'm sure you would.'

Justine was in a combative mood. Not that Lorna cared. She liked Justine's sharp edges – always had.

'Why was Goffman calling you on your cell? How does he have your number?'

'They patched the call through from the gallery.' Lorna glanced over the desk. It was piled with the books and papers that would accompany Justine to Asia.

'God, that guy creeps me out.'

'I think he probably creeps himself out a little.'

'I doubt it. Men like that have zero self-awareness.'

'Well,' Lorna countered, 'what he does have is an unbelievable collection. Probably the best collection of modern art outside a museum.'

Justine made a face. Lorna bit her lip.

'He wants to buy a new Thomas Haller from the show at Claude Berlins,' she said. 'He seems to think I can help him. I guess because he already bought those six Hallers from me.'

That sale, six years earlier, had coincided with the start of their relationship. It had paid for the conversion of Lorna's loft into a writing space for Justine, allowed Justine to complete her second book, sown the seeds – maybe – of Justine's bid for freedom . . .

For a year now, their relationship had been on–off. The faltering had started with a lectureship in Chicago. Justine had gone away for a semester. Since then, she had continued to go away. Her excuses had become less believable until there no longer seemed to be a need for excuses. Busy with her own work, Lorna had shied away from analysing the situation. She'd told herself that she wasn't possessive – that she didn't need a heteronormative structure.

'I remember,' said Justine, her eyes drifting. 'Lead-grey, would-be heroic, male. Just what Goffman would go for.' Her expression lightened. 'Imagine if you and I had been billionaire collectors. We could have built a museum for art that *matters*. The Bedford Olson Foundation. Yvonne Rainer's *Privilege* would have a gallery all to itself.'

'That kind of art doesn't require a whole lot of capital,' Lorna said. 'Dealers would beg you to take some of it off their hands.'

Justine laughed. It was an unguarded laugh that reminded Lorna of the girl she'd met on a visit to Bard College, out on a green hill beside a stucco mansion, as twilight descended on the Hudson Valley and people milled in semi-drunken excitement.

'And we'd fight over everything,' she added, before she had a chance to think better of it. 'We'd never agree.'

In the silence that followed, Justine seemed to scan the room with new acuity: the books that scaled every wall, the mirror by Bill Copley that hung next to the door (stencilled and scored into the design of six cartoon figures), and the Robert Mapplethorpe photograph that hung above the fireplace.

'Can we take that Mapplethorpe down?' she said.

Lorna looked across at the photograph. It was the infamous

shot of a dick hanging out of tailored trousers. Infamous but long familiar. It had hung here, the dick, the picture, since Lorna took out a lease on the first floor in 1997.

'What did I just say? You don't like the same art I do.'

'It's not that. I have a photographer coming round from the *Atlantic*, for a profile they're doing.'

'And they're going to have a problem with a penis on the wall?'

'I need the focus to be on me, Lorna. On what *I've* done.'

Lorna took a step back – crossed one leg over the other. 'And this is happening today? You never said.'

'Yes, before I head to JFK. Beatrix set the whole thing up.' Justine took off her glasses, tousled her dark blonde hair, and plucked at the bobbled surface of her sweater. 'I need to change. Shit. They're coming before nine.' She pulled herself upright on the couch.

'Don't change. You look good as you are.'

Justine had been back in New York for three months, working and sleeping in the loft, finishing her book. Occasionally she'd crept into their old, shared bed. There were moments when they pretended – to each other, to themselves – that nothing had really changed. But the pretence couldn't last. Justine was leaving today for a six-month trip. A writing retreat and a book tour: her publicist Beatrix had organised the whole thing.

Wandering to the fireplace, Lorna caught sight of herself in the mirror. Her hair – brown-black and close to shoulder length, with a few threads of grey – needed cutting. But she looked good, she thought, even in an unironed T-shirt and black jeans, and she was her own sternest critic. A touch pale (it was her dark eyes that did it, and the shadows beneath), but youthful for a forty-six-year-old. Her arms were slender. An old Rolex hung from her wrist like a loose bracelet.

Her focus returned to the Mapplethorpe. The semi-soft cock broke through the open fly, trailed by a strip of white shirt. Uncut and dark-skinned, with a vein running down the shaft like a pleat.

Milton Moore, the model, hung his hands to either side. The picture was problematic now, not because it was explicit but because the model was Black. People said it was objectification. That was why Justine didn't want it on view.

'Milton Moore's dick stays,' Lorna said. 'It's been here since I lived in this one room. Giovanna's room, that's what Thomas used to call it. I won't have our life sanitised for the *Atlantic*.'

Justine rolled her eyes. She seemed about to retaliate when the doorbell chimed.

*

'Boy, is that a Robert Mapplethorpe?'

The photographer was standing in front of the fireplace. Behind her, Lorna and Justine exchanged looks.

This girl – woman – seemed too young to be a professional, Lorna thought, before concluding that *she* was simply older. Far older.

'*Man in Polyester Suit*,' she said. 'One of the first pieces I bought when I came to New York. Strange, isn't it, when you think about it?' She caught Justine's eye. 'Justine wanted me to take it down just now, before you came.'

The girl turned round, newly curious.

'Wait a minute,' Justine blurted. 'That's not what I said.'

Lorna felt a needling guilt. Even at her most ridiculous, Justine had an automatic claim on her love.

'I'm Lorna,' she said, observing the girl from close up. A pretty, boyish girl with short hair. No older than twenty-five. A long-lens camera hung around her neck.

'Maxine.'

Lorna took her hand (warm and busy with rings), aware of Justine's rigid smile.

'I'm sorry. This place is a mess, but you wanted to see Justine's real life, right?'

'You have an amazing home,' Maxine replied.

Justine continued to grin, as if grinning had become an unrelievable affliction.

'It's actually tidier than usual. We've had to sort through a lot before Justine goes away.'

'Hey, Lorna,' Justine broke in. 'Did you want to fix some coffee?' Her voice was sharp and bright.

'Wait,' Maxine said, looking closely at Lorna. 'Aren't you Lorna Bedford?'

Lorna laughed before she could help it. 'Well, sure.'

'I had no idea.' Maxine's hands had closed around the camera. 'I mean, I had no idea you guys were together.' She glanced at Justine, whose smile was contracting finally. 'I should have done my research.'

'Or Beatrix, her publicist, could have told you,' said Lorna, thinking that *together* could disguise various degrees of separation. 'Justine and I met six years ago when I gave a talk at Bard College on how to be an art dealer. Which must be why she's now a best-selling psychologist.'

'Philosopher,' Justine interposed. 'Political philosopher.'

'I go to your gallery often,' said Maxine. 'Ever since I saw your Diane Arbus show in 2014. I wrote my master's on Arbus.'

'Jesus. Was it that long ago?'

'It changed my life.'

There was silence. Something in Maxine's tone had disarmed them all.

'It's irreversible, the impact of those pictures,' Lorna said at last. 'They imprint themselves on you. Arbus does it like no one else. There's a weirdness but also an integrity about those people – the blank-eyed kids, the tragic hobos, gays, Jews . . . It's their vulnerability in front of the camera, I think. Even the celebs she shot look odd – unlike themselves. Like the portrait of Sontag with her son. They're—'

15

'Stripped bare,' Maxine murmured.

'That's it.'

'Lorna, the coffee.' Justine was trying and failing to resurrect her grin.

Lorna nodded, still looking at Maxine, and passed into the hallway. She heard the door closing behind her, and beyond it, Justine's singsong voice taking control.

*

She gazed through the window at the brick-walled yard as the water boiled. The kettle clicked and her gaze receded. This kitchen had been a communal space, back when Lorna occupied the first floor as a tenant. She had bought the house outright in the art market boom of the early 2000s, but had left the kitchen as it was. She liked the aluminium countertops, disfigured by scratches. Art postcards were tacked all over the upper units.

As she located the cafetiere and coffee, her eyes passed over a stuffed spider by Annette Messager and a grease-spotted photograph of David Wojnarowicz buried up to the face in dirt. The Wojnarowicz had served as a bookmark for Justine on trips to Bellport, where her parents had a seaside house, at a time when her PhD research had reached a pivotal stage. An enquiry into Henry James's women was becoming obscured – displaced – by questions of globalisation and the psychology of capitalism. The parlour games of literary criticism, as Justine termed them, were giving way to things that mattered.

Lorna measured out two large spoonfuls of coffee and poured the water in, making a black suspension.

What was this – a relationship, still? A platonic romance? Justine came and went as she pleased, and Lorna pretended not to care, often succeeded in not caring.

She began to depress the plunger, reflecting that this was Justine's first taste of celebrity. Lorna was used to being the eminent one. (*Legendary Chelsea dealer* had been the judgement of *Artscribe* – typically hyperbolic – in the magazine's last survey of '100 Movers and Shakers in the Art World'). But in the last two years, since the success of Justine's first book – a treatise on the God complex in democratic leaders since Reagan – a switch had occurred.

The swarming grounds were mounting a resistance. Lorna pressed the plunger down harder.

Justine's new book, *How to Take Control*, was a self-help manual crossed with a takedown of neoliberalism. This time, Justine had reinterpreted Confucian philosophy in her assault on western ethical systems. The book was hotly tipped, as people said in the industry. A profile of the heretical young philosopher (or psychologist – the terms varied) was slated for the next issue of the *Atlantic*. Then there was the Asian tour. Beatrix had plotted every detail: a visiting fellowship in Hong Kong followed by a five-month parade of lectures, launches, roundtables, readings and residencies encompassing every major city in the region, all of it courtesy of the Pacific Rim Literary Festival.

Justine had said that she needed to escape New York. Lockdown had been like a prison. She needed to reconnect with herself, expand her horizons. Which could only mean that Lorna was a bar to expansion. An anti-muse.

Lorna drove the plunger down hard. It slammed through the cafetiere, hitting the bottom. Coffee projected over her chest and arms. She cried out before realising that the pain wasn't that bad – a sharp, tingling sensation; nothing more.

She used a dish cloth to wipe the mess from her arms, not before wondering whether to leave it there as she carried the tray through, just to see Justine's reaction.

She nudged open the sitting-room door with her shoe. Justine was standing next to the Mapplethorpe with a vulnerable smile (the kind of smile that would never appear premeditated), while Maxine's camera made a rapid kissing sound.

In an instant, Lorna saw that Justine's casual appearance – Calvin Klein jeans, baggy jumper with sleeves rolled up, hair flickering with blonde highlights – was a construction. On her left wrist, she was wearing the silver bangle that Lorna had given her the previous summer. It was a nice touch.

It had been a mistake, Lorna supposed, to fall in love with someone thirteen years younger. The age difference had effected a slow divergence, although Justine refused to admit it.

*

After Maxine had left, something strange occurred – although in retrospect, Lorna decided that it wasn't so strange after all. The glances and remarks of the morning had been leading to it like so many clues.

Justine came upstairs to where Lorna was sitting in the cubicle-like room that passed for an office, reading the first lines of emails. She laid her hands on Lorna's shoulders.

'Will you miss me?'

'You know I will.'

Lorna closed her eyes. Justine's fingers crossed the neckline of her shirt. Lorna began to turn. In a second, Justine had bent down and kissed her.

Lorna stood and they continued to kiss in a way they hadn't for a long time. With joined hands, they wandered – stumbled – into the bedroom, losing their clothes in a swift alternation of unsleeving, unclipping, kicking off and pulling down. They fell onto the bed. Justine's other self, the girl without a persona, was suddenly available.

Lorna pulled Justine towards her, into her, as if their two bodies might be melded. She felt Justine's movements answering her own, felt the smooth friction of Justine's legs as they slid around hers, securing a hold. Their bodies moved together in a tight revolution, close to the edge of the mattress. Kneeling,

Lorna pressed her hands onto Justine's shoulders, then submitted as Justine pulled her down by the neck, clasping their mouths. For a minute or more, unremembered feelings passed between them, tensing and expanding through the motions of their lips, thighs and fingers. Then, as self-consciousness returned, they lay side by side, breathing fast, feeling the warmth of the morning beyond the window. Lorna wondered if it would ever happen again, this kind of closeness.

'By the time you land in Hong Kong,' she said, looking up at the ceiling, 'I'll be on the plane to London.'

'I don't get why you're going,' Justine replied. 'Stay here. Live your life.'

'If I don't show up, it looks like I no longer matter. Like I've admitted defeat.'

'But you *have* been defeated. Thomas jumped into bed with another dealer.'

Justine lifted herself on her elbow and studied Lorna from above. Her areolas were dark, almost brown, against the paleness of the rest of her.

'Not that it matters,' she added. 'Most people stopped caring about him years ago.'

'You're not an impartial observer,' Lorna said.

'I'm right, though. Where's he even been for six years? You made him a star, secured him a show at the Whitney, and then what? He disappeared.'

'He went to Switzerland because – I don't know. It's where he grew up. I guess New York was killing him.' Lorna sat up, crossing her legs. 'You know, it feels like Thomas has always been running away. Even when we were students, when we did everything together, I felt like I couldn't keep hold of him.'

'What did you expect? You're queer and so is he – if he could only act on it.'

Lorna took Justine's hand. It felt cool and compact. She rested it in the crease between her stomach and leg.

Jay had skulked unnoticed into the room. He leapt between them on the bed, parting their hands and regarding them – one then the other – with pricked ears. His eyes, ringed by amber, were like dimmed headlamps. He was a German Shepherd but black all over, with glints of silver at the tips of the fur.

'Do we look weird, naked, to him?' Lorna said, reaching for his head.

Justine drew her knees up to her chest. 'Down, Jay!'

Jay rotated himself and slumped back to the floor. Lorna and Justine watched, enclosed in separate worlds of thought. Lorna's hand traced the smooth form of Justine's lower calf. Smooth and moisturised. Justine never seemed to forget, these days.

'Do you think about what happened?' Justine asked. 'Between you and Thomas?'

'Of course.'

'The baby, I mean.'

Lorna shifted a little, keeping her hand on Justine's leg.

'Of course,' she said again. 'All the time.'

*

Justine was standing on the sidewalk outside the house. Lorna remained at the top of the stoop. Justine clutched the handles of two suitcases. A car hummed behind her.

'Let me come with you.'

'It's better if you don't,' Justine said. 'You're busy.'

'Not so busy that I can't spare an hour at the airport.'

Justine closed her eyes for a moment and drew up her shoulders. Then she scaled the steps, nimble as a child, and kissed Lorna on the lips.

'Stay,' she said. 'And don't forget to water my orchids.'

'The grotesques.'

'Please don't let them die.'

Justine heaved the suitcases into the trunk while the driver chucked a half-smoked cigarette in the gutter.

Once the car had turned onto Avenue B, Lorna stared into the stillness of the park across the road, contemplating the pockmarks of sunlight until she felt a swishing around her ankles. She grabbed Jay's collar.

'Not you.'

She pulled him inside and closed the door. For a long while, she stood and held onto him. Finally, she returned to the sitting room. Before conscience could reproach her, she crossed to the desk and opened the middle drawer. A pile of files concealed a packet of Marlboro Reds, almost full. She prised a cigarette free, then scooped out the matches that had slipped to the back of the drawer.

The act of inhalation brought a universe-stalling rush. She looked at the Mapplethorpe. Justine had noticed that photograph the first time she had come here. Back then, she'd been amused.

'Why do you have that?' she'd asked. 'I mean, it's not like *that's* your thing. Is it?'

They sat back, half lying, on the sofa, kissing between speaking.

'You don't have to be a kink-loving gay guy to like – or own – a Mapplethorpe,' Lorna replied. 'Just because I don't want to suck it doesn't mean—'

She stopped as their lips met, preceded by the alcoholic scent of their mingling breath.

Artists should be praised, she thought now, planting her hands on the empty desk, for imagining people remote from their own lives or desires. (Hadn't Mapplethorpe also made images of women in the nude, just as steely and sexy and funny as the men?) Viewers should share in that imagining.

She looked over at the bookshelves and caught sight of the catalogue – a thick pink spine – that had been published for Thomas

Haller's midcareer retrospective at the Whitney. Screwing one eye closed against the smoke, she went and pulled it off the shelf.

Sinking onto the sofa, she opened the book. She was close to the start of the chronological sequence, in the late nineties, the era of his first abstract paintings. On facing pages were two reproductions, each an expanse of luminous pink, the brushstrokes destabilised in places by the action of a spray can and splashed solvents. The Pink Paintings. She had shown them in 1999 at her tiny SoHo gallery. Joel Blair had reviewed the show for the *Village Voice*, calling the nine paintings *winsome, witty triumphs – each canvas a giddy riposte to the pieties of conceptualism, putting the painterly back into abstraction*. The phrases, ridiculous in their way, had stayed with her.

She took a final pull on the cigarette and dropped it into a mug on the coffee table.

The Pink Paintings had been followed by the Blue Paintings – nearly twenty canvases spanning the turn of the millennium, their paintwork increasingly layered and turbulent. After those came the Day-Glo series. That was when critical opinion about Thomas had polarised into reverence and eye-rolling disdain. The paintings' rising prices had driven the split.

And then, in the last decade and a half, a change. Shadier hues, like troubled skies or topographies viewed at night.

Justine had said that Thomas's art was heroic and male, or trying to be, but looking at the book, Lorna felt that it wasn't either of those things (not in the ways that Justine meant).

She gripped hold of a slab of pages and flipped back to the start, alighting on a double page unlike the others. This marked the moment of origin – a brief moment, often overlooked – when Thomas had painted people. He had allowed only two portraits into the exhibition. The first, from 1995, showed Lorna at a party. She was turning away, captured in profile. A black belt bisected her short white dress. He had copied the image from a Polaroid.

The picture on the facing page dated from the following year.

This time, she had sat for him at his studio flat in Vauxhall. She thought back to the silent hours – how a smile had passed between them like a remark. That closed-lipped smile was what she saw now in the square reproduction on the page, which did no justice to the size of the painting. It had been like an altar-piece. Cast in hazy light, the young Lorna was sitting square-on. Her head and shoulders filled the picture, dark hair tumbling. Her eyes met Thomas's. She'd had a look, at nineteen, that she still loved. A defiant uncertainty.

It had been a battle, that sequence of sittings. A two-month battle that ended with them getting drunk and kissing on the sofa while *Dressed to Kill* was playing on the TV, then making love in the dark, searching for some way of discharging the tension that had built over the hours and days of sitting. Making love or having sex; perhaps the clinical term was the right one. It had lasted all of two minutes.

As she returned the book to the shelf, she noticed that a sheet of paper had been sandwiched between Thomas's catalogue and a book on Eva Hesse. It was a cut-out page from the summer 2017 issue of the *Fire Island Review*.

Too Late for Greatness
Justine Olson

Had she or Justine tucked the article away? Lorna couldn't remember, but the page itself was grimly familiar. There was a photograph in black and white. It was a publicity shot of Thomas in one of the galleries at the Whitney, surrounded by the dark apertures of his paintings. The text purported to be about the death of epic as an artistic category, but the majority of it consisted of a review of the exhibition.

Lorna glanced down the middle column. The words seemed to rise out of her mind as she read.

I looked around the Whitney for truth, maybe a little beauty.

What I saw was an artificial wilderness, all splashed and sprayed. A barren prettiness extending through every gallery. This is cosplay, I realised. He's playing at being Rothko or Motherwell, never mind those who were truly great – Frankenthaler, Mitchell, Krasner. But for the New York Schoolers, art was a serious business. It meant something, even when they were goofing around. Identity, geography, resistance – all of life could be transposed into an abstract key. Even love.

As for Thomas Haller: why did he bother? The question rang in my head as I wandered through his vast, vainglorious retrospective. This is art as pastiche, I thought. Art that has lost faith in art's own possibilities. His paintings are born of the same impulse that makes people want to play jazz or write in hexameters. Just because you can *do it, doesn't mean you should. There's a certain stylishness about the way he swerves from informality to precision. He knows how to modulate his gestures – fine. But it's a sterile virtuosity, and oh so narcissistic. Masturbatory. Worst of all, beneath the metallised lustre, there's an awful gooey nostalgia. Haller is an artist who needs to give up the past. He needs to let the lingering dead be dead.*

There was a subtext, not that Justine would have admitted it, then or now.

Lorna and Justine had only been dating a few weeks when they went together to the opening of Thomas's show. Justine had taken an instant dislike to him: the star artist at the centre of his cosmos. She had hated the early portraits of Lorna before she knew anything about them. That same night, after they got home, Lorna had told Justine about herself and Thomas. The two years in London when they'd practically lived together. The intense friendship that was more like a romance. Their silly, seismic night in Vauxhall. The child.

Justine had burst out laughing, then dissolved in tears. It was one of the few times Lorna had seen her cry. All because of events from long ago that were nothing to do with her. Later, when the article came out, Lorna understood. Thomas represented a chapter in Lorna's past, a realm of memory that Justine could never access. Jealousy and anguish had been sublimated into art criticism. Lorna and Justine had rarely spoken about the article in the years since.

Turning back to the room, Lorna noticed the dark jar of the cafetiere on the coffee table. It hadn't been touched. She poured out a cup and drank the cold contents, then spat. The cigarette butt thudded onto the floor.

3

5 September, 20.58. London

The moment he walked into his hotel room, Thomas Haller knew that Betty was dead. She was stretched out on the carpet beneath the window, in the very place where she'd been when he left. This was a warning sign. But it was the tension in her body – something about the set of her strong limbs, locked in a waking stretch – that made him sure.

He stood by the door, allowing it to swing closed. Betty dead. His loyal, divine Betty, sprawling there in all her majesty. He felt empty, but he knew that grief has a way of stalling its entrance, making you wait.

Reticence had come over him. How often, in recent months, he had watched her as he was watching her now – from a doorway, across a room, cautiously observing her black flank, waiting for the undulations of her ribcage to lift a fraction with an intake of breath (that small, rhythmic movement assuring him that the moment hadn't yet come).

Her fur was no less lustrous than ever as she lay between the undrawn curtains, beneath a sky that had lost all trace of daylight, but her body was absolutely still. The sight of it instilled a matching paralysis, pinning him where he stood.

'Betty!'

The tremor in his voice surprised him. That and the fact that some non-compliant part of him was willing to disbelieve. *It had to happen*, he told himself. *A ten-year-old Rottweiler is living on borrowed time*. At last, he took a step forward.

'Betty,' he said again, in a tone of loving reproach, and crept across the ivory carpet, switching on a floor lamp as he came near. Warm light fell on her coat, burnishing the patches of brown that adorned her muzzle and stomach and front legs like the blots of a Rorschach. He knelt. Her eyes were shut. He laid his hand over her face and used his thumb to open one eye. In place of a pool of cognition, he saw a misted marble. His heart seemed to go light and large all at once. He crouched and brought his face close to her nippled belly.

For ten years, she had come with him everywhere. He had considered leaving her in Switzerland this time, wondering if she was finally too old to travel. But he had been frightened that she might die alone, without him. And precisely that had happened. He pressed his face into her sagging undercarriage until he couldn't breathe. *In a suite at Claridge's.*

He stood up. The telephone on the desk had a speed-dial option for the concierge.

'Mr Haller, good evening, sir.'

'I need towels – hand towels – as many as you can bring. And a decanter. Empty.'

He replaced the phone and plucked two miniature Courvoisiers from the fridge. He emptied each bottle in two gulps, bracing himself before the intakes.

Moments later, there was a knock on the door. He opened it a few inches, shielding the corpse from view, and saw a young man – not much older than a teenager, politely smiling, almost obscured by folded towels. Thomas took them with a nod and let the door swing shut. He had barely set the towels down when another knock came. He sighed, fumbling in his jacket pocket for cash, and opened it.

The young man was solemn now. 'You wanted this as well, Mr Haller?'

He held out a cut-glass decanter with a spherical body and a long funnel. It had a sculpted orb for a stopper. Thomas took the heavy, sparkling object and planted coins and notes in the man's hand, realising too late that the cognac bottles were there amid the money. There was perplexity now beneath the courteous veneer. Thomas broke eye contact and closed the door.

In a surge of determination, he went straight to Betty and slid his arms beneath her. He lifted her, all ninety pounds, and staggered into the passageway that led to the bathroom, catching sight of himself through the bedroom doorway in a full-length cheval mirror. An absurd *Pietà* scene. There he was, in his linen jacket and pink shirt, his face livid with strain. Her corpse spread across his stomach and spilled off the edges of the mirror. Groaning through closed teeth, he tottered through to the bathroom, feeling his knees starting to buckle, and tipped Betty – dropped her as his arms gave way – into the bathtub. There was a horrible thud as she landed, her head colliding with the edge. He gripped his knees, panting with relief, then reached into the tub and bent her legs into the curled, protective stance that she had adopted thousands of times in sleep. She was stiffening but not yet rigid.

He flipped on the tap and ran his hand through the foamy jet, adjusting the temperature. The water splashed over her lips and began to pool around her body, wetting the leathery pads on the undersides of her paws.

He collected the towels and decanter. Standing over the bath, he pulled out the glass stopper and filled the decanter from the tap. Then, with ceremonial care, he emptied it over Betty's head. He refilled it and soaked her body – the upper half that the bathwater hadn't reached. He poured and refilled and poured again.

Taking a hand towel, he began to wash her with methodical motions, progressing from her hind quarters across her stomach and flank, up to her rocklike shoulders. As he reached her face, the motions became painstaking – reverential. With the corner of the towel, he daubed the region of her upper lip. The skin slid up to reveal her canines, yellowing where they met the gum. At once, the white fabric was blue-black. He discarded the towel and took up another, wetting it beneath the tap.

With his finger hooded inside the material, he dabbed at the soft convexities of her eyes. The same dark pigment bled out. He administered another towel to the golden flaps of her muzzle, and the material acquired a browner residue. He could hear his breathing as he worked, heavy but controlled.

The bathwater around Betty's head, several inches deep now and beginning to submerge her mouth, had taken on a muddy, purplish tint. The colour seeped out of her in billows. The assiduous work of four years was undone in ten minutes. Stained towels lay around the bath. Thomas shut off the tap and knelt in silence, gazing down at the water, which had resolved into a pale lilac.

4

Leo trod along the perimeter of the drawing room. In his side vision, the city was a tray overloaded with glasses and bottles. When he turned, the illusion sublimed into a magisterial truth. He saw megaliths of brownstone and stepped marble, and columns of glass like dead-straight plumes. Each building devolved, at a moment's inspection, into finer striations. It was a labyrinth for the eye. You could get lost in that infinite play of light and linearity – find yourself unable to return to your body. Sometimes he felt it beginning to happen, and it took an act of will, a forced coming to his senses, to reel his eyes in.

Somewhere out there, at the midway point of 130th Street, was the derelict Baptist church that he was transforming into a residential complex. *Divine apartments.* A pilot project: Harlem was full of churches. But Leo hadn't been up that way in years, perhaps because the buildings were always covered in scaffolding, ever since Law 11. Or was it because the district contained the campus of Columbia University?

At the corner of the room was a figurine carved from red stone, raised on a plinth. He looked closely at the rounded, simplified body. It had been carved by Henri Gaudier-Brzeska, who died at twenty-four in the French trenches. A lifespan not much more than a quarter of Leo's. And his creative phase had lasted four years. Leo wondered if the sculptor had had a premonition, as he hammered and planed, that time was short.

Red Stone Dancer was a contradictory being. Its torqued

limbs spoke of modernity, and yet it had an aura of antiquity. Leo, too, was young and old. The sculpture seemed to comprehend the divergence that had taken place between his brain and body.

As his gaze took refuge in the mud-red stone, he thought back to the day he had purchased it. February 14, 2004.

He and Ira had met for lunch. The brothers had insisted on maintaining the ritual every six months. That day, it was Leo's turn to pay, which meant La Grenouille.

'How can it be that the building trade is controlled by the mob?' Ira demanded, as their appetisers arrived. 'Since when was concrete a monopoly? Well, what do I know? Here I am with my head buried in linguistic structures, while you're' – he glanced at the wine bottle between them – 'changing the city skyline.'

Leo took the bottle and topped up his glass.

'And how is business, Leo?'

'Business' – Leo plunged his fork into an earthenware reservoir, sending butter streaming – 'is great. I got the zoning removed from that site on the Upper West Side.'

'Oh.'

'It cost me, but I got it done. We're going to build some beautiful apartments. César Pelli's coming in on it.' He bit down on the fibrous flesh of a snail.

'A new Babylon on the Hudson,' remarked Ira. He folded his hands, eyeing the wells of butter that Leo was raiding.

Studying the surface of *Red Stone Dancer* all these years later, Leo recalled how his humours had been out of sorts. Despite his boasts to Ira, the mayor had refused him a tax break on the megadevelopment. And he had been missing Deborah, although that never changed. He watched his breath condense on the stone, remembering how Ira had been brimming with good-natured contempt for Wall Street – Ira, for whom marriage into a rich family had turned money into another philosophical abstraction: his wife, Gloria, was the heir to a canned foods fortune.

'I have a new book out next week,' he had announced, as if it were a point of passing interest. 'With Princeton.'

'The book you've been working on for ten years?'

'Well, it hasn't quite been ten years. And I've published seven peer-reviewed articles in that time.'

'What's it called?'

Ira brought the corner of his napkin to his mouth. '*Saying It Makes It So: Performative Utterances, Locutionary Acts.*'

Leo chewed and swallowed.

'Well, it doesn't roll off the tongue,' Ira went on. 'But not everything is reducible to a piece of catchy marketing.'

'Can I pick up a copy in Barnes and Noble?'

'Ha! I don't imagine so. I entertain no illusions that it will be a bestseller. I'm not that kind of writer.'

'You're not a writer, period.'

'I've published ten books. I think I've earned the right—'

'Ernest Hemingway.'

'I'm sorry?'

'Now *he* was a writer.' Leo sat back.

Ira appeared to search for words among the neighbouring tables. 'Value, in academic publishing, is measured by certain rules. It's not about literary style, and certainly has nothing to do with sales.' His eyes narrowed a little. 'The world isn't all about money.'

'When did I mention money?'

'You didn't need to.' Ira attempted a casual laugh.

Leo slid his fingers around the bowl of his wine glass. 'Well, since *you* mentioned it, how many of your performative utterances have nothing to do with money? How many human interactions *aren't* about money, at some level? It's everywhere. Always has been. You think the Indo-Europeans weren't buying and selling? You think classical Greek art didn't have a price?' He lifted the glass and swilled the dark Pétrus.

'Indo-European is a construct,' said Ira, with the clipped delivery that signalled offence. 'It's a hypothesis. For you to talk about Indo-Europeans is a fallacy of the very kind—'

'Don't pretend,' Leo interrupted, still rolling the wine, 'that your book's too good to cost anything. You academics think you inhabit some version of the Garden of Eden where money doesn't talk.' He raised the glass to his lips and drew wine through his teeth. 'Money talks. Money makes its own performative utterances, every second of every day.'

He signalled to the waiter, who came rapidly with a second bottle. As the man poured, Leo sent his eyes on a pleasure tour of the room. The plush settees and the table lamps seemed redder and golder than ever.

'I love this restaurant.'

'I would be happy to go somewhere uptown next time.'

'I love it here. And you know what? I think Dad would have loved it here.'

Ira tensed. 'I was just thinking' – his words were deliberate, as though he were straining them through a mesh – 'that this is the very last place Father would have enjoyed.'

Leo wondered, not for the first time, whether their father had been a different man to each of them. Fifteen years lay between their births. Bob Goffman, himself the son of a renowned Viennese economist, had been a mathematics teacher, until – in late middle age – he began to invest in commercial property.

'Now that I remember,' Leo said, 'it was Dad who introduced me to this place.'

Ira gave a brittle laugh. 'Tell me – is your enjoyment of that wine simply down to what it's costing you?' He was struggling to maintain an air of unconcern. 'Or the Joan Mitchells that you and Deborah bought – do you only love them because of what you paid for them?'

Leo's heart made an insurrectionist motion.

'You can't measure everything according to its price,' Ira went on. 'There are other ways of calculating worth. There are lives, beyond your own, where money isn't the driving force.'

'Lives like yours, you mean? Floating on top of a multimillion-dollar sea of baked beans?'

Leo felt a smile extend over his face, drawing his features wide. He raised his glass as if to make a toast.

'Everything has a price,' he said. 'And everybody. Yours simply happens not to be very high.'

The light that was spreading over their table flared. The lamp had crashed sideways. Ira was standing, white with fury.

'You're not going to stay for an Armagnac? Hemingway loved a good Armagnac.'

'A man's soul, his status, his dignity – these are things that cannot be bought,' Ira stammered. 'Perhaps you never knew this. Deborah knew, I think, before you got to her.'

The renewed mention of Deborah, so calculated and blasphemous, stalled Leo in his desire to reply.

'Oh, I know she suffered terribly,' Ira said. 'You both did. But it wasn't only that. Something died in her. Her love of beauty in the abstract, her indifference to baser things.'

He held Leo's eye with a stern, pitying look that concealed a deeper malice.

'I suggest you leave,' Leo said.

'You silenced her, Leo. Censored her. The way you never let her *speak* about any of it. Her or any of us.'

Ira shook his head as if no response were possible, and left the room with his posture erect.

Nineteen years on, Leo's hand passed across *Red Stone Dancer* with the touch of a healer. Ira had tried to reunite. Ira's wife had tried. Leo had ignored every call and every letter. The sculpture was a monument to that day.

He had paid the cheque and left the restaurant. A block or two later, he was walking past Christie's, wandering in deep thought, when the doorman put a question to him.

'Are you here for the sale, sir?'

Leo looked through the open doors of the auction house to see a sign on the wall inside.

Masterpieces of Twentieth-Century Art

He hadn't been to an auction since Deborah's death the previous year.

He made his way upstairs to the saleroom and sat at the back. Cocooned by the Pétrus, watching the event proceed, he recognised (how could he have forgotten?) the rhetoric of the auctioneer, that debonair mania. *Red Stone Dancer* was the prize lot for the afternoon. When it was carried in, Leo was amazed by its smallness, or rather, the mute power that its smallness compressed. Through a gap in the rows of heads, between the darting hands that were bidding up the price, he admired the sturdy limbs. There was a concision about the object, something unarguable. The higher the price climbed, the more he desired it. Ira's questions replayed in his head, and he insisted to himself that beauty had a worth. Here was a thing of soul, status and dignity – this *Red Stone Dancer* – and it would be his.

*

The picture in *Artforum* had awakened a feeling. That feeling led him out of the drawing room and along the alabaster byways of the apartment, beneath the unseeing gaze of a Warhol *Liz*.

Leo's bedroom was just as it had always been, a square space decked out in Louis Quinze style. A battalion of cabinets, couches and Bergère chairs fanned out around the quilted promontory of the bed. The headboard was an ecclesiastical marvel of uphol-stered silk and gilded carving. Above, satin drapes rose to the ceiling in a fluted wigwam. Two windows pointed to the north, offering views of the length of the park. A third window pointed east, into the heart of the towery city. Panelled walls obscured the glass of the building's exterior except where these tall open-ings had been cut.

Leo stepped towards his bed. His bathrobe slunk to the floor, detaching from his body like a shed skin. He levered one knee, then the other, onto the pink shelf of the counterpane and crawled across, feeling his hands and knees sink into the satin segments. There were identical cabinets on either side of the headboard. With one hand, he pulled open a drawer and extracted a lilac shawl.

Still balanced on his knees, he brought the material to his face. A vestige of perfume reached his brain like the faltering touch of a finger. *Diorella.* He gathered the gauzy material into a pile and sank his head into the folds. Deprived of air or space to escape, his sigh hardened into a ragged moan.

He glanced back through the aperture of his kneeling legs. His thighs and dick made a quaking M shape out of the room. Or it might have been a W. Bonita hadn't followed. He tried to imagine what he would look like from the doorway. His position, he sensed, was that of an apex predator ready to pounce. But he felt more like an insect stuck on a sheet of flypaper. When had it happened, this diminution?

He folded the material into a rectangle and was about to return it to the drawer of the cabinet when Deborah's face – gazing out from between a hairbrush and a jewellery box – stopped him.

He removed the brush and the little japanned box (her best earrings), before lifting out the magazine and laying it on the bedspread. It was a forty-year-old edition of *Vanity Fair*. The typeface of the masthead betrayed the magazine's age: the jaunty upflick on the *V*, the curlicue of the *F*. So did the phrases that crowded around the edges of Deborah's portrait.

Could you be hypnotised?
How to get off the shelf if you're getting on.

But Deborah herself was as present to him, in that photograph, as she had been the day it was taken.

Deborah Goffman: Chatelaine of Park Avenue

The words extended in a banner of yellow over the top of the portrait. The script was larger than any of the other trailers.

Leo's eyes raked across the cover, registering every detail. He marvelled at the beauty of the room in which Deborah was sitting, long since dismantled. In the background, a turquoise interior scene by Matisse glowed alongside the writhing gold foliage of a mirror frame. The entire space was bewitched by a golden light that intensified like a halo around the woman at the centre.

She was seated, pertly erect, at the swelling end of a chaise longue, dressed in a Halston suit as pink and precise as Mrs Kennedy's, the skirt terminating a little above the knees, the jacket cut in precise alignment with her slender frame. Her left hand was draped over the duller pink of the seat's velvet hillock, its protruding bones and veins atoned for by a trio of heart-stopping jewels. Her legs, planed to sculptural perfection by her tan stockings, were crossed just above the knees (those two knees, he thought, were perhaps the loveliest detail of all – like mounds of water-hewn stone, stacked one upon the other), and descended to a pair of Cinderella heels in beige patent leather. He could make out the interlocking brass letters on top of one shoe. *YSL*. Yves had created the shoe for Deborah. Just beneath, at the base of the picture, lay a Persian cat – a long streak of gaseous white, like a cryptic attribute in an old painting.

His eyes spiralled in – his vision whirling like that of a man intoxicated – taking in her puissant smile (so bright, so sovereign!), the mane of blow-dried auburn hair, the set of her features – acquiring a statelier beauty in middle age, but still betraying the wilder loveliness of the girl from Yonkers he'd married. He dwelled for a long while on the tapering vertical of her nose, and those green eyes, knowing as a lynx's, circled by gossamer threads of mascara.

'That was Deborah Goffman,' he said aloud. 'The chatelaine.'

*

13.23

Once Leo had left for the chiropractor, Bonita went into his bedroom. She straightened the counterpane with swift tugs and plumped the pillows.

Sliding open the drawer of the cabinet, she drew out the shawl. Carefully, as if unspooling a thread, she brought it to her nose. She reached into the pocket of her pinafore and removed a glass bottle. Tipping a droplet onto the lilac gauze, she watched the perfume blot and fade.

As she refolded the shawl, Bonita remembered that she needed to speak with Fritz Schein. She went through to the drawing room and used her iPhone to take a photo of *Artforum*, still open on the page of the Thomas Haller preview.

*

23.14

Waiting for the plane to taxi out, Lorna listened to the noises of pre-flight (electronic chimes, the cabin crew's final checks, a Wall Street trader's furtive instructions regarding flows and crosses), and thought back to the phone call in which Thomas had told her he was going to do a show at Galerie Claude Berlins. It had been eight months ago, on New Year's Eve. He'd mentioned it in an offhand way, as if nothing could matter less.

'Claude's been asking me for ages, and you don't have a London gallery. Nothing's going to change, really. You'll still represent me in the States.'

'I'll believe that when you do another show with me,' she'd said. A casual comeback, masking the shock.

She wondered if she was going to London partly because Justine was leaving. She hadn't wanted to be left alone at home. But there was a belief too (a residual, defiant feeling) that Thomas still belonged to her.

'Can I offer you a drink, ma'am?' asked the flight attendant.

As the young woman poured water, Lorna noticed the fine hairs on her forearm. She picked up Justine's book from her lap.

'You're not allowed to read it till the copy-edit's finished,' Justine had said. 'I want you to see the final version, nothing else. Everything has to be *right*.'

Lorna sank a little in her seat. Justine was an idealist. It was one of the many ways in which they were different. A book where everything was right . . . Lorna turned it over in her hands and felt a rush of protective affection.

Justine would be most of the way to Hong Kong by now. She and Beatrix were spending a few days at Beatrix's family home on the Peak before Justine began her lectureship at HKU. A few days, doing what?

A month earlier, Lorna had come home to find Justine and Beatrix sitting close together on the sofa, Justine leaning back in a stretch that revealed her armpits and midriff. Had something happened – been about to happen? Lorna had said hello and gone into the kitchen, surprised more than anything by her incapacity to react. The thing she'd dreaded for years felt mundane in the moment of becoming real. You don't own a person, she'd often told herself. And hadn't she always been suspicious of hardline monogamy?

She should have a romance of her own, she thought, as the plane began to taxi out. But she wasn't sure that she knew how to do it, where to start. Tinder? She thought of Maxine, the photographer who'd visited that morning.

And what about Andrea, Beatrix's wife? Was *she* okay with this long sojourn? Andrea was an addiction psychotherapist; she had been with Beatrix for fifteen years. Lorna had met her a handful of times. She had a memory of a wilful, principled character.

One time, a couple of years ago, Lorna and Justine had run into Andrea on the sidewalk.

'Justine, Lorna – I *thought* it was you.' Andrea – out of breath from jogging – had flung her foot behind her and grabbed hold of her sneaker, wincing at the stretch. 'When are you guys going to join us on the sponsored run?'

'We're always on Long Island when it happens,' said Justine, giving Lorna's back a conspiratorial prod.

'What sponsored run?' Lorna asked afterwards. 'Doesn't she know that I don't exercise?'

Sometimes, when Lorna came home drunk from a gallery dinner, Justine threatened to set up an appointment with Andrea Driscoll. It was like a running joke, except that it was never quite made in jest.

Lorna opened Justine's book.

For Lorna Bedford, read the dedication, *without whom this book could never have been written.*

The lights were dimmed for take-off. She lowered her eyelids until the cabin was nothing more than a dark tunnel.

Justine had streaked into her life like a comet. A funny, intense, hypereducated comet. Lorna should never have expected to keep hold of her.

5

Spaced from a lack of sleep, Lorna took a shower at Hazlitt's. For a long time, she stood in the purifying heat, shutting out thought.

Afterwards, she sat on the edge of the bed with a towel wrapped around her mid-section like a cocktail dress – the type of dress she would never wear – and took her actual clothes out of her suitcase: black jeans, white shirt, ankle-high black boots, a cropped silk jacket – also black.

She dressed in a shaft of light from the window. It was early yet. She would walk over to Galerie Claude Berlins and check out the show. Maybe Thomas would be around, making final adjustments.

She walked down a silent corridor and took the elevator. She liked the in-between parts of hotels. They were pauses in the otherwise ceaseless diction of reality. The elevator, which was thick with dusky light, was part of this behind-the-scenes realm. A moveable part, bearing her down to the stage.

It was a grey day outside, but warm. She walked along Frith Street to Soho Square. It wasn't the way she'd intended to go. Inside the little park, the plane trees quivered with life. This place was an image of the distant past. In the autumn of 1995, she and Thomas had been students at Central Saint Martins. All she recalled from their first meeting was the place (the Toucan pub: a group of them had gone), and the blue of his eyes. It was funny how a thing like that, a random detail of a

41

person's phenotype, could determine the course of your life. She had felt close to him, uncannily so, from the outset.

She drifted along the path towards the mock-Tudor pavilion, watching pigeons scuttle around her.

It was in Soho Square – they'd been walking here, sharing a bag of Quavers – that she had told Thomas she was pregnant.

He'd stopped on the path and clutched her wrist.

'Are you sure?' And then, as the fact sank in: 'I'm sorry.'

I'm sorry. She could hear him saying it over and over. The prospect of a child had seemed like death.

As they reached the gate at the edge of the square, he hesitated before saying: 'Will you get rid of it?'

'I don't think so.'

They didn't speak about it again for a while. That was the start of his strange, profound indifference.

She couldn't have explained at the time, but it wasn't simply that she was frightened of having an abortion, or that it was getting late. Already there was a tentative pride. Hadn't her parents said that gay people shouldn't be parents? Hadn't she internalised that prohibition, swallowed it whole, and wasn't this, then, the purest transgression? People said that she'd be trapped, but it didn't feel like that. In between the anxiety and nausea, she felt herself coming into being. The child growing inside her felt like a new part of her consciousness.

Looking up just in time, she avoided colliding with a man. He had sunken cheeks, and a sleeping bag was slung around his shoulders. He mumbled something – a word that was more like *bint* than *bitch* – as he shuffled by.

*

On Greek Street, she stopped by a door between shops. It led to the flat, five floors up, where she had lived for two years. She remembered the cold. She had been able to see her breath condense in the air as she lay beneath the window in the mornings. Shifts at the Blue Posts weren't paying enough to keep the heating on. Her parents hadn't spoken to her since she'd taken up with Carmel, a girl of Jamaican heritage who worked in the cloakroom at Turnmills.

It was Carmel who realised that Lorna was pregnant. (What had happened with Thomas wasn't a secret; it didn't seem significant enough to lie about.) Lorna didn't believe it. Her periods had never been reliable, and she hadn't gained weight in months. She couldn't believe either that those fumbling minutes with Thomas could actually have resulted in something. It was her eyes, Carmel said, that gave it away – a slight loss of focus. Her breasts, too. Lorna had never paid much attention to her own contours. A test finally confirmed the fact. She was close to four months gone.

Within days, or so it seemed, she switched from feeling normal to a state of acute, exaggerated pregnancy. Her body started to morph. She was a chrysalis, a grub growing fat and translucent – or, in happier moments, a miracle of nature. She was up most nights, nauseous and giddy with new emotions. Hormones coursed through her like hard drugs. She began to document the change in black and white photographs, hanging the prints on a clothesline in the darkroom at Saint Martins. Her naked body, alluring and gruesome as the angles shifted. A white pebble. A colourless gourd.

Twice she'd gone to the clinic on Dean Street. Both times she'd left with leaflets.

Drunk one night, Thomas raised the idea again.

'What your mother told you,' he said, shouting over the music of the bar. 'You should embrace it. You were never meant to be a parent. You need to do something that matters. Caring for a baby will kill other possibilities.'

She smiled. There was no point talking about it, she said.

*

A few lone men were stationed outside Comptons bar. Flaneurs, except that they weren't going anywhere. Their promenading was of a static, watchful kind.

She was reluctant to see Thomas. Suddenly, she was able to acknowledge it. She walked through the door of Comptons and ordered a pint of lager. The beer slopped over her knuckles as she carried it outside to a brass-plated window ledge.

Drinking in the middle of the day, and who was going to stop her? She swallowed an inch of lager and dimly imagined that she and the character at the next ledge – a taciturn man in a leather jacket – were going to discover a chink in the wall of silence, and begin to talk – about the weather, the news, their lives – before settling in for another pint, then another. She'd once picked up a girl in Greenwich Village that way.

She reached for her phone and punched out a message for Justine.

Are you in love with Beatrix?

She didn't send it. Instead, she left her pint where it was on the brass sill and passed along the road, under the Bridge of Sighs that had once been part of a strip bar. The building was boarded up and graffitied and waiting for development. Soho was gentrifying. Soon, the tawdry vitals would be gone.

*

Galerie Claude Berlins was a new arrival in Mayfair. A year earlier, a building had disappeared from Berkeley Square, leaving a squared-off plot. The space had now been usurped by a stack of concrete, glass and steel – two misaligned storeys, the lower floor adhering to the ground plan of the site, the upper floor overhanging the pavements on either side.

Lorna walked along Berkeley Square beneath a cantilevered projection, then wound her way around the block to Farm Street.

The placement of the entrance on the quieter side seemed a curious act of mock humility.

The bronze-frame door opened with the crack of a breaking seal. Across a lake of polished concrete was a walnut desk. Two young women sat behind it with erect backs. Between them was a vase of white lilies. They glanced at Lorna, then at each other, as she approached.

'Hi,' she said, hearing her voice echo.

She wasn't sure whether the girls had replied. Her attention had already shifted. To one side, through an open threshold, was a vast bright space. Lilac paintings hung around the walls in symmetrical array. The painting that Leo Goffman wanted, with its rift of darker purple, occupied its own wall at the far end.

She crossed the floor, feeling self-conscious. Many galleries had this effect, but here the sense of her body as a stain on the pristine geometry of the room seemed stronger, almost calculated. The gallery was empty, or virtually empty: she heard the clicking of heels. Out of a doorway in the far corner, a figure had appeared – short, smart, determined. It was Sylvia Rosso, Claude's senior partner. Sylvia's hair was different from the last time they'd met. Shorter, with a level fringe that came close to her dark eyebrows. She wore a boxy designer suit.

Their heads swapped places as they made kissing noises.

'You made it past security,' Sylvia said. 'We have guards ready for tonight. They're supposed to be keeping the gallery airtight.' Her teeth flashed white inside red rims.

'They must be on a fag break,' said Lorna. 'I came for an early view. Is Thomas around?'

'He's resting at his hotel.' Sylvia's smile faltered. 'His dog died on Tuesday.'

With a jolt, Lorna recalled a Rottweiler with a beautiful coat. 'I'm sorry.'

'The timing couldn't be worse.' Sylvia fingered the silver necklace that lay against her chest. 'He seems broken.'

They walked in silence to the canvas on the end wall. Within the painting, camouflaged by the uniform tone, were stuttering brushstrokes and hazes of aerosol. And that dark breach, almost cutting the composition in two.

'The *scale* of it,' Lorna said, at a loss for better words.

'Thomas is a genius. It's been incredible working with him.' Sylvia hesitated, then stepped closer. 'I'm going to become his liaison, here. I think he gets on better with women. Well, you should know. Claude's eye is on the bigger picture. And the thing is, with Claude and Thomas . . .' She left the statement hanging, maybe fearing that she'd said too much. 'There's a lot of male silence.'

Lorna went up to the painting, pondering Sylvia's meaning. The dark line was composed of thicker paint, carefully applied with a small brush, as if some accidental effect (the shadow of a tree branch, a crack in plaster) had been traced.

'Is Claude around?'

'He's at lunch. He'll be busy all afternoon.'

At that moment, Claude emerged from the doorway in the corner. There were people with him: a pair of police officers. His broad face was a mask of composure. Sylvia's smile had turned rigid.

'Lorna,' Claude said, holding out both hands but remaining out of reach. 'You're *here*.'

She guessed he was absorbing an unpleasant surprise. His helmet of cropped grey hair glowed in the gallery lights. The officers, a man and a woman, kept pace.

'You'll be joining us at the Connaught for dinner?'

'Well, sure. I didn't come all this way for a Burger King.'

Claude's closed-lipped smile flourished into a laugh, but it was a mime of a laugh – absolutely soundless.

Theories multiplied in her mind. Claude was being investigated – for fraud, for money laundering. An artwork Ponzi scheme? Or was he under protection, having finally made one too many enemies?

'I'm sorry about all this,' Claude said, gesturing with a glance. 'There was an incident the other night involving one of my staff.'

'An incident?'

'One of our associate directors, a young guy.' He lowered his voice while Sylvia went to attend to the police. 'He fell from a building. Not here – his apartment. But don't worry. The opening will go ahead.'

'Did he die?'

Claude closed his eyes, as if to observe a momentary silence. 'It's a tragedy. Everyone's in shock.' Wandering past her, he skimmed the edge of the painting with his fingertips. 'We've kept the news from Thomas, of course. Told him that Luca's sick.'

'Of course,' she echoed, as she came to stand behind him. 'That painting,' she began. 'I wouldn't usually do this, Claude, but I have a client – a serious collector—'

'I've already sold it. Full price, no discount. The whole show's sold, in fact.' Claude continued to inspect the edge of the canvas as though it were a fine piece of joinery.

'Seriously? You haven't even opened yet.'

He looked round. His smile was large.

'Do I have to say it, Lorna? You've had your turn. Thomas wants to work on a bigger stage. His prices are way below where they ought to be for an artist' – the lines around his eyes deepened as he searched for the phrase – 'a painter of his *stature*.'

With this final word, the French accent that Claude had long suppressed broke through.

'And who made him that painter?' Lorna said.

Claude's teeth were a shield. A vague distaste, or some altogether stronger emotion, was building.

'Sylvia,' he called out. 'Is Lorna on our seating plan for the Connaught?'

'Of course,' Sylvia replied, interrupting the police. 'On Thomas's table.'

'Well, then,' Claude said, as if there were nothing more to discuss. His hand, extending from a white cuff, drew an arc across the gallery. 'It's quite a show, no?' He turned to leave.

In that moment, she understood why Claude had wanted Thomas for his gallery. Thomas was predictable; he wouldn't surprise or disappoint. Claude knew what type of work Thomas would make – panels of pure colour filled with plays of light – and he knew that he could sell them. She wanted to hate the paintings, but couldn't. The concentration on a single colour was like a voice hovering around a solitary note. Small inexplicable details (was anything explicable, with Thomas?) made each picture distinct, like the thin line that crossed the corner of one of the lilac fields. It made her think of a telephone cable slicing through an evening sky.

*

Outside, two security guards were now stationed either side of the door. Blank-faced men with earpieces. Nearby, another man was leaning against the wall, smoking a cigarette. He didn't look like a member of staff, more a loiterer. He wore a sagging T-shirt, and had the haunted look of the severely hungover.

'Impressive, right?' he said as Lorna went by, and glanced up at the building.

'Sure,' she replied.

'To create something like this in nine months.'

'Is that all it took?'

'Word is, Berlins found the site and commissioned the architect years ago. But he only decided to build last year.' He dropped his cigarette. 'Who knows why people like that act the way they do?'

'People like what?'

'Masters of the art world.'

'Oh, right. *Them.*'

The shadow of the building fell at a slant over Farm Street. It struck her that the design was similar to that of Thomas's house, from what she'd seen in *Architectural Digest*. Both buildings had an international Modernist air. There was a shared palette of concrete and glass and burnished metal. A preponderance of oblongs.

'You work here?' she asked.

'No, I'm a reporter. *Evening Standard.*'

She thought of what Claude had told her. An accidental death. The man watched her with curiosity. She gave a polite smile and began to walk away.

'Did you know Luca Holden?' he called after her.

She turned back.

'They're saying it was suicide,' he said, with a level gaze. 'Did you know him?'

Shaking her head, she wandered on, through the elegant neutrality of Mayfair.

6

7 September, 17.09. London

'Did you call for any reason?'

'Just to say hi.'

Lorna sat back against the headboard of the bed and hooked a finger into the opening of her shirt, sliding it into the hollow between her breasts. Her phone lay on the bed beside her, on speakerphone. She had gone back to Hazlitt's for a rest, but hadn't been able to sleep, and she'd figured that Justine would still be up.

'Where's Jay?'

'I checked him into Manhattan Woof. I'll collect him tomorrow when I'm back.'

'I've been missing him something fierce,' Justine said. 'My gorgeous boy. The humidity in Hong Kong would kill him. Do you miss me?'

'Sure.'

'You don't sound sure.'

'I was just thinking about stuff.'

'Stuff?'

'This show at Claude Berlins. I always miss you. I follow what you're doing on Instagram. You gave a reading in Cantonese. And you went to the M Plus Museum in Kowloon. See? I probably know more about what you're up to than when you're in New York.'

'Well, you're welcome to follow what I do in New York, too.'

Lorna considered this. Since when had Justine wanted Lorna

to be part of her success? Things had been different when Lorna was the successful one. After Justine got her break, success seemed to be too precious a thing to share.

'How's London?' Justine said. 'Same as ever?'

'The same but different. Soho looks kind of the same, but then you turn your head and it's nothing like it used to be.'

'What did you expect? It would be like me expecting Hong Kong to resemble its old self. This is a Chinese city now. I mean, the place has come back to life since lockdown, but there's no doubt who's in charge.'

'How's it going out there?'

'Oh – fantastic.' Justine was inaudible for a moment. 'I haven't stopped. We've hardly arrived and Beatrix is organising more stuff. Dinner with Liu Zhou at the Hong Kong Club. And readings this fall at the British Club in Beijing and the American Club in Shanghai.'

'Sounds very clubbish. Very – colonial.'

Justine's laugh was a fleck of shrapnel. 'Well, you should know about clubs, being in the art world. Don't get hung up on the names of places, anyway. The crowds here are superdiverse. There are young Chinese, European students, American scholars—'

'That's Hong Kong. Wait till you get to the mainland.'

'What do you know about China? And as for *colonial*! Oh my God, I was trying to explain to Beatrix about that bizarre convention of national pavilions at the Venice Biennale. She thought I was making it up. It's so retrogressive. You contemporary art types make the mistake of thinking that because the art is new, you're a bunch of radicals.'

'You keep telling yourself that,' Lorna said, 'from your gentlemen's clubs in the east. I never said I was a radical. I never took *positions*.'

'Don't I know it? You're a shameless neoliberal.'

'I don't do *postures*. I can't live in a constant state of outrage—'

'There's a lot wrong with the world, Lorna, if the people in your bubble were only aware of it.' Justine laughed again, more drily. 'Did you get Leo Goffman the painting he wants?'

Lorna clicked her tongue. 'There's no way Claude Berlins is going to let me broker a sale.'

'Why doesn't Goffman go direct to Berlins?'

'It's weird. Leo has some kind of block regarding Claude. There must be history there. He insists that *I'm* Thomas's dealer and so I should handle the negotiation. There's something old-fashioned about it. Principled, almost.'

'Goffman, principled? I love that. He's just fucking you around. He likes the idea of a woman doing the running for him.'

Lorna was silent for a while. She wondered whether to mention what had happened at the gallery – the police, the news of an accidental death, the journalist outside . . .

'What's strange is Leo's desperation for that picture,' she said at last. 'His cupidity, I mean. It *could* almost be sexual. I can't work out if he's for real.'

'I wonder if he even knows. When is desire authentic for a man like that? When is desire *good*? Desire for him is a reflex, like needing to shit. It has no value. It's a by-product of envy, loneliness, hate . . .'

'Maybe, but it's no less real for that.'

Justine launched into another subject, and Lorna's gaze dissolved into the sage green and oak planes of the hotel room. Was she becoming oversensitive – too easily offended? From the moment they'd met, she had loved Justine's irreverence. Sparring had always been part of their dynamic, an almost erotic thing.

Justine had walked up to her at Bard College, that first time, and confronted her with a question.

'Come to my gallery,' Lorna had replied, never expecting to see this handsome, bold, precocious girl again. Justine turned up a few days later, on the night that Lorna was opening a show of erotic drawings by Warhol and Cocteau. A stop-gap show: Thomas or one of her other big artists had pulled out at the last minute. Somehow, Justine ended up at the after-show dinner (Lorna didn't remember inviting her), and after that, they ended up at Lorna's house, on the sofa, kissing like teenagers.

7

The pavement outside Galerie Claude Berlins was spilling over with people. The road beyond was like a crowded piazza. Cigarette smoke floated on the breeze, beneath a sky that was turning from pink to deep blue. Laughter and raised voices rebounded off the stately buildings.

Lorna moved through the sea of faces, recognising or half-recognising people – curators, artists, critics. She saw Fritz Schein sailing towards the door, trailed by a cortège of young women from the Lucinda Villa. Not yet forty, Fritz was one of the biggest curators in the business, running the trendiest institution in New York, but never in one place for long. The Lucinda Villa made sure to offset his carbon footprint.

Close to the door, two metal buckets had been filled with ice. A pair of young men were handing out bottles of lager, flicking off the tops. Lorna felt jetlag descending like a first wave of drunkenness. A beer would stave it off, maybe. She took a bottle and drank a few mouthfuls, then placed it in the gutter.

Inside, the foyer had turned into a crucible of breathy heat and babbling talk. The lilies on the desk were shedding their petals. Beyond, in the main space, the paintings were barely visible through the crowd.

'Thomas Haller has entered his violet period!' Fritz Schein cried out, addressing everyone in earshot. 'No – ultraviolet!'

'That would mean his art is invisible,' said a wisecracking man.

'*Thomas* is ultraviolet,' Fritz replied. 'The invisible man! Where has he been for six years? And yet' – his voice ignited with excitement – 'he's everywhere! His name, his influence, his auction records. *Everywhere*, like ultraviolet light!'

Lorna stayed close to the walls. Thomas was nowhere to be seen. Maybe that was what Fritz, in his roundabout way, was getting at. A suspicion was building. Thomas would bail at the last minute – stay hidden in his hotel. Sylvia had already said that he was broken by grief. Besides, there was a frisson in not showing up. It was a gesture worthy of Warhol.

A hand was at her elbow. A firm but respectful touch. She turned to see a young woman, one of the pair who had been at the desk earlier. The girl's hair was long and blonde. Pantene hair.

'Please mind the painting,' she said in a programmed voice.

Lorna had been within inches of one of the canvases.

'Oh, sure. Sorry.'

But the girl had moved on, ready to repeat the words.

Lorna saw Claude Berlins cruising through the room. On the lapel of his jacket was an enamel button of the European flag. His eyes flicked from side to side. As his path came close to Fritz's, the two men smiled full beam at one another, as if encountering their own dashing reflections.

She followed Claude's gaze to an elderly woman. Lorna knew the type. A rich collector affronting old age with her money – dark hair drawn back in a chignon, eyes twinkling with *seen it all before* equanimity. Flanking her like an accessory was a small man in a pinstripe suit. Her husband, maybe, although somehow Lorna doubted it. He was bald, with a deep suntan and gold-rimmed glasses that screened his eyes with reflected light. In a split second she remembered him. Milton Rogers, a movie producer from Los Angeles. A long time ago, she'd sold him a Sam Francis.

He had sighted her in the same moment.

'Miss Bedford! A fellow American in London.'

'I'm British, actually,' she said, raising her voice over the noise. 'I've just lived for years in New York.'

His face crinkled as if she'd let him in on a wonderful secret. 'Come see me in Hollywood. Come to Paramount. That Francis is on my office wall. I'd love for you to see it. Oh, by the way, this is Baroness LaBelle.'

Lorna turned to the woman, but Claude had already interposed himself. He leaned in for a kiss.

'Claude, baby,' the woman said. Her voice was magnificent – textured, probably, by decades of guiltless smoking. 'These paintings are to die for. I love them – the *colours*! I want to die.'

Claude murmured in her ear. Her eyes rolled upward.

'Tell me, is that one available?' She stretched out a hand.

'It could be.' Claude took her by the hand like a Disney prince. 'It very well could be.'

'Come meet my art advisor,' she purred. 'He's just over here.'

As Claude and the Baroness moved away, Milton Rogers touched Lorna on the wrist. A grin of boyish delight had spread over his face.

'Mimi used to be in the movies,' he said in a loud whisper. 'The *grande dame* of neo-noir!'

*

'Please mind the painting,' murmured a girl in Lorna's ear. A different girl this time. She sounded like a testy New Yorker.

A moment later, Lorna felt a hand on her elbow again. She swung around.

The surprise of seeing his face (its very familiarity a surprise), and the weight of his hand on her arm, left her unable to speak for a second. Thomas's eyes circled the room and returned to her.

'I see crowds of people, walking around in a ring.'

'They're walking around for you.'

'Fools.'

His fingers skimmed her forearm and he clutched her hand. His hair, still dark, hung over his brow in a diagonal sweep. He looked older, she thought, and there was exhaustion in his blue eyes.

'This – all this – will disappear,' he said, indicating the mass of people. 'I've seen it drain away before. I belong to the past.'

'Maybe we all do.' She clasped his hand over her own, then detached herself. 'I'm sorry about Betty.'

His smile had clenched.

'When did it happen?'

'Two nights ago, here in London. At Claridge's.'

'You were with her,' she said. The question had come out as a statement.

'Yes,' he said, with an empty stare. 'I watched her go.'

'Then at least she wasn't alone.'

'I could see what was going to happen right before she died. This spasming started. And her eyes . . . It was like she was falling back and I couldn't catch her.'

'And now all of this. Life just charges on.'

He nodded, and she felt his melancholy pass over her.

'I'm glad you've come,' he said. 'You didn't have to.'

'I know. I wasn't sure I would.'

They watched one another. She hadn't seen him in eight months, not since just before Christmas, on one of his fleeting trips to New York – a few days before he'd told her that he would be doing this show.

'How's Justine?'

'She's fine.'

'Really?' He had picked up on something in the speed of her reply.

'I don't know. We're kind of not together any more. She's just gone to Asia – I don't know how long for.'

'I'm sorry.'

'Yeah, right.' She mustered a smile. 'You never liked her.'

'She never liked *me*. I'd hardly met her and she wrote that dreadful essay. To her I'm a symbol of everything that's wrong with contemporary art.'

'Justine thinks in symbols. And trust you to be remembering a bad review tonight.'

'My insecurity is fine-tuned.'

He seemed on the point of saying more. The sadness of moments earlier was receding. He was recovering the self-conscious reserve that she'd never much liked in him. She was aware of Claude's circling movements and the clamour of the room.

'Listen, Thomas. I have a client – I can't tell you who. He's discreet. But this guy's a big deal. He only buys masterpieces. And he wants that painting.' She tilted her head at the end wall. 'It would still be Claude's sale. I'm not doing this for myself—'

'It's Claude's call.'

'Seriously? It's your painting.'

'And it's Claude's gallery.' His voice was level, as expressionless as his face.

'You know that Claude will do whatever you want.'

He watched her for a few seconds. Was there anger beneath the blank? A deeper sorrow?

'I can't,' he said.

*

A woman was easing her way through the crowd, eyes fixed on Thomas. A woman in her early thirties, with unkempt black hair. Lorna saw her first.

'Thomas, hi. I'm Marianna Berger.'

His clear eyes settled on her.

One of the girls from the gallery had come after her and was trying to take hold of her arm. Marianna shook herself free.

'We met once in New York. You probably don't remember.'

She looked southern European or possibly Middle Eastern, but when she spoke, she sounded very English. She seemed subtly agitated.

Thomas gave a nod. 'Berger – any relation to the great man?'

'I don't think so. Maybe. Who cares?'

He glanced from Marianna to Lorna and back. It seemed as if he might laugh.

'My life in New York feels like a hundred years ago. I don't go back very often.'

'I've just quit America too. It wasn't working for me.'

'Are you an artist?'

'Kind of. I make videos.'

'A filmmaker then. Ever heard of Ida Lupino?'

She returned a guarded smile. 'No, but I was in a show at White Columns in the summer. *Chronotopia*. Maybe you heard about it?'

Redness was spreading over Marianna's face. Lorna could feel her unease. It didn't get easier for some artists, the hustling. While for others, like Thomas, success had come early and never gone away.

'I should know more about what's happening,' he said. 'I've stopped looking at other artists' work. I know we're never meant to admit to it, the loss of curiosity. I'm sorry – do you know Lorna Bedford?'

Marianna's front teeth were pressing into her lower lip. She was sexier than Lorna had first thought.

'Yes – yes of course. I've been to your gallery.'

'Maybe that's where you met him,' Lorna said. 'We used to work together.'

There was a hardness to her statement, but Thomas didn't seem to have noticed. His eyes were beginning to flit.

'Say—' Marianna took a step towards him. 'I could come and make a video about you. Sort of like a character study. The artist at home in the mountains.'

'I'm sure you could,' he said. 'And you'd be disappointed. You see, I'm very dull. My paintings are more interesting than me by far. What you're looking at now' – he slid his hands into his jeans pockets and relaxed his stance, seeming in the same instant to break a pose and to strike one – 'is all there is.'

'That's okay,' she said with a laugh. 'I'm interested in surfaces. And I'd get to see your house.'

Her confidence was running too fast, Lorna thought. A flippant idea was hardening into a serious possibility, in her mind. But Thomas would never allow it. He was the most private person Lorna knew.

'You mean a documentary?' he said.

'More like a sequence of fragments. No storytelling. I like my videos to feel like thought.'

Thomas fastened the button of his jacket. 'It's all storytelling, though. All art. All of *this*' – he indicated the gallery with a flick of his fingers. 'What else could it be?' His face had changed. There was an almost pained alertness. He seemed about to walk away when he added: 'I don't allow anyone to record me painting. But as for the rest – I'd consider it. Send an email to Sylvia Rosso.'

*

Lorna watched as Marianna Berger retreated into the crowd. Had she heard the young woman's name somewhere? Probably not. There was something appealing about her, about her lack of respect.

Thomas had fallen into conversation with the Baroness. They were discussing the resort towns around Lake Geneva. Claude was listening with an overcharged grin.

Voices rang through the air.

'Weren't you at the Ljubljana Biennale?'

'Yes! And did you see that performance by Milovan Barbusse?'

'I couldn't *breathe*.'

Lorna felt as if she were waking from a years-long sleep. What was she doing here, among these people? She sensed herself beginning to recoil from the paintings, as though she were afraid of slipping into their lilac depths. She moved towards the reception area. On the threshold of the foyer, she was confronted by Fritz Schein. He seemed to unfurl before her with flailing buoyancy, like a dirigible filling with air. His glasses were two perfect circles, the frames as red as a Rockette's lipstick.

'Lorna! I thought it was you!'

'Hey, Fritz. I haven't seen you in weeks.'

'Not since the Serpentine summer party.' There was a residual German weight to his vowels.

'Not since before. I never go to that.'

'But I was *sure* I saw you. Everyone was there. How could you *not* have been?'

'I don't come to London much.'

'I've been in Europe all summer,' he said, scanning the gallery behind her. '*Eurasia*. The oil fields outside Baku are spectacular, Lorna, like another planet. You know, I'm thinking of making *spectacularity* the theme for Venice.'

Aside from his job at the Lucinda Villa, Fritz was the curator of the next Venice Biennale. He also acted as an advisor to private collections. He saw everything, knew everyone – his existence was a living performance, and Lorna never knew how to react. Was he for real? Delight and exhilaration were the only responses she had ever discerned in him. Perhaps they were the gatekeepers of other, duller emotions that had to stay locked away from view.

'So how was the Serpentine party?' she asked. 'What did I miss?'

'Art is *all* about fashion now.' He drew his phone from his breast pocket. 'Here's me with Bella Hadid.'

Lorna leaned in to see, but light bounced off the surface.

'And look, I made this video.' With a nimble tap, he played a recording.

The picture was dim and unstable. There were bodies, lights, a man's face transfigured by a frantic smile, and then a break from darkness to daylight as the camera moved outdoors. Voices and laughter blended into a tinny synthesis.

'It's a portrait of the art world, and I'm the mobile observer, like Manet!'

'I wasn't aware you knew who Manet was,' said Lorna, blunting her sarcasm with a smirk. 'He's nineteenth century.'

'The art world as pure spectacle,' Fritz went on, unfazed. 'Even Thomas Haller turned up, the great recluse!' He tucked his phone away and his eyes cavorted around the room. 'This show is his redemption, no? His lilac renaissance. His violet hour.'

'You should be on Twitter, Fritz. Or whatever they're calling it now.'

He laughed as if this were the funniest thing he'd heard all night – all year.

'It's true, Lorna. I know it – you know it. Thomas is returning to greatness. *True* greatness.'

*

There was a noise from the door to the street. For a moment, Lorna's brain accepted it as part of the general hubbub. A cackling, hectoring laugh. A drunk woman or man; it was hard to tell. The sound grew louder. She pushed her way closer to the entrance.

She saw a middle-aged man in respectable attire. A dark overcoat hung about him. He was hunched and crying uncontrollably. Onlookers had drawn back from him in a circle.

Lorna stood among them. The sight was appalling. As people watched and waited, the man approached the desk and extracted a card from the vase of lilies. A condolence note: Lorna could tell from the black border and the scrolling text at the centre. *In loving memory*. Names had been written by hand around the edges. The man held the card with both hands and continued to sob. Lorna trained her gaze on his combed hair, his pale neck.

A peculiar quiet had spread around the foyer, although animated talk and laughter still bled in from the gallery.

'Alan,' said the girl with blonde hair, stepping into the space that had opened around him. 'It's me – Sarah. Can I call your wife?'

The man let out a stuttering cry.

'Sarah,' he gasped. '*Why?*'

'I know,' said the girl. 'Come outside. I'll walk with you.'

Claude Berlins had arrived in the reception area. He hovered at a safe remove. Sylvia Rosso slid between the onlookers and positioned herself at his side. Their faces were mirror images of coolness.

Still gripping hold of the card, the man brought his hands to his eyes. He seemed to hold his breath.

'Luca,' he said, and a groan burst from him. '*LUCA.*'

Everyone stood still. All power to react – any capacity to move or speak or feel – had been drained from the spectators. Fritz's head rose above the others, his features a picture of wonder. Slowly his iPhone rose into view, coming level with his face.

Alan's hands dropped. His eyes were sinking into shining wells. Making no noise other than rasping breaths, he stepped towards the lilies as if intending to replace the card.

He tripped. His overcoat flew up behind him and he flung out an arm. The vase sheared through the air, hurling its waxy flowers. Lorna shut her eyes. The sound as it hit the ground was like a car crash. When she opened her eyes, water was streaming over the concrete. Petals floated between segments of glass. Alan was on his knees, then lying face-down in the mess, his black coat open around him. He smeared his hand over the shards and flowers, clawing at the scattered stems. There was a wisp of red in the glistening trail. A whimpering sound came from beneath the coat, out of the depths of his body.

8

7 September, 19.59. London

A sense of reality was returning. People were talking furtively. Thomas was nowhere around. Maybe he'd been whisked away to the Connaught at the first sign of trouble.

Lorna felt the night air through the open door. She walked out of the gallery and into the street. There were longer, deeper shadows now. It was crowded still, but people were drifting into the surrounding roads and alleyways. Taxis turned around the dead-end of roadway in front of Galerie Claude Berlins.

A man was watching her. He was standing slightly apart from the entrance, framed by a segment of concrete wall. For a second, she thought it was the journalist from earlier in the day. The darkness had made Thomas momentarily unrecognisable.

'Did you see that, in there?' she said.

He shrugged, smiling in a way that didn't convince. 'London is full of eccentrics. Always was.'

Their gazes broke and met.

'I stopped by at Comptons today. Do you remember—'

He shook his head. 'I can't talk about the past, Lorna. Not tonight. Not any night. Please.'

'We used to speak every week.'

'Things change. You met Justine. I left New York.'

'But they don't have to. And why *did* you leave? New York

was your life.' She felt an old annoyance burning to the surface. 'Everything was different after the Whitney. Maybe success – that level of success – wasn't good for you.'

She no longer cared what she was saying. She had come to London, it now occurred to her, to say this. She wanted to have it out with him. But Thomas wasn't going to rise to it. His impassivity, that subtle old veil, had descended.

'If this was about having a show in London, I could have given you one. I could have got you a show at an institution. The Serpentine. The fucking Tate. You didn't need to sell your soul to Claude. When did money—'

'When did money what?' His words were exacting.

'Forget it.'

'Dealers, galleries.' He gave a giant sigh. 'I'm indifferent. You know I'm indifferent.'

'Thanks a lot.'

'Not to you personally. I could never be that. To the business side of things, I mean. To the commerce, the politics. All I want to do is paint.'

She laughed, hearing her bitterness ring out in the night air. 'That's such bullshit.' She gestured at the building behind him. 'Is this what you call indifference?'

'It's not about you. This show—'

'Of course it's about me. This is about me and you and twenty-five years of work. The longest relationship of my life. Think of what we've been through.'

As she looked at him, waiting for a reply that wouldn't come, she felt that he was a stranger, someone she didn't know. Certainly not someone she loved.

*

After he had gone, Lorna stood there against the wall, watching people leave. A few feet away, the two young men who had been serving beer took hold of the metal trough by either end and poured the ice cubes into a drain. Pieces of their conversation came to her through the roaring noise.

'No, it was his dad. Luca's *father*.'

'Adoptive father, you mean.' The ice continued to surge. 'Adoptive, yeah. He told me he'd been adopted as a baby.'

They righted the trough, empty now, on the pavement. The boy closer to Lorna stood up straight and placed his hands against his lower back.

'They're all saying it's suicide,' he said.

'Who's saying that?'

'People in there.'

The other one crouched on his haunches and rested his finger-tips on the rim of the trough. 'I saw him the day it happened. He was here, hanging the paintings. Just the same as usual. Laughing, like everything was fine.'

'Excuse me,' Lorna said.

She saw two startled faces. They hadn't realised she was standing there, so close, in the shadow of the building.

She came closer. 'Can you tell me the way to the Connaught Hotel?'

*

She walked through public gardens, a tranquil enclosure hemmed in by mansion blocks, and onto Mount Street. Ahead, she saw the curving facade of the hotel. The guests for dinner would be there by now. She tried to imagine the scene. A tray of champagne in the lobby, a map of the tables (every place assigned), and Thomas hovering beyond reach.

Across the street was a pub. Two men, financial types in striped shirts, were laughing together, then swearing, then squaring up to one another on the pavement. The change in mood had taken place in less than ten seconds. One man was burly and squat, the other tall and slender. The different colours of their shirts, pink and blue, were like plumages.

Lorna slowed her approach. From a distance, she saw one of the men (the taller of the two) felled by a single kick of the other's shoe – a sideswipe across the calves. He looked up from the pavement with an unfocused glare. One of his shirt cuffs had fallen open. The look of loss on his face was absolute, as if all his memory, his whole identity, had been pounded out of him.

A group of onlookers – closer to the scene than Lorna – was forming. The stocky guy wasn't backing down. With his chest inflated, he took another step towards his victim and punted his shoe into the man's stomach. A wheeze of pain burst through the air. As he swung his leg back for a third blow, a group of women surrounded and restrained him.

Lorna walked in the other direction. Whether it was the grim surprise of what she'd witnessed, or the accumulated feelings of the evening, she knew at that moment that she wouldn't go to the dinner. She wandered into Grosvenor Square, which always made her think of an Ivy League campus, and pondered her own bystander apathy. Justine had taught her the term. *The inhibiting influence of the presence of others on a person's willingness to help.*

She sat on a stone bench close to a fountain. It was almost dark now, but two children were playing on the grass: a boy and a girl, aged around ten, chasing each other with piercing yells. They must be from one of the rich families living here, she thought. Expats, probably. A strange existence. She took out her phone, and without quite knowing why, she searched on X for Thomas Haller. There were numerous rehashings of the gallery's press release. *Monochrome palette. Violet études.* And a few photographs from the opening. One picture, posted in the last five minutes, showed the painting that Leo wanted. It was partially blocked by Fritz Schein – his glasses reflecting the gallery lights, an arm flung out across the front of the canvas, and to his side, the petite figure of Baroness LaBelle. But the people weren't of any interest to the poster of the image.

Thomas Haller show at the new Berlins. Will anyone admit this guy is a fraud? #ZombieFormalism

She shivered in the breeze. Around her, the windows of flats glowed out in random sequence.

A few days ago, someone had posted a photo of Thomas and Claude at a party.

Thomas Haller is now represented by Claude Berlins. Hmmmmmm. #Artworld #Patriarchy #MarriagePortrait

Claude was red in the face and laughing. His mouth was open; his eyes were wide. Standing beside him was Thomas, returning a hesitant smile. A single vein was visible on one of his temples. They were together in a crowd, holding glasses of champagne, watched by everyone around them.

It was a photo from the Serpentine summer party back in July. Lorna tapped on the picture to enlarge it. Claude and Thomas were standing in sunlight, not far from a doorway. In the dimness of the interior, she could just make out a younger man.

She perceived a movement in the corner of her vision. She scanned the paths around her, certain that she was being watched, but the area was empty. The children had moved on.

Watching the square grow dark, she thought of the night that she'd given birth. She had worked so hard to blind out the details that only stray fragments remained. The machinery around the hospital bed. Her girlfriend, Carmel, trying to make a game out of the laughing gas. And the pain, like a lodged knife growing in size. Her screams for the epidural and the oozing relief when they gave her the shot in her spine. The way the baby slithered out once his head was free . . .

When Lorna got home from the hospital, she found a note on the doormat. A goodbye from Thomas.

I've gone to Düsseldorf. All the real painters are training at the Kunstakademie. I came to see you at the hospital. They wouldn't let me in.

I'm sorry.

It wasn't until a year later that she saw him again. He showed up in New York – walked into her gallery with a big, blue-eyed smile, holding a stack of Polaroids. He must have thought that they could pick up where they'd left off, as if the child and all the intervening time had been a dream. But something didn't align. He looked thinner; his smile had a note of strain. She knew, in that first bewildering moment, that they were different people. More circumspect. A touch less trusting. Living close to each other in the East Village, they tried to replay the friendship in its original form, reverting to an earlier script. But there was a reserve about their interactions, so slight as to be barely perceptible. It hardened with time, as she became his dealer and he became a success. They both pretended not to have noticed. They talked less and less about what had happened in London, and when they did, it was with rueful humour, as if they were talking about characters in a film they had once watched together.

*

By way of a short crescent, she found herself back at the Connaught. The glazed loggia of the restaurant ran parallel to the pavement. Through the glass, she picked out Claude Berlins. He was standing up – the only standing person in the room – at the central table. There was a glass of champagne in his hand.

She thought of the photo online. Claude's eyes danced around. His free hand fanned and fisted. Seated at the same table, Thomas maintained a fixed smile. *A match made in hell.*

Thomas had risen to his feet. Everyone in the room was clapping. His eyes seemed to travel beyond the restaurant and meet her own through the glass. He was looking straight at her – blankly, acutely. She looked back, feeling like she'd seen his ghost.

*

20.59

She doesn't think I can see her.

Thomas stood at the centre of the restaurant, no longer caring that everyone in the room was waiting for him to speak. How forlorn Lorna looked out there on the street, and yet how beautiful.

And how like Luca. The realisation made him go hot and cold. The words he'd prepared began to issue from his mouth. As he spoke, he had the sensation (it was close to a hallucination) that Luca was there, directly across the table where that Norma Desmond creature was now sitting. He imagined Luca catching his eye, trying to make him laugh at the people around them, enticing him away from the table, into the toilets . . . and then he remembered Luca's face that final time – no longer smiling, already drained of life.

His speech ended with expressions of thanks. He looked at the faces around the restaurant. Rings of them at each table, all turned towards him. Beyond the glass, the pavement was empty.

*

21.00

Lorna walked on. It had been an illusion. The room was too bright, and the night too dark, for Thomas to have seen her. He had been studying his own reflection in the lit glass.

She walked back into Soho, which was noisy and alive – a relief after the tense tranquillity of Mayfair. She was too tired to go into a bar. But the mood of the street was its own kind of drug. She walked slowly, watching people on the pavements as they smoked and drank.

Lying on her bed at Hazlitt's, fully dressed, she flicked through a copy of the *Evening Standard*. On page five was a report with the headline, *Art gallery worker plunges to death*, alongside a picture. The text was brief.

> *Luca Holden, a member of staff at Galerie Claude Berlins in Mayfair, fell from the balcony of his flat in Kennington on the evening of Tuesday 5 September at around eight o'clock. He was found unconscious and was rushed to St Thomas' Hospital, where he died from head injuries. Police have appealed for witnesses.*

The photograph showed a young man, captured close up. The flash of the camera had imparted a sheen to his features and a glint to his teeth (just visible between opening lips). He was beginning to smile. A confident, winning smile, and yet, Lorna thought, there was a wildness there, a dilated quality that registered almost as alarm.

*

23.48

At Claridge's, Thomas took a sleeping pill. He lay on the bed fully clothed, beneath the glaring clusters of a chandelier. He thought of Lorna watching him through the window of the restaurant, and then of Luca's father at the gallery. A streaming flood of water, petals and stems, streaked with blood and gritted with broken glass.

He turned over in bed and hummed tunelessly to distract himself.

It had been in February, before the snow melted, that Luca Holden came to see Thomas in Montreux. He had arrived with his jacket slung over one shoulder, eyes wide from the exertion of the climb, hair messed up by the wind. A work visit: Claude had sent him to look at the new paintings and help make a selection for the exhibition.

'It doesn't seem a very English name – Luca,' Thomas said.

'My mother's Italian.' Luca's smile was open and confident. It was the confidence of a young director at Claude's gallery, but there was something else that Thomas couldn't identify for a moment.

'How long are you here for?'

'Just today.' Luca flung out his hands in a mock-dramatic shrug. 'I'm taking the Eurostar back to London tonight.'

Thomas grew aware, in that first meeting, of Luca's fascination with him. And he was aware of a similar feeling in himself. Conversation came easily. Humour bounced between them. Luca seemed clever, in an unshowy way.

'When did you start working for Claude?' Thomas asked, leading the way up the stairs to the studio.

'Nearly a year ago.'

'And you're a director already?'

'Associate director.'

'He must believe in you.'

'I don't know. It's impossible to know what Claude thinks. He leaves you wondering where you stand with him.'

'He always did.'

Thomas took Luca into the studio and walked around, talking

about his new series, repeating the lines he'd always used about his work. He stopped mid-sentence when he noticed how Luca was watching him, with a hint of irony beneath his earnestness. Thomas saw himself, for a second, through the younger man's eyes. Saw how ridiculous he'd become.

'You haven't mentioned the colour,' Luca said. 'Lilac.'

'Violet.'

'It's what makes these paintings new. I can't think of any other work you've made—'

'It's something to do with living out here alone, that colour. The sense I have that I'm closer now to the end than to the beginning.' Thomas fell silent, surprised by his own admission. 'Come outside. You've seen the paintings. We can choose twelve at random for the London show. Come and see the garden.'

They walked onto the terrace, stopping to look out at the Alps.

'You must have the most amazing parties here,' Luca said, going close to the parapet.

'I left New York to get away from all that. You're my first guest since Covid.'

They went down the steps to the swimming pool.

'Is it heated?'

'Always. Like a Roman bath.'

Luca looked up, startled. Betty had appeared from the forest beyond the pool, a black mass barrelling towards them. She leapt to a halt and barked. Luca laughed. He knelt and the dog loosened her stance, anger relaxing into bewilderment. She padded into his opened arms.

'My leading lady,' Thomas said. 'Bette Davis. Or Betty Grable.'

At the sound of her name, the dog came to him. He knelt in turn, took hold of her head, and held it in the crook of his arm. He could feel her panting breaths. He held her tight until she pulled free and retreated up the steps to the house.

He turned to see that Luca had taken off his shirt, kicked off his shoes, and was peeling off his jeans. His body was tall and slender in the sunshine. He seemed entirely without self-consciousness. Wearing only his underwear – white Calvin Klein briefs – he dived into the water. He swam half the length of the pool before surfacing. Reaching the far end, he gripped hold of the concrete edge and levered himself up on both hands, drawing his back and hips from the water in a slow, sleek motion. He held himself there, aware surely that Thomas was watching. His wet shoulders gleamed. Still balancing on the palms of his hands, his legs suspended in the water, he turned to look back.

9

8 September, 19.17. New York

Lorna sat on the stoop, holding her phone. The sun was sinking and the road was quiet. It was Friday evening in New York and Saturday morning in Hong Kong. Their two voices, tired and bright, seemed to reflect the times of day.

'I skipped Thomas's dinner last night,' she said, tilting her head to catch the stream of the breeze.

'What? Are you serious?' There was a dramatic edge to Justine's intrigue – overdramatic. It failed to conceal her true indifference. Intrigued and indifferent. So many of her reactions had that double character.

'I just couldn't do it.' Lorna held her fingers in the direction of a cat slinking past the bottom step. 'There wasn't one single reason. It just didn't feel right. And Thomas' – she thought again of his face through the window: that blind stare – 'I couldn't get through to him.'

'I'm proud of you. You refused to play the game.'

'I copped out.'

'There's power in refusing to bow to expectations. The liberation in saying no. Look at us, for example.'

'Us?'

'Leading our own lives. Refusing to live in each other's pockets. Being free to – I don't know—'

To fall in love. Was that what Justine meant?

'I don't feel free, not today. I have commitments, millions of them. Another show to sell.'

'You should have been a curator in a museum. Like MoMA, or the Whitney. Thinking about art instead of commodifying it.'

'I'm always thinking about it.'

'Sure, but—'

'Whenever you say that I should have been a curator, or a writer, or an academic, what you're really saying – aren't you? – is that I should have been you.'

'I just meant that you're smart. You see through all the bullshit.'

'Right. Do I?'

'Oh, baby doll,' Justine exclaimed in the Mississippian drawl that heralded a happy mood. 'We pretend to disagree. But deep down, we think the same. We were always so alike.'

For a few minutes, they talked about other things. Justine's insomnia, *Oppenheimer*, the idea (a recurring one) that it all would have been different if they'd moved to LA.

Afterwards, standing at the top of the steps, Lorna reflected that she was in the very spot from where she'd watched Justine leave, two days earlier. Their relationship seemed to exist, now, as an intermittent phone call in which the relationship itself was rarely a subject for discussion. Her eyes landed on the light and shade of the road. She reached in her bag for her door keys.

We were always so alike, Justine had said, employing the past tense. An elegy for what had been? The reality was, Justine had always been different: Ivy League, unfazed, ostentatiously knowledgeable (she read faster than anyone Lorna knew), secure in her principles. Her parents were liberal New England people – her father a pharmaceutical scientist, her mother a cardiologist. She had grown up on a different planet from the terraced street in north London where Lorna's parents had lived and died. Justine could reel off quotes from Adorno the same way an evangelical minister cited scripture at will; she could slip Foucault's name into a random observation and steer clear – just – of self-parody.

Lorna passed into the sitting room. The surface of the desk

was empty apart from a piece of newspaper. It was the page from the *Fire Island Review* containing Justine's article. Lorna scrutinised the grainy photograph of Thomas, standing amid his pictures with a solemn stare. Justine had never liked him. His reputation had been a turn-off before she ever met him. Lorna recollected the awkwardness of trying to introduce them at the opening of the Whitney show, six years earlier: Thomas's charm – failing for once to take effect – and Justine's standoffishness. Justine had walked into the gallery where the two portraits of Lorna were on display, and made a face of exaggerated horror.

'He *painted* you.' The word had a violence about it. Perhaps Justine had already intuited something she couldn't name, and Lorna's revelations later that night – about herself and Thomas and the baby – had the force of a horrible confirmation.

'You must be bisexual.' It was a week or so later that Justine came out with this, while they were eating breakfast in Veselka. 'Or a closet hetero.'

'You look good without make-up,' Lorna replied, deliberately deflecting. 'Sexy. You should go to classes like that.'

'Don't try to change the subject.'

'Thomas loved me – loves me – the way certain gay men adore certain women.' Lorna stirred a bowl of oatmeal. 'Having sex that one time was a sort of pressure valve for all of this *feeling*. And an experiment, I guess. When I think of everything that happened after—' She let go of the spoon. 'I wish we hadn't done it.'

'I wish, too. I can't get my head around it.'

Lorna looked up, finding herself smiling into Justine's fierce, attentive eyes.

'I'm a dyke, Justine.'

'Which is why it grosses me out when I start imagining—'

'Don't imagine then. Or let me just tell you. It was innocent, like a game.'

Justine began giggling. 'Like kids in a fairy tale, you mean? Enchanted woods, treasure in a big ball-sack.'

'There was nothing fairy tale about it. Only, it wasn't quite real. Most of the time we were just kissing. I think Thomas was playing a part. He kept cupping my face with his hand, like this—' She reached across the table and touched Justine's jaw with the undersides of her fingers.

Unexpectedly, Justine blushed.

'It was like he had become a lover in a movie,' Lorna went on. 'Like Montgomery Clift in *A Place in the Sun*.'

'A gay guy playing straight?' Justine posed the question from behind a raised cappuccino. She blew across the foam.

'Something like that. And that's probably what he was getting off on. The roleplay. The idea of being *that* kind of man.'

'Oh boy. Bring me back to reality, quick.'

Lorna leaned forward and took Justine's cappuccino as if it had been an offering. 'Fine. I need to tell you something. I want to get a dog.'

'Tell me this isn't a child substitute thing—' Justine stopped herself, blushing more deeply. 'I'm sorry.'

Lorna rested a hand over Justine's. 'It's okay. This goes back way further. I've always wanted a big dog, like a mastiff, ever since I was a child and my parents told me we couldn't.'

'Your parents were fucking evil. What they did—'

'They were ignorant,' Lorna interrupted. 'Life had defeated them, somewhere along the way.'

Justine's lips drew wide. Spit shone on her front teeth.

'What if I told you I wanted a toy poodle? Or a bichon frise with pink silk accessories?'

'I'd say you were playing at being straight. A proper old Westchester lady.'

Lorna placed her legs like a pincer around Justine's ankle beneath the table and closed them tight.

*

Resting her weight on her hands, she stared down at the *Fire Island Review*, laid out like an archival specimen on the desk. *Too Late for Greatness*. The snarking remarks about Thomas's belatedness had been a way of containing Justine's own hurt. The feeling of having turned up too late in Lorna's life. The review had been a kind of catharsis, although she had always maintained (with an academic's sophistry) that there had been nothing personal about it. Lorna had sensed with unease that she would have to choose between her new girlfriend and her leading artist, who was also the one remnant of her life in London. But only months later, Thomas had announced that he was leaving New York.

Around midnight, holding out against her jetlag, she walked Jay along the sidewalk, stopping as he nosed the base of each tree.

She had been tracking the responses on social media to Thomas's show in London. Among all the opinions she could have predicted were some that were angrier and weirder. Someone with a Warhol *Marilyn* as an avatar (blonde curls replaced by a crazy orange perm) seemed to have a vendetta. Thomas was a shitclown and a fake. He'd sold out years ago. No one would remember his name a decade from now.

She held the leash as Jay balanced on his haunches in a pool of lamplight. The fur on his back glimmered. A turd slid from him, breaking into a lump, then another, until five cartridges had mounted in a lazy pyramid.

A noise was coming from down the street. A quiet recurring wail. Lorna had thought it was a car alarm, maybe a distant fire truck, but now, as she gathered up the shit in a plastic bag, it sounded more human. Jay's ears twitched. Each time, the sound began low, then rose in pitch to a shriek. She looked up and down the sidewalk, but there was nothing to see.

She fumbled for her key, switching the leash between hands. It must have been a hobo, a drug addict. New York had plenty of those. This city was a limbo for society's rejects, and for most of them the cry was silent and endless.

Instead of going to bed, she searched online. She read articles that she had read already. She stared at the photo, now published in various places, of Luca Holden. There was a piece in the *Daily Mail* online that repeated many of the details, but with a new addition. A neighbour had heard music and raised voices from the flat in the minutes before Luca fell.

Raised voices. Questions circled in her head. Why did this story matter to her? It was a strange, sad story, but it wasn't hers. Was it narcissism? He *did* remind her, the boy, of her younger self – of the way she'd looked in those portraits by Thomas.

She walked to the window, searching the darkened street through the shutters. A crying baby. That's what the sound had been. How had she not recognised it?

She tried to think back to the weeks that had followed the birth of her son. She had stayed poor. Carmel kept walking out, kept returning; the reality of a sleepless baby was too much for the girl's free spirit. Thomas had run away to Düsseldorf and Lorna didn't have a number for him. Without being able to admit it, she was terrified of her parents discovering that she'd given birth.

Left alone in Soho with a newborn, she began to go mad. Her life shrank to the confines of her flat. A few people from college drifted in and out, then stopped coming. She realised that her bond with Thomas had excluded other friendships: they had used each other up. She sat for hours on the floor, holding the boy. She hadn't got round to naming him, but was thinking of Jacob. *Jacob and the Angel*, that massive alabaster carving at the Tate Gallery; a fight or hug, she'd never known which. Once a day, she went downstairs to the street to buy crisps and Lucozade. Diana, Princess of Wales, had just died and the whole country was in a vicarious frenzy of mourning.

The baby cried like an animal in a trap. Lorna wasn't producing enough milk, the nurses had said. For weeks, she felt herself sliding in and out of the role she was supposed to be inhabiting. Just as the love was building, and a sense of amazement – this boy was her own, for ever – all feeling was voided. Her mind switched mechanically between states. A painful acuteness, when everything became magnified and granular, and then a haze. The boy went from being hers, Jacob, to being someone else's: a misplaced child.

Awake for days at a time, she distracted herself by listening to sounds outside on the street. One night, while crackheads were attacking a door below, her father turned up. She recognised him, but he was like a stranger. Older and fatter than she remembered, with his combed-back hair falling out of position. He stared at her – through her – with sweat or tears making his cheeks gleam.

'What have you done?' he said, panting out the words. 'What have you *done*?'

He pushed past her into the room and picked up the baby.

'You're coming home. I'm not leaving you here. If I have to drag you out by the feet, I'll do it.'

She remembered how his face had grown larger as he filled the room. How he removed them by force and drove them back to the house in Holloway, where the TV was droning in the front room, just as it always had, and where Lorna's mother was sitting, sobbing, in one of two identical beige chairs. How her own screams had merged with those of the boy.

The following day, she'd seen a psychiatrist. A man of eighty at least, far past retirement age – a family friend. The smell of his breath across the desk was nauseating. He understood one thing, though. *Her natural maternal instincts are offset by longer phases of alienation, phases that in turn induce an agonising sense of guilt.*

The antidepressants zombified her, but the guilt remained.

A single piercing note of feeling. She wouldn't be able to give this child a decent life. She barely knew how to love him. When she agreed to the adoption, relenting to her parents' will, she felt an empty calm. She was recovering control, she told herself; it was the logical course. She refused the counselling offered by social services – there was nothing to discuss. Over the six weeks that it took for the process to complete, even as she surrendered her rights in the presence of a taciturn woman from the agency, she held onto the sensation. Only once the boy was gone did grief arrive in a felling wave, and with it, a new fury towards her parents. She dropped out of Saint Martins and spent her days upstairs in her old bedroom. She wanted to track Thomas down and kill him for abandoning her, or just embrace him until he absorbed her pain. Around Christmas, the numbness came back. Guilt continued to roll in, but it was a gentler agony, and the phases of non-feeling were gentler too – more like relief. It helped to think of the boy's closed eyes: to imagine him asleep somewhere. And Thomas's absence helped her to believe that this, all along, had been the necessary path. But she couldn't forgive her parents, not even after her father (broken in his own inexpressive way) sold his taxi business and gave her half the money. She left for New York without telling them – left a note on the kitchen table, saying that she loved them.

The adoption paperwork, dated 2 October 1997, was in a sealed envelope in a drawer of the desk. It lived beneath Justine's files. But Lorna had chosen not to know anything about the boy – where he had gone or who had adopted him. It was enough to have the information in her physical possession.

She couldn't see or feel him in her mind. Only the sound of his crying remained, and sometimes it came back in disguise.

10

12 September, 11.53. Montreux

Standing at the window, Thomas looked out at Lake Geneva.
He tracked the peaks in the distance. Le Grammont, les Jumelles,
les Cornettes de Bise. The morning sun was on the retreat. A
haze of rain swept through the air.

The days had been uneventful since his return. Claude had
phoned him to confirm that the show was sold out. Sylvia
had forwarded an email from Marianna Berger, the artist
who'd shown up in London. It had been sent at midnight, after
the opening. Berger wanted to make a video about *the real
Thomas Heller*.

He didn't get it. Who was he to her? She couldn't even spell
his name.

For hours at a time, he felt normal. The world seemed
unchanged. Then his mind reeled back. How still it had been,
that evening. Absolutely windless. And the view from Luca's
flat: a violet sky over the city, black by the time Thomas returned
to Claridge's. Was it possible that the life had left Betty at the
very moment it left Luca, their final breaths coinciding?

Thomas walked the length of the sitting room, emptying his
head by a conscious effort. The oblong space traversed the
mountainside like a shelf. Beyond the glass frontage was a terrace
with a low parapet. The room was a sequence of interconnecting
zones: the kitchen and dining area with a round timber table,
the sitting area (a precise-casual arrangement of canvas couches
by Franz West), the maroon piano and the walnut niches of the

library. Opposite the bookshelves, close to the end of the room, was his desk, a sheet of raw plywood that rested on steel trestles, angled towards the window. It was bare except for a supersize iMac.

Luca had seen the ridiculousness of things. The money and hype and power play. He often said that he wanted to set up his own gallery one day, and that the art would be the one thing that mattered.

Thomas tapped the machine into life and saw Betty. Her beautiful, beastlike face filled the screen. Sitting down, he googled Marianna Berger. He found a short biography on the website of a non-profit gallery. She was thirty-two. Six months ago, she'd received a grant from the Rhode Island School of Design. There was a short clip of a video: birds flying over Manhattan.

On another tab was a review he'd been reading the night before, archived on the *Village Voice* website. It had been published in March 1999. *Haller of the Pinks*.

> *The artist's embrace of pink in his first show with Lorna Bedford Gallery is romantic and subversive all at once. His homage to the Colour Field feels double-edged, and knowingly so. There's a heresy about his vaporous spray-paint, a loving exactitude about the way he brushes a wisp of light. Mr Haller's new paintings are touched by – no, blessed with – a capricious humour.*

Where had that humour fled?

Staring out at the mountains, he heard Luca's laughter as they'd walked along the Thames in Woolwich. A boy's laugh, only deeper in pitch and without any taint of mockery. It had been prompted by a remark of Thomas's, something about keeping his swimming pool heated through the winter so that Betty could swim in it.

'That dog would have been worshipped in ancient Egypt,'

Luca said, looking out at the piers of the Thames Barrier. His pupils were constricted by the bright day. 'You would have made sacrifices to her.'

Walking to the piano now, Thomas thought of Luca and Betty, and then (his thoughts splitting into streams) of how Lorna had stood outside the Connaught the other night, staring in at the life he'd excluded her from. He rested his elbows on the piano's lacquered top. Guilt was spreading inside him like a fever.

Something had happened when they became friends. Their existences had been synchronised. Those two years in London, before they both ended up in New York, were a lifetime ago. But certain memories were as clear as holograms. He could see her as she'd been, hear her, almost *feel* the touch of her hair.

He recalled walking with her on Greek Street late one evening. They had been at a gallery opening. Soho was hectic. They stopped at a shop for cigarettes, and Thomas – fooling around – slipped into a photo booth, pulling Lorna after him. They sat together on the plastic stool, Lorna perching on his lap, and he dropped a coin in the slot.

'Pose!' Thomas said in a breathy voice. 'Strike a pose. There's nothing to it.'

Lorna's face – startled, amused – filled the screen in front of them. She was blocking him from view. A light flashed.

'Pose!' he repeated.

She laughed, turning aside as the light flashed again, then turning back to confront the lens. Her shifting reaction was distilled across eight small photos that fell into the dispenser. Two vertical strips of Lornas. She wanted to keep the pictures, but he dropped them straight into his pocket.

He studied his own dim reflection in the piano lid. Lorna must have been pregnant already when those photos were taken. In the months that followed, once she'd told him she was going to have a child, he felt her slipping away. She became withdrawn.

That awful girlfriend of hers, Carmen or Camilla, turned into a gatekeeper. And Lorna no longer wanted to be an artist. That had been the hardest thing to accept. Every time he went to her flat, her camera lay in the same place.

He had applied to transfer to the Kunstakademie Düsseldorf, never imagining he would be accepted. It was where Gerhard Richter taught, and Joseph Beuys before him. Thomas couldn't bear the loudmouth art that was grabbing all the attention just then in London, and, besides, he had more private reasons for wanting to escape. Some instinct told him that he mustn't see the child.

In all the years since, he had rarely thought about his son. The fact that a young man somewhere in the world possessed half of his DNA meant nothing. It was a technical reality, something he knew but couldn't feel.

*

09.03. New York

Lorna walked slowly. She was already so late for work that there was no need to rush. As she reached the shadeless channel of Second Avenue, she broke into a sweat. The vista to the north and south was long and open, as flat as water. It seemed to stretch the length of the city.

Justine had once said, as they walked the same route, that the avenues were epic in a literary sense – that they were capacious, with heroic reach.

'And what does that make the streets – the cross routes?' Lorna had asked.

'They're the epyllia,' Justine answered, with a smile – guileless, almost girlish – that was at odds with her words. 'The mini epics. Slender, neat and Alexandrian.'

Lorna passed along a terrace of nineteenth-century houses, matching properties in complementary shades – pink brickwork, cream stucco, demerara. A slice of Henry James's New York, and hadn't that been her retort, come to think of it, that Justine was trying – with her high-flown analogies – to be like Henry James? They had laughed, then, at the idea of Justine as a leading man of letters.

Even after she gave up her research into James, Justine had liked to pretend, occasionally, to be Gilbert Osmond. Or rather, she had created her own version of him – a cold, snobbish lesbian who spoke in overdeliberate phrases. Gilberta St Laurent (the name was also an homage to *Paris Is Burning*). A finicking lover of old art and old books, an enemy of the new. There had been less of Gilberta over time, although she had reappeared at times, usually to tease Lorna.

'You could intellectualise anything,' Lorna had said, after they'd walked on a block. 'They're roads, for God's sake. Big and small.'

She traipsed up Fourth, feeling the sun's energy sinking through her, and along the southern edge of Union Square. Heading westward, she passed the Mycenaean hulk of the Salvation Army complex. Why, she asked herself again, had Justine left? Was the claimed explanation the actual one – that Justine wanted time to write, time to develop?

From the depths of her bag, her phone was buzzing. The gallery was calling – one of her staff. They were supposed to be installing a show that day. New paintings by Ana Garcia, a young Cuban American artist whose work Lorna had discovered at the Cooper Union graduate show. Ana was a piece of work.

She hit *Remind me later*.

'I will embrace my solitude as a gift,' she murmured, not sure if she'd remembered the line right. Justine could have told her. 'A beautiful gift.'

In front of the Google Building, steam was spewing from an orange and white vent like a smoking firework. The building had once belonged to the Port of New York Authority. The old designation, engraved and gilded in the stone frontage, burned through the steam. After twenty-six years, Lorna still looked at this city with the eye of a charmed outsider.

Her phone buzzed again from the pit of her bag. She ignored it.

She was surrounded now by the industrial units and newbuilds of gallery land. Blocks of condos were rising around the elevated walkways of the High Line. At the corner of West 19th was a coffee and food cart – an aluminium box on wheels, open on one side to display shelves crammed with plastic-wrapped snacks, towers of paper cups, and a coffee machine that resembled a piece of scrap, its chromium casing abraded by years of use. The vendor was sheltering from the sun beneath a propped-up panel. He was Hispanic, maybe Mexican, and he was dressed despite the heat in a thick coat. He looked tired, with lines running vertically along each cheek. One hand was resting on the lever of the coffee machine, like that of a helmsman on calm waters.

*

Lorna Bedford Gallery was situated at the western extremity of West 21st Street, close to the Hudson River. The building had once been a taxi garage. Portals for vehicles had been filled with steel-frame doors and plate glass.

Clutching a coffee, Lorna crossed the street and walked along the opposite side. She wanted to look through the window without being seen. From an oblique angle, she could see Geneva, her sales director, sitting behind the front desk, speaking to someone just out of view. Lorna guessed, from Geneva's fixed smile, that the person was Ana Garcia.

She heard her phone again. They were looking for her at the gallery. She crouched down. For a deranged moment, she imagined Ana striding across the street, right up to her, shaking her by the shoulders (*Where the fuck have you been? We're meant to be installing my show*), only to find that Lorna wasn't Lorna at all, but a huddled-over hobo, one of the lost souls of New York, bent in search of a dime.

She rose too quickly, making herself dizzy.

Just ahead, by a coincidence, a homeless woman was walking towards her. The woman was tall and shrouded from her neck to her ankles in an overcoat of what looked like soiled vicuña. Tilted on her head was a cadet's beret of the same silky material. She clutched handfuls of bags, stuffed plastic sacks that rolled around her. Her complexion was dark and ashen. Her eyes were two shining points.

'You gonna tell me?' she demanded, looking straight at Lorna.

Lorna couldn't be sure if it was a woman after all. The voice was baritone. She gave a polite smile.

'Gonna tell me what you gonna do?'

The words had the rhythm of a lyric. They were only ten yards apart. Lorna stepped sideways. But the woman, or man, stepped the same way, straight into her path, smiling to reveal teeth separated by large gaps.

Lorna stepped the other way. The drifter reminded her of a drag queen from another era. With surprising agility, the stranger blocked her once more, stepping closer. Lorna heard a hoarse titter.

'You just gonna keep on walking? Gonna keep on walking, keep on pretending?'

'Get out of here,' Lorna muttered, without malice. 'I'm late.'

The swaying hands flung their loads to the ground. The bags hit the sidewalk and spilled their contents, which consisted entirely of garments of assorted colours and fabrics.

They were inches from colliding. Lorna saw that the vicuña coat had swung open to expose a near-naked body in a lace undergarment.

'What you gonna do? What you gonna say?'

Lorna veered and the coat skimmed past her as if she hadn't been there, although in the seconds that followed, she heard another whistling laugh. She turned to see that the woman had stopped on the street corner, next to a wire-basket trash can that was overflowing with cartons, cups and paper bags, and was gently extracting something from the pile. A bright purple shawl.

The woman was bunching the material into a coat pocket. Lorna gazed as it kept extending. She sensed that if she kept looking, unless she turned and left, the shawl would never stop unravelling.

*

As Lorna crossed the threshold, she saw Ana Garcia. A small figure at the centre of the gallery.

'Oh my God, you're *here* – finally.'

Lorna held up her hands in apology.

With her dungarees and unkempt hair, Ana looked like a teenage girl. Her face retained the undampened quality of a young person's. Not that she was old, at thirty.

Lorna's attention switched to a painting that was propped against the wall. A swathe of pink paint, gritted with mica, hung like a psychedelic cloud across the top of the canvas. Below was a seam of collaged pages – newspapers, magazines, books – that had been washed with tints of grey and blue to suggest a city.

'It's called *Pink Cloud Over Manhattan*,' said Ana.

Lorna came near, unsure whether to hug Ana or kiss her or touch her shoulder. She opted for the last.

'I love it. But the title—'

'What?'

'It seems kind of literal.' Lorna was walking into a trap, but it was too late to backtrack. 'I mean, is it just a cloud? And does the collaged part have to be Manhattan? Why New York – why not some other place?'

'That's what I'm calling it, Lorna. And where have you been?'

Lorna noticed that four other paintings, identically sized, were leaning in a stack against another wall, each sheathed in bubble-wrap. 'Couldn't you have opened the rest without me?'

'No, I couldn't. I needed you here. Listen – this wall structure isn't going to work.'

'Wall structure?'

'The four walls of the gallery. I can't work with them. They'll kill this group of paintings. Way too perpendicular. I need a long diagonal, right across the gallery, corner to corner.'

Just then, Geneva stepped into the space between them with an expression of controlled alarm.

'*Lorna.* Leo Goffman is on the phone. He says it's urgent.'

*

A red light was flashing on the phone on her desk: Leo's impatience compressed into electronic semaphore. She released the call with one finger.

'I thought I'd be hearing from you.' His voice resounded out of the Cisco device.

'I know. It's been crazy since I got back from London. Listen, Leo, about that Haller painting—'

'About that painting,' he interrupted. '*About that painting.* Well.' He allowed a significant pause. 'I don't know what you did, Lorna. But you're a genius. The painting was acquired by a shell company, Equitone, who have offered to resell to me at cost. I appreciate your discretion. Berlins will never know I'm the owner.'

She glanced out at the brick-walled yard – really a lightwell –

beyond the window. She'd been wondering whether to grow an oleander bush there.

'Congratulations, Leo. Really, though, I had nothing to do with it.'

'I won't hear of it. Modesty doesn't become you.'

'I've never heard of Equitone. And anyway, I thought Claude had sold that painting to some movie star.'

'Suit yourself. Don't take the credit. But I never forget a favour.'

'I didn't do anything,' she insisted, unable to hide her frustration. 'Fritz Schein was at the opening in London. Didn't I hear that he acts as your art advisor?'

'Fritzie was there?' Leo hummed to himself. 'I've never had an advisor. Why would I need one? Fritzie helps out a bit with the collection – he *curates* it. Well, he has a knack, I guess. Makes things happen. Fritzie Forceps, I call him, because he always delivers.' He cleared his throat – a long ejection.

'Well then, he delivered this for you. He secured you that painting.'

'He would never deal with Berlins. He knows what I think of that guy. Truth is' – his voice croaked – 'my wife got to know Fritz Schein when he was just a kid. She adored him. He's a fag, see. She had an affinity for them – some women do. Well, what do I care?'

From out on the street came the beeps of a reversing truck.

'You know I'm gay, right, Leo?'

'Oh, sure, but that's different.'

'Different how?'

'You know how. The Sapphic thing. I mean, when did you last head down to the piers to get buttfucked?'

The question, she guessed, was rhetorical. Goffman was an asshole, maybe a bit of a monster. But he might yet be useful.

'Tell Thomas Haller,' he said, 'that he's invited to the Deborah Goffman Memorial Gala. It's the twentieth edition next spring. Come to think of it, I should make him the honouree.'

'You'll need to talk to Galerie Claude Berlins about that.'

'To hell with that show in London. When someone writes the history of all *this*, you will have been Haller's dealer. *You.*'

'I'm glad you think so.'

'Haller will think so, too. Artists are slaves to their vanity. But in the end, in time, they see things as they really are.' He purged his airways again. 'What do you have on at your gallery right now?'

'Ana Garcia. New paintings. The show opens tomorrow night.'

'I want to see it.' The words were out before Lorna had finished speaking.

'Come to the opening tomorrow at six.'

'I'm eighty-five. I don't do openings. But I want to meet her. I want to see the show.'

Lorna had an intuition that Leo had seen the interview with Ana in the latest *Harper's Bazaar*. The magazine had kindled his desire and this was a predatory manoeuvre. To Lorna's mind, it was a boring article: eight pages of breathy hyperbole about the interiors of Ana's studio, intercut by righteous statements from Ana. But the photographs had redeemed the text – the portrait of Ana in particular, its black and white tonality accenting her freckles.

She nodded to herself as an idea took hold.

'How about you swing by tomorrow morning?'

*

14.39. Montreux

Thomas searched for his name on X. He read through the posts of recent weeks. His eye bounced happily over certain words. *Stunning*, someone had said. *Ethereal*. Then, as he skimmed, he began to catch on harder, blunter commentaries.

Stultifying.

Contemporary painting is soooooo deadpan.

Will anyone admit this guy is a fraud?

The person who'd posted this last question had an odd profile picture. The face of a Warhol *Marilyn* with chaotic orange hair photoshopped on.

He scrolled onward.

A license to print money.

A chain of dollar signs ended with an emoji. The yellow face spewed green vomit. The statement was accompanied by an image of one of his paintings. His heart was running ahead of him, staggering like a drunk.

Thomas Haller is now represented by Claude Berlins.
Hmmmmmm. #Artworld #Patriarchy #MarriagePortrait

This had been posted several days before the opening of his show. It featured a photograph of him and Claude. He remembered the occasion – the Serpentine summer party in July. And he recognised the wan character in the background, almost invisible in the darkness of the doorway.

He zoomed in to look closer, but the image lost its clarity at once. Luca's face turned into a pale smear. His eyes receded, refusing to give up their burning knowingness. What had he seen, or not seen, that day? Straining after a truer image, Thomas pictured him out on the balcony, up on the rail, severe and alive against the fading sky. He sank his head into his hands.

*

Luca had still been a baby when Thomas arrived at the Kunstakademie Düsseldorf. Perhaps not even born.

Only a few weeks into his first semester, Thomas began to feel like an outsider. He didn't care about the end of history, much less the teleology of art. His tutors insisted that painting was dead. The art market was the life-support of a finished medium, they said. And so, out of perversity, Thomas went looking for commercial galleries.

Claude Berlins was one of the few dealers of modern art in the city. His street-level gallery on Platanenstrasse mainly showed European paintings and drawings of the early twentieth century, but it had begun to represent contemporary artists. The first exhibition Thomas saw there was a series of gouache studies by Alexander Rodchenko: orbs and oblongs flying off-course from ruled lines, reminding him of cable cars.

The gallery soon became his hangout. The narrow room, with its parquet floor and minimalist décor, was an antidote to the nightclubs in Cologne where the other students went. In place of ecstasy and electronica, a sequestered space, and hadn't that been the appeal? Since he was a boy, watching guests come and go at the Montreux Palace Hotel, he had been drawn to people with class, with money. The opening nights of the exhibitions were strewn with electric talk. The way people moved – their command of words – was entrancing. Visitors sat at a desk at the back and consulted slides on a miniature lightbox, snorting through a cigarette holder as they bent close. He noticed things he'd seen in adverts and films, like a Cartier bracelet stitched out of tiny diamonds.

More than anything, the draw was Claude, a Parisian in his early thirties. At those monthly openings, Thomas would watch as Claude circulated. The gallerist was tall and domineering, with a square face and hair that curled into ringlets at the edges (so different from the cropped silver of later years). His grey eyes expressed an imperturbable calm. He had a heat-seeker instinct for the people who mattered. Thomas liked to listen in on the dealer's conversations while pretending to admire the art.

Claude had a ruthless kind of humour that tipped sometimes into mockery. He knew how to seize hold of a conversation, switching with ease between German and English and French. His voice was drawlingly smooth, his lips surprisingly full for his planed face. He often wore a black jacket with a sheen to it. Later, Thomas would learn the name of its designer. The engraved pattern on the dial of Claude's watch, a grid of minuscule cubes, reminded him of the quilted box of a perfume bottle.

Claude seemed indifferent to the young art student at first. Then his eyes began to settle on Thomas from across the room, rarely for more than a fleeting moment. Sometimes the two of them would exchange remarks about the art on the walls – Thomas struggling to find the right words – before Claude's attention switched, inevitably, to the next person. Just once, Thomas was conscious of Claude putting an arm around his shoulders.

Even now, decades later, something within him tensed at the memory of that touch.

One night, Claude opened an exhibition of paintings by Sonia Delaunay. Thomas was among the last people at the party. By a trick of words, Claude contrived to make the others depart. He invited Thomas upstairs, into a cavernous room. Art was everywhere, hanging on the walls, stacked against the skirting boards, most of it abstract. The floorboards were dark with varnish. A curtain hung over the single window. There was a large bed at one end, spread over with a tapestry. On one of the walls was a Jean Arp pen drawing: a mesh of torquing lines, swerving like a net in the wind. As they stood together in front of it, Thomas's heart thudded with drugs and anticipation. Guided by the sweep of the lines, their eyes met. They looked at one another and Thomas gave Claude his hands. Claude held them tight – pulled him close.

*

That night was the first time Thomas had seen a naked man other than his father. *Aristocratic* was the word that came into his head at the sight of Claude's muscular nudity.

They lay on the bed. Claude's body was a firm, smooth, agile mass. His cock was like a spell – the hardness, the scent, the taste, the size. At moments, Thomas caught sight of their reflections in a mirror that was propped against the wall to one side of the bed, a gilt-edged oval with a pink sheen. They appeared as semi-abstract snapshots: a tensing thigh, an expanse of back, his own face flushed and pressed close to the bed.

Thomas lay on his back. Claude knelt over him. In the granular dusk, Claude held up a small ceramic jar. He flipped it upside down, releasing a scentless oil. Some of the liquid spattered over the coverlet. Thomas locked his legs around Claude's back. With both hands, he guided Claude's dick until it was pressing against him, into him. He stretched his arms back, above his head, and they joined hands – Claude's large hands pushing down on his own, clutching tight. Thomas was shocked, then and afterwards, by the force of his own desire. It expelled thought – eclipsed pain.

When they woke in the middle of the night, Claude told Thomas that he was in love with him, that he'd adored Thomas from the first time he saw him. Thomas experienced a rush of melancholy that was precious and exquisite, something he never wanted to lose.

They met every night after that. They had sex, usually within moments of being alone together, and then lay for hours on the bed, talking about their lives and their pasts. In a small box with marquetry patterning, Claude kept a stash of cocaine.

'I don't care if people say that painting is dying,' Thomas burst out one night, in response to the edicts of one of his tutors. 'It's what I want to do.'

'And so you should,' said Claude. 'But forget about images. They're sentimental. Abstraction is where your future lies.'

Thomas knelt up on the bed. 'I require a subject,' he said. 'And the subject chooses me, not the other way around.'

Claude lay beside him, his nakedness illuminated by a lamp.

'Let colour be your subject, and form, and tonality. These are the absolutes in art. Everything else is fashion. And you want to be more than a fashionable painter, don't you? You want to be great.'

When Claude spoke in English, his accent had a mid-European cadence. He was descended from French nobility. His parents were eminent, seigneurial people who lived between the Rue Bonaparte and Saint-Cloud. There was a younger sister who had never left the family home.

Claude had received a classical education. If he hadn't become an art dealer, he would have been a scholar of Latin poetry. He had written a thesis at university on Modernist poetry and its debt to Latin literature. He read aloud in different languages: Rilke, Valéry, Yeats, Eliot. His first show at the gallery, seven years earlier, had been a display of Roman antiquities – bronze amulets and other curiosities from Pompeii.

Even as it happened, Thomas was conscious that Claude was shaping him, sculpting his manners and opinions. Involuntarily, he began to speak with Claude's leisurely delivery. He spoke in English more often and picked up on Claude's habit of refusing to give way when another person talked. Gradually, Claude turned him into an aficionado of abstract art. Thomas grew familiar with the arguments of Greenberg and Rosenberg. He echoed and learned to feel Claude's contempt for Andy Warhol and other trickster image-makers.

'Apelles was the first abstract painter,' Claude said one night, lying in bed and stroking his half-erect dick with one finger. 'He was already the greatest painter in ancient Greece when he walked one day into the studio of another famous artist, Protogenes, eager to see the work of a man he'd heard so much about. But Protogenes was out, and all Apelles found was an empty panel waiting to be painted on. So, he picked up a brush and painted a perfectly straight line on the panel, then left. It was a calling card. A challenge – *beat that*. When Protogenes came home and saw the miraculous line, he knew that it must have been left there by the legendary Apelles – who else could have painted a line so perfect? And so, he took up the brush and traced an even finer line in a different colour, inside the line painted by Apelles. A while later, Apelles returned – Protogenes was out again – and he split these two lines with an even finer one, in a third colour. After that, Protogenes admitted defeat. He was good, but not that good.'

As he spoke, Claude reached and touched Thomas all over with his fingertips.

'What I want to know,' Thomas murmured, 'is where the less good artist – Protogenes – kept disappearing to. Why was he always out?'

Abruptly Claude clasped Thomas's shoulders and pushed him down on the bed.

'Be an abstract painter,' he whispered, climbing on top of Thomas. 'It's your fate. I'll represent you. Enough sentimental *pictures*. Seek purity and flatness. Do it – do it – *do it*.'

He repeated the words like a mantra, bringing his lips so close to Thomas's ear that they seemed to touch. Thomas, despite his unease, gave in to his own flickering desire.

*

He wouldn't paint today. All he could predict was a succession of wasted hours. He sent a text message, then walked out into the late-summer afternoon.

The rain had stopped. An autumn coolness was filtering through the pines, emanating from the pockets of blue in the sky.

It would take an hour to walk down the mountain. He trekked at a steady pace, reaching the point where the footpath broadened into a tarmac road.

A view of the town and the lake opened up beneath him. This place was beautiful, he thought, in a way that defied expression. Wherever else he'd gone, Montreux and its surroundings had remained his home. The name came from *monasteriolum*, meaning 'little monastery'. A place to live alone. Six years earlier, when he finally became rich enough, he'd carved his wedge of glass and concrete and zinc into the side of the mountain.

In the distance, through a gap in the buildings, he spotted the domed roofs of the Montreux Palace Hotel. When he was twelve, he had taken to loitering after school in the hotel gardens. He had walked among the guests – the women with their measured gestures, the men with their tailored shirts and Italian loafers. The styles mattered more than the labels, although he began to recognise certain designers: the flamboyance of Versace, the granite hardness of Givenchy. These things, which his parents would have called vacuous, seemed like thousands of tiny accents or touches of a brush. The people's conversations glinted with a significance he couldn't interpret – only feel. He registered everything with growing wonder and disdain. Wonder at the easy elegance of it all, and disdain because these people had everything he wanted without knowing it, without caring. He wished he could learn to be careless like that.

One Sunday, he had pretended to be part of a large Polish family – the daughters all in lace dresses, trailing in a line behind the adults. Imagining himself as their brother, he followed them to the lake, where they boarded a pleasure cruiser. He almost managed to get on board before his rough cotton shirt gave him away.

He passed the Catholic chapel where his mother had occasionally prayed and confessed. Just below, a nondescript terrace marked the beginning of the town. There was a health club, a tabac and a bar with yellow umbrellas.

The bar, Le Mazot, had been there since the time of his grandparents. The glass in the windows was the colour of treacle. He hadn't been inside in months.

Two men were drinking outside, a pensioner alone at a table and a young man standing by the door with one foot hoisted against the wall. The young man was watching as Thomas approached. He was aged around twenty, with short blond hair. His features were delicate – a narrow nose, almost pointed, lips that verged on feminine, a smooth jaw – although his arms and legs, exposed by the singlet and shorts he wore, were muscular.

'You've come back.' He spoke in curt – not unfriendly – German rather than the customary French.

Thomas looked around.

'You're busy,' he said. 'You have customers.'

Otto gave a sarcastic smile. 'Klaus,' he said, addressing the old man. 'Time's up. I have to close early.'

With doddering obedience, the old man set down his drink and disentangled himself from his chair.

Otto went inside. Thomas followed.

A narrow staircase at the back of the bar led to a basement. Thomas went ahead, knowing the other man would follow.

Downstairs was a low-ceilinged room with mirrors covering the walls on three sides. Once, it had been a disco. A stage light hung from the ceiling, fitted with an amber filter. A small bar, emptied of bottles and glasses, ran in front of the unmirrored wall at the end. The countertop had a hinged section and was covered in black leather. The mirrors gave off a rose-gold glow.

Walking in, Thomas saw himself reflected. He registered the other man behind him on the stairs. He crossed to the bar, taking five measured steps. He didn't look round.

It was warm and airless, with the same smell as months earlier:

an odour of abandonment crossed with some other, sexier note. A tang of sweat?

He unbuttoned his shirt and allowed it to slide off him. Unzipping his jeans, he slunk one leg out, then the other, and teased off his socks, feeling the silk ripple over his feet. The warm air touched his back, his stomach, his balls . . .

He set his hands on the edge of the bar, planted apart on the leather, bending forward. He waited, conscious of being watched.

Otto was behind him, a step away. Thomas felt the man's breaths on his neck, and the scanning motion of his eyes. In front, the top of the bar was a platform of tacky black. Beyond, the back of the room was a dark space.

'I guessed you'd be back,' Otto said.

A pulse of sickening excitement travelled from Thomas's stomach to the edges of his pelvis, rippling through his thighs. He pressed his erection into the bar.

The young man reached around – his hand was oddly pale in the darkness – and set down a miniature glass container.

Thomas leaned forward, propping himself on one hand and using the other to depress a nostril. When his head was almost touching the bottle, he inhaled. The vapour hazed through him. He rose on tiptoes. A helium lightness spread from his head to his throat, down to his buttocks, up to his heart.

The sound of Otto's hand on his backside – a sharp, echoless crack – preceded the sensation by a second. It wasn't pain, more a stingless vibration.

'Again,' Thomas said.

'Wait,' Otto replied. 'I'll decide.'

Still on tiptoes, Thomas pushed himself outward and backward.

Otto's fingernail met the base of Thomas's neck, and ran down his back in a long, lazy slice. Thomas tried to remember what shoes Otto had been wearing. He turned his head by a fraction.

'No looking.'

Leather boots, he guessed. Cracked below a layer of polish. Red laces. Pale legs rising out of them. Naked ankles flexing, or white socks. He shut his eyes.

Otto's legs were around his own, closing in on either side. Thomas felt a smear of fingers between his thighs, running upward.

'Not yet,' he whispered. 'The other thing first.'

'Next time,' Otto said. His lips were near Thomas's neck, then touching his ear lobe. The tip of Otto's tongue was in the bowl of his ear, a warm wet plug.

Sinking his head, he inhaled from the bottle and felt Otto's dick prodding with blind intent, then pistoning into him.

*

For years after Thomas had moved to New York, he and Claude had continued to meet, although less frequently over time. Thomas would go to whichever hotel Claude was staying at, and for a few hours it would be the same as in Düsseldorf. The need would come swimming back, blanching out their changed appearances. They would lie in bed afterwards and Claude would talk about his plans for the gallery, which had moved by that time to a gigantic former shoe factory on the Rhine. When they talked about Thomas's art, Claude repeated the same oracular things about painting and purity, but he seemed less interested in the facts of Thomas's life. With slowly descending anguish, Thomas came to realise that he was no longer the blue flame of potential, in Claude's eyes, that he'd been at the age of twenty. He was the kind of painter, Claude would have said, who showed and did well with a dealer like Lorna Bedford.

Six years earlier, the balance had swung. Thomas had been given a retrospective at the Whitney. Critics wrote of his over-looked genius and return to form. His market value began to surge. There were detractors, but the general consensus was that he had risen to the heroic status of Gerhard Richter, Albert Oehlen and Anselm Kiefer. Claude turned up at the opening without warning, wearing a jet-black suit and bearing a bouquet of lilies swathed in cellophane. There was a card tucked inside.

For my Apelles.

Claude showed up in New York every month after that – began to pursue Thomas with a lover's tenacity. It was time, he said, for Thomas to make a move. He spoke of opening a gallery in New York or London.

'You've never had a show in London. I'll launch you there. I'll double your prices overnight.'

One night, when a painting of Thomas's failed to sell at Sotheby's, Claude came to him in the lobby and spoke in his ear: 'Come back to me and you'll never fail to sell.'

Come back. At those words, Thomas felt the tremor of an old desire, far deeper than sexual attraction. A desire that he feared in himself: the need to belong to Claude, to exist in the light of Claude's gaze, only there, for ever.

Thomas resisted until finally his defences failed. Last December, he had gone from Montreux to London for a few days on a nostalgic impulse. Claude had somehow found out and messaged him, saying that he was also in London, by coincidence, and staying at the Connaught. And so they met for drinks. In the bronze light of the bar, over gin martinis, Claude was like his younger self. His eyes were full of humour; his hair seemed darker. He pointed surreptitiously to a jewelled woman across the bar and told Thomas how she was the widow of a Greek shipping tycoon who had once tried to kill her.

'I can do things for you,' Claude said, 'if you let me represent you. Come back to me.' The words were like the chant of a chorus.

Thomas concentrated on the scratches of the zinc-topped bar. 'But I have a gallery. I have Lorna.'

'Who made you a painter?' Claude said, with gentle vehemence. 'Have you forgotten?' He leaned close. 'Lorna has brought you a long way. Further than I'd ever have thought her able. But she can't do any more for you.' He sank his head, seeming to plunge into thought, then looked up with a pensive frown. 'Remind me, wasn't it Lorna's girlfriend who wrote that horrific review?'

Claude sat back and signalled to the barman for two more martinis. At the same moment, a pianist struck up a tune. Claude's fingers mimed the notes on the top of the bar.

'When do you think Lorna Bedford last came inside a place like this?' he resumed, in an airier tone. Without waiting for a reply, he locked eyes with the jewelled widow and blew a kiss over the room. 'Come back,' he said again, and unfolded a piece of paper – drawn from his jacket – on top of the bar.

'You're very sure of yourself,' Thomas replied, trying to suppress the pounding of his heart.

'I won't be able to look after you full-time, of course,' Claude said, placing a lacquered Danitrio fountain pen beside the contract. 'I'm in a different city every week. But I have a member of staff, a young guy, who will look after you. Luca Holden. He'll be your liaison.'

II

13 September, 09.42. New York

Leo called down to Ernesto, the keeper of the subterranean garage beneath the Pegasus Tower, and then headed for the elevator. As the doors slid open, he grabbed an ebony stick, capped with silver.

It was bright and gusty on West 57th Street. Stationed at the sidewalk was his 1970 Lincoln Continental. The engine was turning over. Fumes were bleeding into the September morning. On a day like this, the black surface was a tinted mirror. The glass face of the Pegasus spilled across the car's roof. The reflections of two passing girls flickered over the rear door – doubled pairs of bare legs. A uniformed attendant climbed out of the driver's side with bowing haste. Leo waved him away. Chucking his stick onto the passenger seat, he pivoted on his heels and sank back, through the open door, into the padded leather. He raised both feet and swung them into the car. His knees skimmed the mahogany wheel. In the same moment, his left hand tapped the indented rim – the familiar tap of his wedding band on polished wood – and his feet met the pedals. The attendant closed the door.

With a single backward glance, Leo nosed the car into the tide. Horns exploded from different directions. He fixed his gaze on the far side of the road, at the lanes running eastward, and with three brute twists of the wheel, he spun the Lincoln like a playing card into the opposite stream.

Another horn blared as he flipped the car onto Park Avenue.

Gliding towards the Pan Am Building, he thought of Deborah. They had bought the Lincoln together. Their first work of art. The traffic was moving freely and the sky was a broad canopy of blue above the canyon of the road. He held the car steady at thirty m.p.h.

Right up until Deborah's death, they had bought modern art. It had been a joint venture, a life's mission. Their apartment on Park Avenue, thirty blocks behind him, had grown into a private museum, their *folie à deux*, in which (he searched his memory for the words in *Vanity Fair*) the décor of eighteenth-century France had been set in contrapuntal play with the modernist avant-garde.

'Asshole,' he said, as he swerved to avoid a van.

And there had been a Kandinsky . . . The *colours*! A swishing tumult of greens and blues and mauves. ('Those mauves,' Deborah had sighed.)

He sped up. The Seagram Building passed in a treacly flash.

'Contrafuckingpuntal play,' he boomed, and a fractured roar filled the car as laughter broke from his chest.

He was coming to an intersection. The lights were amber, but people were already stepping into the road. Leo wasn't in the mood to wait. Slowing to a walking pace, he propelled the Lincoln with delicate determination over the crosswalk. Scurrying bodies parted like water around the hood. He had more life than any of them. More life and less time.

He flexed his foot on the gas. The car jumped forward by a foot. Shouts erupted. Someone slapped the rear windshield. Out of nowhere, a woman was standing at the end of the hood, her hands on her hips, eyes alive with outrage. He stamped on the brake.

'Get his licence plate,' she yelled, without taking her eyes off him. 'Someone call the cops.'

She was a fitness zealot, tricked out in green and pink Lycra. Staring back at her, Leo thought of the Beverly Hills Hotel, where he and Deborah had spent their honeymoon. But Deborah was dead, and the sky seemed less blue all of a sudden, and this spectre in green and pink was like a blot on the purity of the day.

'He tried to run me over! Get a picture of him!'

Other people were crowding around. Leo stared at her over the hood – sensed their two pairs of eyes locking in shared disdain. He pounded his left foot on the clutch, then began to depress the gas. The car let out a growl, rising to a whine as he drove the pedal to the floor. He watched as her face clouded with fury, then fear. The car shook from side to side. All around her, people leapt clear.

Leo eased off the gas and released the clutch. The Lincoln sprang forward. He saved it from a stall with a hard pump of gas.

The woman in green and pink wasn't quite clear. He skimmed her – shoved her – with the front-left fender, sending her to her knees. The sound was light but firm. A hard, reverberant *thock*.

He drove on. Switching his eyes to the sideview mirror, he saw that someone was helping her off the ground. She'd live. She should have been quicker, he thought, as he swung onto East 47th Street. Quicker and slower. Slower to accuse and quicker to get the fuck out of the way.

*

10.38

As Leo pushed open the door of the gallery, Lorna thought that he seemed frailer than when they'd last met. Thinner in the face, less steady on his feet.

'How have you been, Miss Bedford?' He flung his stick with fluke dexterity onto the front desk. Geneva sprang back in her seat. 'Your gallery seems smaller every time I come.'

'You haven't been here in years. And that wall's temporary.' Lorna indicated a partition that bisected the room almost from corner to corner.

Leo grasped her outstretched hand. His glare cracked into a smile.

'So. Where's the show? Where's Ana Garcia? Did I come to look at a slanting wall?'

Lorna led him into the segment of space where Ana's five paintings hung in a row. Ana was standing in the far corner, stabbing a message into her phone.

'Hey, Ana, this is Leo Goffman.'

Ana glanced up. 'Hi.' She returned to her phone.

'It's a new series,' Lorna said. 'Variations on a theme.' She indicated the painting closest to them. '*Pink Cloud over Manhattan.*'

Leo was staring at Ana. His hawklike face seemed more ancient than a moment ago. It was graven with deep lines, the lips were bloodless and the ivory-white of the skull shone through. His thinning hair rose in tufts. His pupils had shrunk to microbial spots, like the black nuclei in frogspawn.

'Leo, are you okay?'

His attention shifted at last to the paintings. He seemed to drink them in.

'Looks like quite a show.'

'The hanging isn't finished yet,' Ana said. Her voice was crisp. She hadn't moved from the corner.

Leo looked from Ana to Lorna and back again, with a hint of a smile.

'You know, I used to hang out at the Cedar Street Tavern. All the greats went there. Motherwell, Guston, Rothko . . . Mark was a lovely guy, very funny.'

'Right. All those men,' Ana said.

'That scene—' He drew himself up and inhaled fiercely. 'It was more varied, *diverse*, than people imagine. There's all this crap now about the Abstract Expressionists working in the service of the CIA. Toxic masculinity. Whatever.' He let out a quiet snort. 'Those men were *artists*. And the women, too – damn fine painters. Lee Krasner, Elaine de Kooning. You could even be a fag back then, like Frank O'Hara, so long as you had talent.'

No one spoke.

'One of my few regrets is that I never met Picasso,' Leo went on. 'We knew people in common, like Douglas Cooper. I figure we would have got on. *This*' – he beamed at Ana with intent – 'is why I like to meet the artists I admire. You may not believe it, but I'm a social being.'

Lorna didn't believe it. Leo's sociability, if it had ever existed, belonged to a distant era.

'*Girl on a Ball*,' Leo said, still looking at Ana. 'The masterpiece of Picasso's Rose Period. The little dancing acrobat. The tired old wrestler. Innocence and experience!'

Ana watched him with reserve, before glancing at the phone in her hand.

'Oh, shoot. Lorna, I'm sorry. I have to go – right now. I have to be back at the studio.'

Lorna had known that Ana would bail.

'I'll drive you,' Leo said, his voice abruptly loud. 'I'll take you. My car's outside.'

He waited for an answer with the same riveted expression as before. His lower teeth were visible, bunched and narrow like palings.

Ana dropped her phone into the pouch of her dungarees and walked away without a word. Leo stared at the space where she had been standing.

'How old is she?' he said.

'Thirty.'

'Just a kid.' A steely smile, or the hint of one, appeared on his lips. Control was returning. He gestured at the paintings. 'I get it. Collages but also paintings. Abstract but also not abstract. Bits of – what would you call it? – visual noise. But does it add up to a symphony?' For the first time, there was feeling – a shimmer of sadness – in his expression. 'I should have been an art critic, right? What the hell, I'll take all five.'

*

19.51

Leo stood before the Picasso that hung in the corridor, just outside his bedroom. *Girl on a Ball*. He peered at the blue of the ballerina's leotard. A pinkish blue that sheathed the slender limbs of the girl as she balanced – *posed* (she was conscious, wasn't she, of being watched?) – on the ball of stone. And the guy who watched her: such weariness! The strongman confronted by what he cannot be, by a trick he can't perform. Leo knew that kind of dismay.

What time of day had it been? Evening, he thought. The brink of night.

That's why the strongman is whacked out, why the girl's still full of energy. The circus is over, although – as the man knows, as the kid hasn't yet guessed – it's never over.

A motion down the passageway disturbed his meditation. Through the open doors of the elevator, he saw Fritz Schein. A leather jacket was pulled over the top of his suit.

Leo had a sensation of time contracting, as if decades were elapsing at rapid speed, and then expanding back into regular, passing seconds.

'What are you doing here?'

Fritz stepped into the corridor. 'You asked me to come.'

'Oh, right. Yeah.' Beckoning Fritz to follow, Leo steered himself towards the drawing room, righting his motion by pats of his fingertips on the walls. 'What's new, Fritzie?'

'I just got in from London this morning.'

'London's a backwater, or it will be soon. I want to expand here in New York. Harlem! That church I'm converting – it'll be a prototype. Every church in the district could be a block of Goffman condos.'

'The Baptist place, you mean?'

Leo turned to face Fritz. They were on the threshold of the drawing room.

'The model just arrived from the architects. You have to see this thing. It's *exquisite*. Everything to scale. Miniature blocks of masonry, like the tesserae of a mosaic. The interiors replicated in every detail – anti-gravity glass stairs, Spanish parquet, the pool in the crypt. It opens up like a doll's house.'

'Where is it?'

'At Hudson Yards. Drop by and have a look.'

Leo drifted into the room. *Red Stone Dancer* cut a silhouette against the twilight.

'Do you know why I wanted that place so bad, the moment I heard it was for sale? It was Deborah. She used to go there – up to 130th Street – practically every week.'

'Deborah went to the Baptist church?' There was a touch of amusement or surprise in the question.

'Not to worship. Deborah was a perfect secular Jew. No, she went to help at a soup kitchen in the sanctuary. Can't you just picture her? A saint among the lepers. Joan of Arc, spooning out chowder! I never joined her. It was her thing, see. A pilgrimage. A *mission*. But she told me all about the place. The stained glass was like a Tiffany lamp, she said. A magic lantern.'

Leo found, to his slight surprise, that he was out of breath.

'She went for years until she found out the minister was embezzling donations for some kid in a coma.' A sharp cackle broke out. 'She sussed him out before anyone. She could read people. She saw something in you – hell if I know what it was.'

'So, it was Deborah's place.'

'Always will be. I couldn't let anyone else buy it. And by the way' – Leo strove to control his chest – 'what the hell were you doing at Galerie Berlins last week?'

'There was a Haller opening. I figured I should swing by, just to look.'

'Remember what I told you. Don't go *near* that man. Deborah hated Berlins too, you know. She could read people, like I said. She saw right into them.'

Leo allowed the words to hang in the air, wondering, as he passed between the Giacometti and the Lehmbruck, if all the words that have ever been spoken remain in the air as pulsations. His eyes travelled out to the serene monument of the city at dusk. The monumentality was an illusion. Buildings disappeared all the time – disappeared and regrew. But some buildings stayed put. New York wouldn't be New York without them, or it would be a depleted version of itself. It had been like that after the Twin Towers fell.

His focus retracted. 'The reason I asked you here, Fritzie . . .'

'Yes?'

'I figured there should be a sale, a big event, once I'm gone. Christie's, Sotheby's, whichever. All of the art. I want you to value the collection. Everything in this apartment, everything up in Montauk, the lot.'

'That'll take time. And as you know, I'm a curator – not a market expert.'

'Don't give me that. You buy and sell on the sly. You *advise*. Everyone knows it. I want you to make a valuation.'

'You haven't considered leaving the collection to a museum?'

'I've considered it, sure. MoMA have been courting me for years, and the Met. All those erudite types, borrowing my art, asking me for money, inviting me to dinners. They hate me with a passion.'

Fritz was eyeing the contents of the room. 'I'd need a day, at least.'

'Come next week. I'll be at the chiropractor on Friday. Out of your hair.'

Fritz had turned towards the door. Leo followed his gaze. Bonita was standing there, her hands cupped together.

'*Mr Goffman*.' She spoke in a whisper. 'The police are down-stairs.'

12

14 September, 00.13. New York

Lorna was drunk when she got home. Functioning drunk. There had been a dinner at Soho House for Ana Garcia. It had carried on late. She walked along the hall to the bathroom, slowed down by Jay as he sprang around her in joyful circles. Descending on the toilet, she closed her eyes and listened to the gurgle of her piss.

She took out her phone. There was an unread SMS from Justine.

Andrea Driscoll was run down on a crosswalk yesterday by Leo Goffman. She's been vomiting. Insane headaches. Beatrix is in pieces, wants to go back to NY. Thank Christ I'm with her.

Andrea. Beatrix's wife. The addiction psychotherapist.

'Jesus.'

Lorna sat on the toilet for a long while.

*

Later, she lay on Justine's side of the bed, naked under the sheet. She ran her hands up and down her stomach, skimming her groin, trying to retrieve the sensation of Justine's body – its warmth, its lithe responsiveness. She slid a finger inside herself, then another. The idea that Justine was having an affair filled her with dismal amusement. What was she jealous of? For a long time, Lorna had paid Beatrix no attention, regarding her as just another one of Justine's right-thinking friends. As the two of them grew close, Lorna had been bemused and then irritated, assuming that Beatrix was trying to cash in on Justine's cool. She and Justine used to joke about Beatrix's nasal Brooklyn twang.

Glancing across the floor of the bedroom, she noticed the *Evening Standard* where it had slid from the top of her piled clothes. She had thrown it into her suitcase before she left London. She bent down and flipped over the first two pages to reveal the photograph of Luca Holden. He seemed like a character from the distant past. Was it some chance effect of the photograph – its slight granularity? The boy's expression held her. It had been what prompted her to keep the paper: the feeling that she was looking at a photograph from her own life.

There was a noise outside on the street. Shattering glass. Jay let out a bark from downstairs. Lorna lay very still and listened. For a minute or more she waited, then got up and pulled on a nightgown.

Outside, the air was fresh. The street seemed deserted. But as she descended the steps, she saw a person some distance away, walking eastward. A figure in a long coat. Lorna's eyes tracked back and she saw a broken beer bottle lying on the sidewalk, ten feet away from her. Shards and chips of glass lay in a pool of froth.

Passing back into the house, she glanced at the framed photograph that hung beside the front door. It was one of the few works of art that she and Justine had bought together, a black and white shot by Louise Lawler from the late nineties titled *She Wasn't Always a Statue*. It showed an assortment of antique plaster casts. The white forms were luminous against the surrounding gallery. At the front of the image were two crouching female nudes, both missing their heads and most of their arms.

Lorna and Justine had gone to the Metropolitan Museum one afternoon and found the original statue. Justine had stopped in front of a headless marble figure – nude and locked in a posture between standing and crouching, with one arm angled towards the breasts, but broken off at the elbow.

'It's the Venus in our picture!'

They had stood together and looked at the pitted, blotched stone.

'She wasn't always a statue,' murmured Justine. 'You know, I think the model for this Venus wasn't the youngest. See how she's filled out a bit. Kind of broad in the beam. She has those spare bits on her hips that you have.'

'Go to hell.'

'I noticed when you got out of the shower the other day. It's sexy, to have a bit of that.' Justine began to walk around the statue, flashing Lorna a sly look. 'You'd be a teenage boy otherwise. This Venus has heft – look at those rolls around the belly.'

Lorna tried to be moved by the body, or aroused. She sensed Justine watching her with amusement.

'You feel her vulnerability. She knows she's naked.'

'A statue with emotions,' said Justine. 'I'm going to call her Lorna.'

'I want to touch her waist,' Lorna said. 'The ripply part.'

'Well, go on then. Do it.'

Justine grabbed Lorna's fingers and clamped them to the statue. The stone was warm. Justine's fingers were hard and firm on top of Lorna's own. Lorna tried to pull away. A museum guard was calling from across the gallery, preceded by footsteps.

'Justine, get off!' Lorna began to laugh, despite her indignation.

Justine pulled Lorna's hand away as the guard was nearing, and tugged her through the gallery.

'I can see you as a sexy statue. But you'd be Artemis, I think. A lonely hunter.'

'Is that how I seem to you?'

Justine shrugged. 'Maybe a little.'

Chattering voices filled the air. A group of elementary schoolkids was spreading out between the statues, clutching worksheets, talking in high excitement. One of them let out a shriek, prompting a fierce shushing from the teacher. Lorna watched as the little boy's grin disappeared inside a blush – sharing the pain of his sudden self-awareness. Then she turned to see that Justine was regarding her closely, wryly serious, as if searching for a sign.

*

07.33

The question of legacy was chasing Leo as he swerved and bounced through Manhattan. Colossal forms threw back or sucked in the sunlight. There were no other cars, barely any people. The Lincoln's suspension was sprightly, like a motor-boat's. He tapped and teased the pedal with his toes.

Those mauves, Deborah whispered, and he felt the touch of her lips on his ear.

He held the pedal to the floor. The engine howled. The streets were filling up – with cars, with people – just as he wanted to outstrip the feeling that was taking hold.

He pressed the pedal fast, aiming for the splinter of space between two drifting clusters of pedestrians, and he felt the car dive in a slowly revolving vortex of green and pink. There was a spandex jogging outfit . . . *thunk*. He heard a woman shriek, saw her flying into the treacle panels of the Seagram Building. In the sideview mirror, the Beverly Hills Hotel was on fire – the whole building engulfed in flames.

Air rushed into him and he opened his eyes.

'Sorry to be missing this?' he muttered to the version of Deborah who seemed to inhabit the silence.

'Is that you, Mr Goffman?' It was Bonita, speaking through a gap in the doorway. 'Are you awake?'

He examined the ceiling. 'Yes, I'm awake.'

He assessed the loci and intensities of pain: the usual skeletal throbbing, a neuralgic twinge, the stabbing of an overloaded bladder. He wondered whether to try driving the urine forth with a single push. It might deliver a gushing release. Or not, in which case the agony would double or triple inside the clamped pouch.

For a few seconds, the dream was more vivid than the memory welling up from beneath it. Then the events of the evening returned to him. Two police officers had shown up, all padded and holstered and mean. They had looked odd in the hall of masterpieces – shifty, defensive. *Who lives like this?* He'd detected the question passing silently between them.

He had decided to play doddery, told them about the lights changing and a madwoman running in front of his car and how it all happened so quick.

'I remember nothing!' he'd said. And he'd repeated it until they seemed resigned to the fact. They had taken a statement and left.

He guessed he could expect a lawsuit. But as he rolled on his side, it seemed like the smallest thing in the world. Less annoying by far than his bladder. The colour and turmoil of his dream swam back. One morning soon, he would stay submerged, and this room – his marital bedroom, transposed in every detail from the old apartment on the Upper East Side – would be his mausoleum.

Legacy. What would his be?

He turned over in bed and freed his scrotum from the pincers of his thighs.

Deborah was gone, and soon he would be too. What remained of a person? His body would wither in the mortuary furnace, flesh sublimating with a hiss, bones calcinating into husks, and the collection would be dispersed . . .

The collection: didn't *that* contain something of him, of both of them?

Out of his melancholy came a rousing defiance. There would be an auction, grander than any he'd ever seen, split into day and evening sales, with a catalogue the size of an encyclopaedia. His and Deborah's names would be inscribed on the wall in midnight blue. A picture, too. That photograph taken on the beach at Montauk in '76: Leo with his shirt unbuttoned, Deborah in her printed summer dress.

The proceeds would go to the Deborah Goffman Memorial Foundation. A handsome slice would go to the auction house – that was inevitable. As to whether the sale would happen at Sotheby's or Christie's, well, there was no need to rush the decision. Let them fight it out. The prize was the Leo J. Goffman Collection. It was worth a beauty contest.

'Your clothes are ready, Mr Goffman,' Bonita said from the door. 'Will you swim first?'

'Bring me *Artforum*.'

With his eyes still pinned to the plasterwork, he wondered where he would hang the lilac Haller. The thought came to him that he could have been a great museum curator, superlative, better than Alfred Barr or any of those other pious fucks at MoMA. He was a creative man. Development, too, was an art. Selling – profiting – was its own *jeu d'esprit*.

'I think I threw it out already,' said Bonita after a silence. 'I usually do after a week.'

Breath drained from his body. He strained to lift his head. Bonita was visible in the doorway, placid and utterly predictable in her pinafore . . . exasperating, suddenly, in her predictability.

'Go and get that goddamned magazine!'

He wrenched his head up. Pain scuttled through his neck and back. A cry escaped him. It was a horrible noise, laden with the catarrh of the night.

'Get it out of the fucking bin if you have to.'

He swung his legs out of bed and heaved himself into a sitting position, grinding his teeth against the pyrotechnic agonies in his neck and spine and pelvis, then rose on the balls of his feet.

Bonita took a step into the room, averting her eyes from his swaying nudity. He stamped past her, grabbing a silk nightgown that had once been Deborah's from the back of the door. With a grasping, tugging effort, he shouldered it on.

'The recycling went out last night,' Bonita said, following him into the corridor. She spoke as though she were remarking on the weather. 'But maybe I put it in the general waste.'

'You'll find it.' He strode faster, struggling to tie the slippery garment.

Despite his pace, she entered the kitchen past him. The room was barely known to him. It was vast and antiseptically clean. Sunlight sheared off the edges of the range cooker and the Romanesque hoops of the taps. Bar stools stood like satellite dishes along the central island – a tomb-sized edifice clad in cappuccino-coloured stone. Half the walls were glass: the room occupied the corner of the building. Beyond was a frieze of high-rises, tapering and terminating against a satin-blue sky. The day was blinding. His vision recoiled, jamming with amoebic floaters.

Bonita tapped a panel beneath one of the stone countertops. A waste bin glided out. It was a tripartite silo, each compartment lined with a polythene sack. She began to sift the contents of a red liner.

'Maybe I dropped it in here,' she murmured. 'Yes, it's in here.'

'Empty it!' Leo felt his voice explode. He landed his hand on the nearest marble plane, holding it there to steady himself. 'Empty the damn thing on the floor.'

Bonita raised the bin from its armature. She flipped it to release a slew of trash which slumped onto the floor in a peristaltic tide – potato peelings, detergent bottles, empty drugs packets and a dilute red liquid that streamed across the tiles. *Artforum* slid over the heap and fell open.

'There,' shouted Leo, jabbing a finger while continuing to fasten himself to the countertop. 'It's all covered in shit. Pick it up.'

He watched her as she knelt, hearing the air rush in and out of his lungs. The sun broke over the top of the neighbouring tower. He twisted his neck to evade the glare. The light had silhouetted Bonita, flattening her into a pink-beige shape, a blank presence, absolutely still.

13

16 September, 22.22. Montreux

He could smell Otto's nakedness.

When he looked up, the lamp overhead was blinding. It blotted out the details of Otto's face. All Thomas saw was a strong neck and shoulders, and the outline of the man's cropped hair.

Thomas was kneeling on the floor, facing the bar. Otto walked around him, coming into view momentarily as the light hit his chest. Then he stepped behind Thomas and crouched down. Thomas felt a winding motion around his wrists, the slinky elastic of a stocking. Otto drew the fabric tight.

Closing his eyes, feeling the blood pool in his hands, Thomas remembered the spring. He had gone to London to see the construction site of Claude's new gallery. That was the second time he had met Luca.

They had walked together through the rubble-strewn plot, wearing hard hats and high-vis vests, gazing at concrete piles that sprouted from the ground. It wasn't clear what the gallery would look like. Treading over broken stones, Luca conjured the final forms of things.

'The main space will start here. It'll be huge, like a tennis court. Bigger.'

'Good. I want large spaces between the paintings.' Thomas took a succession of giant steps and flung out his arms. 'Like *that*.'

Luca watched inquisitively. 'I heard that Claude is building this gallery specially for you. For your paintings.'

'Claude would say that to whoever was doing the debut show. When he opened his space in Madrid, it was for Richard Serra – so he said.'

'What's it like to be friends with Claude?' Luca swung one leg in front of the other and back again.

'What's it like to work for him?' Thomas countered.

'He's a monster. But you knew that.'

Thomas wanted to say something flippant, but his insides had tightened.

Afterwards, they went for a drink at the Café Royal. Sitting opposite Luca in the low light, Thomas was able to study his face in detail. A pale face, perhaps a touch narrow. Its shape and pallor were offset by the fullness of the lips. The lower one jutted a little, giving the suggestion of a pout.

'You look like a Florentine,' he said, as a second round of martinis arrived – allowing a thought to spill out. 'One of those early-Renaissance aristos.'

'Thanks, but my mother's Calabrian. She came from a family of farmers.' Luca's smile had the same glint of an affront that Thomas had detected in Montreux.

'My parents were country people too. Rustics. I created myself out of nothing.' Thomas sat back, holding his glass up to the light. 'You could almost be my son,' he added, half as a joke, and at the same moment he caught sight of himself in a strip of mirror behind Luca's head. A man in his forties, no longer young but a long way from being old. He tried to think of how he'd been at Luca's age. An empty vessel.

'I don't see you as much older than me,' Luca replied. 'I've stopped noticing people's ages – guys' ages – when they're between twenty-five and fifty.'

Thomas looked into the velvet dusk of the bar, not believing him. Then he remembered the way that Luca had eased himself out of the pool that day in Switzerland. He could feel the martini stealing into his head.

Luca was tapping the screen of his phone. He tutted.

'Everything okay?'

'Yes. Just an email from Claude. He wants to know how the site visit went.'

'He keeps watch,' Thomas murmured.

'Always. He has a hundred eyes. Magnetic eyes. I've seen the way Berlins sucks people into his orbit, makes them his instruments.'

'That's what's happened to me?' Beneath his incipient drunkenness, Thomas was alert.

Luca set his phone aside. 'I don't think you're so easily caught. You have this containment about you. A barrier.' He leaned over the table a little. 'I want to get past it.'

Thomas was reminded, as he gave a nonchalant smile and changed the subject, of the preciousness of youth. It was a cliché, and yet here was the original fact. Luca had no idea how he looked, just then, as the light reflecting off the table picked out his solemnity (an eager, anxious attentiveness). Would he change in a few years? Despite working for Claude's gallery, he seemed to have little interest in money. Sales were a means to an end, for him, a way of allowing artists to live. All the things that Thomas had been obsessing about for years – museum shows and biennales and prizes – were just noise to this boy.

They had a third martini each, then walked into Soho. Luca was staying at the Z Hotel on Old Compton Street. They went past Comptons bar. Men crowded the pavement outside and music blared through the door.

'I love this place,' Luca said, following Thomas's eye.

'I know it well,' Thomas said. 'Knew it.'

'Let's have another drink.' Luca was already heading to the door. 'I love how *sleazy* it is. Let's go and dance.'

At the point of agreeing, Thomas touched Luca's shoulder and held back. 'You go. I'll save it for next time.'

He walked on to the Savoy, taking his time as he circled St Martin-in-the-Fields. Alone at last, he felt less drunk. His conversation with Luca had been tipping into something beyond the professional, but he couldn't tell which of them had been pushing it that way. Luca hadn't wanted the night to end. Thomas tried to recall when he'd last felt like that: the excitement of the night unfolding, the next day not mattering . . .

The sound of a choir surged from the lit windows of the church. Outside Charing Cross station, a tramp was sleeping on top of the Maggi Hambling sculpture of Oscar Wilde in his coffin, appearing to lie in Oscar's surprised embrace.

*

Otto was shoving something in his mouth. A damp organic bundle. Kneeling, with his hands bound behind him, Thomas opened his eyes and bit down on hard stems. He was holding a bunch of lilacs in his teeth.

The air was a pink haze. He felt Otto's hands on his shoulders, felt himself being turned on the pivot of his knees to face the three walls of mirrors. He shivered to see himself: flowers obscuring his lower face, hands drawn back, eyes wide with what might have passed for alarm. The image was repeated in each mirror. When he looked straight ahead, he saw Otto standing behind him, stretching a tan-coloured stocking above his head.

*

19 September, 10.15. New York

Lorna was on the High Line, walking the route of the former elevated railroad, past a long strip of grasses and wildflowers that grew now around the disused tracks. Justine was on Victoria Peak. The weirdness of cloudy, nocturnal Hong Kong transposed by liquid crystals into the daylight of New York: did it magnify or diminish the distance between them?

Lorna switched her focus between FaceTime and the concrete planks of the walkway, taking care not to collide with slower amblers. Snug in her ears, her AirPods cancelled out the noise around her.

Justine was talking about a lecture she'd just delivered at HKU. It sounded like a big affair. Heavyweight academics from around the world had attended. The theme had been capitalism and its false illusions. The fallacy of individual freedom, the totalitarianism of the neoliberal state.

'Uh huh,' said Lorna as Justine distilled the thesis.

'Of course, the folks from Berkeley hated it. I was using their own theories against them. And, as far as the Chinese were concerned, I was only telling them what they've known for decades.'

'Uh huh.'

'Are you in a rush, doll?' There was an irony to Justine's tone. Behind her, the fluorescent city was misting over.

'No, just walking. I'm listening.'

They were installed, Justine and Beatrix, at Beatrix's family home on the Peak. Lorna had found a realtor's webpage from back when the place was for sale. It reminded her of a nineties office building – white stone intercut with dark glass, arrayed over steep land. There was a terrace overlooking Hong Kong harbour, at the edge of which Justine was now leaning, languid and slightly tipsy. One collarbone was visible above the sagging neckline of her T-shirt.

Lorna thought of the feel of Justine's skin – smooth and taut, with the hardness of muscles beneath. The essence of her sexiness.

She made a sidestep to dodge a striding man.

'You're busy,' Justine said with a smiling sigh.

'I'm running late,' Lorna admitted. 'These last few days have been mad.' She winced to remember Justine's text message from the other night. 'How's Andrea?'

'I was wondering if you'd ask.' Justine's voice fell out of synch with her image. 'She'll be fine. I mean, she didn't hit her head or break anything. It was the shock that got her. But that's not the point. Leo Goffman ran her down on purpose. *Goffman* – your friend! Witnesses are saying he was speeding like a psycho. He has to be made to pay.'

'I'm glad she's okay. And he's not my friend.'

With queasy certainty, Lorna had deduced that Leo had been driving downtown to visit her.

'I don't get why he hasn't been arrested,' Justine said. 'Why isn't it all over the news? Meantime, Beatrix has been going out of her mind with worry.'

'Is she coming back to New York?'

'Oh, I don't think so. Andrea will live. Beatrix needs to be here with me. We have a tour to plan, remember?'

Lorna thought of Justine and Beatrix, nakedly entwined. When was Justine coming back? The question was loud in Lorna's head, but it insisted on remaining there, unvocalised.

'My schedule is crazy,' Justine went on. 'I'm staying up to do a phone interview tonight for BBC Radio 4. *Live.* Will you listen? It's in an hour from now, just after *The Archers*.'

During lockdown, Lorna and Justine had made a ritual of *The Archers*. A ritual and a game. Justine had loved mimicking the farmers' voices. Together they'd conspired about how the plot could be darker, weirder, camper . . .

'Sure, I'll tune in.'

Lorna descended the steps to 23rd Street. She held the phone steady and looked back at Justine. Her eyes lingered on that single clavicle. She had told herself that she was fine with their state of semi-separation – acted as if this were true. But Justine's absence had generated a new restlessness in her this time. An undirected longing.

'What's been happening?' Justine demanded, seeming to scrutinise her anew. 'I know when something's up with you. What are you not telling me?'

'Something in London.' Lorna had reached the sidewalk.

'At Claude Berlins?'

'Kind of. Not exactly.' She felt an inward surrender. 'One of the gallery's staff died two nights before I arrived. A young guy. He fell from his apartment.'

'Jesus. Why didn't you say?'

'I don't know. But I've been thinking about him ever since. Luca Holden.'

'What happened?'

'He'd been drinking. There were drugs in his system. It sounds like he took his own life. Or – it could have been an accident . . .' She arranged the words in her head before saying them: 'I've been thinking about my own boy.'

There was a pause. 'Your own boy?'

Lorna was only half listening. A hidden reservoir of feeling was threatening to break.

'Why are you bringing this up? Is it because I'm not there?'

'It has nothing to do with you, Justine.'

'And what's the connection? Who was this Luca to you?'

Lorna waited. The question of what had happened to Luca was a dark mark, constantly changing shape. Sometimes she caught hold of images. The tower, the balcony, his startled face (an altered version of the photo in the newspaper). The rest was a blank. She hurled herself into a confession.

'That's the thing. Luca was twenty-six, the same age as *him*. And when I saw Luca's picture in the paper, I couldn't believe how familiar he looked – he reminded me, actually, of myself at that age, and I thought—'

'Oh, God. *Really*? This is because I'm not with you. You're starting to fantasise.' Justine lit a cigarette. The tip flared as she drew on it, forming a clot on the iPhone display. 'You always said it was the right thing to do.'

Lorna stood still, staring past the phone at a crack in the ground. 'It *was* the right thing. Thomas and I were never meant to be parents. We weren't even meant to be lovers. We did what we did, and after that . . .'

'What? What happened after?'

'After that we were free. It was a necessary sacrifice, I guess.'

'The Necessary Sacrifice!' Justine's voice was abruptly happy. 'That's the final chapter of my book. So, you've read it. You're quoting me.'

'Maybe,' Lorna replied, with a flash of guilt.

She had just received the hardcover edition of *How to Take Control*. The book was sitting unread on the coffee table at home. The cover image was a silk painting of Confucius, shredded like a torn billboard to reveal an underlying picture: a female bodybuilder, all muscles and fake tits and glistening oiled skin.

Lorna pictured the sitting room at home: the open drawers of the desk, the disinterred folders that lay over the floor.

'I pulled out the adoption documents last night.'

Justine regarded her in silence. Lorna observed the rise and fall of her chest.

'Did you open them?'

'No. Not in the end.'

'Sometimes, you know, it's better to let go.'

14

One block south from the chiropractor, Leo recognised the entrance of Sotheby's. Fate must have guided him here. How many times he and Deborah had passed through this door! Before he could resist, the revolving door had whirled him off the street, into the cream-stoned lobby.

Impressionist & Modern Art Day Sale

A character in a suit was greeting him like he'd never been gone.

'This way, please, Mr Goffman.'

Walking through the double doors at the back of the sale room, he discerned a hum in the air. It was the restive sound of an auction in its final phase.

There was an empty seat, but he stayed at the threshold and scanned the sea of turned-away heads. A platinum crown was visible in the front row. Berlins – it had to be. Fritz Schein wasn't here, of course. He would be over at the apartment by now, making an inventory. When Leo made a request, Fritzie obeyed.

The restrained fervour, the softness of the carpet, the glow of the room: he remembered it all. He was a little underdressed today, in his linen shirt and flannel pants, but what else had changed?

Florian Roth, Global Head of Contemporary Art, was at the podium. He had just brought down the gavel on Lot 200 – an assemblage by Joseph Cornell. It was one of those glass-fronted boxes filled with little objects: a stuffed bird, pebbles, other worthless ephemera. Leo had never cared for Cornell's work. What was the point of all those objects, so finickity and forgettable?

Attendants in aprons carried the box from sight.

Leo continued to survey the room, and began to doubt his decision to allow Fritzie into the apartment alone, or with only Bonita there to keep an eye. But who else could he trust? Deborah had adored that guy from the moment they'd first met him at one of their own fundraisers. But then, Deborah had had love and trust in abundance. Too much of both, if that were possible. With sickening unease, he thought of Fritzie creeping around their bedroom, running his hands over the surfaces of things, rifling through Deborah's drawer. Maybe he had picked up some guy on one of those apps, and the two of them were together this very second in Leo's bedroom, having fooled Bonita with a cover story. With paralysing clarity, Leo saw Fritzie leading a burly stranger around the room, showing it off like it was his own (*This we call the Louis Quinze room!*), slipping out of his clothes and having the guy fuck him right there on the bed. Unravelling Deborah's shawl and using it to choke himself. Or would he have danced over to the wardrobe first and grabbed Deborah's glorious mink coat – pulled it around his naked body before the other guy screwed him? One of them had to be the woman, Leo guessed. He shook his head to expel the vision.

'Our final lot today,' declared Florian, 'is a work of indisputable greatness.'

A wall beside the podium swivelled like a theatre set to reveal a painting.

'Matisse's *Red Interior in Cannes*.'

The hum intensified. This, thought Leo, was more fucking like it. The painting was one of the biggest by Matisse that he had seen; it must have been hidden for decades. French doors in the centre of a red bedroom led to a balcony. A block of marine blue hovered behind scrolling railings.

'This is a major moment for the modern art market.'

Hadn't he stood at that balcony, looked out at the same glittering sea? The memory refused to break through. He nodded slowly, absorbing each detail.

The screens of iPhones were glowing through the room.

'I want to start the bidding here at forty million dollars. Forty million!'

Clutching his mahogany gavel, Florian threw out his tuxedoed arms like a calibrated toy. On the triangle of his shirt, just beneath his bowtie, was a clip-on microphone. Hands darted up. Not Claude's. The megadealer had probably swept up half the other lots, and was content to watch like a glutted predator.

'Forty-one, forty-two, forty-three already!'

Florian gestured in different directions. There was an air of controlled delirium about him. For a moment, his and Leo's eyes met. Leo trembled. Then the auctioneer's eyes darted onward.

'Forty-seven in the room!'

On one side was a platform where Sotheby's staff stood behind a ledge. Leo counted twelve of them, militarily arrayed in designer suits and dresses. A few were murmuring into telephones and giving signals to the auctioneer: a tip of the head, an upflick of fingers.

Leo knew what it would feel like to raise his hand. Even if the bidding went over sixty million, he could afford the painting with ease. The sale of the Harlem church would net him that. *It would be so simple.* He slid his hands into his pockets and watched the numbers on the screen above Florian's head, running away from the bidders in six currencies. Periodically he cast his gaze back to the red room in Cannes and experienced once more a biting spur of memory and desire. But something held him in check.

His eyes grew warm. The past was irretrievable and his time was accelerating. With calm horror, he realised that a tear was sliding down his cheek. A woman in the back row turned and looked at him. He felt the indignity of the single tear, sensed it glistening like a branded mark. He gave a hard snort and the woman turned away.

Only two contenders were left – a man in the centre of the room (Leo could see a stubby, hairy hand, girdled by a silver watch), and a telephone bidder. This absent party was transmitting instructions to a woman on the platform. She was in her early forties, with long red hair and a green dress that shimmered in the stage lights. Her skin reminded Leo of fine porcelain. She motioned to Florian with a flat hand and a half-smile.

Florian's body froze. His arms were locked in a pose like that of an archer. He switched his eyes between the bidder in the room and the red-haired woman. The murmur of the crowd – a rumbling constant until now – died in the air.

'At sixty million dollars, I have all the time in the world!'

Florian's face tightened into a grin. The room erupted in laughter. It was like the canned laughter of old sitcoms. The gavel in his fingers was hovering an inch from the block. Leo watched the space between. He glanced at the woman in green, just as she gave a nod.

'At sixty million dollars – fair warning – *sold*.' Florian cracked the gavel down. 'Thank you, Paula!'

The crowd dissolved into applause. The woman spoke into the phone and broke into a smile that confirmed her beauty. Leo felt his heart strike an unruly rhythm.

15

Le Mazot was a capsule of alternative reality. In the little basement bar, Thomas was in servitude. He was like the lounge
singer in *Blue Velvet*. Another person's toy. The game, the
pleasure, was in submitting, when all the time he was the one
in control. Otto was at his service, an actor in whatever drama
Thomas wanted to stage.

With Luca, it hadn't been a game. Everything was real –
unpredictable. Gone were the rules of the underground room.

Things had changed that night in the spring, when they'd
walked together through Soho. Thomas had left Luca outside
Comptons bar and walked on alone, resisting the temptation
to continue. But the strange, flirtatious energy between them
(all that charged sincerity) was running beyond his control.

Thomas was lying on the bed in his hotel room when he
received a text message.

I followed you.

He contemplated this for a while, wondering if it had been
meant for him.

Followed?

*I wanted to see where you went. You never told me where
you were staying.*

And?

I'm outside the Savoy. Can I come up?

It was close to midnight. Thomas should have said no, made
any excuse.

It's room 205. Give my name at reception.

Walking into Thomas's room, Luca placed something on the end of the bed. An oblong of wrapped paper, torn from a magazine, that unfolded like origami.

They drank whisky and chopped lines on the glass-topped desk. Luca told Thomas about his life – parents, friends, school, the queer scene. A voluble stream. Thomas lay back on the bed, watching the boy from across the room. He felt as if every nerve and organ had been shocked awake.

Luca was talking about how he'd done a foundation course at Camberwell College of Art, then gone through a succession of short jobs. The role with Claude had come about by chance. He'd got talking to Sylvia Rosso at a party the previous year.

'So that's how I come to be here in this room.'

Answering the challenge in Luca's face, Thomas told a story of his life. He described growing up on a remote mountainside. The beauty of it. The loneliness. The sense of separateness that had spread in him like a secretion at the age of eleven. How he had fallen in love with films and film stars, and how – at art school – he'd met Lorna.

'I painted her. It was the best portrait I ever made. The final portrait, too.' Thomas rested on an elbow, lying across the counterpane. Luca was seated at the desk, watching him in the mirror. 'We ended up sleeping together.'

'You had sex with Lorna Bedford?' Luca held a rolled-up banknote in his fingers, rotating it in wonderment.

'She was my Doris Day. I was like Rock Hudson.'

Luca grinned. 'Thomas Haller, the matinee idol. What else don't I know about you?'

Thomas talked on, painting a picture. But he said nothing about Claude. Even under the truth-spilling influence of the drug, he knew where to redact. At 3 a.m., he gave Luca money to go and buy more coke from a dealer in Villiers Street.

When he woke in the morning, it was close to noon. Luca

had gone. Thomas was naked in bed. He felt as if he'd been poisoned. He couldn't remember what had happened, beyond the conversation. For a horrifying minute, he thought that Luca had stolen his clothes, before he found them – immaculately folded – on a chair.

*

9 October, 11.38. Montreux

The real Thomas Heller. That was what Marianna Berger wanted to capture. He imagined himself as a specimen on the psychologist's couch. Would she be his therapist? His confessor?

Seated at his desk, Thomas searched again for her name online. This time, he found a video she'd shown at White Columns a few months earlier. It was on a YouTube page. Someone had filmed the exhibition on their phone. *Hotel* was the title of Marianna's video. Whoever had recorded the footage had stood and watched the entire thing, holding the phone as still as possible.

It began with a view of a hotel room. Yellowish light in a curtained space. The camera was at a depressed angle, maybe on a bedside cabinet. The surface of an unmade bed extended like terrain in the bottom quarter of the frame. Above, to the left, was a dark doorway where a darker presence loitered.

He stepped into the room – an undressed man, visible only as a silhouette.

'Stay here, then, if you're not feeling good.' His voice, calm and decisive, made Thomas aware of the silence that had preceded it.

The camera jolted upwards and sideways to show a woman's bare legs extending across the bed.

'You don't look up to anything today,' said the man, who was no longer in shot. 'You've done this to yourself. Sometimes—'

He sighed, seemingly about to deliver a piece of criticism or advice, before the camera flopped lens-down on the bed. The image went dark.

There were two voices now, hers as well as his, but their words were muffled. Were they arguing? It was hard to tell. She was laughing. Then silence. The camera jolted up again, admitting a view across a fold of the bedsheet. The man was in the bathroom, getting ready. Thomas recognised the clink and rattle of a morning routine. Gushing taps. The roar of a shower.

Music began to play. It was almost imperceptible at first, like sound coming from a distant place, but growing louder. A languid orchestral piece that might have been a film score. In time, it drowned out the noise of the shower. The camera panned across the surface of the bed – shakily, lazily – as if it had merged with the vision of the woman who held it, drifting over her legs, over the convolutions of the sheets, pausing on a strip of pills in gleaming foil. The imprint of a body lurked in the sheets.

The music faded.

'I'll see you later,' the man said from outside the frame. 'Not before three. Try to sort out this room.' There was a long gap before he added: 'You drink too much, Marianna.'

The door closed. The music resumed.

With slow, predatorial movements – she must have been crawling over the bed – the woman gazed through the lens at the residues of the night. There was a shadow-like mark at the edge of the sheet. Discarded underwear on the floor below. A Becks bottle lying on its side.

The light in the room shifted – brightened. The sound of curtain rings cut through the music, halting its luxurious growth. The camera flipped to show the face of a young woman, squinting in the daylight. She had unkempt black hair. Her shoulders were naked. She had a mole on one cheek, and the pallor of sickness or a hangover, but the wan look suited her. She stared into the lens, deadly serious, and began to speak.

But quick-eyed Love, observing me grow slack
From my first entrance in,
Drew nearer to me, sweetly questioning,
If I lacked any thing.

Her voice was cool and clear. She recited without blinking. The whites of her eyes shone in the revealed light.

The camera wobbled: she was switching it between hands. She snapped a cigarette alight.

Thomas waited for her to continue. She watched him through the lens – blew a jet of smoke – and the video ended.

*

11 *October, 06.53. New York*

Lorna sat cross-legged on the floor beside the desk. The room was dim. Through the tilted shutters, a pale light was beginning to intrude. She was holding a hardback brown envelope between the fingertips of each hand, raising it for inspection. It was an old A4 envelope, stained in one corner by a watermark. The address of her parents' house was affixed as a typewritten label. It was beginning to peel off. It would fall away if she picked at it. The glue that was holding the package closed would disintegrate too, in time, and the contents would slide out – insist on being read.

She pressed the envelope between a finger and thumb, guessing at the number of pages inside. Twenty, maybe, and all it amounted to was a countersigned form. But adoption was a serious thing; they'd said so countless times, all the people. She put it down on the carpet. On the floor around her were various coloured folders which had been on top of the envelope inside the desk. Aware that she would have to get up soon – stand up and tidy this room, open the shutters and go to work – she took the nearest folder and sifted through the handwritten pages within. So neat, so exacting. They were the notes from the first semester of Justine's PhD. Her Henry James phase. The notes predated their relationship by a short time. Lorna wondered if this was the writing of *her* Justine or of a person unknown to her, never to be reclaimed.

Under the heading *James on Venice* was a copied-out passage:

> *. . . the waterside life, the wondrous lagoon spread before me, and the ceaseless human chatter of Venice came in at my windows, to which I seem to myself to have been constantly driven, in the fruitless fidget of composition, as if to see whether, out in the blue channel, the ship of some right suggestion, of some better phrase, of the next happy twist of my subject, the next true touch for my canvas, mightn't come into sight.*

Lorna looked up at the shuttered window. The dawn was a little bluer through the slats.

'Next happy twist,' she said out loud, thinking that the words meant nothing when she said them – became almost silly. She felt exhausted and the day was only beginning.

The buzzing of her phone on the surface of the desk recalled her. She stood up. *Justine.* Lorna adjusted her T-shirt and ran a hand through her hair. It was only an audio call, but the movements were automatic.

'Hey, you.'

'Lorna? You have to hear this.' The hardness in Justine's voice was like a wrong note.

'Hear what?'

'That man. Leo Goffman. Your client.'

'Slow down – what about him?'

'He's a murderer. A fucking killer. Andrea Driscoll is in the Mount Sinai Beth Israel. In a coma.' Justine's voice was tremulous now, set to break. 'They say she won't make it.'

Lorna pressed her free hand flat on the desk, sinking all her weight into it. 'But you said she was okay.'

'*Clearly* she isn't. The doctors reckon she suffered from a bleed when she fell. A sentinel bleed, they call it. And now there's been a catastrophic rebleed. *Catastrophic*. Well, go figure. Goffman ran her down one month ago—'

'But she didn't hit her head.'

'What, are you his attorney now? Maybe she did. She was vomiting and had a migraine for days after. Goffman running her down was the start of all this. I can't tell you – Beatrix hasn't stopped crying for five hours straight.'

Lorna tried to process the information. Had Leo caused this? Had *she* caused it, indirectly?

'*Jesus Christ*,' Justine burst out. 'Why hasn't this been reported? Why is no one talking about it? He hasn't even been arrested!'

'Tell me where it happened again – the car accident. What time of day?'

'Nine thirty in the morning. Park Avenue and 48th. And don't call it an accident. Didn't you know that Andrea is on the board of Degentrify Harlem? She's been campaigning for years against Goffman Associates and their landgrabs. He tried to kill her.'

'You really think he knew who she was?'

'He looked her in the eye before he ran her down. He's a psychopath.'

In her mind's eye, glimmeringly, Lorna remembered what Andrea looked like – handsome, with dark eyebrows. The thought of Andrea lying flat on a hospital bed, covered in tubes and a ventilator, became mixed up with other imaginings: Beatrix and Justine jogging together on the Peak, high above Hong Kong, or lying on the beach in swimsuits, Beatrix's stocky build offsetting Justine's slimness, their eyes closed against the sunlight. Beatrix mimicking Lorna the way that Lorna had once mimicked Beatrix, and Justine dissolving into hysterics.

'This isn't real,' she murmured. 'It can't be.'

Justine made a noise of pure scorn, something between a laugh and a sob.

'Thank God I'm with Beatrix. Thank God she has me. If she *knew* that that son of a bitch is a friend of yours—'

'He's not a friend, Justine. This has nothing to do with me. Although' – she sighed, drew breath – 'I may as well tell you that he was driving downtown that morning to meet with me. He came to see Ana Garcia's show. I sold her new series to him.'

There was a pause, just long enough for Lorna to wonder if the call had dropped.

'You have to cancel the sale. *Now.*'

'Before I know anything about what happened?'

'I told you what happened. He ran her down in cold blood. She's going to die. And he's trying to pay his way out of trouble. You sold him Garcia's show? Jesus, I've heard everything now.'

'I didn't know when I sold it that he'd run down Beatrix's wife.'

'She's Beatrix's *ex*.' Justine's retort was squally and rasping, like a spurt of radio interference.

'I thought they were still together.'

'No – and what does that have to do with it?'

'So, is Beatrix with you now?' The suspicion, for so long inexpressible, had sprung out.

'He ran her the fuck down.'

Lorna felt a spasm of annoyance, followed by dismay. Justine was going to use this situation, weaponise it. Lorna was going to be written off as a lost cause.

'I'm sorry about Andrea. Seriously I am. But it's too easy to blame Goffman for anything – for everything – when he's old and objectionable and right-wing.'

'He's a fascist.'

'I don't know what that means, when you say it.'

'Because you don't try to understand me. Some people are plain *bad*, Lorna. Oh Christ, I can't handle this.'

Another voice was audible down the line.

'*What? Tell me. What's she gone and done?*'

It was Beatrix. Lorna recognised her deeper, nasal voice. How much of the call had she been listening to?

'Sold that asshole a load of pictures.' Justine's voice was fainter, as if she'd moved away from the phone. 'The guy who tried to kill Andrea.'

'How's Beatrix?' Lorna asked.

'She's not here.'

'I just heard her, Justine. I just heard you speak to her.' Lorna pinned the envelope on the floor with her toe. 'Are you in love with Beatrix? Is that what's happened?'

Lorna realised that Justine had ended the call. What had seemed like a pregnant pause was just a blank.

*

She walked around the room, looking at her bare feet and thinking – strangely, nonsensically – of those words: *happy twist*. She picked up Justine's book and tried to read it. The writing was sharp and boisterous, just what she would have expected. But her mind wouldn't follow the argument. All she could think of was their phone call. She clutched the book to her chest, running her hand over the spine. A pot of orchids stood in the corner of the room. *Please don't let them die*, Justine had said. The petals were shrivelling and dropping. The grotesques, Lorna had always called them, and now they really were. Crouching to collect them, she thought of a time when she and Justine had been in Bellport, walking on the beach at night. Climbing over rocks with shallow, still pools. The balminess of the night air and only the sound of the waves against their voices. The water freezing cold – but it hadn't mattered.

She tried again to read Justine's book. The chapters had florid titles, which carried a flicker of humour, if you knew Justine. Lorna should have read it the first moment she was able to. Instead, she'd been full of private excuses: Justine didn't want her to; Lorna wasn't smart enough to get it; the book wasn't really for her.

16

7 November, 11.52. Montreux

Thomas set the casket of ashes at the centre of the coffee table. A concrete cube on a larger concrete slab. He made sure the casket was dead central, then stood back and looked at the table and the couches and the room. He'd built this place as a sanctuary, but looking at it now, as he waited for the filmmaker Marianna Berger to arrive, he realised that he'd built it to be seen. The house was a spectacle, all surfaces. A floor of uncracked polished concrete. A wall of glass from end to end, with the blue day flooding in like a miracle. The kitchen at the far end – an arrangement of minimalist sculpture. Everything had been placed at right angles, other than the baby grand piano and the plywood desk, each of them diagonal to the window.

He had created an image of himself in all this. Impeccable, impersonal . . . Who was it for? His only visitor was Mathilde, the woman from the town who cleaned and laundered. He walked across the room and back, feeling expectant. Marianna would have arrived on the 11.30 train. She would come up as far as she could by taxi, and then walk the five-minute stretch of footpath to the steps, which meant – he glanced at his watch – she would be here any minute.

He tugged the cuffs of his shirt from beneath his jacket sleeves, unfastened and tightened his belt. He had left the front door unlocked.

Was this madness, the decision to let another artist – a video artist, as she called herself – into his home? He knew barely anything about her. But he had liked her at the opening in London. Her abruptness, her lack of respect, had appealed. And there was something else. He wanted the house, the view, his motion through the room, to be the makings of a story. He wanted to be captured on film.

He stood beside the window. The quiet of this place needed relieving. Its beauty and brightness, which seemed to build up each day like electric charge, demanded a release. He turned side on, so that he could see through the antechamber (a tunnel through the mountaintop) to the front door.

'*Montreux* comes from *monasteriolum*,' he said into the empty room. 'A place to be alone.' He slid a hand into his jacket pocket. '*Monasteriolum.*'

He sang out the word again, louder this time, like an incantation.

The front door swung inwards to admit a bar of light and the view of a young woman. She had a large rucksack on her back. Either side of her, on the walls of the antechamber, his metallic paintings – three on either wall – came alight. She took a few steps inside and the door swung closed behind her.

'Hey,' she said, sounding out of breath.

Her face was flushed from the climb and her dark hair was a mess. She was holding a Canon video camera in both hands. He noticed that her clothes were casual, almost scruffy. He wondered if she'd heard him speaking in Latin. He kept his hand in his pocket and maintained his stance.

'They didn't tell me about all the steps, your people.' She came towards him with a reserved smile.

'My people?'

'Sylvia Rosso. Galerie Claude Berlins.'

'They haven't been here, any of them. You're my first visitor in a long time.'

She deposited her bag on the floor, keeping hold of the camera.

'I was a bit surprised to be honest,' she said, her words rushing out. 'I didn't think you'd agree to this.'

He wandered past her, towards the coffee table, contemplating the casket. 'I have time on my hands. I'm between exhibitions. And' – he turned to her – 'I like the way you *observe* in your work. You pick up on the power of random things. Sheets on a bed. Light behind curtains. Things that could have been incidental.'

She raised her eyebrows. 'You've seen my work?'

'There was something online.'

She was holding the camera level with her chest. It was like a small TV camera, with a viewfinder and a screen that flipped out from one side. On top was a looping handle with a microphone clamped to it.

'Is that on?'

She twisted the screen around so that it faced outward. A red light flashed. He saw himself being recorded – his sharp-cut jacket and new jeans. There were grey glints in his hair.

'And do you need me to wear a mic?'

'The mic on the camera picks everything up. Act like we're having a chat. Like the camera isn't here.'

'My pulse has never been so low.' He simulated an easy laugh, still watching himself on the screen. 'You know, I always wanted to make a film. When I was a student at the Kunstakademie Düsseldorf, I made a Super 8 recording of a spray can discharging onto a canvas. *Three hundred and eighty-four seconds*, it was called.'

'Yes, I know. Everyone knows that. Your seminal piece.'

'*Seminal?*' He teased out the word to make it absurd. 'No, it was a mistake. I was trying to make a painting that would carry no trace of me. But it was impossible. The spray can was clamped to a vice, the camera was on a tripod, but you could still tell I was there – watching, controlling . . .' He withdrew his eyes from the screen. 'I want this film to be real. Thomas Haller stripped bare. Don't you agree?'

'I want it to be whatever it turns out to be.'

Her confidence was increasing, and too fast for his liking.

She took a few steps across the room. 'Why did you come here – to Montreux?'

He stayed still and tried to picture what she was seeing: the town rising into view on the near shore of Lake Geneva. The preposterous magnitude of the mountains. Soon the snow would fall, but for now everything was green and grey in the sunlight.

'I was born here. This is where I come from, where I've come back to.'

'You're from Montreux? You don't sound very Swiss. Very French, I mean.'

'We spoke German in my family. And I left when I was eighteen. I went to Saint Martins in London for two years—'

'I was at Goldsmiths,' she said eagerly.

'And then I transferred to Düsseldorf. You could be a perpetual student back then. In 1998, I moved to New York, and, well, that's when my life as an artist began. *Ma vraie vie*.' He spoke the words in a thick French accent. 'How's that for Montreusian?'

She didn't laugh – didn't react.

'Someone taught me to speak English a long time ago,' he said, sensing that he needed to retain control of whatever this was, this meeting, this cross-examination. He had allowed her in, but he couldn't cede the power. 'This man had had a classical education. You see, I'm a peasant underneath it all.'

'Who was he?'

'No one you've ever heard of.'

He nodded at the miniature version of himself in the flipped-out screen. Had it been a mistake to wear a violet tie? No, it was just the right colour. Identical to his paintings in London. He wondered what she made of him. Was it fascination that had brought her here, a love of his work? Or some more sceptical instinct?

His eyes returned to the concrete block on the coffee table.

'Is that by Carl Andre?' she asked.

'It's a casket. The ashes of my dog. Shall we go outside?'

*

He stood behind her and elbowed a button on the wall. Between the piano and the desk, a slice of clear air appeared, widening as two segments of glass glided apart. Marianna hovered in the doorway to the terrace.

He tried to see what she was looking at – the town or the lake.

'My father used to take me fishing down there on Lac Léman.'

She turned and pointed the camera back at him. The red light flashed.

'What was that like? What do you remember?'

'Hours of waiting. Silence. He wasn't much good with words, my father. I've inherited that.'

She was smiling, or subduing a smile, in a way he couldn't interpret.

He walked out past her. It was a cold day, but warm where the sunlight fell. The terrace, which wasn't much wider than the path, ran along the length of the house. The parapet barely came to their waists. Beyond the drop was a belt of conifers, their tops almost level with the terrace. He had wanted the house to be invisible from the road below.

Just before descending the steps at the end of the terrace, he glanced sideways. The glass threw back a picture of the mountains and sky, and – close up – his and Marianna's reflections. They were like characters in a frieze. Her camera a sacrificial offering. He would have to deal with those ashes, soon. Today? On camera? His life had turned, in the last few minutes, into a story that he was free to make up. Except that he didn't feel free. He was attending to every motion he made, watching himself. He couldn't get the measure of this Marianna Berger. Perhaps she felt the same about him.

At the bottom of the steps was a paved area with a swimming pool. The sun had carved a slice of dazzling turquoise at one end.

'I've always dreamed of having a pool,' she said, bringing the viewfinder to her eye.

He squinted at the camera's screen. She was zooming in on the surface of the water.

Luca had been the last visitor here, that day when he jumped in. Thomas watched the corpuscles on the water's surface, transmitted through the digital display, then looked at the pool itself. There were leaves on the bottom: it needed vacuuming. He thought again of the ashes.

'Bette Davis swam in that pool,' he said.

'Seriously?'

He turned to her, glimpsing his own face – framed by dark foliage – in the display. Was it ironic or sincere, his expression?

'She was very old by then.'

He beckoned her along a path through the forest, feeling slightly delirious with either glee or dread. An ancient movie star dropping her cigarette ash in the pool – he smiled up at the sky as he went, through the spruces that were as tall as telegraph poles. A bird flapped in a treetop. They came to a clearing. The brighter light made him wince. They were at one end of a narrow shelf of land, carpeted in grass, where the gradient of the mountain levelled out. Blackish conifers cut off the breeze and screened the view.

'This is where I used to come as a child.'

'To play?'

'Not really. I was always alone. To daydream, I suppose.'

He led her towards a conical mound of earth. A hole had been dug that morning. A square cavity with precise corners. He peered in, unable to see to the bottom. Marianna stood beside him, maintaining a curious silence. *Let her be the first to speak*, he thought. Peering closer, he saw a piece of glass inside the hole, wedged into the earth. It was domed, like a tiny umbrella. He wanted to crouch down and retrieve it, but didn't.

She walked away a short distance, guiding her camera in a sweep. 'This would be a good place for an outdoor theatre. It's so quiet. You could build seats in the slope – hold performances during the summer—'

'You could.' He gave the hole a final backward glance. 'But I never have guests. No one ever comes, except the housekeeper.'

She let her camera swing to her side and grinned. 'There *was* a feature in *Architectural Digest*.'

'You've done your research. But that was all about the house. *This*' – he signalled at her to raise the camera – 'is a portrait of the artist, no?'

She held the camera steady, watching him. He walked towards her. His face grew clearer on the screen. He was seeing what the camera saw, in real time: himself and his image synchronised. The garden was a green haze behind him, the sky a thin blue strip at the top. The encroachments of mortality were there around his eyes, in those hairline rivulets – he couldn't hide them in the sunlight. But the eyes themselves were just the same. People had always been mesmerised by them. Luca had told him he had the blue eyes of a huskie.

'Thomas,' Marianna said. 'Are you okay?'

'*Cut!*' He stepped back and relaxed into a smile.

From above the flashing LED of the camera, she returned a blank look.

*

Neither of them spoke until they were crossing back over the threshold to the house.

'I watched your video,' Thomas began. 'The one where you're in bed.' He circled the piano and touched his palms on its dark red surface.

'Oh God. The one where I read the poem?'

'It's extraordinary.'

She lingered in the doorway, untangling her hair with one hand. 'I'm glad you think so. No one else does. No one wants to show it. When you don't have a gallery—' She seemed to stop herself, as if wary of launching into an old complaint. 'I guess I burned my bridges when I left the States.'

'What were you doing there?'

'I was with a guy—'

'The man in your film?'

'Yes. Carter Daily. Maybe you've heard of him? He teaches at Rhode Island School of Design. Writes essays in *Artforum*. I left him back in the summer.'

Thomas recognised the name. Hadn't Carter Daily reviewed an exhibition of his, once? A cautiously positive response, as he remembered.

'You weren't happy, in that film.'

'No.' She hadn't moved from the doorway.

'Maybe that's what made it so good. When I watched it, I had the feeling that I was looking in a mirror. That I'd become you, in some way.'

She nodded hesitantly. 'Thanks . . . I don't really know what I intended.'

'I try not to talk about my work, even to myself. Art should speak for itself. The art I make is separate from me. It doesn't think or calculate. Are you still recording?'

She glanced down at the camera and nodded.

He thought of his early video. The spray can clamped inside a vice, spreading its purple mist over the blank of a canvas. It had been the final piece he made before leaving the Kunstakademie. Claude had said it was a work of genius, a melding of conceptual art and Colour Field abstraction. But it had felt like an ending to Thomas. A moment of closure. He had gone looking for new subjects after that.

'What are you working on right now?' she said.

'I'll show you.'

Beyond the bookshelves was a white door. Thomas led her up a flight of plywood stairs to the studio. The space was like a hangar, close to ten metres across and almost as high. The ceiling was glass and traversed by louvres, tilting slats of white-coated aluminium that sliced the blue into stripes. There was a smell of turpentine in the warm air.

'Where is everyone? Your assistants, I mean.'

'There are no assistants. I've always worked alone.'

He wondered whether to tell her that he hadn't come in here for weeks. Since his return from London, the studio had seemed like a sanctuary from which he'd been expelled. He watched as she trained her camera over the room, homing in on the flecks of paint that ran in a hazy band around the edges of the concrete floor, on the primed canvases that he had left stacked in one corner, on the marks that appeared at intervals on the plasterboard walls – purple coronas around white oblongs where the canvases had hung. There were no paintings anywhere, just three large easels angled randomly across the floor and a wheelable trolley where tubes of paint had been lined up in tonal sequences.

'So, you see,' he said, hearing his voice echo, 'to answer your question, I'm working on nothing. I'm in a waiting state.'

She continued to scan the walls with her camera. This room was like a greenhouse, Thomas thought. Heat pooled in here when he didn't close the louvres. He flicked a switch on the wall and the air conditioning whirred into life. At once he felt a spreading chill.

'This is an outbuilding, really,' he went on. 'I linked it to the house, but it was here for years – decades – before the house was. Maybe you saw it as you came up the steps outside?'

'The giant concrete box, yes.' She ran her eyes around the ceiling. 'I thought it was a substation of some kind.'

'An engine room, actually. There used to be an aerial tramway – a cable car, I guess you'd call it – running from here to Montreux. The Rochers de Naye route.' He gave the trolley a nudge with his foot and watched it roll across the floor. 'This room contained the machinery. Motors, generator, gearbox, a bulkhead for the haul cable.' He sighed before he could stop himself. Remembering felt like such an effort. 'There was only one gondola. It could hold twenty people, but it never held more than three. My father used to drive it up and down, for any or no reason. It was redundant long before it was decommissioned. The mountain's easy to climb, and there's a road almost to the same point. No one needed a cable car.'

She watched him, seeming to expect more. He tried to see inside her head. Were there visions of a cable car gliding up and down the mountain, in and out of the fourth wall of the studio, skimming the jagged edge of the Alps as it went? Or something closer to the wilderness he remembered? For a moment, the emptiness of the room was deathly, like a void he could never conceal, not even if he told her the most extraordinary, exhilarating, redeeming story. He had been a fool to suppose he could orchestrate this thing. What were these moments supposed to add up to, anyway? And how long did she need to form a portrait of him – a day, two weeks, six months? A mild sense of panic came and went.

*

They were back at the antechamber, close to the front door. Six paintings hung around them in symmetrical rows of three, like mirror images on either side of the hallway, their surfaces a shade of dirt-infested gold. One of them wasn't really a painting but a door made of sheet metal, its surface indistinguishable from the others. Thomas opened it to reveal the quilted leather of the rear side. He waved her through. They descended the stairs, between walls of bored rock, down to a soft-lit corridor.

'You dug this entire level out of rock,' she said.

'Kind of. The mountaintop breaks at this point into a crevasse filled with earth. I dug the cavity out – squared off the rock around the edges.'

It troubled him that she didn't say much. The house was a work of art. The garden, too. Perhaps she found it all too much. Too opulent. Artists were the worst, he thought, when it came to envy of other artists. And envy had a way of transfiguring into disapproval, a kind of political antipathy.

The carpet underfoot was dark and deep. The ceiling and outer wall of the corridor had been hewn to a glassy lustre. The inner wall was faced in stained teak. The doors occurred at measured intervals, each one a constructivist marquetry of bronze and steel segments. He remembered the drawings for those doors, the endless revisions. There was so much, as a visitor to this place, that you could never know. To her, it was nothing but veneers. A sensory experience rather than the product of time and love and patience. And *money*: the expense had almost ruined him. It was like looking at a person, he guessed, with no comprehension of the long progression of their life.

He drew alongside her and tapped the nearest door. By a touch-sensitive mechanism, it swung inward. Lights flicked on to reveal a pinewood cell with benches around the walls – two stepped tiers. Heaters clicked into life.

'The sauna.'

When he touched the next door along, it opened with a puckering sound to reveal a space of similar dimensions, clad in amber-like stone.

'The steam room.'

Next was his bedroom. Through the half-light, above his king-sized bed, the Kirchner tapestry of Adam and Eve glowed darkly, like a stained-glass window at night.

'No daylight,' she murmured.

'You sleep better. It's like being back in the womb.' He let the door close and moved on. 'Here's the guest room.'

This room was much the same as his own, except that he'd hung a set of framed drawings over the wall. Naked men and sphinxes by Cocteau. From the doorway, he contemplated their prancing bodies and devilish smiles. A guest room, and never a guest: Luca hadn't stayed the night. With dull wonder, he reflected on the fact that he had never allowed Claude here. He had created the place, even, as a retreat from the world that Claude represented. And yet the gorgeous surfaces – every varnished panel and stretch of carpet, those six paintings of oxidised gold – were a demonstration to Claude. A way of saying: *look what I've become*. It was why he had allowed the feature in *Architectural Digest*, so that Claude would know.

The corridor turned ninety degrees. On the next section there was only one door. Beyond it was a compact cinema – three rows of seats on a raked floor. The air was cool and had an atomised, purplish complexion. The screen hovered as a dim blank. The ceiling and walls were lacquered rockface.

'What do you watch in here?'

'Old stuff. The things I watched as a boy. Billy Wilder. Erich von Stroheim.' He ran one palm across the wall.

She rested her camera on the back of a chair and regarded the cinema screen.

'Who designed all this?'

'Aldo Viertel. A Swiss architect. A *genius*. Oh, I know we don't use that word any more, but he really is. He refuses most commissions. No skyscrapers in Abu Dhabi, just the occasional masterpiece in the Alps. There's a power in refusal, don't you think?'

'I wouldn't know,' she said with what he perceived to be a touch of bitterness. 'You have to be asked, before you can refuse.'

They returned to the corridor. She must have realised by now that it was a loop, leading back to the staircase. Walking in front, he ran his fingertips over the surface of the final door before the stairs, then went on.

'What's in here?'

He turned. She was holding her camera to her face with one eye shut, filming the closed door.

'All right,' he said, and tapped the door open.

He entered behind her, registering her curiosity – it was like a change in frequency – as she walked between the packed contents of the small room. He tried to induce some new perspective in himself, so that he might see everything as she was seeing it, as if for the very first time, like a visitor to his own memories. Music was playing quietly, a breathy saxophone. The space was modest and crammed with furniture, pictures and books. A heavily carved bureau stood in the corner; a stack of leather-bound albums concealed the Sonos speaker from which the music was coming. The walls and ceiling were faced in pine. There was a painting of the Matterhorn, a giant pair of antlers writhing out of an oak plaque, a shaded lamp with tassels . . . At the centre was a Biedermeier table. Like the bureau, it was piled with files and albums.

'I call this the memory room.'

'It feels like another house.'

Thomas walked around the table and looked back at her. She had put the camera down and was gazing at the pair of windows to either side of him – small openings in the pine walls, each framed by red curtains and pelmets. Their panes were filled with pasted photographs – a collage of old snapshots, blocking out the daylight, except – of course – the room was underground, so the windows couldn't be real: had she realised yet?

'It *is* another house. This is my childhood home, Marianna – one room of it. It stood at the edge of the crevasse I mentioned, just below the top of the mountain. We're encased behind the retaining wall. The terrace is directly above our heads.'

'What happened to the rest of it?'

'I demolished it. Everything apart from the cable-car station, but that was always separate – up on the peak.'

Marianna walked up to one of the collages and leaned close, seeming to fix on two adjacent pictures: a handsome man in a khaki suit, captured in an Alpine ravine, and a woman sinking with resignation into a patterned armchair. The colours had faded and coalesced into orange-pink.

'They're both dead,' he said. 'Fourteen years ago, my father. Eleven, my mother. They'd ended up in the same place – a dementia home down in Montreux.'

'I'm sorry.'

'They were old enough. Now that we're all meant to live on and on, going senile is to be expected. I wasn't there, anyway. They hadn't seen me in a long time – wouldn't have remembered me.'

'You can't know that for sure. I mean, a part of the person is always still there.'

'I doubt it. They couldn't speak by the end, either of them. It was like the memory loss was contagious. Makes me wonder how long I've got.' He took one of the curtains between his finger and thumb, tracing the nap of the fabric. 'My mother worked as a seamstress while I was growing up, and an upholsterer. This was the room where she sewed. I used to sit on the floor, right where you're standing, and collect the scraps of fabric. They were like ancient papyri to me. I tried to keep little pieces, but she didn't like me having them.' He smiled and flicked the curtain away. 'The things you remember.'

Marianna had taken up her camera and was holding it close to a photo in the other window. He came near and saw that it was a picture of him as a young man, standing in a stony stream and wearing nothing apart from leather shorts. The grey material crinkled and glinted like sealskin around his thighs. His body was slim and tanned, his hair practically blond. Water purled around his feet, broken into crystal shelves and frothing torrents. His eyes met the camera with unreadable calm.

She kept the camera close to the photo, as if all her concentration had been channelled into capturing the image.

'What's that in your hand?' she said.

'A baby deer, I think. We'd been out hunting, my father and I. That picture was taken in the summer of '95, just before I went to London, when everything was pure potential. The loss of potential is the hardest thing about getting older, don't you think?'

'I guess. Or the realisation that the potential was never really there.' She stepped back to catch him in the frame.

'Oh, it was there,' he said. 'The excitement of knowing that all these people were going to come into my life. The desire to *feel* everything as strongly as possible. It's why I like young people. They still have that.'

He looked into her brown eyes and felt sure that she understood: she was still young herself, closer in age to Luca than to him. To his surprise, she reached out and touched his arm. The contact was only momentary. Then she glanced down at her watch.

'Where are you staying?'

'I booked a hotel for the night. I'm heading back to London tomorrow night.'

'The Montreux Palace?'

'No.'

'Then stay here. Don't leave.'

She eyed him with interest. 'If you're sure – for one night.'

'The room's already made up.'

17

Thomas knew, when he woke, that he hadn't been asleep for long. Maybe an hour – it was hard to tell. After leaving Marianna on the terrace, he'd taken a Nembutal with an inch of Lagavulin. But a rogue impulse deep in his brain had pulled him back from the brink of deep sleep.

He listened to the silence where Betty's snoring should have been. The image on the screen of Marianna Berger's camera was occupying his thoughts. What had possessed him to ask her to stay? A sudden wish not to be alone, or maybe that fleeting contact of her hand on his arm? It appalled him, the idea that he could be moved so easily. The knowledge of her presence in the house – possibly where he'd left her on the terrace, picking at a platter of seafood – made him feel odd. Expectant and tense. Every room of the house was sound-proofed, but he wondered if he could detect the faintest vibrations as she moved around up there.

He wanted this film to be tragic, searching, sublime – all the things that critics admired. And he wanted it to be true. But he was becoming horribly conscious of the way he sounded, and the way he motioned with his hands as he talked. What had happened to him? What had he become?

His fingers met the edge of his iPhone. He tapped the screen, producing a lozenge of light. Against his will, he searched for his name on X, reading back through months of posts. Someone had screenshotted the portrait of him that had appeared in

Architectural Digest in the spring of last year. It showed him on a cowskin chaise longue, sitting up as if roused from a nap, elegantly dishevelled in a blue cotton jacket.

The poster – anonymous, of course – had added a tagline.

The painter as tax exile.

Thomas dropped the phone away from him on the bed. This was why he needed Marianna, and the film. To correct the record. To explain how his move to Switzerland had been a turn inward, into the depths of himself. How he was a man with hidden depths. How it had fuck all to do with tax.

He ran his fingers under the rim of the sheet and skimmed the bristling line at the top of his underpants. His eyes were adjusting. The bored rock of the ceiling was like the sea on a moonless night. A vitreous skin, pinched into ridges and sagging troughs.

A spasm of lust passed through him. He moved his hand to his penis and tried to coax it into life. After a few seconds he gave up. He took up his phone again and swiped back through months of WhatsApp messages. Luca had always emailed him about work things, but after their night at the Savoy, a separate stream of communications began.

Thinking about you.

When are you coming back to London?

Have to see you, T.

Been thinking about our night at the hotel. Haven't you?

To these, Thomas had responded with single kisses or noncommittal likes. And then, one night in May, a string of messages had arrived over a two-hour period:

I have to see you. Come back. I want you.

I want you to fck

Fuck me.

Srry, was drunk.

But I meant it.

In the early summer, Thomas had gone back to London. The gallery in Mayfair was nearly built. The plan was for him to view the building and map out the exhibition. Luca met him at London City airport.

Thomas's first thought was that Luca looked thinner. His hair was longer, its waviness developing into curls. They walked from the airport to the Thames Barrier, then followed the river to the Woolwich ferry. It was a still, clear day. Luca seemed to have a route in mind, and it seemed to have nothing to do with visiting the gallery. The ferry spun them across to the south side of the river – a windy, bumpy interval – and from there they walked through quiet streets until they came to a park.

'I've been thinking about this show of yours,' Luca said, leading Thomas through the park gate. 'What you said about violet – it being the colour of twilight. The colour of endings.'

'Did I say that?'

'Something like that. But the thing is, it's also the colour of first light. Morning skies. And this show, too – it's your comeback. Not an ending, Thomas.'

'I hate that word. *Comeback.*'

'But it's true. People have forgotten how good you are. Even the people at the gallery – Claude, Sylvia – they don't appreciate you. They intellectualise your work, which is fine, the paintings *are* clever—'

'Far cleverer than me.'

'Clever to the point that people stop seeing what's underneath. It's the feeling that matters. Your longing . . . When I first saw your art— I was a teenager. I wanted to cry, and run away, and fall in love – all these things. How many artists can do that to you?'

They wandered over sunlit grass, coming to a circular enclosure that Thomas felt he knew, although he'd never been to the park before. Then it came to him. It was the same park – the scenery was practically identical – as in Antonioni's *Blow-Up*.

Positioning himself this way and that on the grass, he told Luca about the film.

'They have a weird vibe, so many of those old films,' Luca said, as they trod towards tennis courts. 'Everyone spying on everyone. All the death-stares and screaming.' He rolled his eyes dramatically. 'The heavy colours, too.'

'Antonioni spray-painted the grass in this park green for the film. Real grass wouldn't give him the effect he wanted.'

'Imagine that. Painting grass a greener shade.' Luca scanned the ground, then looked up at Thomas with a wide smile. 'Yuck.'

Not far away, a man was slumped on a bench, his shirt open to reveal an emaciated body. He looked old, but wasn't. There were scars on his forearms.

It was turning hot – hotter than it should have been for early June. Thomas's sleeves were rolled up. He could feel the sun's rays. They walked on a slow circuit of the park, beneath spreading oaks. Luca chattered about various things – a nightclub he'd been going to in Shoreditch, the rent hikes in London, a new drama on Netflix. Thomas listened intermittently, drifting more often into thought. He sensed, more than ever, an electricity in the boy's looks and intonation. A trapped energy.

Luca sat down on the grass, beckoning to Thomas to do the same. He flipped off his T-shirt and stretched out his legs. He was wearing a stringlike gold chain around his neck. It seemed to stick to his skin. Thomas wanted to look at Luca's body – his shoulders and chest and stomach, in all their smoothness. But he was aware of the people around them, and restrained his gaze.

A young man passed by. Multiple leads fanned out around him, connecting to dogs of various shapes – a Chihuahua that sprang like a toy on a string, a smiling retriever, a button-eyed terrier . . . They trotted along in tandem, or scurried to keep up. The man himself moved with a light, almost prancing gait.

He had an abstracted air, as if he existed apart from the duller life around him.

Luca and Thomas exchanged a glance.

'Do you have other friends?' Luca asked. He smiled with an openness that blanked out the slyness in the question. 'Friends like me? Like *this*?' He took hold of Thomas's hand.

Thomas felt the same muddling of his senses as he'd felt the last time. A creeping intoxication that he couldn't fight. He looked away. An Alsatian was mounting one of the smaller dogs. He detached his hand from Luca's.

'What time are we going to go and look at the gallery?'

'Fuck the gallery. You know what it'll look like. A gorgeous empty white space. Do you really think I wanted you to come to London for that?' Luca looked away into the distance and drew a finger over his bare chest, as though he were painting a line from his collarbone to his nipple.

Thomas experienced a stirring of lust, and in the same moment a deeper dwindling. All this time, he had been matching Luca's energy, or trying to. He had been fascinated by Luca – caught up in his infatuation, mirroring it back, enjoying the game. Now the feeling was starting to wane, just as Luca's longing (his own word) was intensifying.

*

Thomas got out of bed and walked into the bathroom. In the mirror, he saw a squinting old man. His hair was standing on end to reveal all its greyness. His neck was sinewy.

The lights in the corridor glowed awake. He went into the cinema and sank into his usual chair. This room was the fulfilment of a dream. Aged eight, he had begun to watch the films that his mother let play on the TV while she worked on upholstery jobs. Passing distractions for her, the films had become – for him – objects of wonderment. Before he could comprehend the plots, he adored the colours of the mid-century Technicolor pictures and the steely monochrome of the classics. At the age of eleven, he'd been transfixed by Marlene Dietrich in *Morocco* – bending down, in her top hat and tuxedo, to kiss another woman.

He selected a film. Orchestral music swelled out, yielding to dreamy piano. Familiar title credits appeared, and an opening scene that he knew frame by frame. A heavenly American town viewed from an aerial remove; autumn leaves and a sky like cobalt; a woman pushing a pram on the sidewalk. A 1950s estate car drove into view. It was the same colour as the sky, a low-slung stratum of blue with fins above the rubies of the tail lights. He noted the gorgeous asymmetry of the wheels: a full orb at the front, a semicircle at the rear where the tyre was canopied by bodywork.

And then, Agnes Moorhead stepping out of the car. She walked with a brisk and purposeful stride, like his mother. She wore a dress of bolder blue and a neck scarf of pink and green. Her red hair was in a timeless chignon.

When he was thirteen, he had read in a magazine about the camera that Andy Warhol used to film his daily life. For weeks, he had fantasised about having his own portable Philips Norelco, something with which to transform reality into a movie. He had stood in front of the mirror, practising lines or merely ways of looking and looking away. He made himself cry as he stared at the lens (really an upturned glass), refusing to blink until a tear streamed down his face. He pleaded with his mother to be given the videotape recorder for his birthday. She told him to save up, knowing that he would never be able to.

He heard a sound behind him. The door. Marianna had crept in. Without looking away from the screen, he perceived her as she came level with the second row and then sank into the seat beside him. He turned in momentary acknowledgement – lifted his fingers from the armrest – then looked back at the screen.

Jane Wyman was seated at a table in her garden, dressed in

grey wool. Just an ordinary day, and she was turned out in pearl-drop earrings and cadmium lipstick.

'Perhaps you'd like to share my lunch with me,' she said to Rock Hudson, the gardener – ruggedly handsome in his spotless overalls.

'Just a roll and some coffee will do.' His voice was deep and assured.

'Do you come in here every night?' Marianna asked, as Jane Wyman poured.

He waited for a gap in the dialogue. 'Most nights, yes. For a few hours, when I can't sleep.'

'What are you watching?'

'*All That Heaven Allows.*'

'Douglas Sirk,' she said, with a certain pride – he suspected – at having made the identification. 'Fifties melodrama.'

'His films get called that, yes.'

People thought that it was enough to know a name or to have a reference. But it was better to know nothing. That way, you saw and felt without prejudice. Knowledge was a bore, he thought, and a burden.

'Everything looks so wonderful,' said Jane Wyman, surveying the garden.

A pained sadness came over him. 'It's a work of genius,' he said. 'All of Sirk's films are. Look at those colours. Technicolor was the most beautiful invention, and now it's lost to the world. They can't recreate the technology, the chemicals, however much they try. Those colours are irrecoverable.'

*

00.31. New York

Lorna was dreaming that her son was falling. The boy, already a young man, was tumbling from a great height, miraculously slowly. She had a close perspective, as if she were watching from the window of a nearby building.

At first, the boy's head was the right way up. His feet were pointing downward in a pencil dive. His eyes were closed. But in an instant, he had flipped upside down. The frame rate shifted. His feet were now apart, kicking frantically. He was naked. His body was long and pale as marble. His eyes had opened and were wide with terror. Mouth and eyes were in the wrong order, and his lips had stretched apart to release a howling cry.

The sound of her own cry woke her. Lying in the dark, she waited for the residues of the dream to fade.

*

06.14. Montreux

Before dawn, Thomas went upstairs and took the casket from the coffee table.

He waited as the doors to the terrace glided apart. Marianna's camera was where she'd left it, stationed on a tripod by the window, pointing into the night.

Montreux was a spillage of light at the edge of the lake. On the lower portion of the mountains, dispersed pinpricks formed a blinking constellation. Higher up, the peaks ran in a jagged line, like ripped velvet, across the murk of the sky.

He felt empty – purged of feeling. It was as if the magnitude of the landscape had usurped his interior. The horror and madness of what had happened in London – the smashed fragments of vision and sound, the sickening panic – had receded, like pebbles sinking into a mire, becoming separate from him.

He walked into the cold night. The cold didn't bother him; it never had. Carefully he descended the steps, guided by the gleam of the security lamp, and walked past the pool, bearing the casket in both hands. The woods were dark, but he knew the route.

When he came to the clearing, he waited, observing the hole in the ground. Then he sank to his knees. Bending over the hole, he held the casket level. The palms of his hands were flat on either side of the cube. He parted his hands and the cube dropped. There was a fluttering in the trees. He kept still. The moon was above and behind him, almost directly overhead, and his body was casting a stunted shape on the turf. His arms had become the horns of a bull.

*

After Maryon Park, they had gone to Comptons bar. The place was dark and swarming.

'Everyone knows you here,' Thomas said, as they walked in. He had noticed how men looked at Luca – with a flicker of bored interest.

'No one knows who I am,' Luca said, pressing through the crowd. 'You've forgotten what it's like to be ordinary.'

Thomas bought two lagers and they leaned against the bar.

'Are you two regulars, then?' asked a man with a shaved head and an Adidas jacket.

'I used to be,' Thomas said. 'Before he was born.'

'We're regulars everywhere,' said Luca. 'We're whoring around.'

Thomas allowed his focus to drift, intrigued by Luca's ability to tease him. Perhaps, he thought, there were men here tonight who'd been here in 1997. The ones who never left. The music didn't seem to have changed. Looking back at Luca's face, he was perplexed by the resemblance to Lorna as she had been in their London days. It wasn't just a facial resemblance. It was Luca's acrobatic humour. The way that nothing escaped him.

As they started their third pints, Luca began to talk about Claude. There was a cult of personality at the gallery, he said. People either feared Claude or idolised him.

'It's shitty, being at the mercy of a man like that. It's hard to keep hold of a sense of yourself. You start to think that only the things *he* believes in matter.'

'Resist him,' Thomas said, watching two men on the other side of the bar – one older, one very young. They began to kiss and he felt a squirm of prurient delight. He didn't want to think about Claude tonight.

At some point, as if it were the most natural thing in the world, Luca suggested they go back to his flat.

'Where do you live?' Thomas asked above the noise. ('Better the Devil You Know' by Kylie Minogue was starting to play.)

'Kennington. Just south of the river.'

*

Luca's flat was a large studio at the top of a Victorian water tower. They travelled up in an elevator. The place made Thomas think of the loft he'd lived in when he first went to New York – sparsely furnished, walls of bare brickwork. Double doors opened onto a balcony with steel railings.

Luca sat at the centre of the bed, legs crossed, and arranged lines of coke on the cover of *A World History of Art*, across the face of the mad horse of *Guernica*.

From the corner of the balcony, Thomas could see structures along the Thames: the London Eye, Big Ben, the brutalist shell of the National Theatre. Luca walked out and stood beside him, then levered himself up and spun around to sit on the rail.

'Be careful,' Thomas said.

'I was a gymnast at school. I could walk along this railing and I'd be fine. Why don't I show you?' Luca pushed his body off the rail by a few inches, balancing on both hands.

'For God's sake, get down.'

'I'll be like Philippe Petit between the Twin Towers.'

Thomas pulled Luca towards him.

'It's still early,' Luca said, sliding down into Thomas's arms. 'Let's go and get fucked up. Let's go to Vauxhall. Rude Boyz or Fitladz or Horsemeat.'

'You're making those names up.'

'I never make anything up.' He stretched his arms towards the sky. 'I don't care where. I just have to be out there tonight, free, with you. Let's go to Vauxhall.'

*

09.47

Thomas sat across the dining table from Marianna. He had been up for hours – walking in the garden, rearranging things in the studio. She had only recently appeared from downstairs, wearing a T-shirt with the Pepsi logo printed on it and a pair of sweatpants. She had a dishevelled look about her.

His houseguest. He mulled over the word in his mind as he took a mouthful of coffee and pretended to read the news on his iPad.

Marianna was running her hand over the table's interconnecting planks of timber.

'Are you going to tell me that this table's made out of bits of your old house?' she asked with a smile.

'It's a work of art. A piece by Ugo Rondinone. It's meant to look like something out of a fairy tale.'

She had a day to make the film, he thought. A day in which to capture him. All that morning, he'd had a suspicion that she had followed him outside at dawn, filming him from a distance, holding back so that he couldn't hear. At the time, as he carried the casket to the gravesite, he hadn't been aware of anything.

He had been so absorbed by his own actions that nothing else had seemed to exist.

'What was it—' he began.

She stopped stroking the wood.

'What made you ask me, in London, to do this film?'

She considered before answering. 'I have all kinds of ideas. Usually, they never go anywhere. I never thought you would say yes.'

'But why me?'

She studied the table again, lining up her coffee cup with the cafetiere and the steel milk jug. 'I suppose it was seeing your picture in *Architectural Digest*. And the photos of this place. It all seemed unreal. I had this idea of you as a sort of exile, out here in the Alps. Exiled from the art world.'

He thought of the post he'd read last night on X. Had Marianna been trolling him from an anonymous account? Was it a psychological exercise of some kind, preparation for the film? Or a way of giving vent to her resentments? He wanted to dismiss the idea. He knew it was ridiculous, and yet . . .

'I never liked that term,' he said. '*Art world*. It's marketing speak. There are many art worlds. As many as there are artists. You can make your own art world, if you want.'

'*You* can, maybe. Everything's easier if you have money.' She looked more serious now.

He stood and wandered to the piano. He had put on one of his painting shirts. An old designer shirt, blue with white stripes. The sleeves were rolled up and several buttons were undone. He should go to the studio, he supposed, just for an hour. Try to make something new. Marianna's coming here could be a prompt to action. That was what he needed: a catalyst.

He ran his hand up and down the key lid. 'What you said just now, about this place seeming unreal. Sometimes, you know, I do have the feeling that it's all imaginary. When the lake is full of light. When the sun's hitting the mountains from a low angle. It's like everything's inside my head.'

She came over to where he was standing, picking up her camera from one of the couches. 'Right. Like an image. When I was sitting out there on the terrace last night, I felt like throwing something into the view, just to prove that it was real.'

He lifted the lid and felt the white keys without playing them – their smooth imitation ivory, their regular cracks. The hairs on his forearm were dark. They gave contouring to his wrist. A burnished look, interrupted by the hexagonal bezel of his Royal Oak watch.

She was standing at the opposite end of the piano, in the way of the view. She had placed her camera on the maroon surface.

'What are you doing?'

'Recording you.'

'But I'm not doing anything.'

'Haven't you seen Warhol's *Screen Tests*? The camera watches you as you watch it.'

The red light was flashing. She placed her hands on her hips and took a step back.

She wants to know things, he thought. *Wants to get inside my head.*

'I was sorry never to meet Andy,' he said. 'I came to America ten years too late.'

'Why did you leave New York?' She placed her elbows either side of the camera, leaning over it towards him. 'Why would you leave behind your entire life?'

'I was burned out after my show at the Whitney. Out here in the mountains, I'm at the bright fringe. I'm free.'

'You didn't feel free before?'

'Maybe once. Before—'

'Before you became a massive success?'

He looked straight into the lens. 'Yes. I became a prisoner. It's not like that here, when I'm walking in the hills or painting.'

He studied her for a while without blinking. 'Why did *you* leave New York?'

'It was Providence, not New York. And I told you. I was in a relationship I wanted out of.'

'What was wrong with him?'

'Nothing, really.' She began to laugh, but he thought that he could discern a deeper dismay. 'Carter was clever, popular, charming. He was full of wise advice—'

'And that was the problem.'

'I felt overpowered. I suppose people would say I was jealous. But actually, it was like he was jealous of me. He wanted more and more of me.'

'I've known people like that.'

She turned away to look out of the window. 'I really believed I was in love with him.'

Thomas watched the sunlight on her shoulder.

'I met him randomly,' she went on, 'if these things are ever random. It was at an opening in London. He told me I should apply for this massive scholarship that his school awards. And I won it. He must have had something to do with it, although I somehow didn't figure that at the time. Anyhow, I got out there – to Providence – and soon we were sleeping together, *of course*, and I was staying around at his flat, watching films. He's an expert on Fassbinder.' She turned back with a smirk, as though there were a joke in this. 'We used to watch my videos together. He used to give advice.'

He had got her talking. Something about his eyes – he had always known it – encouraged people to talk. For the span of a second, he thought of Claude, lying on a sun lounger at the Montreux Palace and talking endlessly, about his time at the Sorbonne, about the Humanist revival, about the tragedy of his younger sister who could barely read; and Thomas had lain there – on his front, nearly naked – feeling like an idiot but returning a look of clear-eyed attentiveness.

'This sounds stupid,' Marianna said, 'but Carter made me believe for the first time that I was good at what I do. His approval was—' She stopped, apparently lost for the right word.

'Irresistible.'

'Yes.' She turned back to face him with new animation. 'He kept telling me to give up the lease on my London flat. He wanted me to live in Providence with him. But his guidance, his encouragement, all of that, became a kind of pressure. I looked young enough to be one of his students, and I think that's how Carter saw me. He put me in a show he was curating at White Columns, then paraded me all over the place like I was his accessory.' She laughed again, unhappily. 'Do you know, after I left him, he sent me an email? It was like one of his fucking essays. A sequence of reflections on my immaturity – as an artist, as a woman . . .'

He was conscious of a fluttering of unease. He tried to dismiss the feeling. She had walked out on a man whose eminence she'd feared – or envied. Why should he care?

'Carter Daily,' he murmured. 'I'm sure he reviewed a show of mine once.'

'Forget I mentioned him. I never want to see him again. He's been living in my head like some horrible ghost. And this' – she pointed at the camera with her eyes – 'isn't meant to be about me.' She settled her chin in her hands. 'What about you?'

'What about me?'

'You know – relationships.'

'I've never been much good at those. I've always put art before anyone or anything.'

His gaze drifted beyond her shoulder, back to the mountains. The feeling wouldn't go away. It was spreading all along his intestines. He spaced out his fingers and struck out a staccato chord on the piano. A bright major seventh.

'You can actually play?'

'Why is that a surprise?'

She hadn't answered when he launched into a tune. A succession of major chords followed by a swooping plunge, tripping down the scale into odder, darker keys. She wouldn't need to know that it was the only tune he could play.

'I have to go and work,' he said, sustaining the final chord with the pedal. 'An hour in the studio. That's all. You'll be okay for a while?'

'Sure – I mean, you do know I'm only here for today?'

He closed the piano. The music had only made the feeling stronger. An overflow of adrenaline, something between excitement and dread. The camera, facing him across the piano, continued to flash – silent and inert except for that blinking light.

'Take a look around the house,' he said. 'The rooms, the books – you'll find out everything you need to know.'

*

He climbed the stairs to the studio, two at a time. The room was cold. He'd left the air conditioning on overnight. He went over to the primed canvases that were propped in a vertical stack in one corner.

Luca had wanted him to be someone he couldn't be. 'Stop faking it,' he'd said. 'Stop playing around. Tell me what you're really feeling.'

Taking hold of the first canvas in the pile, Thomas carried it across the room and planted it against the opposite wall. Then he took each canvas in turn, wielding the large stretchers with both hands, and propped them at short intervals around the walls, angling them in places so they caught the sunlight that was streaming through the ceiling. Eight white oblongs reflecting back the day. Hard, bright facets. He felt sweat break on his forehead in spite of the coolness.

It came back to him, the reason why he had fixated, the previous day, on that little piece of rounded glass in the hole outside (buried now with Betty's ashes). As a boy of twelve, he had found a bottle of perfume lying on the promenade in Montreux. It had been in its box, so that he hadn't realised at first what it was. A cylindrical box made of sturdy white card, slightly scuffed, its surface dimpled with a quilted pattern and inscribed in gold: *Le Dix. Balenciaga.* The weight of the box gave it away: he could feel the heavy bottle inside, knocking this way and that. It had been dropped, he suspected, by one of the guests at the Montreux Palace. He slipped it into a pocket before anyone noticed. Only once he was home did he take the box out and unfasten it to release the bottle: a gorgeous, fluted capsule with a domed stopper that he had to pull hard to release. It was already three-quarters empty. He sprayed a single jet on the inside of his wrist, the way he'd seen his mother do at the department store. The smell made him think of the hotel. The bottle itself was like an excised piece of the place (as much of it as he'd glimpsed through the entrance): the lobby lights, the polished panelling. He didn't spray any more, fearful of his parents detecting it – and of wasting the scent.

For a year, he kept the bottle in the deepest recess of the space beneath his bed. He removed it only when he was alone, and allowed himself to release the spray on rare occasions – those moments of heightened hope or sadness that were beginning to afflict him. He would stand the bottle on the window ledge in his room, and watch the sun setting through the prism of the glass, through the amber slab of remaining perfume. Occasionally he would turn the bottle, taking care to wipe away his fingerprints with a cloth, so that the light shot through the glass and spread in ripples across the wall.

He couldn't remember how or when he'd lost it. Only that when the time came to clear out the house in the aftermath of his parents' deaths, he had found the stopper at the back of a cabinet in their bathroom. The glass umbrella was caked in dust.

He thought again of that domed chunk in the hole. How had it ended up there? In the rubble from the house? Maybe, after all, it had been something else. For a while longer, he stood and watched the magic lantern he had made out of blank canvases and light. It was better than anything he could paint today.

*

When he came back down to the main room, it was empty. Marianna had gone outside or downstairs. Slowly, reflectingly, he cleared the breakfast things from the table, pouring the coffee grounds from the cafetiere into the waste disposal unit. He liked the crunch and gurgle of the metal teeth.

This house was a masterpiece, and she appeared barely to have noticed. Not an object out of place, everything atomically precise; empty space itself had a sculptural volume between the planes of concrete and glass. It was a medium for the ever-changing light.

He went downstairs and made a circuit of the corridor. The door to the spare room was open, the bed unmade. He continued, having guessed where he would find her.

The door to the old room of the chalet was off its latch. He heard music as he entered and saw pink light suspended in the scalloped shade of the floor lamp. Marianna was standing so still – turned away from him, leaning against the table – that he didn't register her for a second. Around her, spread over the table and piled on the floor, were stacks of forgotten papers and bundles of photographs: loose prints, stuffed envelopes, rolls of negatives. A cool light was rising from the desk in the corner. He edged into the room and saw that she had plugged in the lightbox. One of his albums of photographic slides was open beside it on the desk. She had emptied the contents of one page (a polythene sheet filled with slides) over the surface of the lightbox. He knew, without needing to come any closer, what the images looked like. Each slide contained a single colour. Shimmering green with a cleft of shadow through the middle. Turquoise interrupted by darker swathes, like regions of deep sea. An expanse of creamy pink. He hadn't looked at those slides in twenty years. The album contained hundreds of similar pictures.

He wondered what she had thought as she pored over the lightbox – if she'd realised that the colours were those of his paintings. But she wasn't looking at the slides any longer. Motionless beside the table, she was holding a pile of Kodak prints in her hand, staring at the top picture.

Coming closer, still undetected by her, he saw what she was looking at. A close-up of red grooves in white flesh. Lacerations, open and bleeding in direct sunlight.

'I should have thrown those away.'

She started. The photographs dropped from her hand and fanned across the carpet. Other prints showed bleeding forearms, a scored thigh, skin that was smeary with blood – and then the subject in full: a boy of twelve or thirteen, stripped to his underpants and crouching on uncut grass. Behind him was a timber chalet with a pitched roof. His limbs and shoulders were pitted and scored with cuts.

'I was just looking through your stuff,' Marianna said in a trembling voice. 'Shooting B-roll.'

Thomas gazed down at the pictures, hardly recognising the child. Teeth marks spread across the boy's knee like pink tyre tracks; he was looking up at the camera with shining eyes. Had it been fear or plain unthinking shock?

Marianna crouched and gathered up the prints. There was a cool, controlled panic about her as she scraped them into a pile, stood back up and handed them to him. At the bottom of the stack were two prints that were differently shaped from the others – at once they slid apart in his hand. They were photo-booth prints. Two strips of square images, all showing a young woman. Her hair had been practically black, back then. He could tell that Marianna was glaring at him, expecting an explanation. But he couldn't stop looking at those small squares, that changing expression. He felt his lips recede around his teeth.

'That was Lorna Bedford,' he said.

'And the others?' There was a hardness in her voice, but it was closer to fear than anger.

'That was a long time ago.' He slid the pile of prints into the back pocket of his jeans.

'Is it you – the boy?'

'Why don't we go upstairs? You should film some more on the terrace. Or I'll take you out on the mountain where the cable car used to run. There's so much you haven't seen yet.'

'I think I should go,' she said. 'There's a train at six. I think I need to leave.'

*

17.02

Thomas sat at his desk and studied the two strips of pictures. The colours seemed fainter in the brighter light upstairs. Lorna aged nineteen. And he'd been there, right behind her, although she was blocking him from view. She stared out from the long-ago night, her eyes meeting his across a twenty-seven-year breach.

Lorna was hurt. But what had he expected? She was hurt because he mattered to her. They still mattered to each other. Her girlfriend was a pig; he could well imagine *her* calling him a fraud and a sellout and those other things he'd read online. But Lorna had a conscience – that, if anything, was her biggest problem.

Sliding the photos to one side of the desk, he took out his phone and sent a message to Otto.

Free tomorrow?

18

9 November, 09.01. New York

Lorna drove along Broadway with the radio turned low. She didn't often drive to work – the Nissan Sentra was really Justine's – but she hadn't slept much after waking in the night. The car was a layer of protection against the day. A newscaster was predicting worse to come for the economy. There had been protests in New York and LA. She watched the road ahead, vaguely expecting an angry mob to invade the lanes. The traffic lights turned red.

She closed her eyes and felt the sun on her eyelids. The inquest for Luca had recorded an open verdict. Suicide hadn't been ruled out. She had gathered from a few of the reports that the Holden family lived in west London. She had found the road on Google Street View. Two rows of detached Georgian properties, some of them streaked by ivy. She pictured a bedroom, abandoned years earlier but kept as it had been when the boy was a teenager, crowded with the stuff of a young life. A privileged young life, to be sure. Did that lighten the tragedy? For some people, Justine's kind of people, there wasn't much 'pity and fear' in privilege.

The radio cut out. Her phone rang through the hands-free system.

'Lorna, it's Geneva. I have Thomas Haller on the line.'

Her heart stumbled. 'Put him through.'

The line changed pitch. She knew that he was there, listening for her.

'Are you there?' he asked.

'I didn't think I'd ever hear from you again.'

'*Ever?*' Thomas laughed. The sound reverberated through the car.

'What more did we have to say?'

'There was a time when we spoke all night. It was like we could never run out of words.'

'I thought you didn't want to talk about the past.' She accelerated as the lights changed. 'I shouldn't have come to London – it was your big night with Claude. I figured no one would miss me at the dinner.'

'Well, it wasn't quite a no-show, was it? You saw me through the window, giving my speech.'

She opened the car window by an inch. She had persuaded herself that he hadn't been able to see her out there on the street. That he'd been cocooned in the light of the restaurant.

'I heard that your show sold out before the opening,' she said.

'Who told you that?' He sounded different: the cajoling humour had gone.

'Claude did.'

He waited before answering, so that her disclosure seemed to grow in significance. 'The show sold out because Claude bought in half of the paintings. He sold them to himself. He needed it to seem like an overnight triumph.'

'Is that what you called to tell me? That Berlins is a charlatan?'

'I called to say I'm sorry.'

The sun was in her eyes. The car in front was too close. She hit the brakes just in time.

'Go to hell. You threw me over for Claude. You threw away everything we had. You've been walking out on me your whole life—'

'We were children,' he interrupted.

'You left me to go mad. And still I forgave you. I forgave

everything.' She struck the steering wheel with her fist. 'Justine had you sussed. You care about nobody – nothing – only your image . . .' Words were flying away from her. 'You're not *real*.'

'Lorna,' he said. 'Please listen. You don't get it. The thing with Berlins – it was never about money, or reputation—'

'Then what was it? Are you in love with him?'

The seconds in which he failed to answer were like a joke gone wrong. In that stretching instant, the southeastern corner of Madison Square Park was a mess of road signs and swarming life that she couldn't fathom.

'Yes,' he finally said. 'I mean, I thought I was.'

Coming to a halt at an intersection, she rested her forehead on the top of the wheel.

'You never told me.'

'I never told anyone. It happened the year I went to Düsseldorf. It happened, then it ended – or it seemed to. I came to New York, started over . . .'

'But why would you keep it a secret?'

'Because it always felt like one. Something I should have stopped, but couldn't. And something *he* didn't want people to know about. We kept seeing each other in New York, when he was over there. One-off meetings that went on for years. I couldn't let go. Or he never allowed me to.'

'He chased you.' She crunched the car into gear.

'No – not for a long time. He didn't need to. He knew how I felt about him, and you see, in all the years I lived in New York, when you were representing me, he didn't care much about my work. It was only after the Whitney show that—'

'You were finally worth something to him.'

'It wasn't as cynical as that.'

'Come on. All he cares about is your selling power.'

'It felt like the fulfilment of a promise, like I'd lived up to his expectations at last. He began pursuing me, asking me to show at his gallery—'

'And why didn't you resist him?'

'I tried to. I went to Switzerland. But he has this, I don't know, this hold. Ever since we were young, it's been there – an almost physical thing. All his knowledge and judgement, like particles of light.'

'Jesus.'

'I know it sounds mad. I've hated myself for feeling this way. But when Claude believes in you, it's like being on a stage with all the lights up: you can't see anything else. I was twenty and he told me I would be a great artist, that I'd go all the way. I never stopped craving the feeling he gave me in Düsseldorf.'

'And my belief in you meant nothing?'

'That was different. You know it was. You were my friend. The love was equal.' His voice was growing quieter. 'Please forgive me, Lorna. I was only a boy.'

'Maybe you were, but how have you not learned? How does he still have this power over you?'

She drove on in silence, listening to the muffled, fractured sound of his breathing. She felt like an idiot for not having guessed. Or a liar. Hadn't she known this, at some level?

'Something happened in London,' he said at last, in a near-whisper. 'Before my show.'

'Betty?'

He waited. 'No. Yes. It doesn't matter.'

'The boy from the gallery. Is that what you're talking about?'

'Who?'

'Luca Holden. The one whose father burst in—'

'Oh, that.'

'Did you know him?'

'Not really. There are so many staff at that gallery. I was only there for a few days.'

'It was tragic.'

'Bizarre. Things like that just don't happen, until they do.'

She dug her teeth into her lower lip. How could she explain, to Thomas of all people, her feeling about Luca? She could barely articulate it to herself.

'What was it, then? What were you going to tell me?' She scanned the storefronts to either side of the road. Taco Bell. Envy Nails.

'Oh, nothing. Just something I thought would make you laugh.' He went silent. When he spoke again, he sounded calmer – practically his normal self once more. 'Do you remember that night, when we were on Charing Cross Road? We'd been at an opening. Wolfgang Tillmans. We went to that sleazy gay bar—'

'Seventy-nine CXR.' She cuffed the wheel gently and sped up, clearing Broadway.

'That was the one. And then we went to buy cigarettes and ended up in a photobooth.'

'I remember. But why are you asking? What's the point?'

A young man was crossing the street. He was dressed in a trench coat – a fitted number, belted at the waist, like something Vivien Leigh would have worn.

'I'd better go,' she said, before Thomas could answer. 'I'm late.'

19

9 November, 12.49. New York

Leo walked along Central Park West, casting his eyes about like a man on the hunt for something. He never arrived dead on time. Let the other guy wait; there was weakness in being the first to show.

He caught sight of a piece of paper scudding along in the wind. Giving his body time to change shape, he bent down and intercepted it, pinning it to the sidewalk with his index finger. A fragment of the *Post* – something about Trump and Biden. Leo thought of the time he and Deborah had gone to dinner at the White House, the November night in 1985 that Princess Diana danced with Reagan.

It was a beautiful day, blue and cool. When the breeze lulled, he could feel the warmth of the sun. It filtered through the thin polyester of his zip-up jacket. Fall was a time of fading, expiring, but it always made him brisk with optimism.

*

Florian Roth was already at Pendavis, seated at Leo's usual table. Their eyes met as Leo crossed the restaurant, grasping the backs of chairs.

'Congratulations,' Leo said, as he gripped hold of the other man's hand.

'Thank you, Leo. But what for?'

Leo lowered himself into the chair. 'That Matisse sale. Sixty million dollars. You're a conjuror. You're – what do they call it? – a *demiurge*.'

Pleasure gleamed over Florian's face. 'I thought you were going to bid for it.'

Leo remembered how he'd watched from the doorway. That freak tear.

Through the restaurant window, the trees of Central Park were shedding russet leaves. Kids were scrambling on the rocks. Phosphenes, bright as comets, seemed to chase after them.

'Well, what's going on? What are we here for?'

Florian laughed. It was an eager, petitioning sound. 'I hope you can tell me. Fritz Schein wanted us to meet.'

'Ah, my *curator*. Whatever the hell that means. I'm his bit on the side. The Lucinda Villa aren't paying him enough, I guess.'

Florian laughed again. Up close, his face appeared misshapen – too narrow. A Habsburgian head, all edges and elongations. It made Leo think of a stone finial, one of those sculpted pineapples.

A waiter was asking about water.

'I'll have a glass of Pol Roger.' Sitting back, Leo watched the waiter hasten between the linen islands. 'I like this place. Reminds me of the eighties. Everyone on the up.' He looked back at Florian. The star auctioneer was wearing a silk suit – grey with purple gridlines. 'How old are you?'

'Forty-two.'

'Time races by. Feels like just the other day that I was here with Roy Cohn, talking about buying the Algonquin. But then – and you know, time is funny like this, *contradictory* – it feels like for ever ago.' He curled his fingers around the chromium armrests.

'It's a beautiful hotel, the Algonquin,' said Florian. Had a ripple of uncertainty disturbed his aristocratic poise?

'Even then – when was it, 1982? – I wasn't young. Older than you are now. You see, a life contains within it multiple lives, whole eras, fucking eternities. I can't believe I've lived this long or seen this much.'

Leo stared at the man across the table. The sale of the century was on the auctioneer's mind. *The Leo J. Goffman Collection.* Leo pictured Florian at the podium, arms spread wide, as Picasso's reinterpretation of *Las Meninas* spun into view on the revolving wall, drawing a gasp. What a shame that he wouldn't live to see it.

'Tell me, Leo – I should know the answer – did you get it, the Algonquin?'

The waiter had returned with water and champagne. Leo tracked the pearls of gas rising in the flute.

'It was my anniversary present for Deborah. Our first ten years.'

*

18.56. Montreux

Thomas was always the first to undress. The smartness and precision of his own attire, the casualness of Otto's: the disparity suggested a power dynamic, which removing their clothes would reverse.

He stood in the red-tinted light of the bar and waited as Otto instructed him to remove his jacket, his shirt, his trousers.

'Pass me the belt.'

He held it out behind him, without turning.

'Shoes. Underpants.'

Thomas kicked his discarded clothes aside. He stood completely naked, facing the bar. Holding his back straight, he imagined his reflected image in the mirrored walls behind him. A pale pillar, grotesquely pale in the garish light. A pillar of salt. An object to be used.

Otto's hands were on Thomas's hips, then on his buttocks and thighs. Otto's lips were close to his neck.

'Get on the bar.'

Thomas placed his hands together on the leather surface and

raised himself off his feet, like a gymnast on a pommel horse. For a second or two, he held himself suspended, his feet a few inches from the floor, until the muscles in his back and arms began to burn.

With a brute thrust and an upswing of the legs, he deposited himself on the bar top, rolling onto his front. His arms hung off the sides. His face pressed into the warm black leather. The narrowness of the surface forced him to hold his legs together, imprisoning his half-hard dick in a tight cavity.

In his peripheral vision, he perceived Otto as an encroaching dark shape in the red. He adjusted his head a little. Otto was standing at the bar, still clothed. A long black strip trailed from his hand. Thomas's belt.

Otto took the loose end in his other hand and coiled it around his fingers.

*

13.17. New York

'At my age,' Leo said, 'you reach a state of natural melancholy. But the drive to acquire hasn't left me. I own more things than I could ever count, but still I want more.'

A young woman in a blue dress had left her table. She touched her forearm with the fingers of the opposite hand in an uncon-scious – self-conscious – way as she crossed the restaurant.

'Well, that's the nature of a true collector,' Florian replied. 'I mean, look at the de Menils—'

'I used to be like that about sex,' Leo continued. 'I would look around a room like this, full of beautiful women. I'd look at that girl over there, and I'd think to myself, I *know* what it would be like to have her. But I'd still want her.' He eyed his untouched champagne. 'Do you think that men or women get greater pleasure from lovemaking?'

'Leo, if you'll allow me to cut to the chase—'

'Allow you?' Leo looked up and chuckled. 'I could deny you nothing.'

'What are your plans for your collection, when you – I mean, in the end, when the time comes . . .' Florian shifted in his chair, seeming to lose his resolve.

Leo smiled into the room for a while. 'After I met Deborah, I never looked at another woman again. I became a real man, just like that. No longer a lusting animal.'

'What an incredible woman your wife was, Leo. What a collection you built.'

'A natural melancholy! That's my state of being. And by melancholy, I don't mean depression, the American malaise. I never had a therapist. Melancholy can be a blessing, a heightened state of insight. Like existentialism. Or Buddhism. Freedom from the ego. God, I'm starting to sound like my brother.'

The waiter set down two plates, arrayed in abstract-painterly style with scallops and pea purée.

'I just bought another Thomas Haller.' Leo speared a scallop with his fork. 'Claude Berlins practically begged me to buy it.'

'You surprise me, Leo. From what I'd heard, you and Berlins have never seen eye to eye.'

'Begged,' Leo repeated, conscious of an abrupt surge of – what was it? Anger, or exhilaration, or pungent sadness? 'You should have seen him. Berlins would prostitute his own daughter for a sale, if he had a daughter. But the painting's a stunner. Like a sky at dusk. Like a piece of silk . . . I know, *I know*, the image is incidental with Haller. There is no image, only paint. I should have been an art critic, right?' He bit off half the scallop. It didn't taste of much.

'Haller's market has never been stronger,' Florian mused. 'But he's an absent presence these days. Why do you think he disappeared at the height of his success?'

'Why does anyone do anything?' Leo said, chewing. 'You can't get inside a guy's head.'

'That's true enough. Truer with Haller than most. I've always wondered.'

'Wondered what?'

Florian leaned closer. 'His paintings are beautiful, but what are they about?'

'He's a damned fine painter. What else is there to know?' Leo held up the other half of his scallop to the sunlight.

*

18.58. Montreux

It was nothing new, this juxtaposition. Otto clothed, Thomas naked. The one vertical, the other prostrate. But it never failed to elicit a shiver of delight. Was it intellectual, in some small way? A reinvention of Manet's *Le Déjeuner sur l'herbe*, with himself as the nude courtesan – gazed upon, focalised . . .

The meditation broke with a crack. The impact of the belt was painless, for a fragment of time. His lower back twitched in protest; his feet rose from the bar.

At once the belt descended on the tops of his thighs, and this time the pain was scalding. He heard his own cry pierce the small room, deprived of an echo. It was a peculiar, dissonant sound, a roar that transformed in its final phase into a sharp falsetto.

The belt struck him across his body from hip to hip. Nausea blocked his throat and plunged the wrong way, into his chest, down to his groin, like electricity looking for an outlet. The redness of the room intensified, then faded. The belt was swinging from Otto's hand. Thomas clamped his eyes shut. He wanted to beg for an end to it. The belt cracked and a cry erupted.

With detached fascination, he listened to the sound that came out of him. It was more sustained than before, gaining in strength, almost operatic . . . A luxurious burn was spreading. He wondered, somewhere deep in his brain, if he was hearing the sound echo and re-echo, or if those sounds were fresh screams, released with every hurl of the belt. He pressed his teeth together in a manic grin, so hard that he thought they would shatter.

*

13.40. *New York*

Leo dropped his fork into his spaghetti and wound a coil from the midst of the mussel shells.

'Ever since it was suggested to me that I shouldn't eat shell-fish – not that my parents were orthodox – but ever since I was given to understand it's not the done thing, well, I've just loved the stuff.'

He met Florian's eye, then glanced down at the dish. 'Looks like a Delacroix, right? *The Death of the Sultan*, one of those crazy excessive ones.'

Florian laughed on cue. Leo could tell that he was thinking about the auction, wondering how to steer the conversation around to it once more.

Let him wait. Let the whole world wait a while longer.

'Deborah and I used to see art everywhere, out in the world.' He raised the coiled spaghetti and held it suspended. 'We were down in New Mexico years ago, at a hotel near Taos. It was a hellhole, the heat at night was insane. But in the early morning, with the sun rising behind the red blinds, our bedroom was a Rothko. It was like being *inside* a painting, a panel of red at the end of the bed and nothing but darkness all around, and my wife's body beside me, naked.'

The spaghetti tumbled back. He drew a fresh coil onto his fork and lunged to capture it.

'Collecting was our life,' he went on, through a full mouth. 'When we were young, we knew very little. I guess you could say we had no taste.'

'I'm sure that's not true.'

'But money can buy taste. People say that like it's a bad thing, like they've found you out. But money can acquire you an eye if you use it right. Just look at Isabella Stewart Gardner. Look at Vanderbilt. Deborah and I started going to galleries, to auction rooms. We bought small, then we bought bigger. Imps and Mods. Pissarro, Braque, Modigliani—'

Florian began to speak.

'The Russian Constructivists! A fucking *spellbinding* Kandinsky. When Deborah died, I carried on. I never lost the momentum. Just the other day I got five paintings by Ana Garcia.'

'Ah, Ana. She's a genius.'

'Picked them up from Lorna Bedford. There's one where she's made a hole in the canvas with her boot. There's a violence about it.'

'Her work is daring. As is your entire collection.'

'There's a violence,' Leo repeated. 'People should acknowledge brutality.'

'Of course.'

'It's inside each one of us.'

The colours and textures of the restaurant had intensified: the blonde wood panelling, the sheen of blow-dried hair, the dyes and fabrics of clothing.

'The art market's capricious, don't you think?' Leo said, training his gaze on Florian.

'That's one word for it.'

'You think you know what the market's going to do. You reckon you can pet it and it'll lick your hand. But then it bites you and draws blood. Charges you like a bull.'

Florian made a brittle noise, not quite a laugh. 'Except that the art market isn't a real being, Leo. I mean, we all *talk* about it as if it were a creature, or a god – a *force* with taste and agency—'

'That's precisely what it is – a creature. A beast. A schizophrenic mess of competing desires. We *worship* it, but we can't tame it.'

Light splintered as if the room were a mirror that had silently shattered. Voices surged in a chaotic flood. Leo felt his dick pulse and squirm. A waiter walked past with two martinis on a tray. The ellipses of the glasses were grotesque saucer eyes, strafing through the air, wet and lunatic. In an instant, the spectre had disappeared behind a woman's shining hair. She sat and fondled the narrow strap of her dress, listening to the drawn-out story of an older man.

'Leo,' Florian said.

With a rush of adrenaline, Leo felt the presence of the thing again. He pursued it, but it evaded him like a whining fly. It stole through the air, catching up the energy of the place, guzzling everything in its path, but guzzling so daintily – with such gentility, for this was Pendavis – that it was invisible to everyone. In a flash, it had skipped over the pearls that hung around the woman's neck, dispersed in the veneers of the man's teeth.

'Leo.' Florian's voice was urgent. 'Are you all right?'

Leo's senses contracted. He focused on Florian's face and called his brain to order. It took long seconds for words to form.

'I get tired. I'm old.' He drew a crust of bread through the oil on his plate. 'You know what Jean Renoir said when he heard that Picasso had died?'

'Remind me,' said Florian. The eagerness was gone from his voice.

'He said, "What an un-Picasso thing to do."' Leo dropped the bread and slapped the table with both hands. Energy was coursing back through him like a drug. 'Death didn't become him! I tell you, they'll have to prise the life away from me cell by cell.'

'Of course. You're like a man in his sixties.'

'Still, I have to think about things.'

'That's eminently wise.'

'Things like my estate. Like my *art*.' He watched Florian with a steady gaze. 'When I die, it goes up for auction. All of it. The Rothko, the Warhol *Liz*, my Barnett Newmans, my Louise Nevelson, my Joan Mitchell, my David Smith, all the contemporary stuff as well – Thomas Haller, Ana Garcia, my five Richters, the girl in the black dress by Alex Katz. I want a sale in two halves, like an opera. Paintings first, then sculptures, over two successive nights.'

'Well, that's an unconventional split, but there's a certain elegance—'

Leo landed his hands on the table again. 'A deluxe catalogue! The most beautiful book you ever saw. Ivory bond paper, a velvet cover, an essay on the Goffmans as collectors by Yve-Alain Bois or another one of those theorist guys. And I want the whole art world to show up.'

'It would be an honour, Leo.'

There was a warmth to Florian's statement, a sudden gravity in his bearing, a luminosity in his eyes.

A tickling sensation fluttered across Leo's brain. He waited a beat.

'What would be an honour?'

'To hold this auction. The sale of your and Deborah's extraordinary collection.'

Leo pressed his hands to the tablecloth. He held his body erect.

'Who said anything about you holding it?'

Florian passed his tongue over his lower lip.

'You think you're the only auctioneer in this city?'

'Well, no, but I assumed—' A phantom smile was spreading over Florian's face. He seemed to be sinking into his own violent blush.

'You assumed,' Leo intoned. 'People always *assume*.' He injected the word with stress, making it portentous and silly. 'You're right about one thing, mind. It *is* an extraordinary collection. Art was our life. Still is my life – I don't have a family. No heirs. No one to gift with an inheritance. And so, the collection has to go the way of the rest of me, where all the atoms of my body go, back into the universe. Into circulation. No heirs.'

He nodded at his own words. Through the window, over in the park, kids were still playing on the rocks, but they must be different kids by now. He had a giddy apprehension of the passing of generations, all of them flickering down like leaves.

'You have a brother, though, don't you?' Florian asked. 'Doesn't he teach at Columbia?'

Leo fixed his attention on the red-leaved carpet of the park. 'I haven't spoken to my brother for close to a quarter of a century.'

'I'm sorry. I shouldn't have asked.'

Leo turned back. 'Why not? Why shouldn't you?' There was a mocking softness in his question, and behind it, a gripping, twisting conflux of feeling. He suddenly wanted to be sick. 'We haven't spoken in decades. *Tell me*' – his voice was growing hoarser – 'what kind of man does that make me?'

He knew that Florian wanted to look away. He wouldn't allow it. Not for the first time, he was aware of the stabbing power of his eyes.

'What kind of man?' he repeated, holding his voice steady. 'What kind? Tell me.'

'I don't know.'

'*TELL ME.*'

The words had leapt from him. The air seemed to quiver. From a nearby table came a high-pitched cry. Then there was no sound at all. It was as if all life had been sucked from the room.

PART II

20

21 February, 13.00. Montreux

Thomas Haller stood in his studio. On the wall in front of him, three tall canvases hung in a row. The same violet base layer covered each one.

The light in the studio was low; he had closed the louvres overhead to produce the kind of half-light that lingers after sunset.

He walked slowly towards the central canvas, squaring up to the unfinished – barely started – painting. Not a painting but an idea.

He shook the spray can in his hand, producing a hard rattle, and sprayed a paler shade (close to pink) over the top quarter of the canvas. It spread in a broad, filmy swathe. Drawing his arm in an arc, he made another pale incursion further down the canvas. Pinkish light swerved through the violet. His eyes watered.

He stood back. It was too considered, he thought. Too exact.

He began to fire the spray paint in spurts all over the canvas, mottling the surface with agitated motions. The acetone was in his blood, strumming his nerves. Its tang was in his throat.

He threw the can on the floor and took up a brush. It was already loaded with grey paint. In a single flourish he scored a horizontal line, straight as a rail, across the canvas, cutting off the bottom quadrant. He sighed in wonder at the fluke precision.

Turning away, he went to the centre of the room, where a projector stood on an elevated stand. He switched it on. Light and colour struck the central canvas, matching its proportions exactly. He felt the heat of the beam – heard the whirr of the fan. Motes spilled through the light.

The night last summer when he'd gone to Vauxhall with Luca consisted, in his mind, of a single picture. The bars they'd gone to, the people they'd chatted with, were all a dark impression. The one image, the only part to have clearly resolved, belonged to the end of the night, when he and Luca wandered, staggering, into the open space behind the Royal Vauxhall Tavern. A place of miniature hills and valleys, running alongside the railway arches. It was warm that night, with a breeze. They crossed a region of grass, then dipped into a canyon where bodies appeared and faded like glowing lights. Voices were audible, and other sounds besides. Breaths, whines, the wet clicking of tongues. In his wired state, Thomas felt that he'd walked into a nightmare. Luca slid off his T-shirt and shorts and walked alongside him, naked apart from his trainers.

Luca stopped abruptly and placed his hands high above his head, against a tree, pushing out his hips.

'Fuck me.'

His body was a slender shape against the tree. Thomas fumbled his trousers open, undid his shirt, tried to tease his dick into life while running his other hand over the warm, smooth surfaces of Luca's body. Someone was watching. Multiple people. He tried for a minute or longer – heard his own breaths quickening against the silence of Luca's expectation. He couldn't do it. The desire was there, but none of the reflexes. Sweat poured over his forehead and he buried his head in the depression between Luca's neck and shoulder.

'I'm sorry.'

*

Turning back to the canvas – transformed, now, by projected light – and stepping towards it, he was struck (almost surprised) by the intrusion of his own shadow: a narrow body cut in two by the grey bar, silhouetted against the pink and purple. Dazed from the chemicals, he saw the painting as a cinema screen. A twilit episode, a balcony scene, and Thomas was the solitary character, wandering across the frame. He watched his own shadow move.

What he needed was a director. He thought again of Marianna Berger's video of the hotel bed. A view of blank space in which nothing happened. But then, from time to time, chance incidents. Small details. Could his life be like that, on film? A blankness out of which meaning, truth, complexity, feeling, would all come into being by random touches?

He went down the plywood steps, through the main room, onto the terrace. The sky was clear. The snow was receding from the hillsides, leaving sporadic patches of green. It felt like spring, except for a coldness in the air that caused his breath to billow. He descended to the pool and went into the woods.

He had left Marianna frustrated, the last time. Those old photos he'd failed to explain. He had wanted too much to be in control. He had tried to see the film, every frame and angle of it, before it existed. Besides, what had the film been *about*? A portrait of the artist at home, doing nothing, saying next to nothing. Now he had a project. A subject worthy of a film. A thing to redeem him after the long months of glacial brightness outside, and in the studio, an aching hopelessness.

The clearing beyond the trees was newly mown. It felt more than ever like an enclosed formal garden. The trees were practically black, but the grass was a pool of light: it seemed to have been lit from within, like a slide on a lightbox. He could trim the turf to carpet-like perfection, he thought, and plant box hedges to make a knee-high maze. He walked to the end of the plot, to where the evidence of Betty's grave had almost disappeared. The grass was growing back over. Soon there would be nothing to mark the spot.

*

07.49. *New York*

After fifty lengths, the pool was as warm and cocooning as amniotic fluid. He could do worse, Leo thought, than die in this stuff.

Sometimes, as he swam in the mornings, he looked back on the events of his life and felt things. Things like pride, desire, shame and regret. Yes, regret: he couldn't deny it. But he had it mastered. Usually, before long, a deathly numbness spread through his body, seeping into him from the chlorinated plasma.

Stepping onto the poolside, dripping with water, he felt as if he were waking from a dream. He had passed from deep memory to the reality of himself, a naked eighty-six-year-old. He heard his own exhausted breaths as he turned to survey the paintings on the walls, the settling water, the city beyond . . .

Nothing existed outside *this*. The past had been extinguished. The future was nothing more than a hypothetical present. And he didn't believe in an afterlife.

He grabbed a towel and tied it around his waist, feeling his hipbones projecting like buttresses.

Memory be damned. He preferred the pristineness of the senses (the apprehension of *now*) to the waters of memory with their concealed emotional currents, their tedious riptides of regret. Perhaps that was why he liked art. It insisted on a present-tense encounter. It belonged to the realm of the senses. Each encounter was a new encounter.

On which subject – where the hell was his new Thomas Haller? The painting had been held up in UK customs for months. Leo's birthday had passed. Brexit was the excuse, as usual. Fritz was communicating with the intermediary, Equitone, the shell company that Lorna Bedford had claimed to know nothing about.

Leo stepped into the elevator, chattering with cold. He liked Lorna. She was a dark horse. For whatever reason, she didn't want him to be in her debt. She was one of the few people, he reflected, who didn't fall down before him in deference.

The elevator doors parted again, delivering him into the stone-lined passageway of the upper floor. For reasons he couldn't now recollect, he had stayed at the apartment all through the winter. His house in Naples, Florida, had stayed closed. At the Pegasus Tower, he had busied himself with plans for the Baptist church in Harlem.

'Don't give me a mimsy-pimsy building,' he had said to the architects. 'I want something that people are going to love or despise.'

He traipsed along the corridor, realising that he'd forgotten to wear his slippers. Through the threshold to the drawing room, the sky over Manhattan was a spotless blue.

'I don't do mimsy-pimsy,' he said out loud. 'Never have, never will.'

He was conscious of a chill on his bare shoulders. He had forgotten his bathrobe, too. On he went, through the room, girdled in a towel. He had the sensation that he was materialising and dissolving by turns. At moments he was reminded of himself (*there*, in the blue laminate of Donald Judd's boxes, thrown back as a broken column of shadow selves). At other times, he slipped into nonexistence. Rothko's darkness had a way of annihilating him, drowning thought with colour-feeling.

The September issue of *Artforum*, five months old now, remained on the coffee table. Often, as he half listened to his architects' commentaries on soil tests and airflow, his gaze settled on the cover image, a heap of gold-wrapped candy, and the words of a song repeated in his head.

Sweets for my sweet, sugar for my honey.

He stopped by Brancusi's *Bird in Space*. He could see his face in the polished bronze, stretched almost beyond comprehension. But it was the surface itself that stole his attention, those thousands of tiny scratches, visible only in the region of the metal where the light happened to be concentrated. The marks swept in thronging formations, cohering around a single point. When he moved his head, a new effusion of marks rose into view, swirling around their own axis, as if *that* – and only that – were the true centre point.

In the prison of the apartment, art provided endless escapes. Shortcuts into the infinite. For months, he had been waiting for deliverance. Losing your car was like having your legs cut off.

He heard footsteps in the passageway.

'Bonita, is that you?'

A fleck of spit landed on the Brancusi. He wiped it with his thumb, into the grain of the marks.

'Yes, Mr Goffman.'

He reorientated himself with small steps.

'What have you been cleaning this sculpture with? What product, what *cloth*?'

She was standing in the doorway with an untroubled expression.

'No product, only the duster. The same as always for the Brancusi. Ostrich feather – always ostrich.' She regarded the sculpture. 'The same as Mrs Goffman told me when you bought it.'

There was understated pride, or defiance, in her ability to remember.

As he stared at her, the space between them seemed to enlarge elastically. Bonita became tiny, a doll's house maid that he might be able to pick up and snap. Then the room bounced back to its usual proportions.

'Always ostrich,' he murmured.

*

14.11. *Montreux*

Standing at the centre of the grass where the light was strongest, Thomas tilted his phone against the glare. He had Marianna Berger's number saved. It rang twice before she answered.

'Thomas?' She sounded distant. Faintly alarmed.

It was random of him to be calling, he supposed.

'Is this a good time?'

'It's fine. I'm out walking.'

'How funny. So am I, out in the garden here. Where are you?'

'I doubt you'd know it. Vauxhall Cross.'

'I know it very well. You forget, I lived in London once. And I had a studio in Vauxhall. It was different back then – no high-rise flats, no sky pools.'

'I live on Kennington Road,' she said, in a flat voice. 'That hasn't changed.'

Very close to Luca, he thought. Too close. What did the coincidence signify? That everything was connected, and the causality of things a piece of intricate circuitry too pervasive to see in its totality? No, he told himself. There was no logic.

'How are you?' she said. 'How was Christmas, all of that?'

'Oh, the same as usual. I went down to the Montreux Palace. Got drunk. Walked back up the mountain. I've been holed up here ever since.'

'Is there snow?'

'Always. It's Switzerland. And how about you, how have you been?'

'The same. I'm broke. I can't find a gallery. Still waiting for my break.'

He primed himself to sound casual. 'What happened to my biopic?'

'I couldn't see a direction for it, I guess. I'm sorry I didn't get in touch.'

'I waited for you to call,' he said, walking in a tight circle on the grass, smiling into the trees. 'I waited for days – weeks . . . Is she coming back? Is this film going to be made? Is she still alive?'

'Come off it. And it's not a film. I don't shoot on celluloid. The stuff I make – it isn't cinematic. *Film* sounds too formal. Too—' She paused, and he heard a banging and mechanical whining in the background: London sounds. She groaned in feigned disgust. 'Too conscious of its own importance.'

'The reason I called,' he began, then waited. Bowing his head, he felt the sun's energy concentrating on his neck. His shadow was a stub. Had he lost some weight? His clothes felt loose around him.

'Yes?'

'I have some news.' He waited again. 'Fritz Schein called me last week. He wants me to represent Switzerland in the Venice Biennale.'

His voice was calm, almost offhand. But the words, spoken aloud in the silent capsule of the garden, seemed to tremor around him, hovering in the air like dragonflies.

'You're doing the Swiss Pavilion? In Venice?'

'It's very late in the day, of course. It was supposed to be Franz Hefner.'

'Yes, I saw in the *New York Times*. A heart attack.'

'Right. He was such an old boozer. And he hadn't completed any of the work that he was planning to show. So – Fritz has asked me to do the exhibition. I guess he's thinking we can show the paintings that were at Galerie Claude Berlins.'

'And will you?'

'Of course not. This requires something new. Something big.'

'Isn't Fritz curating the main Venice exhibition too? The one in the Arsenale?'

'Yes, he's all over it. Who actually gives a damn about diversity? They don't call him a supercurator for nothing.'

'The Swiss Pavilion at the Venice Biennale,' she said, with affected gravity. 'So, this is it. The climax of your career.'

He laughed drily. 'Or *a* climax. The thing is, I want more. I always want more. Everything. Maybe too much.'

'And you rang to tell me this? I could have just read it in the *Art Newspaper*.'

She hadn't lost her harsh edge, he thought. That note of reprimand.

'I want to talk about the film.'

'*Video*.'

'It got cut off, last time. You say it didn't have a direction. But this, the Biennale, gives it a new angle. A hook, isn't that what they call it?'

'I don't know. I mean, I have no money. I don't think I'll make my rent this month, never mind come to Switzerland.'

'I'll pay your air fare. Come and stay for a night or two.'

'I don't know,' she said again. 'I'm not even making art at the moment, to be honest. I haven't been doing anything. It all gets harder, all this stuff, the longer I go on . . .'

'*Come*. It's beautiful here in the spring. You have to see it. We'll be like the lovers in *A Farewell to Arms*. And bring walking boots.'

'Let me think about it.'

'I'll have Sylvia Rosso send you a plane ticket. How's early March?'

*

10.31. New York

Lorna passed under the red canopies of Veniero's with Jay beside her. His eyes flashed up every so often, as if to check that she was still there. She was late dropping him at Manhattan Woof.

The leaves were waxily green against the red of the terraces.

The sidewalks were stainless apart from a few spots of gum. This place had become desirable in the time she'd lived here. Even the clouds of marijuana smoke seemed atmospheric, ambient. The neighbourhood had gentrified. But then so had she. When she thought back to the early years of her gallery in SoHo – the parties, the drugs, the sense of freedom intercut by despair – she saw that it could never have lasted. Most people were destined to become a little less real.

Andrea Driscoll had died the previous week. It had been a foregone conclusion, but the news was still a shock that wouldn't be absorbed. Lorna had texted Justine and not heard back. Then Justine had sent a series of messages on the subject of Jay: his food, his exercise regime, his joints supplements. The silence over Andrea was a rebuke.

Lorna tracked her reflection in the panels of a parked UPS van. Was Justine really as narrow as that – to suppose that Lorna was in some way complicit? There had been (perhaps still were) other parts to her. Like humour and love. And goofing around.

'If you go to London and chase after Haller,' Justine had said, in the haughty tone of Gilberta St Laurent, her Jamesian alter ego, 'it will be in defiance of my deepest desire.' That was the morning Justine herself went off to Asia, shedding her old life like a costume. Lorna couldn't shake the suspicion that the whole thing with Goffman had been convenient for Justine. A reason for breaking finally, after all the months of going away and coming back.

She paused in the sunlight. How narrow, she thought, her life had become. It *seemed* so full. There were lunches with clients, studio visits, parties – endless parties. A masquerade of purposeful activity. Her life with Justine had eclipsed other people. Relationships could be selfish like that.

*

She had crossed 21st Street and was about to open the door to the gallery when she sensed someone close behind her, then passing in front of her. A figure in a hood, pacing up to the window and slapping the glass with both hands.

'Come out here!' The voice, a furious yell, was a girl's. 'Get the fuck out of there and speak to me, you little bitch.'

The girl was addressing one of the staff at the front desk – Daniel, the new sales assistant. Flushed with alarm, he glanced at the girl, then at Lorna, and then hurried across the gallery, disappearing into the staff quarters. His shirt was hanging out behind an unpressed jacket.

'That's it,' cried the girl. She smacked the glass again. 'Run away!' This last word, simultaneous with a kick of her leather boot, came out as a near-scream.

Through her shock, Lorna felt a glimmer of amusement. Inside, Geneva was still seated at the front desk, peculiarly impassive, her attention flicking between Lorna and the hooligan.

'This is my gallery,' Lorna said. 'I'd thank you to stop beating up the window.'

The girl turned and looked at her with startled curiosity, then gave the glass another kick, slamming it with the sole of her boot.

'Right, I'm calling the cops.' Lorna felt ridiculous, standing there with her cappuccino and iPhone.

'You're calling the cops on me?' demanded the girl, coming closer. 'Fuck that. You should be inviting me in. I'm an artist.'

Her hood had slipped off to reveal short hair. She wore a tight leather jacket over the top of her sweatshirt, unzipped and unbuttoned at the cuffs. Her expression – parted lips revealing another fractional parting of the front teeth – was hard to interpret.

Lorna could have come out with the usual line, that the gallery wasn't looking to represent anyone new.

'How do you know Daniel?' she finally said.

'Some party, I don't know. He owes me. He told me you guys were going to show my work.'

'I don't know anything about that. I'm sorry. Did you misunderstand?'

'I understood very well,' said the girl, with affected crispness. 'And I understand now.'

Lorna was aware, as the girl spoke, of her physical shape. Short and slim, but with a hint of strength inside the arms of the leather jacket. Almost masculine, but sexier than any boy, with subtle convexities in the chest and waist. And a growing hint of mirth in her expression. Some weak, errant part of Lorna wanted to say that it was all true. They would give the girl a show; it hadn't been a drunken lie by one of her staff.

'I'm Em,' the girl said. 'You going to call the cops or what?'

'Lorna. And no, not if you leave my window alone.'

'*Your* window . . .' Em was stepping backwards, still watching. 'It's the window of whatever asshole you pay your rent to.'

'We have an opening here next Wednesday,' Lorna said. 'Come by, if you want.'

Em's smile was broader now, but with an undercurrent. Their eyes remained linked for a moment longer before she turned and crossed the road.

*

Lorna stared into the lightwell beyond her office. The oleander that she had planted outside the window was growing but yet to bloom. It had been a mistake. The sun only struck that spot for an hour a day.

Her phone lay on the desk in front of her. She waited, imagining it might ping – that Justine might have decided after all that she wanted to come back. *I was never in love with her!* Or maybe Justine would call in the next few seconds to say that Andrea hadn't died, and it had all been a huge mistake. Lorna had an urge to tell Justine what had just happened, about the odd encounter out there on the street. Justine would have an interpretation. A way of framing it.

Lorna waited and nothing happened. The gallery phones were quiet today. Emails, too. In the end, she searched online for Luca Holden. There hadn't been any reports for weeks. She knew everything there was to know about the young man's death. She still had the copy of the *Evening Standard* from last September; it lay on the floor by her bed. But she didn't need to look at it. Luca's picture kept returning to her, as she pondered scale models of art-fair booths, as she walked in Manhattan, as she slept. It was fixed in her mind, like the photographs she'd developed years ago at Saint Martins, hanging them on a clothesline to dry.

Scrolling down the Google results, she noticed something she hadn't seen before. A radio programme. She saw the names Luca Holden and Alan Holden, and then the title of the programme: *Woman's Hour*. It had been broadcast a few days earlier. She clicked to listen, and jumped through the recording in short increments, picking up snippets of stories that made her feel nostalgic for London. Maybe it was just the voice of the host. Lorna could have sworn that the same woman had hosted this show in the nineties.

The woman's delivery was suddenly solemn. She was introducing a new segment, talking about suicide and grief.

A different woman began telling a story: how her daughter, a teenager, had taken an overdose the previous year.

'I don't think she meant for it to work,' the woman said. 'It was a cry for help. She'd done it before.'

As she listened, not daring now to jump forward in the recording, Lorna scanned the emails in her inbox. She'd received a reminder about the Deborah Goffman Memorial Gala on March 7. And then, in a few weeks, Venice. She had been sent a hand-addressed invitation from Thomas to the opening of his show at the Swiss Pavilion, a might-be olive branch.

'Alan Holden, you lost your son Luca to suicide last year,' said the radio presenter. 'Tell us what happened.'

Adrenaline welled from Lorna's chest to her head. She held herself still. There was a pause that seemed unnaturally long. She turned up the volume.

'I find it hard to use the word suicide. It's the word that has been assigned to my son's death.'

Lorna thought of the man at the opening in London, maddened by grief. And now this tone of sad authority. She couldn't join the two.

'I'm having to reconcile myself to the reality of it,' he said. 'I have doubts—'

'Doubts that he meant to take his life?'

'All kinds of doubts. It's not clear what happened. It was eight in the evening and he fell from the balcony of his flat, that's all we know for sure. Whether he jumped, or managed to slip over the edge . . . The police believe he was with someone. Perhaps more than one person. His phone went missing that day. But no one's come forward to say anything, so it seems we'll never know.' He paused, and again the silence seemed to balloon. 'He'd been drinking, taking cocaine . . . I can accept he was in a vulnerable state – out of his right mind. It was an accident, I suspect, or maybe just an idiotic thing he did without fore-thought.'

'What was Luca like? How do you remember him?'

'He was—' (Lorna held her breath. A phantom grief was rising in her.) 'He was extraordinary. His mind was *made* of ideas. He wanted to create things, to work with artists – he had this excitement, an inexhaustible optimism about art, about the future. And when I think back, it was always there, that blazing energy.'

'From when he was a child?'

'From the moment he became ours. We adopted him when he was a baby, you see, in rather tragic circumstances. His parents had died in a car crash – his mother was a cousin of mine, just a girl herself. Luca wasn't quite one year old at the time. And although he couldn't yet talk, he had a gleam of intelligence. A *curiosity* about the world, and a restlessness. We adored him, possibly more than if he'd been our biological son. He was a gift. But then, at the same time, he always had a quality of – I don't know – separateness. Specialness. This sense of belonging only to himself.'

He hesitated again.

'It was hard, when he left us to live alone. He was so private – there was so much we didn't know.' He tutted, as if at a minor annoyance. 'We were very close, but there were things he wouldn't ever talk about.'

'I'm sorry,' Lorna said, speaking into the silent office.

The presenter shifted to a third guest. Lorna gazed through the window. Hadn't she known that this would be the reality? The knowledge that she'd coveted for months – coveted and resisted – had withered into banality at the moment of possession. The fact that Luca had been a perfect stranger, nothing to do with her, was like the mere semblance of a resolution. It was as if reality were a dreary imitation of truth. Hadn't he *become* her son, in her mind, in her imagination, and didn't that inner reality possess its own stubborn significance? It was mad to think so; she knew it. But the questing feeling was still there. Maybe life (her life, at any rate) was meant to be like this. An endless search for something she wouldn't find. Justine had called her a lonely hunter.

She clicked out of the web-player, back to the Google results for Luca Holden. There was an old report in MailOnline, with the picture she knew so well. She zoomed in until his pupils were pixels.

'What happened to you?' she whispered.

21

2 March, 09.33. Montreux

Thomas stood at the centre of the studio, at the precise midpoint of the floor, and rotated himself to inspect the eight canvases. Eight violet variations, sprayed in multiple layers, each overscored by a network of darker grey lines. The lines seemed to hover like an airborne mesh – repeating verticals topped by a single horizontal. He had painted them freehand, but they were as straight as if he'd used a ruler. Sometimes, he had framed the arrangement with a larger encompassing oblong. For two weeks, the series had been consuming him. He had given up the outside world. He hadn't seen Otto. For hours at a time, nothing had existed outside the countless layers of spray paint and the repeated attempts at dead-straight lines. Every time he failed – whenever a line wavered, even slightly – he wiped it off with turpentine and tried again. Kept trying, until the thing was perfect: like a musical stave turned endways.

Now he felt like he'd woken into harsh reality. The paintings weren't working. They were terrible. He was dizzy from the spray paint, and boiling hot. He undid the fly of his jeans and shoved them off, over his bare feet, then unfastened the buttons of his shirt. Narrowing his eyes, he tried to imagine the paintings onscreen, in a film. What sense would they make to anyone but him? What sense did they make to him?

Marianna Berger had arrived late the previous evening. She had come to see these pictures. His Venice suite. She was here right now in the house, asleep in the guest room. He felt a scuttling of his nerves. As soon as she had arrived, she had asked to see inside the studio, but he'd put her off.

'Tomorrow,' he'd said. 'You'll see them all tomorrow, when there's daylight in there.'

First thing that morning, Claude had texted him.

Need to know what you're painting for Venice. Send pictures.

There had been two additional messages in the past hour.

Show me.

Now.

The room was filled with daylight. Too much of it. The paintings were worse than anything Thomas had ever made. A mass of rehearsed gestures. There was an assurance about those lines and dissolving hazes, but underneath it all, a loss of faith. They were like parodies of his London show, except for the superficial distraction of the floating lines. And the worst thing of all, the thing he *knew*, as he stood there, with grim certainty, was that Claude would like them. He would praise their rhythm and minimalism.

But then it wasn't Claude's disdain that Thomas could sense, right now, like an insistent whispering in his consciousness.

The air conditioning had broken. Sweat trickled on his back, between his buttocks. He felt his throat closing and fought against the sensation. Anger had usurped every other emotion. He thought he would scream, but didn't. Instead, he strode to the wall and grabbed a canvas with both hands. Holding it aloft, he ran down the stairs, tilting it sideways above him, out to the terrace and down the steps to the pool.

A very light rain had begun to fall, pattering over the surface of the water. He flung the canvas out, as though launching a boat, then ran back up to the studio and grabbed the next painting in the sequence. By the time he had run up and down for every painting, some of them were beginning to sink beneath the surface and he was groaning for breath. Sweat was pouring over him, the cool air bringing no relief. He went to the timber shed just inside the woods where the housekeeper kept the pool vacuum and net, and he took a metal can from the floor. A box of matches lived on top of it. Returning to the pool, he gave a final glance to the overlapping panels. Rectilinear continents, colliding and submerging. Segments of a sinking raft. The anger hadn't quite gone, although it was mixed up now with a savage exhilaration. He unscrewed the can and flung petrol over the surface of the pool. The smell reached his brain.

He lit a match, half wondering if he would go up in flames himself, and flicked it over the pool. With a whipping, sucking rush, the petrol ignited. For a few seconds, it was as if the water itself had caught fire. He watched, feeling his open shirt and underpants clinging like sodden rags to his body, breathing in the mingling odours of petrol and burning canvas.

He ran back to the shed and took out the net on its long pole. Holding it over the water, he prodded the flaming canvases – drove the net into the centre of one painting and tossed a blackened husk into the air. Glancing up at the terrace, he saw Marianna. A still figure in a Pepsi T-shirt, holding her camera up to her eye.

Petrol was skimming the surface of the water like mercury. Keeping the pole steady in one hand, he lifted the can and flung an arc of fuel across the pool. It ignited with a roar before it hit the paintings. He could hear Marianna calling out to him. Gradually, as he watched the fire, her voice grew more insistent, until she was standing right beside him. She lowered her camera.

'What the hell are you doing?'

The surfaces of the canvases had burned away, receding into black skins that stuck to the stretchers. Shoals of flaking matter drifted over the water.

'They weren't working.'

'Couldn't you just have thrown them away?'

He turned his hand over in the light. It was stinging. He must have scorched it as he poured the petrol. Marianna put her camera on the ground and took it in her own hand.

'You're hurt.'

'Not really.'

'I thought—' Her eyes were wide and shining. 'I thought you were going to jump in there, drown yourself.'

He fought to control his breaths. 'Imagine if I had. Imagine if I'd done that and you hadn't been there to film it.'

He pictured the scene. His body floating face-down on top of the half-submerged canvases, limbs outspread, as the last of the flames died. The film's closing shot.

'Let's go for a walk,' he said.

'Like this?' She glanced at his semi-undress, then her own.

'Sure – just grab some boots and a coat. We're not going to meet anyone.'

*

They passed the clearing where Betty's urn was buried, and into the forest beyond. Thomas walked ahead, allowing memory to guide him. Light fell through the trees in flakes and blots. There was no snow left here. The ground was spongy with needles. The coming spring seemed to rise out of the earth and to breathe through the forest. His hand smarted from the burn, but he didn't care. He felt released. Marianna might have regarded it as mad behaviour. A melodramatic show. But he'd had to stop those paintings from existing – to eradicate them.

He had nothing, now, for Venice. The realisation brought none of the horror he would have anticipated, out here on the mountain. They walked in silence. He had pulled on walking boots, a pair of shorts and a Balmain puffer jacket that he had hardly ever worn. It felt odd – stiff and tight. A touch too high fashion for the Rochers de Naye.

'Damn,' said Marianna from behind him.

'What is it?'

She looked pained. She was wearing trainers that weren't quite adequate for the terrain, and the sweatpants she'd slept in. He had lent her an old duffel coat.

'I forgot to bring my camera. It's still down there by the pool.'

'Leave it. If anything happens on this walk, anything good, we can reenact it.'

Her eyes narrowed. He walked on.

The path steepened and the temperature fell. It was years since he had taken this route, but it was just the same. The mountain rose in a near-vertical wall to one side. On the other, Lombardy poplars formed a dense mesh. The path twisted and the screen of poplars fell away. The concrete box of the studio, nestled on its promontory, was visible in the middle distance. Beyond, Montreux and the lake were like models of themselves.

They came to a grassy headland scattered with rocks. Recovering his breath, he pressed his hands on the small of his back. Hot from the climb, he could still feel the winter – its residual sting – on his face and legs.

'This was all covered in snow a month ago.' He took her hand and pulled her onto a rock for a better view.

Her dark hair blew around her face; she pushed it back. He thought for a moment that he could sense a sadness in her. Some deep, enervating lack. Things hadn't turned out the way she'd wanted. She had allowed herself to be trapped by events, by people. Time had pulled her plans out of shape. But who was he to judge?

'Why did you do that?' she said. 'Down there by the pool. It wasn't for the camera. You didn't know I was recording you.'

He kept his eyes on the view. 'Sometimes I want to destroy everything I've done. The house, my art, everything I've ever made. What would it be like to be left with nothing?'

'It would be shit.'

Her directness was like Luca's, but without Luca's innocence, without his love of life. Would Luca have ended up like this, his pleasures dimmed by experience?

They went on, past a pair of mountain huts that were like dozing beasts. They were fake, Thomas told her. Pieces of stage scenery concealing wartime bunkers. They were data centres, now.

For a while, the trail followed the course of a stream. Cattle stood motionless in the surrounding fields. Another wooded slope, steeper than the last, led to a ridge. It was too high now for trees to grow. The air was thinner. In the far distance, above the Alps, the clouds were static cascades.

At times, they had to use their hands for balance on the rocky incline. Then, as if a dream had broken, they came to the summit. They were standing on top of a jagged outcrop of rock. A crucifix, spliced from two large pieces of timber, rose over them. A few metres in front, the ground fell away in a cliff.

They looked out at the vista: the rolling expanses of green, patched by snow and belts of pine forest, swerving down to the lake. In the distance, he could make out the serrated edge of Le Grammont.

'This is called the Dent de Jaman,' he said. 'The mountain sticks up like a tooth. People began climbing up here in the nineteenth century. *Alpinistes*. Montreux had its fair share of recovering invalids and nervous wrecks back then, too. A few of them made it up here – they came and drew.'

The view was spellbinding. More so than he had remembered.

'To have lived in the nineteenth century!' he exclaimed. 'When people had clear visions of history and the future.'

'Watch it,' she said. 'You're starting to sound like an arch conservative.'

They wandered between the stones.

'I used to come walking up here with my father on Sundays, when the cable car was closed. We would walk for hours.'

'What were your parents like?'

He studied her again. She had fastened the duffel coat up to her neck. Her arms were folded against her chest. She had stopped bothering to push away the hair that blew across her face. She was around the age his mother had been, he supposed, when she'd had him.

'They were from the two different halves of Switzerland. My mother was French. My father was German. When I was young, I loved them and hated them. They were bourgeois, moralistic, very *Swiss*. So eager to be respectable.' He found himself smiling. 'You know, my background – my past – is very boring. I wish I could tell you that my parents died out there on the Diablerets glacier – fell into a ravine – and that their bodies are still out there, frozen. Nothing like that ever happened. Really, I had an ordinary childhood. Not unhappy, but dull. And lonely. No siblings, no family apart from my parents. My father worked long hours. My mother – well, she was remote in a different way. They weren't interested in other people. That's why they lived up here, manning a station for a cable car that no one wanted to use.'

He peered at a cluster of chalets in the valley below. Something was prompting him to talk about himself in a way he hadn't before, not with Marianna. Perhaps it was the relief of the fire, or the high altitude, or the fact that she had forgotten to bring her camera.

'I struggle to remember any of the details of my childhood,' he went on. 'It's like my life didn't really start until I went to London, started at art school, met Lorna—'

'You must remember something.'

He turned back to her. 'You want to know about those photos?' He watched her for a moment, sensing a quiet defiance. 'All right. My parents were strict with me. Strict about where I went, about who I saw.'

He lowered himself onto his haunches, resting his arms over each knee.

'I was fifteen. I'd just watched *Rebel Without a Cause*. I had this weird feeling that I was Plato, the boy who loves James Dean. And there was a boy at school, older than me, more popular . . . I guess he was Jim Stark in my mind. I knew that he hung around by the lake every Saturday night with his friends. So, one night I pretended to my parents that I was going to bed, and then I crept out of the house. I found him around midnight, but he wasn't with his usual gang – just loitering on the promenade. Of course I pretended I was only passing by, and waved at him, and that could have been it. But he invited me to walk with him. We smoked cigarettes, talked about—' He smiled and turned the palms of his hands upwards. 'I don't even recall. Some girl he was in love with. Nothing happened – we walked for hours, our sleeves brushed.' He sensed his smile receding. 'As I climbed back up the mountain, the sun was rising. It was cold, even in the summer, so I pulled up the hood of my coat – it covered most of my face. I'd reached that little clearing below the house—'

'The burial ground.'

'Yes. And I saw Magda, our Rottweiler, across the grass. From the way she was watching me, I knew that something was wrong.' He dislodged a rock with his hand. 'By the time she'd realised it was me, it was too late.'

He pulled up the sleeve of his jacket. With one finger, he traced a puckered pink ridge that ran along the underside of his left forearm.

'I'll never forget the force in her jaw. I thought she'd kill me. It was an incredible, terrified rage. Something she couldn't control. She'd thought I was an intruder. When she understood what she'd done—' He gasped for breath. 'I've never seen guilt like that in a creature's face. The anguish.'

'What happened to her?'

'My father said she would have to go. The whole day, I begged him to change his mind. You see, I didn't blame her. I didn't love her any less. I begged him until I wept, but the next morning he took her away and had her shot.' He shrugged, as if to dismiss the memory, and rose to his feet. 'He took photographs of the wounds, as a reminder. The rewards of disobedience. But I forgave him. I forgave both of them, my mum and dad. I hope they forgave me.'

'Forgave you for what?'

'For abandoning them. I left for New York and never came back. I let them die in a care home down there in the town. I couldn't bring myself to see them as invalids. Smell them, feel their bones through their clothes . . . The idea of having no memory, nothing left in your head – it terrified me.' He kicked the stone and it rolled off the edge of the cliff. 'Getting old is the worst thing that has to happen to us, don't you think? Worse than death. If you're young and full of hope, and then – one day – that's suddenly *it*, you lose your life' – he snapped his fingers – 'is that so bad? Haven't you already had the best of everything? You never have to face the indignity of losing your looks, your mind . . . The prospect of ageing is frightful to me.'

'I can think of more frightful things.'

He felt his features being distorted by a pained grin. 'You mean foreign wars and people being tortured and disease and injustice and all of that. More terrible than losing yourself piece by piece? I'm not so sure.'

He gazed out, wincing at the sunlight, thinking that the view was becoming somehow more immense, less easy to comprehend, the longer he looked at it.

'People think this place must be a paradise to live in,' he said. 'But it's a tough kind of paradise. The solitude gets to you.'

22

2 March, 14.15. Montreux

After lunch, they sat on canvas chairs on the terrace, with Marianna's camera balanced on the parapet in front of them between two glasses of wine. Lake Geneva was a disc of pearly grey in the afternoon sunlight. A pleasure cruiser streaked across the water, its flags flapping.

Thomas topped up their glasses from the bottle. He felt exhausted. He was relieved, still, but there was a background hum of anxiety. The real world was still there. Claude's messages were waiting to be answered. He tried to distract himself by telling stories. He described the time he had got drunk with Dennis Hopper in the East Village; then he recounted the occasion – it had been at a benefit on the Upper East Side – when a press tycoon had exposed himself, accidentally or on purpose: no one had been able to tell.

Wrapped in a blanket, Marianna listened with a guarded expression. He began to wonder if he had said too much up there on the mountain. Or perhaps she was getting bored, thinking that he was reverting to type with these practised anecdotes. She had closed the flip-out screen on the camera so that he could no longer see himself being recorded.

'People say I'm a brilliant mimic, you know.'

Her eyebrows lifted. 'Really? I can't imagine that. Who can you do?'

'David Hockney.'

He stood up and shuffled along the terrace a few steps, puffing at an imaginary cigarette.

'Death awaits you even if you don't smoke,' he mumbled.

At last, she laughed. It caused her face to relax – her eyes to widen.

'And how about this?' he said, straightening his back. 'Who's this? *Be an abstract painter, Thomas! Do it!*'

She laughed again, but with a new reserve, an incipient tension, as though she knew she were being tested.

'I don't know. Who is that?'

'Claude Berlins.'

'Right – I mean, I don't think I know what he sounds like.'

'He sounds just like that.' Thomas looked back at her, conscious of an embarrassment that the wine was failing to erase.

'When did Berlins ever say that?'

'He didn't. I made it up.'

He sat down and refilled his glass. Neither of them spoke for a while. With a dismay that seemed to suck the air from him, he realised that he had wanted her to be like Luca, who had seen everything with a bright, undaunted humour – when really she was just a person in her own regard.

'What are you going to do?' she said, breaking the silence.

'What do you mean?'

'Your paintings for Venice – the ones you destroyed. The ones I came here to make a video about. What's going to happen?'

'I don't know. I'll think up something. I have seven weeks.'

'That doesn't seem long.'

He took a mouthful of Frascati and swilled it through his teeth. Fear and annoyance flitted through him like horrible tittering children.

'Tell me about *you*,' he said, turning to her with a serene smile. 'Your life. I want to know the whole story.'

Falteringly, holding her glass steady on her knee, she told him about her childhood in London. Her family had lived in Clapham. Thomas remembered the grand old houses along Clapham Common, bordering the dark open terrain – how he used to study their Victorian features as he walked by.

'Oh God,' she exclaimed. 'I *know* how it all must sound. So clichéd. I don't have any of the glamorous trauma you need as an artist.'

'But I like middle-class English people,' he said, keeping his distaste pressed deep down. (Maybe it was just envy – an inevitable envy of a life unlike his own; the same thing she felt for him.)

'I hate being thought of as that.'

'I mean it. People like Laura Baxter in *Don't Look Now*, or the Wilcoxes in *Howards End* – they're strange and wonderful to me.'

Except, he thought, she wasn't like one of those characters. She had too much cautiousness about her. He had begun to sense, in all her silences and non-reactions, a resentment of his success. Probably she considered the house vulgar. His work, to her, was showy and apolitical. He knew what people like her – artists like her – thought. She had the readymade opinions of her tribe. He preferred the version of her he'd seen in her video: the fragile girl who refused to get out of bed and broke into poetry.

'Tell me more,' he said, goaded by the wine or some deeper compulsion. 'I want to know more. What happened after you left home?'

'I studied classics at UCL, for a bit. Then I dropped out and switched to art at Goldsmiths.'

'Classics,' he murmured. 'Do you like Catullus?'

'Greek tragedy was more my thing. When I went to art school, I made a video about Cassandra – me as the crazed prophetess, telling the truth while no one listens. It wasn't good. I've stopped putting myself in my work.'

'But you're always in your work. We all are. We're more truly in our work than we are in our daily selves.'

Her sceptical frown had returned. 'You sound just like Carter.'

'You know, your Carter Daily reviewed a show of mine once. Years ago, one of my exhibitions at Lorna's gallery. People respect him, no?'

'Oh God, please don't.'

'Don't what?'

'You're going to invite him to your party in Venice, aren't you?'

'Well – he'll be at the Biennale anyway.'

'But you don't have to invite him. Not after everything I've told you.' For a second, she looked downcast, almost imploring. Then she stood, picked up her camera and walked along the terrace, stopping at the top of the steps. 'By the way, who was that guy clearing out the pool earlier?'

He watched the back of her. She was standing in the very place from where she'd witnessed the fire. She had brought the viewfinder to her eye.

'What guy?'

She kept her camera angled on the pool. 'The young guy with blond hair, wearing shorts and a vest.'

'His name's Otto,' he said in a level voice, rising from his chair. 'Like you said, he was here to clean the pool.'

'But who is he?'

'A kid from the farm down below.'

'A friend of yours?'

She turned. Was there a restrained irony there, he wondered? He felt a smarting heat in his neck. It was possible that she had seen something that day when she left the house in a rush, appalled by his old photographs, and went down to Montreux to catch the train. He had gone that same evening to Le Mazot. What if she'd hung around and caught sight of him?

With a grin, Marianna came back along the terrace. She put down her camera and pulled out her phone. She typed into it.

A song began to play. She turned the phone round so that he could see the screen. It was the scene from *Cabaret* with the boy from the Hitler Youth singing 'Tomorrow Belongs to Me'.

'That's who he reminds me of.'

Something about the way he was staring at her caused her grin to fade. She stopped the song.

'He does jobs around the town,' he said at last, straining to sound casual. 'He dug Betty's grave last year. He works sometimes at a bar on the Route de Caux, on the way into Montreux.'

'That old Hansel and Gretel place where no one goes? I thought I recognised him. I heard it was a meeting spot for the Union démocratique du centre.'

'The owner's an old queer alcoholic. Never there. Otto keeps it going for him out of' – Thomas set down his glass and gave a shrug – 'love, I guess.'

He pulled out his phone and typed a message. A reply came within seconds.

'I have to go out,' he said. 'Just for an hour.'

*

Thomas descended the steps to the mountain path. He passed along corridors of foliage and open ridges. The afternoon was warm, but with a breeze to temper the heat. The path turned into a road. He glanced up to see a strip of glass and concrete slicing through the conifers. He had an instinct that Marianna was watching him through her telescopic lens, but he was too far away to see.

He had said too much. Told her things he shouldn't have. And yet, he could tell, she regarded his honesty with scepticism, as though it were just another mode of performance. A way of deflecting enquiries, of bouncing back an image of himself.

He came to a bend. A meadow tumbled over the mountainside. Two barns, timber structures with red-tiled roofs, glowed in the sunshine. They had always been there, just as they appeared now. Hadn't he hidden inside one of them as a boy? Those barns belonged to the past, and yet here they were, as real and concrete as anything he'd seen. On an impulse, he ran – sprinted along the road between high walls of pines. He didn't care if a car swung around the next bend.

The past. What was it? A collection of images in his head? It was gone for ever, irrecoverable, and yet he could feel it. The view broke open again. He stopped to recover his breath, clasping his hands on his knees. In the distance, Lake Geneva was a giant blue eye. It gave him a feeling of deep, excited longing – a longing that he knew wouldn't be satisfied by feeling the water on his skin, by hearing it splash, by drinking it . . .

*

The town rose into view. From a distance, Thomas's eye alighted on the pinnacle of the Église du Sacré-Coeur, a stone cruciform. He had been confirmed there at the age of eleven. The church, with its muscular carven Christ and stench of incense, had made him aware for the first time of what it could feel like to be profane. To respond not to the liturgy, but to the sex and brutality that were everywhere in the building – in the agonised martyrs, in the svelte angels – beneath the thinnest veil of solemnity.

He had returned to Montreux many times. The town had a way of flinging him out and reeling him back, this funny *elsewhere* place with its overlapping casts of characters: the retirees, the jazz aficionados, the moneyed, the respectable. But only two of his returns had the character of homecomings. There was the time, seven years earlier, when he had left New York and come here to build the house. And there was the day in the summer of 1998 that his mind had learned to conceal the way a magician holds an object inside his cuff. The memory belonged to this very stretch of road.

He had been nearing the end of his year in Düsseldorf. His life had become concentrated, like a single spot of focus in a blurry photograph, in the curtained room above Claude's gallery. At the academy, his days passed in a trance. Claude was the only person who mattered, practically the only person he spoke to. No one else seemed real. The relationship had become like a drug. As Thomas walked early one morning along the Rhine, on his way from Platanenstrasse to the student lodging that he barely used, he was able to see himself from a fractional remove. He told himself that he was in thrall to Claude Berlins. He was still attracted to Claude, but the nights above the gallery were becoming too loaded with feeling. The anticipation and release were a kind of violence, and the release was only ever temporary. He fed off Claude's attention and feared Claude's ridicule. One day, instead of going to the academy, he had sat in the public library and studied a book of poems by Sappho, memorising lines, just so that he could make a few casual references – and Claude had hardly noticed.

Contemplating the yellow waters of the Rhine that morning, Thomas told himself that he needed solitude for a while, or a simpler kind of company. His mother's banal questions, his father's self-satisfied opinions. Besides, he was running out of money and would soon be without a place to live. He thought of Lorna. Their time in London already seemed far away; it was like a remembered dream, something he might begin to invent and reshape as memory failed. He knew that she had given up the child and gone to New York (he had heard the news from a mutual friend), but he had no way of tracking her down.

He decided to go home to Montreux. It would just be for a month or so, until he could save some money and find a studio in Düsseldorf. Claude accepted the news with ease, saying that a month was nothing. He had a gallery to run, a show to sell.

On his first morning back in Montreux, Thomas went down to the lake. He swam, feeling the sun on his shoulders through the cold water. At the point when he'd gone almost too far, he raced for the shore in a sprint of front crawl. Afterwards, walking up the Route des Monts, at the place where the road began to incline more steeply, he saw a figure approaching from the other direction. A well-dressed man; his linen suit was pressed and pale as bone.

It was as if Claude had materialised from nowhere, in subtly different form. He seemed more domineering in the prettiness of the resort town.

'So, this is where you live?' were his first words. 'Not in the town itself?'

'Above it,' Thomas replied. 'A long way up.'

Claude absorbed the information with parted lips. Thomas wondered how far up the mountain Claude had walked – whether he had set eyes on their house. Claude looked towards the town and explained that he had taken a room at the Montreux Palace. He had decided to close the gallery for a month, possibly longer.

In the weeks that followed, they spent their days by the pool at the hotel, making up stories about the other guests, or lying in bed and watching the lake change colour through the balcony doors. Thomas lied to his parents about where he was going. Basking on sun loungers, they talked of going to Morocco. Claude told Thomas about a house he had found the previous summer, while driving through the desert.

'It could be a small museum, with gardens. Buildings on multiple levels, some of them made from red mud. All joined by tiled steps. Orange trees . . . It's an old garrison – what's known as a *ksour*.'

'I could design new sets of tiles,' Thomas said. 'Islamic, geometric—'

'You're a painter,' Claude interrupted, rolling onto his front and adjusting the waistline of his swimming trunks. 'Not an artisan. An *artist*. Remember that you have a talent. And a purpose.'

Two different systems of logic were at work. Their days together in Montreux were endless and numbered. They knew that Claude would go back to the gallery in the autumn, but the fact was rarely mentioned. One night in September, they leaned together on the railing that bordered the lake, watching the sunset.

'This is all the time left to us,' Claude said. 'This summer.'

'Why?'

'I have to go back to Düsseldorf – to the gallery. Back to my life.'

'But why can't this carry on? I could live with you—'

Claude shook his head. 'That isn't the life I want. It's not what you want either. You're not a hausfrau. Relationships' – his eyes skimmed the surface of the lake – 'aren't for people like me and you. They're a comfort blanket – bourgeois. If you want to live, and succeed, and go beyond all *this*' – he looked back towards the town – 'you need to be free.'

'I could get a studio in Düsseldorf.' Thomas had dreamed up the scenario already: a cheap warehouse space on the Rhine, and Lorna coming to visit.

'Get your own life. You're a painter, think of your lineage. Rothko, Motherwell, Clyfford Still – New York is the place for you.'

Claude touched Thomas on the shoulder. A firm, sustained clasp. Thomas leaned close until their faces were virtually touching. He listened to the birds over the lake and drank in the smell of Claude's cologne, which seemed to come from the silk scarf he had wound around his neck, over the top of his T-shirt. A design of grey and blue cubes. Thomas skimmed his lips along the fabric, then sank his face into it.

They stayed like that for a moment only, before Claude stepped back. He pulled the scarf from his neck, smiling blankly. In another second, he had flung it out on the water.

'Why did you do that?' Thomas watched it sinking. 'I would have had it.'

'You worship *things*. It was only a scarf.'

*

Thomas had come to Le Mazot. He wandered into the main bar. It smelled of wood and beer. Five old men were drinking around a table, engaged in a good-natured quarrel. They were working men, not affluent Montreusians. Men like his father.

Otto met Thomas's eye and poured him a beer. Thomas sat outside and waited for nearly an hour.

At last, the men left in a shambling file. Otto switched off the lights inside. *Fermé* flipped into the window.

Thomas passed behind the empty bar. Otto had disappeared.

He went through the door and down the stairs. The basement bar was empty, too, but the light was on. He inhaled the musty odour of the room as he began to remove his clothes, folding them in a pile – jeans, underpants, socks – catching sight of himself in the mirrored walls.

Unbuttoning his shirt, he became aware that Otto was in the doorway behind him, watching. Upstairs, Otto had been dressed in his usual clothes – a loose T-shirt, beige shorts. Now he was virtually naked and strapped in a kind of harness.

Wearing only his opened shirt, Thomas faced him. Otto was wearing lederhosen. Grey leather crossed his torso in an H shape, with silver buckles at the intersections. The muscles of his upper legs and stomach swelled around the straps and breeches. There were floral forms on the leather shorts, embroidered in silver thread.

Thomas planted his hands on Otto's stomach and held them there, against the warm skin. He slid his fingers inside the leather waistband. The space within was hot and confined. His finger-tips passed over bristling hair.

Otto lowered his arms. Lazily, with one hand, he opened the double buttons of his shorts to release his cock. Thomas knelt. Veins ran like rivulets. He touched the domed smoothness and then slid his hand further down – gripped softly, then hard. He took the weight on his tongue, sealing his lips around the head, and ran his hand to the base. At the furthest recess of his throat, he felt its mass and taste.

Otto flung his head back and groaned.

The room was as warm as a sauna. Sweat was tickling Thomas's face. The sweat on his hand passed to Otto's cock, mixing with the sleeker fluid that oozed from the tip. He drew his fingers down, repeating the motion over and over, allowing the coarse hair to buffet his hand. With his other hand he clasped Otto's buttocks through the shorts, pressed them as if he might puncture the leather with his fingertips.

Otto let out a whining sigh. Thomas sat back. There were hot shooting splashes, too quick to see before he felt them land on his shirtfront with pattering thuds.

*

He took a roundabout route back to the mountain path, through the town. He wanted to avoid the Route des Monts. In the window of a women's boutique, a man in a skimpy T-shirt was fiddling with a gauze dress stitched with metallic flowers. A headless mannequin lay on a velvet stage.

He set off up the hill. The road steepened and the houses drew further apart. He breathed deeply as he climbed. The day seemed to glare brighter. All around, the light was clustering, building like charge in the grass, in the leaves.

It had been like this the afternoon of the Serpentine summer party, the previous July – Hyde Park a reservoir of green light.

Before the party, he and Luca had gone for a walk along the lake. Luca had run his hand over the pitted stone of the giant Henry Moore arch, on the section where the sunlight was strongest. Thomas had walked behind, conscious of the picture: Luca framed by the aperture of the sculpture, the water beyond. Luca seemed to be conscious, in turn, of being watched. He stood there motionless, holding the pose.

'I hate these art world occasions,' Thomas said, to kill the stasis. He felt hot in his linen jacket.

'Then why are you going?'

'I have a show opening in September. Did you forget?'

Luca turned and took one of Thomas's hands, then the other, and pulled him near – smiling at Thomas's momentary resistance. He was wearing a T-shirt beneath his jacket, the neckline of which dipped to reveal his smooth chest. The T-shirt was thin, like crepe paper. Thomas felt old. The brightness of the day, and the greenness, were a reminder of lost time. *Elegiac* was the word that came into his head. Claude had used it a lot. Luca belonged to a different genre. A happier, more vigorous one. This thing felt impossible. There were twenty years between them. Perhaps that was all there was to it.

'Claude wants me to be there at the party, getting noticed,' Thomas said, uncoupling their hands.

'*Claude*,' said Luca with disdain. 'Wait with me. What's the hurry? Let's walk for a while.'

Thomas gave in and walked on.

'Are you still thinking about what happened that night in Vauxhall?' Luca said. 'It doesn't matter, you know. You were high. I was high.'

'I'm not thinking about anything.'

They came to the rose garden. Entering by a gate, they passed along paths bordered by flowers as gaudy as confetti.

'This is the Hyde Park cruising spot.' Luca flashed Thomas a look.

'It always was,' Thomas replied, looking ahead down the path.

'We could be cruising right now,' Luca said, with amusement. 'I could be your catch.'

How experienced was he? Thomas wondered – how innocent? Luca wanted Thomas to believe he'd lived in Felliniesque underworlds. Was any of it real? Luca's lack of restraint, his freedom from embarrassment, everything that Thomas had loved at the start, had turned into an irritant in the summer heat. The boy seemed to believe that he existed apart from reality, as if life's rules didn't apply to him. He'd had it too easy. His fearlessness was just another form of naivety. This had to end, Thomas told himself. And yet Luca's presence was like a spell, even now.

Luca had taken his hands again – the same luring motion as before – and this time he pulled Thomas into him. Luca's eyes had closed. He brought a hand to the back of Thomas's head and held it, running his fingers to the base of Thomas's neck.

Many hours later, after the party, they took a taxi back to Kennington. Their night together passed like a dream, such that Thomas could only recall random snapshots of the whole. Luca's lower lip, wet and trembling. The way he shut his eyes to kiss. The cavern of his armpit. The lack of shame – a smiling, sexy candour – and Thomas's own dismal inability.

Thomas woke in the night amid a turmoil of sheets. Luca was strewn across the bed, startling in his naked availability. The doors to the balcony were open. Beyond, the night was as still as death.

*

There was a dull ache in his calves by the time he reached the steps to the house. He felt weak from the climb. He had been gone for hours. Marianna had probably been looking for him all over the Rochers de Naye. She would surely have given up and left by now. He mounted the steps slowly, glancing at the square concrete mass of the studio protruding from the top of the promontory. Its outward-facing wall was inset slightly, like a removable panel.

At the top of the steps, the reverse side of the house resembled a bunker sunk into the earth. A concrete wall contained the steel front door. The sun had retreated from this side of the mountain already, but the metal was warm to the touch. He entered the code on the numerical lock: 10086. The door unbolted with a whirr and swung open. The space between the antechamber and the far window was dim. At once, he saw her camera on its tripod – standing at the centre of the window, silhouetted by the mellowing day.

'Marianna,' he called, walking into the room.

He stopped. His lightbox, the one he kept downstairs, was lying on the floor beside one of the couches. It had been plugged in. Its rectangle of white light was like a window. Littered on the fluorescent surface were photographic slides, at least thirty of them. Bending over, he recognised the little panels of colour. She had been rifling through his old materials. To one side of the lightbox was an iPhone in a turquoise case. His heart went queasily light, before he remembered that he had wiped the memory.

He went on a few steps and saw that she had deposited books all over the couches and the coffee table. Art books from his library, most of them flung open. He heard something at the end of the room. A persistent rattling.

'Marianna,' he called again.

Beyond the bookshelves, in front of the door to the studio, she was kneeling on the floor. She had found his box of spare keys, the one he kept in a kitchen drawer, and was trying each key in the lock, rattling the handle.

'There's nothing in there,' he said. 'I burned them all.'

'I can't figure you the fuck out,' she said, continuing to tug at the handle. Her hair was hanging over her temples so that he couldn't see her face.

'Stop,' he said. 'Come here.' He put out his hand.

Ignoring him, she rose and walked to the centre of the room – straight to her camera. She twisted it on the tripod like the head of a doll, pointing it at him.

'Where have you been?' She was glaring with a savageness he hadn't seen in her before, or never so clearly.

'The time got away from me, I'm sorry.'

She moved behind the camera and watched him through the viewfinder.

'What's that all over your shirt?'

He looked down. The material had soaked through in places. He could feel it sticking to his skin. He brought one finger to his chest, as if he were touching a wound.

'Who are you, really?' she said, apparently half to herself.

He glanced at the camera. 'You've seen everything there is to see. You've ransacked the place.'

'I didn't come here to see a house.'

'All right, then.' Thomas kept one hand on his chest and bowed his head. Slowly, with a swivel of the shoulders, he eased the shirt off. He drew one arm free, then the other, and allowed the shirt to slide away. Across his chest was a dark red stripe, running diagonally.

'What happened to you?'

The red light of the camera flashed. He touched each elbow with the opposite hand and kept still. His hair had swung over one side of his brow. In his mind's eye, he was a model – thin and androgynous – or a woman in a painting he'd once loved, holding herself before the artist's gaze. The stance was artful, and then, by a fractional shift, it was incidental – not a stance at all, just the posture of a boy uncertain of his body. He looked straight at the lens and had the sensation of breaking clear of the surface of a pool and taking a desperate breath.

Embarrassment returned. He laughed to hide it. His arms dropped to his sides.

'How's that for a screen test?'

She unscrewed the camera from the tripod. For a moment, he thought that she would hurl it at him. But she just switched it off and placed it on the floor, then began to dismantle the tripod. Behind her, through the window, Lake Geneva had turned pale. Darker bands, frilled with ripples, cut across the smoothness. A motorboat was trailed by a waterskier. He felt a plummeting sadness.

'I'm sorry.' He bent down and picked up the shirt. 'I'm sorry for running away. I'll make it up to you.'

She heaved her shoulders into a long shrug. 'I just don't think this is going to work.'

The skier had fallen. The boat idled on the water. He sat down on a couch between the books, giving in to his exhaustion.

'Come to Venice in April. It'll be different there. It's going to be the climax of everything.'

'But you don't have a show.'

'I've made a show in less time than this before. I'll do it again. You'll see. As soon as I have an idea, and some time—'

She tutted. 'Time is *all* you have out here.'

'Usually, yes. But I have to go to New York next week, for the Deborah Goffman Memorial Gala.' He delivered the words with mock reverence.

She laid aside the tripod and came towards him. 'The Goffman Gala? Everyone goes to that. Couldn't you have got me an invite?'

'It's just a ritzy benefit. Believe me, I don't want to go. I hate the art world. I'm an outsider to all that. But I'm the guest of honour.'

'Try being me. Then you'll know what it feels like to be an outsider. I've been passed over by virtually every gallery in the world.' She sat down heavily on the opposite couch. 'Is Fritz Schein going to be there?'

'He'll be running the show, from what I've heard.'
'Then do something for me. One thing. *Please.*'

*

In the evening, they sat in the cinema. Thomas touched a button and the lights dimmed. He had prepared the film the night before. The title credits blazed through the darkness against a backdrop of raining diamonds. The score was bluesy and languorous, teetering on schmaltzy. He had heard it many times. Hundreds, probably. But it still roused a soaring longing in him.

Directed by Douglas Sirk.

He relaxed into an alert torpor.

A beach scene, Coney Island, 1947. A blonde woman in a pink headscarf had lost her little girl. Minutes later, all smiling relief, she found the child under the pier in the company of an older child and a Black lady called Annie Johnson. The girls ran off to play. The women sat and talked. Lora Meredith, the blonde, assumed that Annie was a childminder. Annie explained that her daughter, Sarah Jane, resembled her father.

'He was practically white. He left before she was born.'

In the same instant, Annie was offering her services as a maid to Lora.

'Seems to me, Miss Meredith, I'm just right for you. You wouldn't have to pay no wages.'

The scene changed. Annie and her daughter had moved in with Lora. Thomas watched with a benign, forgiving disbelief. Would Annie's daughter really have been able to pass as white? Would Lora really have taken in Annie and the girl just like that? But it was only a story, after all, and the movie streamed on, dissolving his doubts in Technicolor. Every frame was a thing of beauty, exactly lit, a montage of surface and depth.

Lora Meredith was a down-on-her-luck widow who craved

success as an actress. She was loved by a man called Steve, a photographer.

'My camera could easily have a love affair with you,' Steve said, holding her chin and turning her face with presumptuous tenderness.

Lora loved him back, but she turned love aside for the sake of her dream.

'Maybe I should see things as they really are, and not as I want them to be,' she said, crying under Steve's cool gaze. She wore a pearl necklace and black frock, its neckline carving her head and chest into a portrait bust.

Thomas thought of his life in New York. Cast out by Claude into the world, he had resolved to make it on the art scene. Nothing else had mattered. Becoming successful was a way of repairing things with Lorna – and a way of holding onto Claude's regard, even from a distance.

Steve wanted Lora to give up her ambitions and marry him.

'Steve, you don't know me at all. I still love the theatre.' Lora rested her head on his shoulder, closing her eyes. Her lips were scarlet. Her hair projected from a shawl like a strip of lit platinum. 'I want more. Everything. Maybe too much.'

Marianna leaned over to Thomas and whispered: 'I've heard you say that.'

He experienced a mild jolt. He had forgotten she was there. He kept his eyes on the screen.

Lora soared into stardom. She pretended to fall in love with a Broadway director who gave her a break. A decade flew past in a succession of marquee signs and magazine covers.

Now she was living in a beautiful house upstate. There were shelves of leather-bound books, a vast stone fireplace, a baby grand piano. The place was a cliché of mid-century luxury, with painted panoramas behind the windows.

He was all too aware now of Marianna's presence beside him.

He could sense her passing judgement. She considered the film a sickly-rich affair. She wasn't attending to the details.

And he could admit, there *was* something overwrought about the story. An excess of ambition, desire and pain. But the look of the film was its own reality. The glowing surfaces, mirror images, fabrics, *things* – not a reflective barrier, but a world you could enter and be defined by. Colour was a source of crisis. Annie's daughter, Sarah Jane, now grown up, was more ashamed than ever of her mother's race. Sarah Jane had a secret boyfriend. When he discovered that her mother was Black, he beat the girl up on a dark sidewalk, slapping her with all his strength until she fell in a gleaming puddle.

Lora was lying on a couch, attended by faithful Annie. The heroine wore a pink gown with grey fur around the shoulders and forearms. She lit a cigarette. Annie, ailing now, spoke about her plans for her funeral and the friends she wanted to come.

'It never occurred to me you have any friends,' said Lora to her saintly maid.

'Miss Lora,' Annie said, 'you never asked.'

How much, Thomas wondered, did Marianna know about him? He had told her about his childhood. Perhaps she knew about Otto, or had guessed. But these were no more than fragments. Why hadn't she asked more about his art? Why hadn't he told her more? He wondered where Lorna was, right now. At home in the East Village, probably, without Justine. He tried to remember her face, and his mind threw back a confused, oscillating image. Lorna in the photobooth; Lorna as she'd been in London a few months earlier.

Lora Meredith rose from the couch and her plush gown swayed behind her. The material flashed and rippled, falling away from her waist in broad striations. The colour, alternating between mid-pink and rosy white, was the same as in one of the Pink Paintings.

'You painted her dress,' Marianna said.

He thought of the slides he had seen scattered on the lightbox upstairs. His archive from the 1990s. A sensation of relief and scorching exposure came over him. It was like a car door being opened in the heat of the desert. But hadn't he wanted to be found out? He had left the albums of slides lying around, the last time she came.

There was a pause – the dialogue continued – before he answered.

'Yes.'

'Your Pink Paintings were based on that dress?'

'That dress and others like it. All from movies.'

'I saw the slides.'

'Then you know. You know more than anyone.'

Claude's words returned to him: *Be an abstract painter.* So insistent, so absurd; why should he hide like this?

He brought his head close. 'I was never an abstract painter. Just a painter of details – surfaces. A miniaturist, although I work on a large scale. Everything I've ever painted is a small fragment of a larger view. All my works in the nineties came from films. I froze the frames' – he pressed pause, arresting the view of Lora in her gown – 'and made photographs. Then I painted them.'

'And after that? What about the darker pictures – the blue and purple ones?'

'They're all images of one kind or another. Skies, water, shadows. Things I've photographed. Things I've seen. Those paintings in London were the sky at twilight, interrupted by a tree branch or the cable of a cable car. I've found that by abstracting the details just a little, I can make the sources invisible. You stop *seeing* them as pictures.'

He pressed play. The film continued, shifting to a nocturnal scene. A girl ran across a lawn to a waiting car.

'I adore the way Sirk does the night,' he said. 'So artificial, that blue light. But utterly believable.'

'So, all this stuff about you being an avowed abstractionist, non-representational, the heir to Rothko—'

'It's a lie. But a seductive one. Who wants to know that I'm obsessed with the play of light on a dress, or the colour of Lake Geneva at sunset?'

He gazed at the film without hearing the dialogue.

'This doesn't go in your film,' he said. 'Nobody can know.'

23

6 March, 07.53. New York

Leo was on his knees.

His head was close to the ground. The beast's breath was hot and rancid. He felt its bristling muzzle on his ears and neck. Its teeth were piercing his scalp like filed fingernails. Limbs closed around him, pinning him down, penning him in.

The beast was trying to fuck him. Its erection struck his thigh with the force of snapping elastic. He tried to get up, but his knees wouldn't obey. He flung back his hands and kicked with one leg, but the animal was nimble. His foot skimmed a matted flank. The fur was like mink, only drenched in oily grime.

A crackling filled his ears. He brought his hands forward again, dropping them to the floor, and in the same moment he was aware of a blinding pain. It surged from the pit of his groin through his pelvis. The animal was inside him. He felt his body revolt and submit in less than a second. Where had the fight been?

Exhalations gusted around his face and neck in time to the clumsy shoves. The beast was all around him, inside and outside, invading and ingesting him with its whole vile body. Its mouth was on the crown of his head, the teeth sinking down to his skull.

Leo howled and hurled himself forward, just as a warm rush was blasting out, spraying, pooling . . .

The sheets around his legs were wet.

He lay for a long time in the cooling spillage, breathing hard, staring at the stucco swags and garlands on the ceiling. Sunlight, breaking through a gap in the drapes, flecked the edges of the moulding.

At last, he yanked his limbs across the damp mattress, heaving himself into a sitting position.

The telephone on his bedside cabinet blasted out a ring. He snatched the receiver.

'Yes?'

'Mr Goffman' – it was Bonita, calling from the front lobby – 'the shipping company have arrived.'

'Who's here? Why didn't you wake me?'

'They're early. Your new painting is being delivered, the Thomas Haller.'

'It's *here*? The Haller painting?' He was wide awake.

'The men are going to hang it next to your Agnes Martin.'

In the dimness, Leo saw bearded faces chuckling in the ormolu of the mantelpiece clock. Above the fireplace, directly across from his bed, a Baroque mirror with a twisting frame rose ten feet to the ceiling.

'No – have them bring it to me. I want it on the wall in here, right opposite the bed, in place of the mirror. And Bonita, another thing.' He wedged the phone under his chin and rummaged on the top of the cabinet. 'I have some rings of Deborah's. The sapphire, the ruby, the etched gold one with the platinum. Take them to the jeweller. I want them expanded and reset.'

He replaced the phone and dropped the rings back on the cabinet. They made a clinking sound, like coins.

The phone rang again.

'Well, what is it? Are they bringing the painting?'

'Leo, this is Gloria.'

'What?'

'Gloria Goffman, your sister-in-law.'

Gloria Goffman. He hadn't heard her voice in years. The

starchy intonation was a knife straight out of the past, stabbing through his equipoise. The wetness around his buttocks had turned horribly cold.

'Ira wanted you to know,' Gloria's voice went on, 'that he was elected yesterday to the American Academy of Arts and Sciences.'

There was something gruesome about her self-control. A measured tenor that was also strident, belligerent, malign.

'Why are you calling me?'

'Because of Ira. He's been elected to the American Academy. He wanted his brother to know.'

Leo could hear a man's voice in the background. Ira's voice. *'Is he there? Did you tell him?'*

'You ring me on his behalf,' Leo said, mimicking Gloria's solemnity, 'to tell me this?'

'Ira wanted you to know,' she repeated. 'It's an important day for him – for the family. You're still his brother, Leo.'

He thought of Ira's life at Columbia in all its liberal dignity. Great minds, ethical thoughts, a little piece of Eden around the Memorial Library.

Bonita had opened the bedroom door. She stepped back to reveal two youthful men in polo shirts. Behind them was a tall plywood crate, positioned endways. He beckoned them in.

'*The American Academy*,' he proclaimed into the mouthpiece, keeping his attention on the men as they steered the crate through the door on wheels. He jabbed his hand at the mirror and waved. 'Well, it beats me. Ira was never what you'd call a *scholar*.'

'What do you mean, Leo?'

'*What's he saying?*' Ira demanded in the background. '*Did he say I'm not a scholar?*'

'Not like our grandfather. The great Max Goffman of die Universität Wien. Now *he* was a scholar. A genius of economic theory. He should have won the Nobel, but there are politics to these things. As for dear old Ira, he never came close. We all know it. Let's not pretend.'

Sitting against his pillows, he gazed at the men in their trim shirts and jeans, wheeling the crate to the centre of the room and placing ladders either side of the fireplace. Would they smell the piss?

'Your brother—' Gloria began.

Ira's voice was abruptly clear down the line: *'Tell him! Tell him I made the Academy.'* There was a stuttering, cackling sound. He had begun to weep.

'For the love of God, Leo,' came Gloria's voice – less controlled than before. 'Your own brother.'

'Tell him I'm the Jacob K. Heirston Professor of Linguistics!' Ira's words fought against his sobs.

The men on their ladders were inspecting the fixings on the back of the mirror.

'Just get it off the wall,' Leo yelled, feeling a rush of delirious excitement. 'Get the damned thing down. I want the painting up there now. Fuck the mirror, I don't care if you break it.'

'I'm sorry?' said Gloria. 'Are you there, Leo?'

'Professor,' Leo declared, 'must mean something different from back in our grandfather's day. Professor Max Goffman. Now *there* was an academic, the like of whom—'

Ira's sobbing had become uncontrollable. It was a hideous, hilarious sound.

'Your brother is a great academic, Leo,' said Gloria. 'And he can hear everything you're saying.'

How that woman loathes me, Leo thought. And how he loathed her back. The passage of years had done nothing to diminish the feeling. With his free hand, he reached under the covers.

'Gloria – the only difference between my brother and a great academic is that he isn't one.'

He replaced the phone and watched as the men tilted the vast mirror off its fixings and bore it down with tensed faces, descending their ladders in painstaking tandem. As the glass lurched downward, he saw himself reflected. His legs were thin ridges beneath the sheets. The soaked area was like muslin. His legs, genitals and stomach were blearily visible through the translucence. He was surprised by how small he appeared in that desert of sodden silk.

24

The car swooshed along, jerking to a halt at lights or where the traffic jammed. Thomas thought of the years he had lived in the East Village and SoHo. The names evoked a blur of parties, bars and studios, streaming with people. He had lived with a permanent hangover, but it had been an energising nausea.

He had entered a sort of trance, observant but woozy, by the time the taxi pulled up at the Pierre. He allowed himself to be directed through the hotel entrance, into the chequered lobby, over to the desk.

'Room one-eight-seven, sir,' said the man at reception, handing him a keycard.

Another man, younger than the last, accompanied him in the elevator.

Should he try to sleep? It seemed a dangerous option: the alcohol from the flight was metabolising. He wouldn't wake up if he lay down.

Inside his room, he went straight to the minibar, expecting the bellboy to leave.

'I have a note for you, sir, from another guest.'

Thomas came forward. Who, other than Sylvia Rosso, knew he was here? He took the folded paper from the man's hand.

Below the Pierre letterhead was handwriting in block capitals. *ROOM 91.*

He recognised the slanting script.

*

It took several journeys up and down in the elevator before he found the right floor. He passed along the corridor at a dreamy stroll that contradicted his thudding heart.

He tried a handle only to find it locked, then saw that it was the wrong door. He took a few extra paces to where the correct numerals gleamed out. This time, the door gave way.

A short passageway led into a high-ceilinged room. The light was low. Between draped windows, Claude Berlins sat in an armchair. He wore a bathrobe that reached close to his bare feet, a black silk gown adorned with gold palm leaves. His hair was newly cropped and his face was darker than usual, more deeply tanned and shaded by the gloom; and yet his eyes were clear and large.

Thomas allowed the door to swing closed behind him.

'What are you doing here?'

'I wanted to see you.' Claude's voice was level except for an almost indiscernible jaggedness. 'It's been a long time.'

'I thought you were in Rome.'

'I will be. I'm flying tonight.'

'And this was your plan, to meet me first – in this place?'

Claude smiled dimly. 'Why not? Don't you remember how we used to meet at hotels?'

'They were never as flashy as this one.'

'No. I didn't want to be seen. I suppose it was very nineteenth century of me.' Claude cast his gaze around the ceiling before returning it to Thomas. 'You look tired. Your hair is greyer.'

'I'm not going to dye it, if that's what you think.'

'You look a mess, Tom.' Claude rose from the chair. 'You can't go to the Goffman Gala like that. Here—' He strode to where Thomas was standing, flipped open the door of a wardrobe and drew out a long coat of what looked like vicuña. 'Wear this. Keep it.' He thrust it into Thomas's arms.

'You've been distant from me,' he went on, walking back into the room. 'More distant since London. Since the night your show opened. Your comeback!'

'You know I'm grateful.'

'I saved you the embarrassment of a half-sold show when I bought those paintings in. Why won't you tell me what you're painting for Venice?'

'I can't talk about my art, you know that.'

'I'm your gallerist now, don't you think I should know? You hardly speak to me.'

'I hardly speak to anyone.' Thomas contemplated the folds of the curtains. 'I started some paintings. I destroyed them. They weren't working.'

Claude came close. Their bodies were practically touching.

'Is that whole affair – what happened in London – getting to you? That boy—'

'No.' Thomas felt his teeth give a single knock.

'You haven't said anything, have you, to anyone?'

'Of course not.'

'Not to Lorna Bedford?'

'Why would you ask that? *No.*'

'Good. I told you nothing would happen, and nothing has.'

Claude rested a hand on Thomas's upper arm. Thomas stepped back, breaking the contact.

'Don't resist me,' Claude said with mock portentousness. 'Don't run away. It's absurd to try.' His eyes were alive with feeling. 'I'm here for you, Thomas, I always have been. Have you forgotten?'

'Forgotten what?'

'The way I noticed you in the crowd – saw something in you. The moody art student who kept turning up at my openings.'

'It seems so long ago, all of that.'

'A one-room gallery in a European city, and no attachments. I miss it. The simplicity of it. I've created a monster in Galerie Claude Berlins. I have no choice but to keep feeding it.'

'It's you, the thing you're feeding.'

'Maybe. But now you're part of it, at last. Forget all that stuff about being over the hill. Your market never suffered. And we'll make you a star again. The leading abstract painter in the world. I have plans for you, Thomas – for us!'

He felt Claude's consciousness envelop him. A sensation of grief and idiotic mirth possessed him, then went.

'Got any whisky?'

Claude indicated a mahogany cabinet. Concealed within was a refrigerator stocked with miniatures. Thomas took one with unsteady fingers. Opening it, he drank from the neck of the bottle.

'You know,' he began, 'I used to think for years that you didn't really give a shit about me, except for the hooking up.'

Claude hadn't moved. His gaze was serene.

'I never gave up on you. I was with you; didn't you feel it? I was waiting.'

'Waiting for what?'

'For you to come out of your chrysalis.'

Thomas drank again, finishing the bottle. He walked a few steps towards the window, feeling Claude's eyes on the back of his head.

'I thought . . .' He fell silent.

'Thought what?'

'That when you began to represent me, things might be different.'

'Different?'

Thomas turned. There was a hint of humour, or possibly contempt, in the lines of Claude's face.

'We're not conventional people, Thomas. Greatness requires sacrifice. I told you that. What were you thinking?' He began to laugh. 'That we'd set up home on Fire Island?'

'I don't know.'

'You have a hankering for petty comforts. You always did.'

'It must be the Swiss peasant in me.'

'Besides,' Claude said, 'I could never be with an artist. A dealer, a great one, needs to be impartial.'

With delicate force, he took the empty bottle from Thomas's hand. Dropping it in a wastepaper bin, he sat back down and spread his hands on the armrests.

'I heard that you're having a film made about you.'

'How did you hear?'

'I get to know of things. Is this a good idea? This filmmaker, this *artist* – whoever she is – probably resents you. What does she even know about you?'

'She's building a picture.'

'And how complete do you mean that picture to be?'

'It's not your concern.'

'Oh, but it is. Your image is my concern. I represent you now. I could have organised a profile in the *New Yorker*. I could have asked Tom Ford to make a film.' He laughed again – a brittle, hacking sound. 'You'll be posing nude for art students next. Is that what you want to be? Somebody's bitch?' He spat the word.

Thomas took another whisky from the fridge.

'What are you going to Rome for?'

'I'm opening a gallery there.' Claude's words seemed hollow, like an absurd cover for what was really being communicated. 'Do you want a glass? Ice?'

'No, thanks.'

'It's a beautiful space, in a vault of the Castel Sant'Angelo. We're showing late works by Kounellis. How I love Italy . . .'

Claude rose from the chair and bowed his head. A scratching sound issued from his throat. Thomas wondered if he was starting to sob, then realised that the sound was one of irrepressible glee. When Claude looked up, his face was warped with exhilaration.

'Building the London gallery has opened my eyes. There are opportunities all over Europe. New collectors. I'm expanding my horizons. Venice! I'd love to open a space on the Giudecca. Paris, too – I've found a warehouse in the Marais. And then, Switzerland . . .' He stepped closer. 'Montreux.'

The pleasure in his expression was mingled with sadness and regret and other feelings that Thomas couldn't distil. They were standing inches apart, at the edge of the room. Thomas was conscious of being observed up close. The consciousness brought with it a quiver of nostalgia.

Claude extended a hand. Involuntarily, Thomas took it in his own. Claude grasped him hard. In the dimness, Claude's face was ageless, or multiple ages, seeming almost youthful before the tautness of the skin betrayed him and a fine webbing showed through. The room seemed to grow. The air glimmered as though the lights were failing. Claude let go, but his stare had grown acute. Slowly he spread his arms, unthreading the cord of his gown. The gold and black material split to disclose his body. It was taut – well-tended – but unmistakeably old. The muscles were half-concealed beneath a carapace of rippled skin. His erection was the single remnant of youth, solid as a tower, purplish and polished at the top, with a glaring black eyelet.

Thomas was voided of the raging, conflicted feelings of seconds earlier, sensing only the rush of whisky in his head. He watched as clear fluid beaded from the hole, swelling into a tiny marble that balanced on the tip. For a moment longer it grew, then it rolled off its perch and distended into a silklike strand that swayed in the air.

25

7 March, 19.14. New York

He felt a spray of rain as he stepped out of the taxi. Shouldering on the vicuña coat, he crossed Fifth Avenue. There was a crowd outside the Metropolitan Museum. It extended along the sidewalk. Out of the mass came the frantic cries of paparazzi.

A red carpet, bounded by ropes and railings, threaded its way through the crowd. An attendant waved Thomas onto the route. None of the celebrity-gazers was interested in him.

A man and woman glided onto the carpet in front of him. The woman wore a dress of platinum fronds – a broken net over her nudity.

At the call of a photographer, the couple fell into casual, artful poses. Flashes spattered like fireworks.

Nearing the steps, Thomas sensed that something was wrong: the crowd was noisier and angrier than it should have been. Among the gawkers was a hostile faction. He caught sight of a cardboard placard.

PUT GOFFMAN IN JAIL

The words were daubed in black freehand. They jumped up and down. Other words tottered on sticks.

JUSTICE FOR ANDREA
LEO GOFFMAN RACIST
ERADICATE THIS CREEP

This last imperative had been scrawled over a blown-up picture of Goffman, a rare image of his disinhibited grin.

The rain was intensifying. Thomas hurried up the steps.

Wailing broke out. He couldn't decipher words, only agonised noise. To his right was a young woman in a combat jacket and a wool hat. She had wrenched apart two segments of railing. She ran in front of him, holding up a sign on a pole.

MURDERER

The word had been spelled in bright red capitals.

She looked straight at him, her eyes shining.

'Murderer!'

Other people were streaming through the breach in the railings. Her followers. He tried to run and tripped. He was on his hands and knees, his wrists throbbing. The cardboard sign descended on his shoulder blades. He closed his eyes.

'Murderer!'

Scrambling to get up, he tripped again and his teeth bashed together. He braced himself for a stampede, groaning as the yells of the woman and other protestors – a growing band – tore through his head.

Security men were closing in.

'Stick him in jail!' the woman cried as the men pulled her back.

The noise was abating. Back on the street, cars were honking. Someone had begun to laugh. Thomas stayed where he'd fallen, his hands extended above his head and his legs stretched over the steps. He felt the pressure of someone's touch on his shoulder. It was too gentle – too gently persistent – to be an attacker. The hand eased him onto his back. He lay with his face to the sky and saw Lorna. Her face, caught in the glare of a floodlight, was pale above a black shirt, unbuttoned to reveal a necklace of square silver links. Her eyes were dark and sceptical.

'Thomas, are you all right?'

'I fell,' he gasped. It was a dazed, weary, witless statement of the obvious.

'Get up. You'll do.'

He felt her arms slide around his shoulders and under his knees, as if she meant to lift him.

'I'm sorry,' he whispered. 'I'm so sorry.'

'You'll do,' she repeated.

'Pose!' shouted a photographer from beyond the railing. Thomas looked for the source of the command, but all he saw was a cascade of flashes.

*

19.24

There was a mood of subdued intensity in the Great Hall. Voices rose in a roaring murmur to the arches and domes. Guests in ballgowns and tuxedos drifted towards the Grand Staircase or hovered in groups. They moved with the self-regard of party-goers, conscious of being looked at.

'It's just as well I found you,' Lorna said, raising her voice. 'Those protestors were ready to fuck you up. Who did you borrow the coat from, anyway?'

Thomas slid his hands into his pockets.

'How do you know it isn't mine?'

'You've changed, but not that much.'

He hadn't been at risk of serious harm, she thought. An overhyped protestor, full to bursting with hatred of Leo Goffman, had made Thomas a target. A middle-aged white man treading the red carpet in a fur coat: he had been a good enough proxy. Seeing Thomas at all had been the real surprise. They hadn't spoken since he'd called her in the car that day and told her about Berlins.

Servers waited with drinks. Glasses of champagne hung in

furrowed trays, effervescing beads on a giant abacus. Negronis glistened in tumblers.

'I'm starring in a film,' Thomas said, apparently wanting to lighten the mood. He took a cocktail and drank half of it in a gulp. 'Do you remember that artist who came to my London opening, Marianna Berger?'

'The video artist?'

'She came to visit me. That idea she had of making a film. I said yes.'

'Is that a good idea?'

'Why wouldn't it be?'

'It's not like you to open your house to a stranger.'

'No. I suppose. But things are different.' He sighed deeply, then glugged the rest of his drink. 'Don't you start to wonder – to worry – what it's all going to amount to? I've realised lately how alone I am, how short my time is. I've never kept a diary. There's no record of my life, except for random photos and my paintings – but what do they really tell you? What will people say about me, in the end? What will my memorial be?'

'No, I never think like that.'

'You're lucky, then.' He drifted a few steps ahead of her.

Milton Rogers, the fêted Hollywood producer, swept by.

'Lorna Bedford! When are you going to come see me at Paramount?'

He winked and sidled into the crowd.

'*Thomas Haller! Who would have thought?*'

Joel Blair, the perma-smiling critic, was striding over with hands outspread. He wore a yellow suit that accentuated his sunless pallor. He gave Thomas a kiss on each cheek and embraced Lorna.

'The old pro!' His glasses twinkled.

'Who are you calling old?' she said, with just enough levity to get away with it.

Joel simpered wordlessly and turned back to Thomas. '*So!* You're set to be the top lot in the auction tonight. And the *honouree*, I hear.'

Lorna followed his eyes to a painting that hung close to the main entrance. *Untitled*, 1995.

'Try telling that to the mob outside,' Thomas said. 'They wanted to kill me, not honour me. I knew that Goffman has his enemies, but this?'

Joel came closer. 'Didn't you hear? Leo ran down a woman on Fifth Avenue last year – put her in Mount Sinai. She's just died, after being in a coma for months.'

'Ran her down? Deliberately?'

'Well, that's the thing. What's *deliberate*? Those folks outside think it was. And even if he didn't do it on purpose' – Joel's voice grew conspiratorial – 'we all know that he's a bullying misogynistic prick.'

'Do we?' Lorna interjected. 'I mean – is he?'

Joel eyed her with suspicion. 'Fact is, he's managed to keep it out of the courts and out of the news, so no one knows what happened. That's why the protestors are mad.'

'And here we all are, guests at his party,' said Thomas.

'Well, I only came to write it up for *Artforum*.'

'The woman he ran over – is she Black?'

Joel's smile morphed from quizzical to crestfallen. 'Why would you ask that?'

'The signs out there. One of them said, *Leo Goffman Racist*.'

'Ah, well' – relief had spread over his face – 'that's because of his colonisation of Harlem. All the housing projects he's razed and turned into luxury condos.'

'Are my ears burning? Are they? Well?'

Leo had welled out of the depths of the room.

'The maestro!' Joel declared.

Leo seemed, to Lorna, to have grown in stature, but there was a volatility about his movements, an almost manic alertness, as if he'd dropped an amphetamine. A triangle of purple silk rose from the breast pocket of his tuxedo.

'The only maestro around here is this guy,' he said, pinning his eyes on Thomas. 'Our honouree! Your paintings are the diamonds in my collection, sir. And as for the masterpiece we're auctioning tonight, well, the Met should be buying it. I'll talk to Dora Jacobson.'

Thomas began to reply, but Leo was gesturing towards the people, the hall, the entire museum.

'It isn't the Met Gala, but we do our best! Dinner is at eight in the Charles Engelhard Court. Then the auction, with your painting as our final lot, and *stupendous* works by Cindy Sherman, Julian Schnabel, Jeff Koons . . .' He faced the crowd with a wild stare before clapping his hands. 'A roulette table in the Greek and Roman gallery! Acrobats from Georgia. All as Deborah would have wished. Well, there she is, watching over us.'

He signalled to where a row of columns separated the hall from the Grand Staircase. Erected in front of the colonnade, on a tall plinth, was a sculpture carved from ice. It was a life-size statue of a woman – Deborah – pushing a boy in a wheelchair. A smile was detectable on her glassy face. The boy held up his hands in imitation of the Christ child.

'Oh boy,' murmured Joel Blair.

Lorna looked on in dull wonder. The tableau had been chiselled with impossible precision. Deborah's shoes were like Cinderella's slippers, the heels hewn into fine stalactites.

'It's the best piece of art I've seen in years,' Thomas said, apparently without irony.

'No kidding, right?' cried Leo, and then, with a calcified smile, he turned to Joel. 'I'll have you know, sir, that the kids serving here tonight are from the Harlem ghetto.'

'Amen to that,' Joel said – and then, as Leo stepped away, he glanced with merriment at Lorna and Thomas. 'Doesn't that just prove my point about colonisation?'

Like everything else about him tonight, Leo's hearing had seemingly been over-tuned. He turned at once.

'If you don't like colonisation, you should get the fuck out of this museum. It was built on imperial power.'

'Hold on, Goffman. I didn't mean—'

Leo touched Joel's jacket, drawing his fingertips in a derisive caress over the yellow fabric. He was wearing more rings than usual, Lorna noticed, including some with coloured stones.

'You didn't mean, you didn't mean,' he repeated in a rueful tone. 'You art critics never mean what you say, do you? It's why I only look at the ads.'

He traipsed away, into the party.

'I kind of like that guy,' Thomas said.

'He'll get what's coming for him.' Joel was scanning the room for someone else to talk to. 'And anyway, what the hell happens to his collection when he dies?'

'That's anyone's guess,' Lorna said.

*

Thomas had gone to find another drink. Lorna thought of how she'd found him on the steps, spreadeagled on the red carpet. He had seemed agonised, like a martyr. Could she forgive him? Had she already?

A chasm opened in the room. A body flipped and flew through the space with mind-stilling speed – somersaulting, cartwheeling, then slowing in elegant rotations to a halt. Lorna perceived a woman in a skin-tight leotard. She was taller than anyone around her, with a stare of intense concentration. She stood upright – feet rooted to an axial point – and unfurled her limbs in sinuous arcs. For a second, it was as if her gravitational pull might swallow up the party. Guests stood in rapt silence.

Someone broke into cheerful laughter. People began to clap. All around, the sounds of the gala continued to bubble.

Wandering beneath the ice sculpture, Lorna observed Joel Blair again. He was preoccupied by something on the floor. She realised that he was following the path of a black cable that led from the base of the plinth. He walked with cautious steps, the way a child tiptoes along a wall, through an archway to one side of the staircase. The cable terminated at an unmarked door.

*

Lorna climbed the stairs, passing beneath the statue of Perseus with the head of Medusa. She was about to enter the gallery with the giant Tiepolos when Leo reappeared in the doorway, rising out of the crowd. His dress shirt was studded with black beads that reminded her of pigeons' eyes.

He took her by the arm. She felt his long fingers pressing into her. He seemed paler; his eyes were vaguer. For an instant, it was like he was holding on for dear life. Then his fingers relented and he wandered to the balustrade that overlooked the hall.

'Is Ana Garcia here tonight?' he asked, without looking round.

Lorna stood beside him at the ledge.

'She couldn't make it. I'm sorry, Leo.'

He nodded at the vast room.

From this vantage, Lorna could see that the plinth beneath the ice sculpture contained a machine. Vents ran across the top panel.

'It's a cryocooler,' Leo said, watching her. 'Designed by the best mechanical engineers. Keeps the sculpture pristine.' He ran a pair of fingers over his lower lip. 'I had a guild of ice sculptors work on that thing for weeks. It's a replica of a bronze statue. The original stands outside a hospital for kids in London.'

'Right,' she said. 'I guess that explains the boy.'

'The boy? Oh, right.' He laughed huskily. 'But to recreate

such a thing in ice! The delicacy of the craftsmanship, Lorna. The slenderness of the joins!'

They watched the milling guests below. Platters of canapés were moving through the room like scattering freighters.

'Those protestors outside,' Lorna said. 'They're calling you all kinds of things.'

'My grandparents died in the Holocaust. My grandfather was strangled. Do you think a few misguided kids are going to upset me?'

He felt no guilt, she told herself. Life was tragic. Terrible things happened every day, and the worst things imaginable had already happened.

Fritz Schein had appeared on a platform at the centre of the hall. A young woman was standing beside him, pressing the buttons on a microphone.

'Old Fritzie,' Leo said, smoothing his jacket. 'I remember what he *used* to be like, before all the supercurator crap. He used to come over to our place on Park. And you know what? He was normal. *Boring* normal. I guess that was the problem. Who wants that? Who wants to *be* that?'

'If you think so little of him, why is he hosting your event?'

Leo's eyes narrowed and his smile gathered strength. 'Oh, but I admire him greatly. That man *is* the art world.'

A shudder passed through her. In the same moment, she noticed that the white corner of his shirt was protruding through his fly.

'I've known him since he was a kid. He turned up in New York aged eighteen. Desperate to please, in awe of everyone. I guess Deborah was like a mother to him.' He stopped and contemplated. 'Maybe I'm too critical. Correction, I *am* too critical. My wife' – he stabbed a finger at the sculpture – 'saw the best in everyone. She would have liked you, Lorna, very much.'

The surface of the ice seemed glassier – wetter.

'That's a fine painting by Thomas Haller up for sale tonight.' Leo indicated the canvas that hung on the opposite side of the hall.

It had come, Lorna guessed, directly from Thomas's storage. The canvas, six feet by eight, extended across the wall with the swagger of a history painting. It was a panorama of indigo. Dripping, dense pigment gave way to watery interludes where the canvas was visible through the wash. Clots of puckered blue lay over the surface, as if Thomas had squeezed out the tubes and left the paint to sit there. It made her think of Monet's *Water Lilies*. Fat flowers floating in a shoal.

'Very fine indeed,' Leo said. 'But not half so fine as my lilac abstract.' He touched the silk pocket square on his chest and gave a baleful smile.

'Leo, listen. I had nothing to do with getting that painting for you in London.'

'What do you mean? You *procured* that painting from Claude Berlins.' He stressed the word as if to endow it with legalistic force.

'No, I didn't. Berlins refused to deal with me.'

She was relieved to see that he was more bewildered than angry.

'Fritz Schein was at the opening,' she went on. 'It can only have been him.'

'Impossible. Fritz is like family.' Leo laughed without mirth. 'He knows I'd turn him out in the cold if he so much as *spoke* to Berlins. We look after each other, see. He's loyal – to me, to Deborah. She hated that man with a passion.'

'Deborah hated Claude?'

'Ever since he refused a sale to her. This was back when he was a small-time dealer in Düsseldorf. He wouldn't sell a drawing to an unknown woman with a Jewish name. She wasn't aristo, see. She wasn't old money.' He took a glass of champagne from a passing tray. 'Someone knew that I wanted that painting. Who the hell was it? Mr Equitone, or Mrs . . . Ha! Sounds like a mystic, right?'

'A medium, yes.'

'Who could have done it? Who *knew* . . .'

He was staring at the ice sculpture. He stood very still. The champagne in his glass tipped and began to spill.

*

19.51

Thomas stood at the end of the hall with a glass of champagne – his third.

On the platform, Fritz was making an address. His voice boomed out, subduing the general murmur, as he declared that this was no ordinary charity ball but the furtherance of a lifelong mission, a *saintly* mission, although that word hardly seemed appropriate to Deborah Goffman. When had a saint ever been so sassy, so cool?

The champagne was dulling Thomas's mind, but the feeling he'd had on the steps was still there.

He noticed Leo Goffman through a break in the crowd. Leo had turned away to inspect a long table of cured meats and cheeses. Behind the table was a chromium vice with a pig leg stuck inside. Every so often, bodies shifted to block the view, but Thomas had noticed a curious expression on the old man's face. A locked grimace, as though the party had registered as a sustained, gruesome shock.

He watched as Leo spread his fingers above a platter. There were rings on his hands, jewels a woman would wear. Leo pressed all ten digits into the Parma ham and mopped them together.

Raising his voice, Fritz warned that the art world would die of elitism if people didn't wake up. This gala was a wake-up call. It was time for a radical redistribution. It wasn't enough, any longer, to be cool. If Deborah Goffman were alive today, she would be woke and proudly so. Applause erupted.

'And now, please welcome our patron and host, Mr Leo Goffman.'

Fritz descended from the stage, his eyes dancing inside the red frames of his glasses.

Still chewing, Leo sauntered past him and scaled the steps with a prancing attempt at agility. Someone passed him a microphone.

'Welcome to you all, welcome, welcome. My wife would have been eighty-two this year. Seems young, all of a sudden, doesn't it?'

There was a brittleness to the memorised words.

Thomas edged his way to where Fritz was standing, still flushed from his address.

'Nice speech.'

'You're *here*,' Fritz whispered in happy agitation. 'You missed two planes. What happened?'

'I met a friend in Montreux. We drank all night together. Talked about growing up on the Rochers de Naye – a beautiful wasteland, we agreed. He wants to recruit me to the UDC – you know, the fascists.'

Fritz repressed a giggle. 'Oh Thomas, be serious. Why were you late?'

'Work on the Venice show.'

'You must tell me what you're doing. I *am* the curator of the Swiss Pavilion.'

'Deborah changed the face of philanthropy in this city,' Leo intoned. 'Correction, she *was* the face of philanthropy. She dedicated her life to others. No one will ever know the extent of her sacrifices. No one . . .'

Thomas watched as Leo ceased to speak or move. The old man had been hypnotised, it seemed, by the ice sculpture. The faces of Deborah and the child were hard to make out. The whole thing was shimmering. The grilled panel underneath the ice was overflowing. Water was spreading on the stone floor.

'She weeps to hear me,' Leo said. His hand, still clutching the microphone, had dropped to his side so that only those standing close to the platform could hear.

'Christ, we need to get him off the stage.' Fritz's eyes darted from side to side.

'Don't let me out in public if I ever get that bad,' Thomas said.

A man with a white rose clipped to his tuxedo shushed them. Thomas thought that he recognised the hawklike face from news clips. A former Trump staffer? It amused him to think of the strange assortment of people at this event. Only Leo Goffman could have achieved it.

Leo pulled at his silk pocket square until a bloom of material had spilled across his chest. Then he trod to the edge of the platform and descended the steps, swaying as he went. Attendants rushed to help but he swiped them away. There was a belated pattering of applause.

Thomas brought his mouth to Fritz's ear. 'Any chance of a pick-me-up?'

Fritz turned to him with a fading smile. 'Here?'

'Sure, why not? You're lit up already.'

'Keep your voice down. This is a charity event. It's *work*. I'm presiding.'

'I'll tell you what I'm making for Venice.'

Fritz looked around, then gestured to Thomas to follow. They exited into a side lobby.

'I keep having to remind myself that this is Deborah's night,' Fritz said, as they walked down a flight of marble steps. 'Everything I do for Leo, I do for her.'

'You make it sound like he's your overlord.'

'He asks a lot. I had to set him up with a criminal injury

attorney – the best in New York, and the most expensive. The thing is, he has no one else to help him. There's only his maid.'

'And a multinational real estate firm,' Thomas said.

'Goffman Associates?' Fritz gave a sideways glance. 'That fell by the wayside. Leo sold the firm years ago to a Chinese consortium, although I wonder sometimes if he remembers. All he has left is an office in Hudson Yards and a small development in Harlem. And his art collection.'

They crossed another lobby and arrived at washrooms that nobody else appeared to have discovered.

*

Leaning against the toilet wall, Thomas listened to the rustling sounds of Fritz's preparations on top of the cistern.

Fritz was a chameleon, he thought. He half wondered whether to come onto him right here in the locked cubicle, just to see what would happen. He could try to kiss him, grab his ass . . .

'I'm surprised you're not making another film tonight,' he said. 'It's nothing if not a spectacle, this Goffman Gala.'

'The Serpentine film is a one-off,' Fritz replied, still bent over. 'I've just had it remastered by a studio in Brooklyn. They've done something incredible with the filter. The violet colour is amazing, like pale fire.'

Fritz stamped the white deposit with the edge of his credit card.

'The folk in the Amazon who extracted this for you,' Thomas said. 'Are you redistributing privilege to them, too?'

'Leave off, Thomas. What's with you tonight? You're all on edge.' Fritz swept the powder into two fat ridges. 'Tell me, then. What are you painting for Venice? I have to write a press release.'

If only Fritz knew the truth, Thomas thought. An empty studio. An imagination stripped bare.

Fritz's billowing hair descended to the cistern. He snorted.

Standing up straight, he flung back his head, eyes closed, like a man about to be executed.

Thomas slid his plane ticket from the breast pocket of his jacket and rolled it into a tube.

The drug hit his brain. Nausea rippled through his throat. He swallowed, tasting the bitter powder as it caulked his tonsils. He pressed both hands on the tiled wall and thought of Claude, enthroned in that room at the Pierre.

'Are you okay?' Fritz asked. 'Want another one?'

'I killed someone.'

Fritz's pupils were like dark marbles. 'What did you say?'

'I dreamed. A vision. Jesus, this is strong.'

'Venice!' Fritz cried. 'You *have* to tell me what you're painting.'

Thomas closed his eyes and tried to slow his thoughts.

'I'm going to make one more.' Fritz turned back to the cistern and began fidgeting with the paper wrap.

Thomas thought of Lorna's face out there on the steps, so wan and beautiful in the floodlight. With the touch of her hand, she had drawn him back to the world. His fingers squirmed on the tiles. He thought of Leo Goffman and the puckered ham.

'Paintings of wounds,' he said. 'Religious pictures.'

'Now you're just mocking me. Be serious. This is the Venice Biennale!'

'I mean it. You'll see.'

*

21.02

Leo looked around frantically for anyone to blame.

The statue of Deborah was melting. No one seemed to have noticed. Her orbitals were shallow recesses. The pearls of her necklace were pustules. Water was streaming over the floor. As for the kid in the wheelchair, no one could have figured out what he was meant to be. The icicle-thin spokes of the wheels had broken all over. The boy's head was listing at an unnatural angle.

Leo stared at Deborah's hands where they clutched the handles of the chair, and saw two glacial mounds. Her rings had vanished. Her fingers were gone. He stepped through the water, feeling the plish-plash on his leather soles, and became aware of a current of hot air. It reminded him of stepping from a plane into the heat of the Sahara, a long time in the past.

He was falling. As his legs released him, he felt the coarseness of a boar's muzzle on his neck and face, and the attentions of its granular tongue. Its teeth were diamond-hard, made for tearing.

*

21.02

Thomas was running through the museum. He had to find Lorna. But she wasn't anywhere to be seen. He hurried through the maze of galleries, passing artefacts that seemed like so many corpses, dug up and encased for leering eyes.

He saw someone he knew and the man stopped him, crying: 'Haller! You were with me in Kassel.' The man's face had been pinned back at the corners.

Thomas pushed past, but at once an elderly woman in couture had stepped into his path.

'I'm gonna bid for your blue picture! Such a great cause.'

People stared as he fled. He came to the glass atrium with the Temple of Dendur. The night sky was a grid of purple. A cocktail bar had been installed around the ancient building. Its surface glowed like a freeway. The sides were decorated by sphinx heads and papyrus columns cast from fibreglass. A real palm tree, made monstrous by floodlights, reared up behind, casting serrations over the temple. The bar staff seemed to be nude except for Cleopatra wigs and crescents of segmented gold around their shoulders.

He was back at the Grand Staircase. The crowd was noisier, with a different energy from earlier. A clearing had formed. He saw Leo Goffman lying in a pool. The fingers of the old man's hand were curling inward. The red and blue of his rings glinted in the water.

*

21.03

Lorna had guessed what was going to happen. Leo, who had been groping at the ice statue like a drowning man – clutching it, hanging from it – had fallen to the floor.

A moment later, the ice boy in the wheelchair nodded. The head slumped forward, fell off the shoulders and landed with a tinkling crunch on the lap.

Leo was lying in the water beneath the statue. Lorna crouched and shook him by the shoulder. She could feel hot air blasting out of the plinth.

He opened his eyes and stared at her. He'd had some kind of seizure; his eyes confirmed it. He was looking at her with radiant, devastating calm.

'He's dead!' a man cried. 'Leo Goffman is dead!'

'He's not dead,' said Lorna.

A noise was issuing from Leo's throat. It was a soft, restive growl, reminding her of a car heard from a distance at night.

26

14 April, 11.40. New York

It was Sunday. Lorna was lying on the sofa with the lights off. In two days, she would fly to Venice for the opening of the Biennale. She observed Jay as he stood from sleep, doddered between piles of books, and settled with a tumbling thump into another doze. She hadn't heard anything lately from Justine. Even the messages about Jay had stopped.

A long time before Justine, before the birth and the adoption, Thomas had been the closest person to her. But other realities had come along. He had run away to Düsseldorf; she had gone to New York. For a while, she had figured that she would never hear from him again.

She thought of the day (she remembered the date and the time: eleven in the morning on October 2) that he had turned up in New York; the way he had walked into the second-floor room of the SoHo tenement where she had her gallery, standing casually in front of the desk until she looked up. They embraced and held onto one another for a long time. It was easier to do that than to look at each other or talk. In the end, he laid a stack of Polaroids on her desk – panels of satiny pink, flecked by deeper mauve – and asked her what she thought.

'What happened to your portraits? The photorealist stuff?'
'That was all a dead end.'
'So, the Kunstakademie Düsseldorf got to you.'
'It wasn't the school,' he replied, seeming not to share her

tentative amusement. 'I've had enough of images – of *things*. This is what I am now. An abstract painter.'

She spread the Polaroids in a fan on the desk, somehow knowing that the paintings would be a hit. It was the fall of 1998 and colour was back in. Richter's squeegee paintings were causing a sensation in the auctions. And there was a mood of romance in Thomas's new pictures, so different from anything he had made before.

*

She heaved herself off the sofa. Jay followed her down the hallway and lay by the bathroom door after she'd gone in.

Had it really been like that when Thomas came back, or was she subtracting details? Hadn't there been an ache of dismay and a suspicion that she could never forgive him? Becoming his dealer had made it easier, given her a part to play. From then on, the friendship had been an acting out of roles. And there had been a fatalism about the decision, at least for her. A feeling that they were destined to look after each other, since they hadn't been able to care for the child.

Sitting on the toilet, she thought about the gala. She retrieved the image of Thomas's face as he lay on the steps. Had there been relief there? A craving for deliverance? Or had he just been drunk and wired?

And who the fuck had he borrowed that coat from?

She flushed the toilet and returned with Jay to the front room. She pondered why she was going to Venice, and whether it was to see Thomas again, and whether she could feasibly go to Venice and *not* see his exhibition. For a few seconds, as she settled back on the sofa and closed her eyes, she wished she had a place to run away to.

*

In the early days, she and Justine had gone each weekend to the beach. Sometimes to Orchard Beach in the Bronx. More often to Long Island, where Justine's parents had a gingerbread-style house in Bellport.

'Maybe we should give up the city,' Justine said as they sat in the garden one night, beneath a tree. 'Come and live by the sea.'

'And live on what?'

'We'd get by.'

'Says the girl who's never been hungry,' Lorna said.

'Do me a favour. You're the one with a house, and money, and renown.'

'You've never had to fight,' Lorna said, with weary affection.

'Not like you, you mean?' Justine hit back. 'You old prize-fighter.'

'I do feel like everything's a battle. All of life.' Lorna looked past Justine into the night.

'You're getting to sound like my mother. Every observation carries a moral.'

'Oh, don't worry. There isn't a moral to anything I say. I am a mother, though, remember? Somewhere out there is a boy I gave birth to.'

'Lorna. Stop. He's no more your son than I am.'

'I have the adoption certificate somewhere,' Lorna went on. 'Sealed from when I gave him away.'

'Leave it alone. He doesn't belong to you.'

Justine leaned close – the breeze was growing cold – and slid her hands beneath Lorna's T-shirt. The branches of the tree rustled. Stars were visible through rifts in the clouds.

'We could throw parties at this place,' Lorna said, after a while. 'If it was ours, I mean.'

'I don't want to throw parties, or give parties, or whatever the saying is. I don't want to be one of those glitzy society dykes. I want you to myself, Lorna, all of you.'

Lorna felt Justine's hands on her shoulders. Their faces were close, but it was so dark that Justine was just an impression.

After a silence, Lorna said: 'Will you love me for ever?'

Maybe she'd been thinking of the Carole King song, but the words came out wrong.

Justine scrutinised her through the dark. 'Who asks questions like that? I love you now. What else is there?'

'The future.'

'One of us will get sick and die, then the other one will go on alone – or something like that. What's the point of thinking about it?'

'Will you stay with me, though?'

Justine laughed and drew back, rising on her heels. She hauled Lorna up, and they crossed the garden to where the sand dunes began. There was no fence or barrier. They ventured onto the beach. Then, on a shared impulse, they raced into the darkness, stumbling across the sand, laughing and calling out – each to the other – to slow down. Justine pulled Lorna, then flung her ahead, a projectile that she refused to release. As they neared the shore, she let go. They staggered the few final steps to where the water swayed up and down the sand, a white line in the night.

Visible as a shape against the moonlit sea, Justine pulled off her T-shirt and shorts and shoes, then ran past Lorna, plunging through the water. She stood thigh deep.

'Come in!' she shouted.

'Isn't it freezing?'

Lorna unbuttoned her shirt and let it drop to the sand. She undressed, feeling the air on her body, and stepped through the shallow water.

Justine fell back and began to swim away. Lorna sank into the water, gasping at the cold, and swam after her, pulling hard with her arms.

'Swim to me,' Justine called out, treading water.

Lorna had nearly reached her when Justine pulled back. Lorna threw herself forward and Justine kicked away. Lorna dived through the water and this time Justine allowed her to grab hold. She enclosed Justine in her arms and held her tight. They were out of their depth, suspended in the ocean. Like pale jellyfish, Lorna thought. Dumb creatures. Seawater splashed in her eyes. She gripped Justine's hips between her legs, and their lips met.

*

11.50

'Faster!' he yelled. 'Faster!'

Rubber straps clung to Leo's thighs and shoulders. Suspended in the harness, inching towards the water, he felt time decelerate. His shouts were distant. Some perverse logic was at work: the commands were making Bonita, or the universe, go slower.

Through the glass, Manhattan was more beautiful than he'd ever known it. A tall trapezium of land crammed with splints and pillars, flanked by iron water, with the mid-green inset of the park.

His eyes dropped. The water beneath his feet seemed more immense than the city. It was as if he'd soared miles in less than a second, and was looking down from a place of ice-cold ether. His hanging limbs and strapped-in crotch lost their heaviness.

'Faster!'

The crane whirred. On the poolside, Bonita held the lever of the remote control.

His toes were virtually touching the pool. The water was glaucous in the midday light. The reflections of the six paintings had extinguished its transparency. His fatless legs dangled like tentacles. An eighty-six-year-old newborn.

'Faster, Bonita! Drop me in quick.'

He thought of what he'd seen when he came round, lying on the floor of the Met. For a brief interval, he hadn't understood or cared to understand the excited babble, the colours and shapes, the descending discs with their glistening insets and dark openings. Disordered impressions of the world – or maybe just the reality of things, before judgement imposed its designs. And then the clear sight of Lorna Bedford's face.

Had it changed him, almost dying? Something had changed. In all his decades of atheism, he'd never realised that the spiritual life was hiding in plain sight, there where he'd least expected: in the substance of things, in the tangible matter. That copy of *Vanity Fair* in his bedside cabinet – it wasn't just a memento of Deborah. It *was* her. Out of nowhere he remembered something he'd heard or read a long time ago (this state of suspension had set his thoughts in freefall). The statues that the ancient Greeks made of their gods weren't, after all, statues of gods. They *were* the gods. The statue itself, *divine*. He saw now, with a clarity that staggered him, that his life of acquisition – the buildings and art and antiques, all of it – had been a quest to find host vessels for his soul, objects large and plentiful enough for the evolving, expanding spirit matter of Leo Goffman.

'Faster, I said! Turn up the speed.'

'It only goes this fast, Mr Goffman,' Bonita said. 'I can't make it go any faster than this.'

*

11.50

Bonita pushed the miniature lever, directing the crane. She heard him shouting and held the lever firm. His toes were touching the water now, tacking the surface to their undersides.

Once the water was up to his shoulders, she would halt the descent and give him time to unbuckle the rubber harness. Then she would pick up the steel pole that lay on the poolside and hold it out as he swam, near enough for him to cling to.

Switching her attention between the lever and Leo's drooping body, she tried to calculate how long he would need to unbuckle himself. Longer than it would take for his head to be immersed if she kept the crane in motion.

She eyed the ungainly equipment: a robotic arm composed of white-sheathed pistons and steel joints, a metal chain, a rubber truss. Would he float if she dunked him? Would he disappear beneath the water? She imagined his furious, frightened response. Then a stranger vision interceded. Leo sinking without protest, resigned to his fate.

'Faster, Bonita!'

What if she were to pause the crane just where it was, with nothing more than his ankles beneath the water, and leave? She could walk out of the apartment, out of the tower, and take herself to Saks for the afternoon with his credit card.

The fact of his utter helplessness seized her with such force that, without meaning to, she let go of the lever. The crane juddered to a halt. Leo gasped as the chain jolted upward and the harness tightened. She watched his face contract with pain, and a peculiar calm came over her.

27

16 April, 11.00. Venice

Venice!

As Lorna walked to the landing stage beyond the airport terminal, the smell of the lagoon hit her.

She boarded the vaporetto and sat in the canopied section at the back. The chugging of the boat, its meandering movement onto the open water, awakened feelings that only existed in this place.

Sunlight was breaking through the clouds, pressing against her brow. Wasn't there something sexual about the impact of Venice on the senses – the rush of desire, the loss of intellect, the balmy reflectiveness that came after? In Justine's old notes, she'd read something about Venice as a sentient being, conscious of human affections. *You desire to embrace it, to caress it, to possess it* . . . She wanted to be possessed. She craved the self-erasure of a love affair.

Her trips to the city, every two years since 1999, had marked the course of her adult life. Many times, the Biennale had restored her faith in art. It had shown her where art was going and what art could be. Those revelations had felt more pointed against the radiant calm of Venice itself. But in the last decade, the Biennale had grown more predictable. The revelations and disruptions were still there, but they came amid a tide of hype, money and manic consensus about what was hot, what mattered, *who* mattered. The art had become a given. What people came to see was the art world.

The boat sped up, bucking the waves. To one side was the narrow spit of the Ponte della Libertà. Small islands came and went. At the edge of the main island, houses with walled gardens bordered the canal.

Some tattered fibre of optimism was springing back to life. It was impossible to feel cynical out here on the water. The boat motored into the city, ducking from the main waterway into a canal where bridges sliced the water into segments. Steps slimed with moss led out of the canal into stone portals, some of them gridded with iron bars.

*

17.25

Thomas walked in an unhurried way across the Piazza San Marco. Ahead were two pillars topped by a winged lion and a saint whose name he couldn't remember. Beyond, the lagoon was virtually white, the colour of fresh ash. The air was pleasantly stale, the way it often was in Venice, and all around him people were at leisure – laughing, chattering, idling. Work and pain didn't exist in this hallowed patch of Old Europe, between the porticoes of the Doge's Palace and Sansovino's library.

It was the night before the opening of his show. The paintings were hung. Claude had been texting and emailing since New York. Thomas had resisted. There had been a single missed call just this afternoon. He would see Claude tomorrow at lunch. He would see everyone then. For now, he had agreed to meet Marianna Berger. This film of hers, whatever it proved to be, must be finished. He thought of Claude's hostility. Was that the reason Thomas wanted to see the thing through, never mind what Marianna thought of him? He stood at the edge of the water and watched the boats, the islands opposite, the nearly cloudless sky . . .

'Hello, Thomas.'

He turned. Marianna was standing beside him, holding her camera. Her hair was tied back. He had never seen it like that. She wore a dark pullover with a white Peter Pan collar over the neckline. She looked older, he thought, but something else was different besides. There was a deep composure about her. The acerbity seemed to have gone. He wasn't sure if he preferred this new nunlike guise.

'You crept up on me,' he said.

'This is where you said to meet.'

He sighed and gave a weary smile. 'Let's not film tonight. Let's just talk. You can finish the film tomorrow, at the grand reveal.'

They strolled back in the direction of the campanile, looking (Thomas supposed) like a husband and wife. Marianna bought a gelato and threw it to the birds. They fluttered around the pink mess without eating it.

'I've never been to Venice before,' she said.

'I think it must be my hundredth trip.'

'I'm not sure I see the romance. It's like an old dirty museum. I've been walking about all day, watching the art world types.'

'Is it Venice you don't like or the visitors?'

'Both. They seem like a weird match.'

He ranged his gaze over the people around them. 'Where are you staying?'

'The same hotel as you. I hoped we'd bump into each other.'

'I've hardly been there. I've spent days – it feels like days – at the Swiss Pavilion.'

'I heard that you haven't let anyone in. No journalists, no one at all.'

'Not until the opening tomorrow. Just the guys who hung the paintings.' He listened for a moment to the piano music that was trickling towards them from Caffè Florian. 'It feels like, until I let people see it, the show isn't real. Like it could still be inside my head and nowhere else.'

'Well, it'll be in everyone's heads tomorrow.'

'But until then . . .'

He stopped walking. She looked at him with the same cool composure.

'Yes?'

'Until then, I won't have to think of it as a disaster. Or a sensational success. Or as *anything*. It can just exist in my mind without a judgement attached to it.'

'Come on. Everything you make – everything we do – is for an audience. We're artists.'

'Maybe. I mean, yes, in the past. This time, I'm not so sure.'

He was distracted by the sight of a boy of around eight, standing a few feet away with his arms outspread. Marianna switched on her camera and raised it to her eye. A pigeon had landed on the boy's head. Others came to land on each arm until five birds were competing for whatever grain his fists concealed. The boy grinned at Marianna's camera, then threw the seeds away. In a flapping rush, the birds were gone.

In the space beyond the boy's head, Thomas saw Claude sitting at a café table at the far end of the square. Claude was watching him, or seemed to be: the distance made it hard to be sure. He sat at ease, one leg draped over the other. His hands rested on a Panama hat in his lap. But his face didn't align with the picture of repose. By a shift of the evening light, a transient brightening, he seemed transfigured. The features were his, but the tanned skin was like parchment. His nostrils were dark holes. His eyes were pale and his lips had retracted around his gums. For an instant, the sound and motion of the square disappeared, like a theatrical routine abruptly suspended. Thomas turned away. Marianna had wandered into the crowd, still filming. He strode to catch up.

'Let's go back to the hotel,' he said, conscious of the restrained alarm in his voice. 'I'm done walking in this tourist trap. All these flying rats.'

He paced away. She hurried to keep up.

'What is it?'

He didn't reply. Ahead, the basilica glimmered like an incense burner. They were nearing the alleyway that led to their hotel. Marianna glanced back across the square. Thomas went ahead of her. Had Claude really seen him from that distance? At last, as he entered the passageway, he looked behind him into the square, through the narrow aperture of the buildings. But the view was blocked by birds, and then by Marianna – coming towards him with her camera raised high, set to record.

*

After he and Marianna had parted in the lobby of their hotel, Thomas went walking. He walked a long way through familiar – then increasingly unfamiliar – streets, coming to the Canale di Santa Chiara. To one side of the road was an expanse of railway tracks, forlornly empty in the evening sunlight. Parked railway trucks were stacked with timber. The cut wood was letting out a sweet sharp odour.

He felt warm in his linen jacket. He undid three buttons of his shirt to release the heat. A cruise ship had docked on the water. Lights glowed behind its hundreds of windows. He tried to count the little squares.

At the age of twenty-one, he had decided that he wouldn't be able to fall in love. Not with one person. In New York, he'd had hundreds of encounters. He felt a safety in numbers, and found those numbers in Bryant Park or Washington Square (beside the railings, in the dark), or on summer trips to the needle-carpeted groves of Fire Island. For most of his life it had been like this – and he had been lucky, in the early days, while many others hadn't. Near encounters or actual encounters:

sometimes the pleasure was simply in the hunting or being hunted.

No one found him along the railway tracks. After nightfall, he returned to San Marco and stood again at the edge of the lagoon, feeling the saline air move through him and listening to the babble of conversations. It was cooler now. The lights of the boats bobbed on the water. He had been there ten minutes or more when he glanced to his left and met a man's eye. The man returned a desolate stare. Thomas walked away. When he came to the middle of the square, he turned to see that the man had followed from a distance. Thomas went on, through the gateway of the clocktower. When he turned again by just a fraction, he caught sight of the man's striped T-shirt. He crossed a footbridge and they passed along opposite sides of a narrow canal. In less than a minute, the city had grown almost silent. Their footsteps pattered, not keeping time. The man was tracking him more closely. Again, their eyes met. Thomas saw that the man's face was handsome, but not overly so (that was good), with a narrow Roman nose and hair that clung in black curls to his brow.

They came simultaneously to another short bridge. The man crossed it in a few bold paces, and they walked side by side, so close that their forearms skimmed.

*

Entering his hotel room late in the evening, Thomas saw his phone. It was lying on the desk where he had left it that afternoon. There were fourteen missed calls. He drew the curtains closed and sat on the bed. The hotel phone on the bedside cabinet began to ring.

He picked it up.

'Where have you been?' Claude sounded quiet, as though he were a long way from the phone.

'Walking. Clearing my head. Why does it matter?'

'Are you drunk?'

Thomas teased off his shoes with either foot and lay on the bed, feeling the mattress creak beneath him.

'I went to the Swiss Pavilion this afternoon,' Claude said. 'To see your show.'

'It's closed.'

'So they told me.'

'No one can see it until the opening. Tomorrow at three o'clock.'

'What is this – a joke? Your own dealer refused entry.'

Thomas listened to his own exhalation and thought of the man he'd met, whose name he hadn't asked, whom he would never see again.

'I have to go inside,' Claude said. 'I have to see the paintings. How can I price them? How can I sell them?'

'This show is different. Not for reputation or sales. It belongs to me – only me – until the public opening.'

'You sound like a child.'

'I mean it. I don't care if it wins the Golden Lion.'

Claude let out a clattering laugh. 'You'd better care. You'd better care that it wins every prize in the Biennale. This isn't just about you, or have you forgotten? Who made you what you are? Who gave you the Swiss Pavilion?'

'Fritz did.'

'Because of your show in London. Your show with me. The show you very nearly wrecked—'

Claude stopped and waited. Thomas felt a tremor of nausea, then nothing. He pressed his lips shut.

'How easily you forget,' Claude said at last.

'And what about Lorna?'

'What about her?' Claude's voice felt abruptly close. Thomas imagined Claude's lips touching the mouthpiece of the phone.

He looked at the ceiling. There were concentric brown marks in the wallpaper, like spilled coffee.

'I betrayed her when I signed with you.'

'Betrayed?' The word was thick with mock amazement. 'That was a business thing. She's a second-rater.'

'She's my oldest friend – or was. We were precious to each other. We were—'

'Listen to me,' Claude broke in, sounding almost panicked in his anger. 'If you intend to make it, really make it, you need to suffer and make other people suffer too.'

'All of them?'

'Let her go. You're precious to me. Isn't that enough?'

'If you meant it . . .' Thomas traced the ring marks and tried to remember the places he'd been that night.

'And what the hell is that girl still doing with you? The pretend filmmaker.'

'There's nothing pretend about her.'

'Get rid of her. She's an embarrassment. And a liability.'

Thomas stayed silent. It was just like Claude, to think that someone could be made to disappear. And hadn't he heard Claude say those words, or similar ones, about Luca? He lay very still, waiting for the feelings that had built in him to dispel.

28

Thomas scanned the numbers on the doors, looking for Marianna's room. The hotel was small but cavernous, with terrazzo passageways that all looked the same. He arrived at an echoing corridor that seemed to be a dead end. On the wall ahead was a Venetian mask. The eyeholes were filled with the sludgy Anaglypta of the wallpaper behind. Red ribbons hung from either side. On the adjacent wall, invisible until he came close, was a door. Marianna's room. He knocked and waited, then tried the handle. The door was unlocked.

The room was hot and dim. Her bed was unmade. Through the balcony doors, Marianna was sitting on the stone ledge, turned towards the canal below. She wore a sleeveless white dress. Her legs were visible between the balusters.

'I came to get you,' he said. 'We'll be late for lunch.'

She didn't move at first. Just when he'd assumed she hadn't heard, she twisted round. She had a tired, wild-eyed look.

'I'm not coming.'

He stopped midway through the room. 'Why not?'

As she looked back, he had the sensation once more of witnessing a different version of her. The beatific calm of last night was gone. She reminded him of when she'd knelt at his studio door, desperately trying to unlock it.

'You tell me,' she said. 'Your gallery emailed me this morning – told me you're withdrawing consent for the video. I no longer have your permission, they said. So that's it?'

'Who emailed?'

'I don't know. Some rude fucking assistant.'

Ahead, through the unlit space, the balcony was a box of light. He could feel the warm spring air. Church bells were clanging.

'Ignore it,' he said. 'It's all power games.'

She swung her legs back to the near side of the balustrade. 'You mean you had nothing to do with it?'

Not wanting to discuss it, or to think about what it meant, he glanced around the room. On the rumpled sheets of her bed was a laptop. It was open and wired to her camera. A video was playing silently on the screen. It showed a man in a striped T-shirt, viewed from below. A gondolier driving his pole into the water in a slow cyclical motion. The video had been shot, Thomas guessed, from the seat at the centre of the boat. The camera remained fixed on the man as the buildings and sky moved around him. From beneath his straw hat, he returned its gaze with surly patience.

'You make ordinary things look strange and new,' he murmured. 'The way light falls on objects. The surface of everything is alive.'

He stared at the screen for a long time, thinking of the man from the night before: he hadn't been dissimilar.

'But what's underneath?' he went on, thinking aloud. 'Where's the story – the feeling? I want to know who he is, what he's thinking, not just that the sun looks lovely on his arms.'

Her face had gone from pale to red.

'It's just something I was trying out. It has nothing to do with you. But thanks. You think it's superficial. At least now I know what you think of my work.'

'I didn't mean—'

'It's fine. Leave it.' She planted her hands either side of her on the parapet.

He could feel her hurt and outrage as though the heat of the day had transmitted them. He came closer to the door. There was a magazine on the floor of the balcony. It was *Artforum*, lying open to display two adverts. One was for a Carl Andre exhibition. On the facing page was a photograph of the Los Angeles skyline, faded and grainy like an old film still.

SEX AND THE CITY
Curated by Fritz Schein
Getty Center, Los Angeles, opening July 1

'If you'd spoken to Fritz in New York, like I asked you' – Marianna's words were taut – 'he might have included me in that show.'

'I'm sorry. I forgot.'

'If you gave a shit, you wouldn't have forgotten.'

Thomas raised a hand to shield his eyes against the light. 'You shouldn't worry. It sounds like a lot of froth. Fritz has changed his mind about that show five times at least. At one time it was going to be about feminism. Then it was urban living in the wake of posthumanism.'

'What's that supposed to mean?'

'It's all so that he can include his own video. You know, the one he made of the Serpentine summer party last year.'

She stared at him.

'Listen, Marianna. No one's going to help you in this game. You have to fight for what you want. You have to suffer.' He smarted to hear himself repeat Claude's words.

'What have you suffered? You've had a midcareer show at the Whitney. You're *rich*. You're not going to help me, that's for sure. Not the way you feel about my work. *Vacuous* – isn't that what you meant just now?'

He didn't speak. Sweat prickled along his hairline.

'You've been playing a game with me all this time,' she said. 'You ask where the feeling is, where the truth is. Well, what about you? You wanted me to make a portrait of you, but you don't want anything revealed. It's like you're watching yourself in the mirror, *constantly*.' She looked away in smiling contempt, down at the canal, before turning back. 'And what's the deal between you and Berlins?'

He opened his mouth but no words came. His consciousness was sliding over itself in unstable layers.

She laughed. It was a terrible, sparkling laugh.

'I'll see you at lunch,' he said, stepping backwards into the room. Turning to go, he caught sight of her laptop screen again, and that picture of the gondolier in his endless mechanical rhythm.

*

12.58

As she crossed the lobby of the St. Regis, Lorna became aware that someone was standing in her path. He wore a cream suit and held a Panama hat to his chest. The cropped silver hair, the suntan, the varnished handsomeness: there was something deadeningly generic about Claude Berlins. And yet he couldn't have been anyone else.

He motioned her to one side.

'Have you seen Thomas?'

'No. I only got here yesterday.'

'He should have been here an hour ago. Do you know where he is?'

There was a hint of sternness to the question. Lorna noticed a film of sweat in the groove of his philtrum.

'I told you. I haven't seen him since I got to Venice. Hasn't he been installing?'

'Something's not right. He gets funny before exhibition openings. Nervous. He goes and does stupid things.' Claude glanced along the lobby, pressing his lips tight. 'He considers you his friend. What's he told you? What's this about refusing to allow me into the pavilion?'

The wetness above his lips was spreading. An odour of sandalwood was rising out of him.

'I don't know more than you. He'll show up – he always does.' Her frustration was growing. 'What is this, anyway? He left me for you. Why would I know where he's got to?'

Claude studied her in silence, palpating his hat. Within seconds, his fever of panic seemed to dissipate, leaving behind a stony amusement.

'*Left me for you.* What strange words to use. You make it sound almost— unprofessional.' He drew a handkerchief from his jacket and dabbed his face with the folded edge, still watching her. 'What people like you forget is that an artist has agency. Thomas wanted to come to me. He saw where the future lay. Isn't it enough that he's invited you today?'

His smile was a parade of white veneers. Fleetingly she wondered what he would look like if he weren't a wealthy art dealer – if, say, he had been adopted as a baby by peasant farmers. Or an ordinary couple from north London.

'Don't you see,' Claude went on, 'that I can do things for him? The paintings in the Swiss Pavilion will be five hundred thousand dollars each.'

'But you haven't even seen them.'

'I don't need to. I know Thomas. I know his art, and I know its price. Which of your clients is going to pay that?' He ran a finger along the black band of his hat. 'He's outgrown you. There's no shame in it – if you just accept the fact.'

'Fuck you,' she said, causing a passing guest to tut. 'You don't give a shit about Thomas. You never have.'

Claude hummed playfully.

'He told me what happened in Düsseldorf.'

'And still you think he belongs to you.'

'I don't think anyone belongs to me.'

'No? I heard a rumour that you claim still to represent him in the States.' Claude held his arms wide, then planted his hat on his head. 'Very well. Represent him today in Venice, along with me. Consider this exhibition, Thomas's pavilion, yours or mine to sell. Whoever's faster. No discounts.'

'You're not serious.'

'I'll have Sylvia send you a consignment within the hour. If you sell a painting – any painting – before me, then it's your sale. If you sell the entire show before I do' – his smile broadened – 'well, you've won.'

'Why would you offer me that?'

'Why do you think? Thomas will know that I let you in on the sales. And he'll know – when I sell the entire exhibition, which I will – that he made the right choice coming over to me.' His pupils were like pinpricks inside his grey irises. 'Don't get me wrong, Lorna. I love you. Thomas *loves* you. But this is business.'

With a touch of his hand on her back, he prompted her to walk.

They came to the threshold of the terrace. A humid wind was blowing. Guests were circling. Laughter juddered through the air.

*

Fritz Schein's red glasses were as bright as a toy in the sunlight.

'I'd like to propose a toast. To Thomas Haller's exhibition at the Swiss Pavilion!'

Glasses were raised. *Cheers* were said.

'All will be revealed at three o'clock!'

There was a fluttering of applause across the terrace of the restaurant. It couldn't dispel the general unease. From every table, people were looking at the chair where Thomas should have been seated.

Lorna was at the centre of the main table. It was a long,

narrow table facing the Grand Canal. Claude sat directly across from her, with Fritz beside him. There were two empty places to her left, bearing cards with the names of Thomas and Marianna. Collectors and curators filled the other seats. Joel Blair, the Pulitzer-winning critic, was on her right, already chattering about the different national pavilions – this one not political enough, that one political in quite the wrong way – and the likely candidates for the Golden Lion.

Through her Ray-Bans, the Grand Canal and the sky above Santa Maria della Salute had resolved into the same hazy turquoise. It was uncomfortably hot. She had shed her jacket to leave a white T-shirt that probably looked inadequate. She fanned herself with the printed card that itemised the five courses of lunch. In front of her on the table was a wicker wreath, woven all over with poppies and wildflowers. She guessed it was intended as an emblem of Switzerland.

No one knew where Thomas was. Lorna could tell, from intermittent glances at Claude, that his unease had returned. He was barely speaking. His eyes kept flitting to the door of the hotel. Just that morning, Lorna had noticed that trolling posts had begun to appear on X and Instagram again. Last night, someone had posted a picture of Thomas walking in St Mark's Square, with a snarky comment about crapstraction.

A glass vial containing amber-coloured foam was set down before her. She tried some using a tiny silver spoon. It dissolved on her tongue with a savour of fish.

Claude beckoned down the table to Sylvia Rosso, who came at once to stand behind him.

'I knew this would happen,' he said in an audible whisper. 'We should never have allowed him to stay at a different hotel.'

'Shall I call the police?'

'Don't be ridiculous. This is all premeditated. Attention seeking.'

Lorna wasn't so sure. She suspected that Thomas had got

drunk and overslept, but she wondered also if his absence signified something. The young artist she'd known in London would have been dazzled and elated by the prospect of a party in his honour. Never late. Over time, Thomas had become the moneyed ghost of his earlier self. What did he care about, any longer? She rested a hand on the seat beside her, thinking that it was strange that she had been placed next to him. The idea came to her that she would never see him again, and that this was a sort of funeral reception, only no one had realised.

'Thomas is an avant-garde painter,' Fritz was saying, addressing the table at large. 'An avant-garde painter for the twenty-first century!'

'He's the greatest abstract painter of his generation,' Claude interjected, as if Fritz had started a contest. 'When everyone else was flirting with pictures in the nineties, Thomas gave us a new purity. An escape from *personality*.'

His eyes landed on Lorna. In his Panama hat, he made her think of a character from *Death on the Nile*.

'He's forward-thinking and backward-feeling,' Fritz proclaimed. 'An epic painter for our epoch—'

All around them, voices were dwindling. People were turning.

Thomas stood at the threshold to the hotel, watching the gathering like a casual observer. His hair was newly cut – short at the sides and swept back from his brow. He wore a linen jacket over a blue shirt that chimed with his eyes. His jeans had a tailored fit, and his shoes – black trainers with gold eyelets – were clearly brand new. And yet, Lorna thought, he looked tired.

Someone began to clap. As Thomas crossed the terrace to his seat, there was a slow ripple of applause.

'Our epoch,' he echoed, as he sat down. 'What's that, then?'

Fritz's eyes skipped over their audience. 'The era of contemporary art, I mean. This golden age.'

Thomas glanced over the table, the terrace, the canal. 'Is *this* the golden age? And what, by the way, *is* contemporary art? A period? A movement? I was never sure.'

'Why are you so late?' said Claude. His words were brittle. 'Why have you kept us waiting so long?'

Thomas sat down, appearing not to hear. He picked up the card that marked his place (his name inscribed in scrolling script), and held it up for inspection before tucking it into the side pocket of his jacket. He poured himself a glass of water with what Lorna perceived to be exaggerated leisureliness. Claude watched him – watched them both – from beneath the brim of his hat.

'We're in an era of multiple movements – countless realities,' said Joel Blair, to Lorna's right. 'No more isms! That's what contemporary means. Just ask those kids on TikTok.'

'Which all sounds a lot like postmodernism,' mused Carter Daily, who was next to Joel.

They were masks of comedy and tragedy, this pair, thought Lorna. Joel wore a constant grin, whereas Carter, who taught in one of the US art colleges, had an air of weary nihilism. He seemed untouched by the sun, with dark rings beneath his eyes.

Claude's silence was like radiation. Lorna wondered if anyone else could feel it. Thomas was surely aware, but he looked out placidly at the Salute across the canal, acknowledging nobody.

As conversations split, she turned to him.

'What kept you?'

'I couldn't bear the idea of a grand introduction.'

'Come off it, you love these occasions.'

'Do I? I'm looking forward to going back to Switzerland – escaping.'

This last statement had been loud enough for Joel Blair to hear.

'You think you can escape from the art world, Thomas, but you're it.'

'And Switzerland is the centre of the art world,' Fritz said. 'Think how many *kunsthallen* there are in Zürich.'

'Switzerland is a microcosm of the art world,' corrected Carter in a toneless voice. 'It's full of money, it's neutral on global political issues, it's elegant, sophisticated, *secretive*. And relatively insignificant, so far as the rest of the world is concerned.'

'What the hell is the art world, anyway?' said Thomas, without retracting his gaze from the basilica.

Claude spread his hands on the table. The alacrity of the movement drew everyone's attention. There was a queer expression on his face, a sort of pained ecstasy.

'Everyone desires an escape. It's not human *not* to want to run away. I've just bought a house in Marrakech for my retirement. It's beautiful – unimaginably so. And do you know, I actually went there once, as the guest of Yves Saint Laurent and Pierre? It was their house – the Villa Oasis. It has the bluest walls. The rooms are like jewels. And now it's mine. Think of the parties! And the spread in *Architectural Digest*. Just *think* of it!'

Claude was looking at Thomas. The trembling solemnity of his words – their spiralling passion – had defied a response. What he'd said was preposterous, a fantasy invented out of thin air, and everyone must have known it. Lorna felt a wild laugh ignite and die in her chest.

'Like you'd ever retire,' she said.

Claude returned a vacant look, before standing and walking away.

It seemed as though Claude meant to leave the party. But in a few seconds, Lorna saw that he had risen to greet a young woman who had arrived late. He guided her to the place beside Thomas that had been intended for Marianna. She was tall and in her mid-twenties, and wore a plunging silver dress that seemed excessively glamorous even for this occasion. She must be a collector, Lorna thought, or the daughter of one. She heard Claude address the woman as Olga.

'Where's Marianna?' she whispered to Thomas, as conversations revived.

'I wish I knew.'

Olga was glaring at Thomas and Lorna in turn. Perhaps *she* was one of his internet trolls. A beautiful malevolent visitation.

'Which of you is Toma Haller?' Olga demanded. In her long fingers she held an iPhone sheathed in white snakeskin.

Thomas met Lorna's eye. From the night they'd first met, he had been able to send out a signal like this, an ironic telepathic smile, even as his face remained expressionless.

He offered his hand to Olga, but already she was angling her phone to capture their two faces in the display.

'For Instagram,' she said.

*

The sun was almost directly overhead. The hotel staff had erected umbrellas across the terrace, but the light and heat seemed inescapable.

Dishes piled with tiger prawns were set down along the table. Waiters transferred the glazed and charred crustacea, pincered between utensils, onto plates.

Since his outburst, Claude had continued to watch Thomas with a curious intensity. As he conversed with Fritz, or attended to the Italian collector on his right (a sort of wizened Audrey Hepburn), or attempted small talk with Olga across the table, he kept looking back as though he had some urgent message to convey.

Everyone was talking about Fritz's exhibition at the Arsenale. Lorna had gone that morning to the VIP preview of *Artists of the World Unite*. Aside from the national pavilions, it was the main event of the Biennale: a massive display of contemporary art spread across the former shipyards. She had arrived to find Fritz surrounded by a party of guests, talking about the

Exposition Universelle of 1867, André Malraux's *musée imaginaire* and the Tower of Babel. She had wandered alone. The scale of the project defied comprehension. There was art she recognised, much more that she didn't recognise. Art that moved her, art that left her cold. She hadn't been able to decide if the whole thing was encyclopaedic or wildly indiscriminate.

Carter Daily spoke of the show's anarcho-pluralism. The word *kaleidoscopic* passed up and down the table, gaining and losing a sparkle of irony. Thomas seemed not to be listening. Two prawns lay on his plate with a sprig of rocket.

'Say, Fritz,' Joel Blair began. 'What was that wall of names at the entrance to the Arsenale?'

'Workers of the Biennale unite!' Fritz drew a shape in the air. 'I wanted to expose the lie that we all collude in. The lie of the individual. The *collective* is the only thing that exists. That wall contains the name of every worker at the Biennale – the art handlers, the fabricators, the curatorial teams—'

'And your name's written larger than anyone's.' This came from Sylvia Rosso at the end of the table.

'A revolution,' Fritz declared, smiling past her. 'That's what we need. A swift and bracing change. And it must be televised!'

A waiter lifted Fritz's plate away. The prawn husks gleamed like shavings of lacquer.

'That could be your next show,' said Carter. 'The coming revolution.'

'My country had a revolution,' said Olga, without looking up from her phone. 'It was shit.'

'I'm serious,' Fritz went on. 'Change is needed. And it begins here, in Venice. The Biennale must never again be curated by a white man.'

'Now that you've had your turn,' said Joel.

'I acknowledge my complicity in the unjust state of things.'

'Oh Fritz,' Joel simpered. 'You're just an old-fashioned Marxist.'

'A neo-Marxist, to be sure.' Fritz's attention darted around the table. 'What about you, Lorna?'

Her non-participation had made her conspicuous. She was aware of a gravitation of attention towards her.

'What about me?'

'Are you a Marxist?'

'Marxist, neo-Marxist, it's all just rhetoric, right?'

She looked away from Fritz towards the canal. The water was feverish with light.

'I'll take that as a no. Lorna Bedford is not a Marxist. Who knew?' Fritz's voice was giddy, on the edge of hysterical.

Claude began to laugh.

'What does Marxist mean?' she said, feeling a spur of provocation. 'That I've internalised every line of *Das Kapital*?'

Beside her, Thomas placed his fingertips around the rim of his water glass and turned it slowly on the tablecloth.

'It means whatever you want it to. That's the point. He's a curator of words.'

His statement was like an intonement, disembodied and exhausted. Fritz's face rebelled. For a moment, his exuberance had subsided beneath some other feeling. Lorna glanced down at the links of her watch. In the sunlight, the scratches were mad hatchings etched by a lunatic.

'Marxism, for you, has to do with rejecting the social order, or thinking that you're rejecting it. It's a way of giving your sentiments validation – the ballast of history and philosophy.'

Her voice was becoming choked. She knew that she was arguing not with Fritz but with Justine. The obstreperous version of Justine who lived (alongside all the other versions) in her head.

'You don't believe in living through your beliefs,' Fritz retorted, his smile rallying. 'You don't believe in praxis. What we need is a rupturing of the social fabric. A dismantling of the systems of oppression. A radical remaking—'

'There are injustices everywhere,' she shot back. 'The world is fucked up. As for how you address that' – she chased after the words she desired – 'it goes beyond writing names on the wall or calling yourself a Marxist. Do you really want society to be razed and rebuilt? You seem to have done just fine.'

Fritz's smile had grown perplexed. It wasn't confusion so much as distaste for her entire way of speaking, as if she'd flouted the rules of whatever game they were playing. Claude was watching her with amused disdain.

From across the water, the bells of Santa Maria della Salute chimed. She could feel perspiration breaking over her body. Venice shone with satin brightness.

'Nothing makes me more suspicious than purity of heart,' Thomas said. He settled his gaze on Claude. 'Whose heart is pure?'

Lorna watched as Claude's expression fractured. She felt Thomas's hand touching her own beneath the table.

*

The entire gathering, every table, had gone quiet.

Lorna looked up to see a young woman standing between the main table and the door to the hotel. She wore a white dress that was soaking wet and clinging to her skin. Her hair was sodden. It was Marianna Berger. In one hand, she held a pair of high heels by the spikes. With the other, she clutched at her dress. A trickle of blood had dried on her shin. She didn't move. Her stillness was hypnotising, like an act of rebellion against the party. Lorna scanned the faces around her, and saw – above the wreckage of half-emptied plates and scattered glasses – expressions of embarrassment, annoyance, amusement . . . Claude's face contained all the reactions at once.

'We wondered where you'd got to,' Thomas said at last.

'Someone pushed me in the canal.' Marianna's words quivered through the air.

A waiter had appeared with a large napkin. She snatched it and flung it away.

'Are any of you listening?' Marianna let go of the shoes and they clattered on the paving beneath her.

'What is this?' Claude muttered, leaning towards Thomas. 'What have you done?'

'She's an artist,' said Carter Daily. 'I used to know her.'

Thomas had shifted his attention to a distant spot on the water.

'I could have drowned.' Marianna's voice was louder. At the other tables, people had begun to murmur.

Fritz reached for his iPhone. 'Is it a performance?'

'You're a fucking performance.'

Fritz's hand hovered midair.

'I could have drowned,' she repeated. 'And none of you care.'

Music – a dance track – was emanating from a source that Lorna couldn't locate. The girl was in shock, she figured, and the shock had spread like a virus to every table. People could only watch, captives to the situation.

'My camera's wrecked. My video—'

Thomas turned to her. 'You hadn't backed it up?' He had lowered his voice to counter hers, as if wanting to confine matters.

'No. It was all on the memory card.' Her eyes tripped along the seated guests to Carter Daily. 'And what the fuck is *he* doing here?'

Claude sat back and placed his hands on the tablecloth. His composure had returned.

'That's the thing about video art,' he declared. 'So ephemeral. It's why I never show it. You're not going to lose a *Thomas Haller* in the canal.'

In a chain reaction, people laughed. This, Lorna guessed, was meant to be an ending. Sylvia Rosso had appeared alongside Marianna, ready to lead her away. Thomas was staring out at the water, his self-possession a shield.

But Marianna had broken into a horrible smile.

'Look at you all! What do you know, any of you, about this man you're celebrating?' She ranged her eyes around. 'Who do you think Thomas Haller is? All he cares about, the only thing he loves, is his name. He *craves* all this' – she swept up the party in a rolling glare – 'like an addict. Craves your adoration. Without it there's nothing. *Look*—' She stabbed her hand in Thomas's direction. 'It's like he doesn't exist. If this exhibition doesn't win the Golden Lion, he'll kill himself. Oh, and as for all that shit about avant-garde purity' – she gave an agonised groan – 'he paints little sections of dresses, stockings, scarves . . . film stills! Sandra Dee's frock in *Imitation of Life*! Lora Meredith's shawl! A sleeve in a mirror! He's had you all fooled. He's not avant-garde, he never was. Thomas Haller is pure fucking *kitsch*.'

Around the terrace, people laughed again. But the laughter was more confused than before, a discharge of unhappy feeling. Thomas hadn't moved. There was a tautened quality about him, as if he might shatter into pieces. Looking over at Claude, Lorna observed a gleam of pain.

At last Thomas laughed, and the sound – a single sharp ejection – commanded silence. He rose from his seat and faced Marianna. His eyes were like creatures roused to pulsing alertness.

'You're insane,' Marianna said. 'You're a—'

Her voice fractured as he came at her. She stumbled back.

Claude had rounded the table at a striding pace. He stepped between them and tried to grab Thomas by the arm. Before he was able to, Thomas had caught hold of Claude's hand in his own. He clutched it hard. Marianna watched from a few feet away, her mouth a dark shape.

'Let go,' Claude said, beneath his breath.

Thomas's face was calm now except for a slight hint of pressure in his closed lips. He began to twist Claude's hand, holding it so tightly that it seemed he meant to break it.

'Let go,' Claude gasped, his shoulders beginning to cave.

Thomas's knuckles had turned white. Lorna held her breath. Claude had begun to claw with his free hand at Thomas's forearm when abruptly Thomas let him go – threw his hand away – and walked off, away from the tables, over to the edge of the terrace where rotting stumps protruded from the water.

In the seconds that followed, the pounding of dance music was clearer, together with the chug of boats on the canal. Across the tables, between the unspeaking guests, sunlight had splintered into shards and specks. It clung to the silverware, the stems of glasses, the rim of an ashtray where a burning cigarette – kissed pink – had been wedged. Olga was holding up her iPhone and rotating her glass of champagne. She was emoting dumbly to her own image on the screen. This, Lorna realised, was the source of the music: Olga was lip-synching for Instagram.

Slowly, and then with growing fervour, people began to chatter. A man at another table had retrieved Marianna's shoes and was holding them up like earrings, arousing laughter. Already, Claude was wheeling between the tables, clasping his hands on the shoulders of guests as if nothing had occurred, although the film of sweat was back, covering his whole face.

Sylvia Rosso had taken Marianna's hand. 'The shock's got to you,' she said. 'And the *heat*. It's like a day in July.'

Marianna yielded, allowing herself to be guided towards the hotel. She left a trail of water on the flagstones as she passed between the tables.

*

From San Marco, Lorna caught a vaporetto leaving for the Giardini. Thomas's exhibition opened at three o'clock. She would have time – just – to see it alone. Sitting at the back of the boat, she watched the buildings and landing stations that bordered the lagoon in a straggling line.

Everyone had taken Marianna for a madwoman. But there were things she had said that Lorna couldn't dismiss. Hard, polished stones of truth. And hadn't Thomas succumbed to a kind of madness? Lorna tried to recapture the look on his face as he had run at Marianna, and then, in the next instant, turned his anger on Claude. He had become someone else; not the man who had placed his hand on hers beneath the table. *Who do you think Thomas Haller is?* The question grew into a refrain as relentless as the motion of the boat. He had always been secretive about the sources of his work, coy about the word *abstract*. Was it possible that she had been complicit, without knowing it, in a gigantic lie about his art?

She wanted to order the boat around – to go back to the St. Regis and drag Thomas away from the party, free him from Claude's clutches. To shake him out of his senses, hurl him in the canal . . . Yes, she thought: she wanted to kill him.

29

The Swiss Pavilion was a simple structure in pale brick. Out of its horizontal roofs rose two glass canopies: one pitched, the other arching. People were hanging around the forecourt. A photographer was adjusting his lens. At the door, the security guard seemed to recognise Lorna. He waved her through without a word.

She passed into the first of the pavilion's white-walled spaces. Paintings of the same size hung around the walls: ten oblong canvases, each dominated by a creamy flesh tone and overspread by crimson streaks and blots. As she trod the border of the empty room, she observed how the red pigment broke out in jittery splatters or hard diagonals. Thomas had thrown the paint or brushed it in fine lines. It made her uncomfortable, the intimation of blood, but Thomas would say, of course, that she was projecting.

There was another gallery, separated from the first by an empty courtyard. She wandered across and stopped in the entranceway.

She was confronted by her own face, repeated around the walls on nine square canvases. Each picture was the size of a small billboard, nine feet along either edge.

The pictures were painted from photographs – close-ups of Lorna's head taken at fractionally different moments. The execution was meticulous, the brushwork barely visible. The young woman in the pictures was solemn, then smiling, then halfway between the two. Laughing, finally. Her head was turned slightly in some paintings, front-on in others. The colours were a mixture of blanched and saturated – her face pale, the collar of her leather jacket as black as spilt ink. The background was a fuzzy orange curtain, falling in pleats.

For a few seconds, all feeling stalled. The effect was one of annihilating clarity, like setting eyes on a pristine sky. The veils and distortions of time had gone.

Nine Muses was the name of the series. Thomas had hung the portraits around three walls. Tracking from left to right, she saw that the final picture, at the end of the right-hand wall – in which seriousness had given way to open laughter – was a repetition of the picture preceding it, only fainter, like a fading echo.

She walked close to the middle wall, where the central painting showed her eyeing the camera from a three-quarter angle, a hoop earring suspended from one ear. Here, her smile was guarded. Laughter was still waiting to break.

Following the arc of the earring, she remembered where the pictures came from. That photobooth on the Charing Cross Road, where they'd sat together on the stool. She looked at herself around the walls, and felt his affection, his adoration, as a forcefield. He had applied the paint so minutely that she could hardly make out the marks until she stood close. Only then did she perceive a mass of tiny flecks. She marvelled at the intricacy, and her sense of amazement was inseparable from one of heartbreak.

*

A path led from the Swiss Pavilion into the depths of the gardens. It was a gravel route with national pavilions on either side. Hackberry trees formed a broken canopy.

Unsure of where she was headed, Lorna walked through a growing crowd. Most people were drifting in the opposite direction. She saw ranks of sunglasses, pressed linen shirts, floating dresses, faces she didn't recognise but instinctively knew. The shoes were works of art in their own right. At the sight of a pair of pink satin platforms, appended by tiny padlocks on their straps, she looked up. Baroness LaBelle was coming towards her. Milton Rogers, her pinstriped companion, was talking in her ear.

'How *are* you?' the Baroness cried.

At once, Lorna realised that the Baroness wasn't addressing her, but someone close behind. She walked on. How *was* she? She'd drunk too much at that hideous lunch.

Did she miss Justine? She missed someone to laugh with, that was for sure. Her aloneness was a new sensation, just then, in the bustling gardens. *What will I do with myself?* She almost said it out loud. Then, a few steps onward: *I'm old, or I will be soon.* She thought of Justine's naked back. The way her sweat broke in minuscule beads.

The green avenue was muggy. The crowd was thinning out. Coming close to the lagoon, Lorna tried to envisage the reaction to Thomas's paintings. People would be stunned, admiring, maybe a little amused. Claude would be outraged. After his prolonged colonisation of Thomas Haller, the abstract painter, this group of photorealist portraits (this *love letter*) would seem like an act of insurrection.

A woman was pushing a wheelchair in Lorna's direction, walking with the same straight-backed poise as Deborah Goffman's ice effigy, except that the chair was empty. The woman had ringleted black hair and a serene face. She was accompanied by a man who shuffled alongside her, a much older husband. He was wearing white sneakers, beige chinos, a white linen shirt with short sleeves, and a red baseball cap. Aviator sunglasses masked his eyes.

Coming closer, Lorna made out the words embroidered on the cap in white.

GOFFMAN ASSOCIATES.

She peered at his face, shaded by the unbent brim.

'Leo!'

Leo and Bonita stopped together.

'Why, if it isn't Miss Bedford.' His voice was frail. His hairless arms hung loose from the cones of his shirtsleeves.

'I didn't know you were in Venice.'

He clutched her hand. His fingers were cold.

'I've taken a little palazzo on the Grand Canal. I never miss the Biennale.'

Lorna caught sight of herself in his mirrored lenses. She had never seen Leo in Venice.

'How are you?'

'I'm alive. *Thriving*. I mean, I have a little trouble with stairs, but what of it?'

Bonita stood apart. The chair was a heavy-looking thing, high-backed and perpendicular and trimmed with chromium.

'They tell me,' Leo said, 'that Ana Garcia is here.'

'Ana? Here in Venice? No, she's not.' Lorna watched as his lips began to motion a response. 'Maybe you heard she'd gone to Venice? She's in Venice, LA. She went there to do a residency.'

'That's too bad,' he said at last. 'I was going to invite you and Ana to a party tonight. Thomas Haller, too.'

He began to walk again. Lorna went with him and Bonita followed.

'I read in the paper—' She hesitated, then forced herself on. 'I read that the lawsuit against you has been dropped.'

Leo adjusted his baseball cap. 'The causative link was too slender. That woman on the crosswalk—'

'Andrea Driscoll.'

'Right. She died from a subarachnoid haemorrhage.' He drew off his sunglasses and peered into the distance. 'Now, what the medical examiner said was – she must have had an underlying condition, a cerebral aneurysm, undiagnosed. What happened on the crosswalk, well, maybe that triggered a minor bleed – the stress of the incident. *Maybe*. But she didn't even hit her head, Lorna. Four weeks later, the aneurysm bled again, *catastrophically*. Well, it's a tragedy, but who's to say it wouldn't have happened anyway?'

Lorna walked beside him in silence.

'People like to make sense of disasters by ascribing a *cause*,' Leo said, raising his voice on the final word. 'By ascribing *blame*.'

'Those protestors at the gala, you mean? The signs, the chanting – do you think that's what caused you—'

'To have a stroke?' He glared at her, then smiled. 'Quit looking for reasons for things.'

They walked on in their convoy of three: Lorna and Leo, straining to match each other's paces, and Bonita a couple of steps behind, wheeling the empty chair.

'Leo – I'm sorry that Ana isn't here.'

He seemed to subject her words to close inspection.

'I'm sorry if you were expecting to find her,' she added.

Still he cogitated, and she felt a chill of sadness.

'Why don't I come over later anyway?'

'Don't you have other places to be?'

'Well, sure. There's an extravaganza at the Gritti, and three other things at least. But I could come by around eight.'

'It's the Palazzo Archento. Bonita can give you the address.' He pulled out his phone and inspected it for a moment, his hand shaking. 'Say, where is Thomas Haller's show? It's all I've been hearing about.'

*

People were crowding outside the Swiss Pavilion. Fritz was giving an interview to a TV camera. Just ahead, Claude Berlins was walking through the entrance. His hand was suspended over the lower back of Olga, his Russian heiress.

Lorna guided Leo into the gallery with the abstract paintings.

'These pictures are extraordinary, right?' she said, as people flowed around. 'They remind me of the Pink Paintings of the late nineties. Different palette. More carnal. They're like Hans Hartung's later works. And, you know, in a different way, they do make me think of Helen Frankenthaler. There's *feeling* in the colour.'

Leo made no reply.

Claude and Olga were in the corner of the room – Claude expounding, Olga returning a bored pout. Leo didn't appear to have seen them.

'They're not his worst,' he finally said. 'But all I can think of is raspberry ripple ice cream. Hey, isn't that Bob Shapiro?'

Lorna left him and walked across the courtyard.

Faced with her own image once more, she felt naked – defenceless – and yet she was conscious of a rising exhilaration.

Claude and Olga had entered behind her. Claude's eyes narrowed as they met Lorna's. His expression gave nothing more away.

'I want these for my boat,' Olga declared. 'All of them, for the *Axioma*. What's the price?'

'Four and a half million,' Claude replied in a near-whisper, 'if you want all nine.'

Lorna's exhilaration died as she foresaw the paintings entombed on Olga's superyacht.

'I want a discount,' Olga said.

'No discounts. This is the Venice Biennale.'

'I want ten per cent, Claude.'

Leo shuffled in. Claude's face changed as he registered the old man's presence. For a moment, Lorna thought that she could discern a furious alarm. Leo walked on. His eyes were fixed on the painting at the centre of the group, the one where Lorna was turning to reveal an earring. He stopped midway through the room. She was aghast to see that his eyes were shimmering.

'You won't believe me,' she said, in a rush of embarrassment, 'but I didn't know anything about this group, these *Nine Muses*. Thomas never said a thing.'

'Muses don't know,' said Leo in a trembling voice. 'They just *are*. Like memories, or movements of the spirit.' He scanned the pictures with fierce concentration. 'Or maybe we don't know what muses think. Maybe they know everything and all we see is a face.'

Across the room, Claude was in furtive discussion with Olga, but he had seen that Lorna and Leo were talking. Every few seconds he glanced their way.

'I take it they're for sale?' Leo said. 'All nine?'

'I can't do a discount,' she answered, keeping her eyes on Claude. 'The price—'

'The price is the price. I'm old. I'll pay. Just tell me they're mine.'

She shook Leo's hand, and Claude's eyes met hers. She nodded to him. In the seconds that followed, she noticed a stripe of scarlet appear on Claude's neck, where the skin met his collar. As she looked back, the colour was spreading upwards, engulfing his face until he was glowing with anger or embarrassment or dismay; but on he went, whispering placatory nothings to his client.

*

After Leo had gone, Lorna hung around the entrance to the pavilion, watching the crowds pass back and forth along the avenue. Fritz was still talking into a TV camera. Thomas was nowhere to be seen. She looked across the broad gravel path and saw, on the opposite side, Claude standing beneath a tree, separate from any clusters of people. He seemed to have lost his hat somewhere between the hotel and here. He looked as sunned and suave as ever. His cream suit had the smoothness of latex. But as he rolled on the balls of his feet, moving out of the shade of the tree, his skin appeared stained. His hair had turned practically white in the sunlight.

She crossed the path towards him.

'Where's Thomas?' she asked, as he noticed her.

His eyes performed their old ensnaring trick, or tried to. He placed one hand over the other. He was wearing a signet ring inset with a dark gem that could have been ancient.

'He's tired. He couldn't come. What a shame, Lorna, for both of you.'

'You magicked him away.'

He didn't laugh, and she realised that she hadn't intended to be funny.

'It's confirmed,' she said. 'Leo Goffman is taking the nine portraits.' She smiled in spite of herself. 'I guess this means I've won.'

He gave her a rueful, searching look. 'You'd already won, Lorna. It's you in the paintings.'

He walked off, into the unceasing flock of art pilgrims.

30

17 April, 19.45. Venice

'Come out on the balcony,' Leo said. 'It's beautiful at this hour.'

Walking with a stick, he led her through a parlour. It was a large space on the first floor of the palazzo, hung with tapestries and filled with carved furniture. A pair of doors led to a loggia. They passed along the walkway, followed by Bonita. Open portals, separated by columns, overlooked the Grand Canal.

Lorna rested her hands on the balustrade. San Geremia was visible in the distance with its dome and sandstone belltower. Above, the sky was fading to purple.

'I always drink Bellinis in Venice,' Leo said. 'Will you join me?'

At Lorna's assent, Bonita returned to the shaded interior.

'Funny place, Venice.' He came to stand beside her. 'The western extremity of the Byzantine empire. The eastern tip of old Europe. The route to Islam. Look at those palaces over there. Moorish.'

The buildings were losing their definition in the dusk.

'Where are all the other guests?' she asked.

'There are no other guests.' There was unease just beneath his candour. 'This is it. Welcome to my party. We're celebrating, aren't we? I didn't think I would buy another work of art in my life. Let alone nine paintings of *you.*'

'The day turned around when I met you.'

His teeth gleamed. 'It hadn't been going well before that?'

'There was a lunch for Thomas. You know the kind of thing. A gathering of art world personalities.'

'Of course. I'm one of them. *The personalities*. Except that people don't warm to mine.' He smiled bleakly at the water. 'I saw him there at the Swiss Pavilion, Claude Berlins. Trying to hustle a sale. I guess we beat him to it.'

Lorna wondered whether it had been love or hate that had moved him to buy the portraits – love of the art or hatred of Claude. Probably both. She turned to see Bonita bearing a silver tray. Glass flutes, each carved with a latticework of grooves, were filled with pink liquid.

'Here's to our sale,' she said.

'Here's to you. Muse of Thomas Haller.' He studied her. 'When I was lying on the floor at the Metropolitan Museum, after my stroke, I *saw* that portrait of you. The one with the earring. What I mean is, I saw the part of you that Haller sees.'

She held a finger to her earlobe, empty now.

'Hell, we all need something. For most people it's love. You're married, aren't you?'

The question took her by surprise. 'Yes. I mean, kind of. We've separated.'

'You're young enough.'

'Young enough for what?' There was dismal humour in the question. 'I'm nearly fifty.'

'You have time to expand your life. I feel like I'm walking down a corridor that's getting narrower with every step. And emptier. Where did everyone *go*? The only person I speak to every day is Bonita. Though I'm not sure she sees herself as my friend. I guess I don't treat her as one. How *do* you treat a friend? I'm not sure I ever knew. I've got too used to having my own way. That's where Deborah used to step in. She knew how to cut me down a little. I guess if we'd had kids . . .' He closed his hand around his glass, sluiced the liquid. 'A daughter could have taken over from Deborah. Kept me in check.'

Seagulls were flying low. Lorna felt herself descending, resistless, into the affairs of Leo's heart.

'It's a beautiful evening,' was all she could think to say.

'I adore Venice.' He spoke with the husky machismo of a man ambivalent about confessing his adorations. 'Just look.' He directed his gaze along the canal. 'It's good to be here. It stabilises the senses. Venice is a repository of consolations.'

'Henry James?'

He nodded. 'And people say I'm a philistine.'

'I only know because my partner – my ex – knew James inside out.'

'Tell me about her.'

'Justine was – is – the smartest person I know. Beautiful, although she'd hate to hear me say that. Fearless, which is such a cliché, I know, but she just doesn't give a damn. I loved that about her. It's funny – I thought that I would always be with her. Even though we bickered and disagreed about everything. I could never quite believe that someone like her had fallen for me. She made me feel good about the things I'd done' – she laughed drily – 'when she wasn't railing at me for being a sellout. I guess if we'd both stayed just the same as we were those first two years, before she became a runaway success . . .' She was silent for a while. 'That makes me sound jealous. But it isn't that. More that I couldn't keep hold of her. I felt her changing, slipping away from me, and I couldn't do anything to stop it. I should have paid more attention, seen it coming. She got closer and closer to her publicist, and then they ran away together to Asia. Happily ever after, right?'

Leo attended to everything with silent fixity.

'When I try to figure out how that relationship started—'

Andrea's coma brought them closer than ever, she wanted to say. *A shared tragedy – a shared enemy. If you hadn't driven downtown that day—*

But hadn't she persuaded him to come to the gallery? Wasn't she implicated, somewhere, in all this?

'Funny coincidence,' she said with airiness. 'Beatrix – the publicist – used to be in a relationship with Andrea Driscoll.'

'Andrea,' he murmured, taking a moment to place the name. 'What happened there, it makes no sense. Tragedies rarely do.'

Lorna saw that he had nothing more to say. The whole matter had been unfortunate, to his mind. Senseless. He had been passing by in his car. The fender had clipped the woman's knee. Maybe he should have been more patient. The causative link, as he'd said before, was slender.

Leo's concentration appeared to settle on the windows across the water, some of them beginning to glow through the twilight.

'You miss Justine,' he said.

'Yes.'

'It's in Venice that I miss Deborah most. It was here' – he ran his hand along the ledge – 'that we used to talk about our lives. This city is a truth serum. The water, the air, the *beauty* of it.' He sighed, perhaps sensing the word to be inadequate. 'It takes down your defences. It draws confessions. I think that's why we felt so close here, so connected. Fact remains, though, I was still alone, and so was she. You live alone in your head. You'll die alone. We only see parts of each other.'

A motorboat was cutting a groove through the oily water. The reflected lights guttered. The noise of the engine dissolved. For a minute there was silence, broken only by the rhythmic slap of water and then – almost too faint to be real – a woman's cry.

'Look at that sky,' Leo said, not seeming to have heard. 'What a colour. I like this time of day the best, between light and dark, when time grows precious. When the world reminds you of its strangeness. I'm going to die soon, Lorna.'

She was about to interject with a protestation, but the quiet of the evening checked her.

'I can predict the future like that, see,' he went on, with a trace of a smile. 'I always had the gift of prophecy. I've had close to ninety years, and I want more. *Many* more. What kind of madness is that?'

'You're a collector,' she replied. 'Your desire refuses to be satisfied.'

'That's for sure.' He turned his empty glass around in his hand. 'Another drink?'

'Sure, why not?'

*

It was close to midnight. She had stayed at Leo's longer than she meant to. It was still warm. A weak nocturnal glow hung in the air like mist.

Justine had sent a series of messages – her first contact in weeks. She had seen reports online of Thomas's show and was convinced that he had used photographs *she* had taken as the sources for his portraits.

You're wrong.

Lorna typed the reply as she meandered over a piazza.

He took them. Or a machine took them – a photobooth. I remember the night it happened. It was twenty years before I met you!

Justine replied at once.

Well, I took some very similar ones. I know I did.

Behind the protest was a softening, Lorna thought. The anger that had followed Andrea's death seemed to have spent its energy.

Another message arrived.

Such a weird thing, this Venice show. WTF is he painting you? Is this the apex or nadir of his career?

Lorna posted a laughing emoji.

That's what everyone's asking. Maybe both.

What does that mean?

He's done something that no one expected. Least of all me. Something emotional. Not like him at all.

Justine didn't reply, this time.

Before long, Lorna became lost. She knew that if she persisted in one direction, she would reach a square, or a shop, or a bridge that she recognised. This city often played a game of hide and seek.

She walked along a street lined by shops – people were still drifting and pausing at the lit windows – and then slipped into a labyrinth of alleyways. She found herself on a deserted path running alongside a canal. A solitary gondola was tied to a post. Ahead, just before the canal made a blind turn, was a bridge. The reflection of a lamp hovered in the water. The sound of her footsteps on the stones echoed back at her.

She had walked past someone. She continued a few steps, then turned to see a young man alone in the shadow of a building. She had passed within feet of him. He hadn't moved.

His face was round and childish, but with a heaviness about the eyelids. His stance – leaning against the wall with one leg hitched up – seemed like a proposition. After a second or two, he levered himself off the wall and slouched away.

Before reaching the bridge, she paused at the edge of the canal. Her eyes passed from the water to the buildings and up to the sky, and she had the sensation of leaving her body on the canal side and floating into the air. Her senses extended like radio waves.

A person was drawing alongside her. She saw the face of a young man, different from before. His smile was crooked. His eyes had an awestruck glint; he seemed to look past her even as he drew closer – too close. He was raising one hand, palm outward, as if to stop her or embrace her. A sound was coming from him, although his lips hadn't moved. A hurried, inane muttering. He wore a tight striped T-shirt.

His hand made contact with her arm. His fingertips clamped around her.

The man crashed backwards into the water. The noise of the

impact jolted her. She had pushed him with both hands. She could feel the pulsing recoil in her arms. The man sputtered and flailed in the canal. His pale arms were gleaming against the grey-green. His movements made her think of a panicked bird. He seemed smaller, down there, almost like a child.

As she hurried away, she thought it was odd that she hadn't heard anything as she fled – no sound of splashing or struggle. It was as if the water had swallowed him.

*

18 April, 00.02

Thomas found his way to Campo Santo Stefano, and from there back to his hotel.

Inside, he found it hard to ascend the stairs. They kept skidding away from him, listing like the deck of a ship. He took the banister in both hands and tried to swing himself upward. He pulled hard and let go. The sensation of spinning on his ankles, weightless as a ballet dancer, gave way to a rushing descent and a flipped view of the marble steps. His head hit the stone.

Slightly less drunk and clamping a wet towel to his head, he wondered how he had got from the staircase to his room. He tapped through social media feeds on his phone. People had posted photos of his show. He saw words like *genius* and *triumph* and *heartbreaking*. He clamped the towel harder until he felt water straining out.

Now that he'd registered for an account on X, somebody kept tagging him in posts. Somebody with a chain of letters and numbers in place of a name. He recognised the profile photo: Warhol's *Marilyn* with a giant ginger wig. It made him think of Art Garfunkel.

@ThomasHaller @SwissPavilion WTAF?! Retrograde blue-chip bullshit $$$ and people are saying he's a genius.

@ThomasHaller why? WHY?

Why *what*? He giggled. It was a shrill, peculiar sound.

He tapped to view the profile and scrolled through a long chain of posts. Words and phrases that he didn't understand and didn't like glinted out. *Aggro-centrist. Strawman. Educate yourself.* He wondered if this masked poseur could be Justine Olson, Lorna's partner.

He dropped the towel and typed into his phone.

I won the Golden Lion.

He stared at the words. Within minutes, replies began to appear.

Congratulations!

Sensational news.

You're a genius @ThomasHaller

Moments later, the phone began to buzz. Claude Berlins was calling.

The buzzing stopped. Thomas lay back and allowed his head to sink into the pillows. Through the wobble and shimmer of his drunkenness, he caught hold of a memory. He had a clear vision of the woven coverlet on Claude's bed, with its scene of Eden. Closing his eyes, he switched to the image of himself and Luca in Maryon Park.

Struggling to lift his head, which was horribly heavy now, he looked again at his phone. The praise had multiplied and none of it meant a thing. He scrolled down until he saw what he'd known he would find.

Fucking bullshit. Judges haven't decided on a winner yet.

31

22 April, 11.55. New York

All morning it had refused to rain. Leo walked the single block to Baglioni's, carrying a tightly wound umbrella that doubled as a walking stick. He struck the sidewalk with the metal tip, watching for sparks. He'd told Bonita to dump the wheelchair in the Adriatic.

Another lunch date – another auctioneer. He thought back to the previous occasion. That fawning mess, Florian Roth, had been desperate to clinch the sale of the century! Well, the sale was Leo's gift to dispense. He tried to remember what Melissa Dion was like. *Artscribe* had called her the most powerful Black woman in the art world. He'd only met her once. But auctioneers were predictable. He knew their desires.

He walked into the Rockefeller Center and along the Channel Gardens. He loved the optimism of the buildings. They were extolments, in steel and stone, of international trade and private enterprise. His eyes jumped along the fountainhead sculptures. Nymphs, tritons and other bronze beings spouted water into pools. On the ice rink, a few lone skaters were whirring in ellipses – late for the time of year. They made him think of flies trapped in a strip light.

*

Melissa was ten minutes late. She walked into Baglioni's with calm haste but no apology.

'Don't get up,' she commanded.

321

Remaining in his seat, he sized her up. A woman in her forties or early fifties, dressed in a business suit with a wide-lapelled white shirt. She was striking, he thought. Beautiful, but with a certain froideur.

'The most powerful Black woman in the art world,' he said.

She scrutinised him as she sat down. 'I don't pay attention to those descriptions. The art should be the news story, I always say, not the auctioneer.'

A waiter arrived and offered them water. Something about his skinny, freckled arms made Leo feel unwell.

'You've been in the news yourself,' Melissa said. 'Or rather, you've managed to avoid being in the news.'

'I don't know what you're talking about.'

She smiled in a not entirely pleasant way. 'It's been all over social media – not the mainstream news. That crowd of protestors on the night of your gala. Maybe you never saw them. Did they usher you into the Met through a back route?'

'They took me out through the front, on a stretcher. I had a stroke that night.'

'I'm sorry, yes. I did hear. How are you now?'

'I can't do stairs. And I have a urinary tract that's boobytrapped with razor wire, but that's nothing new. I used to wonder why old folk obsess about their ailments. Now I know. *Death*. It takes you over, piece by piece. A killer blow is what I want, not a million pricks.'

'Something like a brain haemorrhage,' she said, without a smile.

He felt a thrill of anguish. She disapproved of him – detested him! She was one of those who blamed him for the Driscoll woman's death. But still he had something she couldn't resist. That was why she'd come.

'Fate is cruel and apathetic. What can I do about it?'

'You wanted to talk about your collection.' She signalled to the waiter. 'Let's order.'

'I'm not afraid of death,' he went on. 'It's there. Always has been, for everyone. It's stalking closer now.' He felt his mouth widen in a tragic smile. 'Well, I do what I can. I swim every morning.'

'Right.'

'Butt naked.'

'So did you want to discuss your legacy?'

'Is it possible to imagine being dead?' He tried to catch sight of himself in her pupils. 'To visualise the world when you're no longer in it? I wonder. Maybe it's easy. Maybe you just have to look around you.' He steered his eyes around the restaurant, over the stripped planks of the floor, the diners seated at the bare wooden tables, and the gigantic mound of ice on which fish and crabs had been laid in a nacreous carnival of blind eyes and upreared claws. 'Everything would look like it does now, except it wouldn't be *you* seeing it.'

The waiter was back at their table.

'Give me the salmon,' he said. 'And a glass of Chablis. By the way,' (addressing Melissa again), 'I just gave a hundred thousand dollars to the Democrats.'

'The skate,' said Melissa. 'And sparkling water.' She looked back at Leo with arched eyebrows. 'Seriously?'

'It's nothing to me. Nothing to them. Like tossing a dime at a hobo. Truth is, I've never been political. Although, back in the seventies, my wife *did* host a meeting for the Black Panthers at our duplex on Park.'

Melissa leaned forward a little and returned a business-like smile.

'Tell me about that in a minute. Your advisor – Fritz – mentioned that you're considering a posthumous sale.'

'Fritzie Forceps, yes. He always delivers.'

He began to laugh, then stopped. Three young women were filing past the table, chattering noisily. Their dresses floated.

'Hannah and her sisters. The Three Graces! I used to own a

Canova, before I got tired of all that *conquest of appearances* crap.' He turned back to Melissa. 'You know, I always wanted kids.'

She fastened a button on her jacket.

'*Three*,' he declared. 'I wanted three. But one of them a daughter.'

'How about three daughters?'

'Funny thing is, I only see one. I mean, when I look at my unlived lives. It's like I'm out on the freeway, coasting down the middle lane, and I see the vehicles side to side of me. Sometimes I can see into the cars, the people driving them, the passengers. *One daughter*. That's how it is, glancing over at the lives you didn't lead. Can't do it for too long, though, or' – he clapped a fist into his open palm – '*boom*. You weren't looking. Too much sideways glancing. You have to keep your eyes on the road ahead, otherwise—'

'You run someone down.' She smiled in the same unpleasant way as before.

A waitress swept by, bearing two identical plates. There were pink slices of what looked like smoked duck alongside clouds of mashed squash. The waiter returned with their drinks.

'Just the one daughter,' he murmured. 'Sometimes – in my dreams, never when I'm awake – I see her so clearly that it's like she exists out there in the world. Other times' – he raised his still-closed fist to his temple – 'she's just in here.'

'I want to talk about your art.'

'*Sex* was the problem, Melissa.' Leo regarded the serious, handsome woman across the table. 'Or, if not exactly a problem, a place of mutual – what would you call it? – *diffidence*. We had too much respect for each other, Deborah and I, too high a regard. We idolised each other. The Chatelaine of the Upper East Side, that was how I thought of her before *Vanity Fair* ever called her that. My sweet chatelaine! How could I reduce her to a sexual being? *How?* I mean, we tried, but it was complex, the sex act.' He sighed and consulted his age-stained fingers. 'We were the furthest thing from animals. Like Adam and Eve before the Fall.'

How could he expect her to understand? There was a control about her expression that fascinated and appalled him.

'A sale, yes,' he said, exhaling at length. 'The art sale of the century. I mean, it can't all be buried with me, can it? I'm not a pharaoh, nor was I meant to be.'

He picked up his glass and sucked at the Chablis. Melissa's serenity was unnerving him. Florian Roth had been a mouse he could play with. This wasn't a game, or not his game.

*

The waiter laid down their plates. Leo stared at the salmon steak on its pyre of lentils, dribbled with hollandaise – a touch that seemed daring, outrageous, like globules of cloud scuttling over an orange-pink sunset. To insert a utensil would be an act of desecration.

He drove his fork through the salmon. The resistance was minimal. The fish split into slippery shavings.

Turning slightly, he saw two ladies at a neighbouring table, both aged in their seventies. In their gilded aspect, they were different from the other diners. Both were looking at him. Maybe they had known Deborah. For an instant, he thought he saw (or heard, or felt) something foul and brutal. It was stalking him every day, that sweet-tongued, mean-eyed boar. Cute when it chose to be, but still a fucking beast.

'Isn't that Leo Goffman?' he heard one of the women say.

'My God, he must be a million years old by now,' the other whispered.

'Ninety at least.'

'I'm eighty-six,' he blurted, staring at his plate. 'And teach your friend some manners.'

His utensils, clenched in either hand, were tremoring like tuning forks.

Melissa was standing. 'Leo, I feel like I'm wasting my time. Shall we call it a day – reconvene?'

He stared at her. What a relief to be rebuked. He was a man who needed to be affronted. Chastised. So few people knew it.

She had drawn away from the table. He raised his knife.

'Wait. You need to hear this. I have three Barnett Newmans. *Three*. Two Ellsworth Kellys – premium pieces, mid-sixties – and an Yves Klein. Beautiful – the bluest blue you ever saw. A Picasso, you know the one – the best version he made of *Las Meninas*!' The knife was pointed straight at Melissa. 'And that's just the paintings. There are sculptures – Gabo, David Smith, Gaudier-Brzeska, Brancusi. A *Bird in Space*!'

'Leo, I know.'

'And that's just the modern stuff, only a fraction of it. There's all the contemporary art, too – my Jeff Koons *Bunny*, which I never even wanted. (Deborah said, *Buy it! You won't regret it!*) Sixteen Thomas Hallers. *Sixteen*.'

Tears were running down his face. A hot, soul-corrupting flow.

'Leo, let's continue this another time. I have a two o'clock. You know where I am. You know that we'd be proud to handle the sale of your collection.'

His knife dropped on the table with a thud. 'A deluxe catalogue. Hard-bound. Lined with silk.' His voice was withered. 'Papal red edges.'

'Let's put a date in the diary.' She was signalling to the waiter. She had covered the bill. Not even the privilege of paying had been left to him.

'I'd want that guaranteed in writing.'

'Goodbye, Leo.'

'The pages,' he said, and closed his eyes. 'The edges. A deep papal red.'

32

27 April, 09.04. New York

As Lorna walked along the street with Jay, a man in blue overalls was watering the squares of earth beneath the maples. Each
tree was fenced in by a tiny iron grate. The space behind was
packed with flowers. Water trickled over the sidewalks.

She had been living in a world of hypotheses. No sooner had
the truth about Luca been clarified than she'd propelled herself
down a new line of fantasy. She had been searching for reports
of a drowned man in Venice. A gondolier, maybe. The fate of
her assailant had split into multiple strands. He had drowned.
He had swum away. He had heaved himself from the water and
slunk into the night. She had made him up. The previous night,
she had tidied up the drawers of the desk at home, placing
Justine's various folders in a kind of order, part thematic and
part chronological; she had left the adoption paperwork at the
top of the pile. It had occurred to her that she could open the
envelope, right then, and search online for the child – the man
– if she wanted to: the name of the adoptive family would be
in there. Instead, she settled for googling *Jacob Bedford*. She
knew that he would never have retained her surname or even
the first name she had given him. But high up in the results was
a LinkedIn profile for a man in his twenties of that very name
– good-looking, dark-haired, smiling in a way that reminded
her a little of herself. He lived in New York and worked as a
lighting technician at NBC . . .

She passed Veniero's and walked on another block, uncertain

of how she meant to spend the weekend. It took less than three hours to get to the beach on the Long Island Rail Road. She tried to remember which terminal it was that they'd always caught the train from.

She was walking beneath the marquee of an old nightclub when her phone buzzed. She pulled it from her jacket and saw one of the Pink Paintings on the screen. Years ago, she had saved the picture so that it flashed up when he phoned.

'I've been trying to reach you,' she said, resting one foot on a step.

'I know. This isn't too early?'

'It's morning here. I'm out already. Did you see my messages?'

'Yes – I'm sorry. These last few days have been a blur. I'm still hungover. I've been hungover for a week.'

He sounded the same as ever – detached, as though he were talking about someone other than himself.

'How come I didn't see you at the pavilion?'

'I never made it.'

'You missed your own opening?'

'I got drunk at some bar. It doesn't matter. It was your show, really.'

She scanned the townhouses around her, their red bricks muffled by ivy and ponderous shade. 'It was beautiful – but unbearable, in a way. I felt like I was looking at my own memorial.'

'I haven't read any of the reviews. I've no idea whether I've been trashed or showered with praise.'

'A bit of both.' She stopped on the sidewalk and looked up at the new leaves on the trees. 'Why don't you come and see me?' The words had come to her like a revelation. 'Come to New York for a few days. We can talk about it all, properly. Everything. You could stay up in the loft—'

'I can't.'

'But why? I can't believe you're up to much.'

'I can't,' he said again. 'I have an exhibition to prepare for. Claude wants me to show at his new gallery in Hong Kong.'

The air seemed heavier. The clouds overhead were hanging in a dense formation, excluding the blue.

'I thought Claude would have dropped you after Venice. Those portraits—'

Thomas laughed, but with a forlornness. 'He says I've blown apart my credentials as an abstract painter. And he hasn't forgiven me for the claim I made about winning the Golden Lion—'

'Fuck the Golden Lion.'

'Fuck the Golden Lion,' he echoed. 'But the thing is, Claude never lets go. Haven't you realised? All those years in New York when I worked with you, he was circling – biding his time. I can see it now . . . Try to shake him off and he holds tighter. If he loses, it's only temporary.'

'So, what happens now?'

'He says I need to be resurrected in a new market. He reckons China is the place. The show's in two weeks.'

'That's insane. What kind of work can you make by then?'

'Precisely the kind that Claude wants. Production-line art. We've outsourced it to a fabricator in Zürich.'

'You know, you could just say no. Walk away.'

'It's too late.'

There was a tremor, she thought, in his voice.

'But your Venice paintings were a breakout. You resisted Claude. That day at the lunch—'

'The freedom's only ever an illusion. When Claude allowed you to sell those paintings to Goffman—'

'That wasn't part of his plan. He wasn't banking on Leo walking in.'

'It doesn't matter. He's framing it as a pay-off. A final act of generosity to you. He wants you out of the picture for good.'

'Fuck him. What do you want?'

'I don't know. Maybe to go away. To Mexico – the desert. Or a provincial town somewhere. I could get a job at a gas station.'

'I can see that working out.'

He didn't reply. The siren of a fire truck wailed from a long way down the street. Jay raised a leg and began to piss. She watched the stream as it dripped to a halt.

She walked on a few yards, then crouched down on one knee and took Jay's muzzle in her free hand. She wanted to feel its smooth underside, its warmth. Whatever outrage she'd felt had been spent. Everything she'd wanted to say to Thomas in Venice felt meaningless; it would be like arguing with a ghost or a person in a dream. He was in love with a vision – an image – like the kneeling Venus that she'd found with Justine that day at the museum.

'I'll tell you what I want,' he said at last. 'I want you to come to Hong Kong. It'll be hell without you. Please say you'll come.'

*

5 May, 19.44. New York

The evenings were always long in New York. His other residences – Montauk, Naples, the palazzo in Venice – offered ways of passing the time. But a hundred floors above Midtown, he didn't feel the same temptation to step out and perambulate. New Yorkers were a threat. At any moment, he might be pushed in the gutter.

He sat in his oxblood swivel chair, watching night fall by small increments, like tints being added to watercolour paper layer by layer.

He used to be one of them, the threatening mass, charging along the sidewalks with places to be. Once, when he'd been walking along Madison with Deborah – a clear day, after rain, the air boisterous with breeze and light – she had stopped dead on the sidewalk, forcing him to stop too, and she had begun to laugh.

'For God's sake, Leo. What is this, a race? Why are you walking so damned fast? I can't keep up. Slow down. We're not in any hurry.'

He'd been about to protest that they *were* in a hurry, that she'd taken too long – as ever – getting ready. But her humour, combined with the sharp beauty of the morning, induced an alternative action. He leaned over and embraced her, right there in the street, held her tight for a moment, saying nothing.

He remembered the feeling of her fur coat as he pressed her close, and the scent of the shawl around her neck, and how his hands sank to rest on her shoulders. That had been the day she'd told him she was pregnant.

Slow down.

The summit of the nearest building released a fiery gleam. Everything else – the hundreds of oblongs and spires – was retreating into depthless purplish gloom.

Perhaps he would listen to the radio, or watch television, or call Bonita and ask for a whisky sour. Maybe later. For the time being, he rose heavily and went to look at his art collection.

He drifted past two Barnett Newmans. Their expanses of dark red, split by cracklike fissures running from top to bottom, made him think of the heat of New Mexico. He trod onward, his feet seeming to skim the carpet, and ran his hand over a bronze by Isamu Noguchi. It was an abstract piece, all clefts and hard corners.

He crossed the room to touch another sculpture. His hands rested on the brushed steel. It was warm to the touch.

Wandering more slowly, obeying Deborah's decades-old command, he went along the passageway to his bedroom. He'd cheated time with this room – transplanting it, exactly as it had been in the Park Avenue apartment, into the Pegasus Tower. He stared at the middle window. Bonita hadn't drawn the curtains yet, and pink-blue light filled the glass.

He turned to face the Thomas Haller painting, which seemed now to have bled into the room, and he dropped to his knees. He felt the carpet underneath him, all around him, like a rippling sheet. *Slow down*. It wasn't difficult after all. No sensation of falling. Why hadn't he listened? This was how it should feel, being alive – how it should always have felt.

*

20.01

Bonita knew that Leo was dead before she'd fully opened the door. He was lying on his side by the fireplace. His mouth was open. She went to stand beside him. His eyes were closed. His hands were clasped over his chest, one on top of the other, like the hands of a saint. Slowly she crossed herself. He was inhumanly still. It made her realise how noisy and animate he'd been, even when sleeping.

'*Descanse em paz*, Leo,' she said, dropping the *Mr Goffman* of four decades' use. What did a corpse care?

She glanced at the bloodless skin, stretched over the framework of his brow and nose, then at the hands in their mimicry of penitence. God could be ironic, she thought. But then, how much better than Leo had most of the saints been, when it came down to it, once you stripped away the legends? They'd all been sinners. Being a saint virtually required it.

She went to the bedside cabinet and opened the drawer. She lifted out the copy of *Vanity Fair* and placed it on the bed, then drew out the shawl that had been Deborah's. Kneeling on the floor beside his body, she took one of his cold hands in her own, lifting it by an inch, and twined the material around it, then around the other hand, unifying them in a figure-of-eight knot.

33

Standing at the base of the Pegasus Tower, Lorna was struck by how uninventive it was. Four facets with chamfered corners, swathed in bluish plate glass. And within, a megasystem of ducts and cabling and elevator shafts. She had heard stories of how the waterworks groaned and periodically exploded.

The lobby, lying beyond a revolving door, was a shrine of alabaster and dark teak. A shrine whose spirits have fled.

'I'm here to visit the home of Leo Goffman,' she said to the suited concierge.

The glass gates that ran in a line between the lobby and the elevators slid apart. One pair of elevator doors was already open.

*

When the doors drew apart, she saw a woman, slightly smaller than herself, standing in wait. Bonita. Her face was sombre and alert. A single dark ringlet had escaped from the tousled mass of her hair. It hung close to one eye. She wore sweatpants, a T-shirt and worn-out plimsolls.

Lorna held out the envelope containing the certificate for the *Muses*, realising that flowers would have been more fitting.

'I'm sorry. I don't mean to intrude.'

'You're not. It's good to see you.'

'This' – Lorna indicated the envelope – 'I guess it belongs here. To the estate. I wanted to bring it myself.'

Bonita gave a nod and took it.

'I'm sorry about Leo,' Lorna said. 'These things are a shock even when they're expected.'

'Everything was a shock while he was alive. Now it's just silent. Empty. Come—'

Bonita led Lorna across the hallway and along a broad corridor paved in creamy-golden stone and hung with paintings. There were Modernist landscapes: a Fauvist harbour scene, a blossoming orchard in a cloisonné style. The place was empty, as yet, of flowers and tributes.

Lorna stopped beside a painting that was larger than the others. It was a picture that she knew from countless reproductions: Picasso's *Girl on a Ball*, of a seated wrestler watching a child acrobat as she balances.

'Leo bought that painting for Deborah,' Bonita said.

Lorna wanted to linger, but she felt the gentle psychological tug of her usher. At the end of the corridor was a pair of oak doors. Bonita rested her hands on the brass knobs and the doors swung apart. Lorna saw into a bright arena – a space that seemed to float in the upper air of the city. She retracted her gaze and began to identify the sculptures that were laid out in a phalanx. David Smith's steel boxes shone like a colossal, faceted crystal. In one corner, a red stone figure, probably by one of those European Modernists, squatted in an ungainly dance.

The carpet was spongy underfoot. Lorna looked down at the off-white shagpile. It made her think of packing foam.

Bonita was watching her as she drank in the details.

'I'll make coffee,' she said. 'Will you have one?'

'Sure. Thanks.'

Lorna sat down on a dais of silvery velvet and tried to imagine Leo in this place, an old man in a hall of mirrors. Her eyes shifted to the surface of a coffee table, stacked with art and design books. An old magazine lay at the centre. She saw the patina of age in the sheen of the cover before she made out the image. A beautiful lady, aged around forty, seated in a sumptuous room (*how eighties*), hair primped and pompadoured, eyes alight with confidence, teeth revealed in a beatific smile (the teeth, charmingly, a little too large for the face).

Deborah Goffman: Chatelaine of Park Avenue

It was an issue of *Vanity Fair* from September 1983. Deborah had been aged around forty in that photograph, younger than Lorna was now. Staring at the woman on the cover, Lorna tried to imagine what she'd been like. She picked up the magazine and began to turn its pages. The adverts, with their smug assurances and prissy typefaces, dated the magazine. She flicked through a profile of Karl Lagerfeld – still dark-haired but already brandishing the fan. Then a clump of pages flipped over in one go to reveal the cover story.

Lorna saw the same radiant face: Deborah was standing off-centre in the double-page image, holding a tea tray decked with porcelain. But the composition of the image was what startled her. It was an elaborate reconstruction of Velázquez's *Las Meninas*, staged in what looked like an oak-panelled, stucco-corniced room of the Goffmans' duplex. Leo was there, off to the left, playing the role of the artist in the Spanish masterpiece, standing to one side of an easel bearing an invisible picture. He was youthful, probably around forty-five, with dark hair that was thinning but sleekly combed. He wore a double-breasted suit and a striped blue and white shirt with a red tie. He was smiling – a broad, easy, American smile.

And between them, a child. A girl of perhaps seven, a pretty child with dark hair that poured out from behind a black velvet band, cast in the part of the *infanta*. She stood there in a lace dress, resting a hand on the arm of the sofa. True to the original painting, her expression was shy, a touch uncertain. Her head was turned in the direction of Deborah, but her eyes were on the camera.

They'd even included a mastiff. It lay in the foreground, its mouth gaping.

Deborah Goffman and her family at home at
800 Park Avenue.

With a quickening pulse, Lorna read the text. It was a typical frothy feature, the story of one of the city's leading patronesses – a benefactor of the Met Opera, the Whitney, the Frick, the New York City Ballet.

'Does Lilith like the ballet?' I ask Deborah.

Lilith – Lily – now seven, is Deborah and Leo's only child. She skips in and out of the room, curious and reserved, watching her mother with wide eyes.

'Oh, she adores it! She's taking lessons. Leo drives her to ballet class twice a week.'

A daughter, and he had never said a thing. In fact, hadn't he said that night in Venice that he regretted never having had children?

Bonita was coming towards her, holding a tea tray in a peculiar random echo of Deborah Goffman in the magazine.

'Oh, that,' she said, stopping for a moment. Lorna heard the coffee cups rattle in her grip. 'You found it.'

'They had a daughter. I never knew.'

'Hardly anyone knows.' Bonita set down the tray and poured coffee. 'Milk?'

'No, thanks.'

'Mr Goffman – Leo – never talked about it. The people who remember, friends of his and Deborah's – he stopped seeing them a long time ago.'

'What happened to her?' Lorna stared at the family portrait.

It was a pastiche, verging on ridiculous, although the child's eyes were a stray moment of candour.

Bonita shook her head slowly, as if Lorna hadn't needed to ask. She sat beside Lorna on the edge of the sofa.

'It was so long ago that without that magazine, I could believe none of it had happened. Leo kept it by his bed. He worshipped the picture of Deborah on the front. But I don't think he opened it in forty years.' She looked around the room, around the pinnacles of the city, before focusing on Lorna. 'This second life of his, his whole life after he left Park Avenue, was an effort to forget.'

'To forget about Deborah?'

'Oh no, he lived on the memory of Deborah. To forget about Lily. He and Deborah were never able to forgive themselves.' She took a cup of coffee from the tray. 'The girl suffered from night terrors. She used to wake up and not know where she was – still dreaming but awake. I slept in the next room, and if I heard her, I always came running. That night, I heard nothing. Lily got out of bed and managed to climb up on the windowsill. It was higher than her head – I don't know how she got up there. But she did. And the window was open.'

Placing her coffee back down, she took the open magazine from Lorna and brought it to her chest, shielding the cover with both hands.

'It was the summer after this magazine came out. A man walking his dog found her at five a.m. Leo was already up and dressed. He ran down the stairs, ran out onto the sidewalk. I watched him pull off his jacket and throw it over her. The look on his face – it was like he'd gone insane.'

'Grief is a kind of madness.'

'They both went mad, in that case.' Bonita set down the magazine. 'Deborah was never the same again, and she lived for another twenty years. And Leo – well, it was only a few weeks after the funeral when he was suddenly just *over it*. He went back to work and that was the end of it, for him. He didn't want the child mentioned. I had to pack all her clothes and toys away, everything. Leo told Deborah that they couldn't live in the past.'

'And you stayed with them, through all of this?'

'They needed me more than they realised, Leo especially. After Deborah died, he went to live in Montauk. He felt closer to her there. And then he built this place.' She ran her hand over the silver fabric of the couch, leaving swathes of shadow. 'Like I said, he needed to forget. More coffee?'

'Thanks, yes.'

Bonita looked down at the magazine. 'That's the only photograph I have of Lily. Leo removed all the others. Destroyed them. He filled his life with the art he bought.'

Lorna glanced back at the girl, posed in the role of Velázquez's *infanta*.

'There was a time when I thought he'd brought all of her toys back out of storage. There were bunnies and bears on the floor of the drawing room here. Mickey Mouse, Donald Duck. Turned out it was an installation. That guy in LA who made all the things out of old soft toys.'

'Yes, I know the one.'

34

16 May, 23.34. Montreux

The security light flicked on as Thomas left the house, metallising the steps down to the footpath. On either side of the track, the trees were like dense matter moulded from darkness.

After a few minutes, he cut off the path into the forest, using his phone to light the way. Weaving through the maze of pine trees, he flashed the beam this way and that, hearing nothing apart from the crackle of his footsteps.

He saw a red light flashing in the undergrowth. Fixing his eyes on the point, he walked towards it. The light flicked out of view, then reappeared. It seemed to have moved.

He walked faster, straining not to blink.

He scrambled through ferny undergrowth, tripping and almost falling, arriving at last at the edge of the forest, where it met the road. He stumbled down a steep incline onto the asphalt. Far below, the lake was like a sleeping animal, beaded by twinkling lights. Out on the water, a red light was bobbing and twinkling as a boat glided across.

He trekked for close to an hour. The road into town was deserted. There was an ache in his legs by the time he banged on the door of Le Mazot.

*

Thomas could see himself in every mirror. He knelt on the floor, naked apart from his boots. The rubber heels dug into his buttocks.

Otto came into the room, dressed in a T-shirt and shorts. His legs were smooth, as if he'd waxed them.

'Take off my shoes.'

Thomas untied the laces, using his fingernails to loosen the grimy knots. The sneakers were dank and warm where he slid his fingers around Otto's feet. He pulled them off. The smoothness of Otto's skin was synthetic. The young man was wearing flesh-toned pantyhose.

Otto undid the button at the front of his denim shorts. They dropped to his ankles. Beneath the glossy gauzy fabric, he was shaven and erect.

Thomas raised his hand. Otto took it and drew it to where the elasticated waistband circled his hips. Thomas slid his fingers beneath the ridge, bringing them close to where Otto's dick lay trapped in nylon.

'Take them off.'

With both hands, Thomas drew the tights over Otto's thighs, feeling the material slide like liquid. The sliding accelerated as it cleared Otto's knees. The tights lost their tensility, began to pucker and collapse. Otto stepped out of the shrivelled garment.

Thomas took the fabric in his hands and ran it over the tip of his own dick. Then he raised it, teasing it into a long straight line, and wound it around his neck – once, twice – and handed the two ends to Otto.

In a swift, brutal motion, Otto had pulled the ligature tight. Thomas felt the blood pool in his face. The flow of air halted in his throat. The room glowed and darkened around him. Holding the nylon tight, Otto stepped behind him. Thomas widened his eyes to the sight of his own naked body – kneeling and multiplied by three. Otto was standing over him, arms drawn wide, the stretched material in his hands like a crossbar. By an act of will, Thomas made himself remember.

*

He had finished installing his paintings at Galerie Claude Berlins two days before the opening of the exhibition. In the late afternoon, he went with Betty to Hyde Park. Luca had suggested that they meet at his flat that night. In the taxi from Mayfair to Kennington, Thomas felt that he was fated to keep returning to that single-roomed apartment with its brick walls and sparse furniture.

Luca at once seemed distracted, embracing Thomas only briefly before retreating into the flat. They were no longer in the public realm of the gallery. It was the first time they had been alone together since July. Thomas watched as Luca moved about, arranging drinks and filling the silence with talk about the dinner on Thursday. Perhaps Luca was wondering what would happen once the show was open, once there was nothing more to plan. They wouldn't see each other so much; that was almost certain.

The door to the balcony was open, admitting the warm evening into the room. Thomas lay back on the double bed that faced the doorway, resting his head on the pillows, and told himself that it couldn't go on, in any case, this thing. Luca's energy needed some other outlet. His irreverence, his scorn, his sincerity, his admiration – all of it was becoming excessive. A dangerous buildup. Thomas needed to free himself from the boy's need, or his power, whichever it was. And yet whenever they were together, it was like smoking or taking drugs, a shortcut into feeling young again.

Luca was fiddling with the sound system. A song began to thump out: 'Freedom' by George Michael. He began strutting, half dancing, around the room. But something was different. His usual easy humour was a performance tonight.

'You're not happy,' Thomas said. 'What is it?'

Luca spun around to the music, raising his arms. His T-shirt sleeves slipped down to reveal his biceps.

'Are you surprised?'

'It's because I didn't answer your messages, right? I said I was sorry. I was busy with work – the paintings. That's how I get before a big show. Everything else stops mattering.'

Luca turned to face Thomas. His hands were on his hips.

'You've never answered any of my messages, unless it's a work thing. What's new? I have to pretend that the gallery is our only connection. That none of *this* has actually happened.'

'That's not true. You know I like you.'

Luca made a face. 'Do I? Do you?'

Thomas heaved himself up on the bed. 'What's got into you?'

Luca stood near the door and looked out at the view. 'You going silent on me was a good thing, actually.' His voice was calmer – strangely so. 'It gave me a chance to think about things. About the last time we were together. About that party at the Serpentine.'

'What about it? We got drunk. We came back here . . .'

'It didn't mean anything to me at first,' Luca said. 'And not for a while after. But the things you said, you and him, kept coming back to me.'

'I don't know what you're talking about.'

Luca crossed the room and turned the music down. He picked up a tumbler of whisky and Coke and took a large gulp.

'I was standing with you and Claude outside on the grass.'

'And?'

'You were talking about the show. The number of paintings. Claude with his usual obsessive shit about selling to the right people.' Luca raised his arms again in an extravagant stretch and watched Thomas. 'But then he said something weird. He said, *I told you this would happen*' – Luca put on a French accent, far stronger than Claude's – '*I told you I would represent you*. It seemed like he didn't care if I heard. And then he asked if you remembered the Montreux Palace.'

Thomas ran his fingers over the bedsheet. 'What did I say?'

'You said yes. You said you remembered everything.'

'Well, so what?'

'There was something odd about the way you said it. I couldn't figure it out. I thought you were talking about some art event. It wasn't until the other day, when I found a picture of us all standing there at the party – Claude and you and me – that it made a kind of sense.'

'What picture?'

'One of those social diary photographs. I found it online. It was the way you were *looking* at him. It made me think of your voice when you answered him. It was like – I don't know – like you were in love.'

'You're drunk, Luca.'

'I understood why you'd kept me – *us* – a secret. You didn't want Claude knowing.'

'You're wrong.'

Thomas stood and went to him. He held out his arms to touch Luca's shoulders, and Luca repelled him, clapping the palms of their hands together. He walked onto the balcony and leaned back in the crux of the railings, spreading his arms wide. Thomas stood at the end of the bed, just inside the door.

'I've been waiting to see if you'd deny it,' Luca said. 'And you haven't. *You can't.*' He cried these last words into the sky, then looked back at Thomas, pivoting his wrists in a way that could have been playful. 'You're in love with him. Or you were. I don't think it's love any more. You're just his slave now.'

Thomas felt a rush of fury, so strong and unexpected that it made him dizzy. The evening sky, the whole world, was like a suffocating coverlet trapping his anger and sadness.

'Luca. You're a child. You don't know a thing.'

'I know this. I can *see*.' Luca was gripping the rail with both hands. His trainers lifted a few inches into the air.

'Get down off there. Listen. This thing between you and me, it can't go on.'

Luca was seated up on the rail, balancing there, using his

fingertips to hold himself steady. 'Because of Claude? He's warned you off, hasn't he? Told you to cut with me.' He stared with parted lips.

'That's a lie.'

'All this time, I've been telling you about his grotesque power – and you're under it.' He raised his arms in the air, gripping a vertical railing with his shoes to maintain his balance.

'You're *lying*.' Thomas took a step towards the doorway.

'I don't think so.' Luca gazed back from his elevated perch. He was like a figure on a trapeze. 'You're a lie. Your life's a lie.'

The sense of entrapment broke. Thomas had the peculiar sensation – one he'd never experienced before, or never as strongly – of feelings rushing out of him, as if his lungs were expelling them. The massed emotions of years went out. A separate force, one that seemed to come from outside him, propelled him to the door. In that fraction of time, Luca's expression went blank.

Thomas flung out his hands and caught himself on the edges of the doorway. The momentum of his body pulsed in his hands. He realised, with delirious horror, that he would have hurled himself straight into Luca if he hadn't stopped.

But it didn't matter. Luca's eyes had turned large, like those of a boy in a cartoon. His hands were raised to stop Thomas and his mouth was open. He seemed to lean back lazily, then batted his hands. The sound of his cry came last of all, as his feet slid clear of the railing.

The song, which had been thudding quietly all this time, came to an end. Thomas was aware of the silence in the room. Beyond, there was nothing apart from the dull whistle of an aircraft, and then – somewhere closer – a car's horn, swelling a little and then dying. He put on his shoes, did up the buttons on his shirt, and checked himself in the mirror. As he left, he noticed Luca's phone lying next to the sound system. He took it, switched it off and dropped it in his pocket.

35

5 June, 20.35. New York

As she walked home, for no special reason, Lorna took a detour into Tribeca. Maybe it was that she wanted to see different streets – a different facet of the familiar city. And she had no reason to be home early.

A building was rising at the corner of Walker Street and Broadway. It was still a latticework of steel in its upper sections, but the first-floor windows were glazed and filled with light. Something was happening inside. People were crowding in the concrete interior.

Through the open door she could smell cigarette smoke. She went in. Most of the faces around her looked implausibly young. Their expressions – quick, alert, suspicious – disorientated her. Fluorescent strip lights hung down on chains. Music was playing. It sounded like a disco track from the rhythm, but the melody was lost in a swell of voices.

There was an ice bucket close to the door, filled with bottles of beer. She took one. Hovering near the bucket was a woman with a heavy fringe and a crocheted jersey. She was older than most of the crowd, maybe in her thirties, and was talking in a loud voice about Art Basel and an installation by Maurizio Cattelan.

'So predictable,' she was saying. 'So fucking predictable.'

So, this place was a gallery, at least for tonight, although Lorna couldn't see any art. She wondered how the news had escaped her. The art world was spinning faster than she could keep up with.

Everyone was moving to the centre of the room. She pushed her way close to the front until she saw an open space where a young girl with very short hair was standing. The girl's face was unmade-up. Her features were delicate and angular. She was draped from her neck down to her ankles in a fur coat. It looked like mink – a dark, monstrous pelt with an oily sheen. Underneath, she was wearing hard-edged leather boots. Beside her was a plain wooden chair, like a café chair, and a large amp with a cable that snaked across the floor.

The girl was standing erect and still. Suddenly the music was louder. An eighties song burst out, pulsing and synthesised. She began to dance. Raising her hands, she swivelled her arms and paced forward. Her staccato strut was accompanied by thrusting movements of the shoulders and a defiant upward tilt of the head. She came close to where the crowd was standing, then spun around and paced back, over to the other side of the clearing. She spun around once more, returned to the centre of the ring, and leapt onto the chair. Rising above the crowd, she flung out both arms, rotating her hands in time to the beat. The fur coat flared.

Someone whooped. A moment later, the crowd erupted in cheers and yells. The girl bounced on her planted feet, bending her legs by timed degrees until she was crouching, the coat tumbling over the edges of the chair. Her face broke into a smile. There was a slight gap between her front teeth. Lorna felt the drumbeats passing through her.

The music cut out. The girl had flung away the coat to reveal a white vest and drainpipe jeans. Her eyes bore straight through the crowd, through the room, out to the street. She jumped to the ground. With one hand she gripped the back of the chair and flipped it upside down. She held the chair in the air. A second later, she'd hurled it on the floor. It clattered like a gun going off, bouncing into the crowd. People jumped back. A man cursed.

The girl leapt after the chair and picked it up with both hands. For an instant, her gaze landed on Lorna. She seemed to shrug – it was a subtle motion of the eyebrows more than of the shoulders – and then marched with the chair towards the entrance. People stepped back to make way. Someone tripped.

A few feet from the window, the girl stopped, rolled on her heels, and with all her strength, flung the chair into the glass. It bounced off and struck the ground, somersaulting over.

'Fucking *yeah*,' someone cried.

The girl retrieved the chair and hurled it again at the glass, this time with a scream that made Lorna bite her lip. The girl lifted a booted foot and slammed it into the window. The glass wobbled slightly.

Someone tried to grab her. She pulled away. Sweat was shining on her forehead. She ran back to where the chair had landed. This time, she propelled it straight into the crowd. Lorna heard screams. Turning, she saw a woman's face. It was the woman with the fringe and the knitwear. Blood was running across her cheek, pooling messily around her lips, staining her teeth.

*

Still clutching her beer, Lorna walked to the next block. She drank several gulps, wondering if the alcohol would jump-start a response.

She sensed somebody standing behind her. It was the girl – the performer. Lorna felt her eyes open wider. The girl was watching her, calm now.

'Hi.'

'Hi,' Lorna replied.

'I'm Em.'

'We've met before. You were trying to break my gallery window, just like you were trying in there. Does it ever work?'

'Not in this part of town.'

Lorna chucked her beer bottle into the road. It smashed with a dull clink.

'I guess that would have been something,' she said. 'If the whole window had shattered.'

Em watched as the last of the beer streamed into the gutter. 'I knew it wouldn't.' She looked around at the buildings and released a long, staggering breath. 'I'm done. Want to take a walk?'

Lorna followed her gaze to the cathedral pinnacle of the Woolworth Building. The sky was clear and practically dark. Lamps were casting a glow along the sidewalks.

'Sure.'

They began on a northward course. For some time, neither of them spoke. They walked with leisurely intent. Every so often, their hands brushed.

'Where's home?' said Lorna. 'Which way are we walking?'

'Home is nowhere right now. It's all over the city.'

'And your parents?' Lorna hated how the question sounded. Prim, like a question a parent would ask. 'I'm sorry, you're not a kid. And it's none of my business.'

'It's okay. They're a long way from here. I moved. I got out in the world.'

'I never spoke to my parents after coming to New York,' Lorna told her. 'It's like I've always been an orphan in this city.'

After a long time, they came to the East Village, where the streets all seemed deserted, the houses closed up. Lorna had a deep, stirring sense of closeness to this girl about whom she knew nothing, coupled with a twinging sadness. The empty street seemed to exist inside her as well as around her. Their feet kept time, and for a brief moment she felt herself stepping – lightly, as if on tiptoes – over the years of her life.

They walked all the way to her house, as she had known they would. As they scaled the steps and crossed the threshold, she wondered if they would stay up half the night and drink and talk, but almost at once – by mutual assent, with hardly a word exchanged – they went upstairs and undressed.

The room was dark. Lorna didn't switch on the light. They held each other tight in the silence. Lorna felt the girl's mouth on her own. Their bodies touched at different points like wires crossing. Her fingertips slid down a back that was smooth and wet with perspiration in its middle groove, then descended to the deeper groove below. Their mouths separated. Lorna felt Em's hand repeating the movement down her own back, more insistently. Fingers were moving under her, into her. Their short sighs mixed together. They kissed again. With slow, relenting motions they lay down.

*

6 June, 06.55. New York

They had been lying awake, their legs interconnected beneath the duvet, for close to an hour. Daylight was shimmering in the gap between the curtains.

'What I don't get is *why*,' Lorna said. 'Why did you throw it in her face?'

Em stretched her arms high above her head. The duvet pulled away from her, revealing her shoulders and chest.

'Why does anyone do anything? Why should I explain?' She looked into Lorna's eyes and flung her arms back down. 'I'm an artist. Not *your* type of artist.'

'What's my type of artist?'

'Oh, *you* know.' Em drew her fingertips over Lorna's shoulder and neck, skimming the edge of her throat. 'One day, Lorna Bedford, I'll come to your gallery and do a performance. I'll drag a block of lead across the floor, pulling it on ropes, screaming my head off. Then I'll melt it in a furnace, and everyone will get fucked up on the fumes, and I'll throw liquid metal in the face of every asshole who's come to watch.'

'You'd poison yourself with the fumes.'

'I'd be wearing a gasmask. And nothing else. Picture it.'

Em slid her hands beneath her head. Lorna propped herself up and looked at the girl's sculpted arms, the armpits with their patches of bristle.

'Maybe that *is* my type of art,' Lorna said. 'Or are you just trying to turn me on?'

She lay back down next to Em, and found herself in a strange place between bewilderment and pleasure.

'Maybe you should, though,' she said.

'Should what?'

'Do a show with us, at my gallery.'

'Are you serious?'

'We have a gap in the programme this summer.'

'You need to know: nothing I make has a point. Not one I could put into words. Or a value . . . And nothing is ever finished. Not really. I'm never satisfied. Making art is like sex, like desire.'

'How does that figure?'

'You can never catch hold of the thing you want.'

'Haven't you caught hold of me?'

Em climbed on top of Lorna and took hold of both her hands, pinning them against the pillows. 'Not all of you. That's what I'm trying to say.'

She kissed Lorna.

They lay together for a while, not speaking. Lorna thought of her obsessive belief that Luca was her son, and then of her actual son, wherever he was. She looked through the gap in the curtains.

With a nimble kick, Em propelled the duvet to the bottom of the bed, revealing Lorna's nakedness to the light. She watched Lorna – scanned her entire body – with tender interest. Lorna felt the tracking motion of her eyes.

'Why don't you play hooky today? Stay with me. We could – I don't know – go to the beach. Anything you want.'

Lorna turned to face her. She smiled as she allowed her gaze to dwell on Em's eyes, on her features, on her body. She glanced back through the window at the sky, feeling its heat and promise. Beneath, the leaves of a tree were a magic lantern of green shades. They would fall in a few months, but for now . . . She sat up, resting on the edge of the bed, and looked at Em.

*

On the train back, she studied the scratched glass of the windows, and beyond, the reeling views of the Bronx. The hours of sunlight had made her drowsy. Beside her, Em had stopped talking. Lorna turned and saw that the girl had fallen asleep. Slowly, Em's head tilted towards her, coming to rest on her shoulder. They plunged underground. Lorna watched the two of them in the darkness of the window opposite, until she too began to sleep.

Then, out of nowhere, Em was standing, holding Lorna by the shoulders, gripping her tight, looking straight at her. They had come to 125th Street.

'I'll call,' she said.

The train doors closed behind her. Lorna tried to catch sight of her through the window, but the platform was busy with homeward commuters. The train moved into a tunnel. She fought to keep hold of the image of the girl's face and the events of the day. Already a stranger had taken the seat beside her. She continued for two stops before getting off. The subway had been taking her too quickly away from where she'd been. She wanted to make time stand still, at least for a bit.

After surfacing, she walked into Central Park. The gentle warmth and the new leaves on the American elms produced a queasy, deep-down feeling in her. She thought of a time, on mornings long ago, when she'd walked through Manhattan to go to work. Back then, the beauty of the park had been enough.

Ahead of her on the path, a little girl was riding a bike – approaching at speed. The girl couldn't have been more than four years old. She swung the handlebars one way and then the other, veering wildly, then fell to the ground. The bike clattered onto its side and the wheels spun.

Lorna stood still. There were no adults in sight, although someone – a parent – was surely there beyond the curve of the path. The child's eyes met hers, shining with tears. But the anticipated flood didn't come. Was it the coincidence of their gazes that did it – the child's realisation that she had an audience in this unreacting stranger? Lorna wondered if she were witnessing one of those small pivotal moments of childhood: the moment at which the girl's view of herself would adjust, in an irreversible way, to take account of how others saw her. All thanks to the presence of a tired-looking woman who was walking alone, playing truant.

She walked on with an inward smile. It was pure vanity to think so.

At the edge of the park, not far from the Museum of Natural History, was a single-storey pavilion with a zinc dome. She went inside. The lobby of the Lucinda Villa was empty except for a young man who sat at the ticket desk. The glass double doors into the gallery were blacked out. The Lucinda was between shows, she guessed – closed to visitors. A side door led into the gallery's bookshop, which was also practically empty. A man in a trench coat was bending over one of the tables, holding a book and giving out intermittent snorting laughs.

She looked at the shelves of art magazines. All of them were there, the big-hitters and the small-timers. The *Fire Island Review* was poking out of one slot. The cover of *Artforum* consisted of a black and white film still from *Privilege* by Yvonne Rainer: a woman in a black sparkling jacket embracing a man in a suit (the man's face invisible to the camera). Justine had loved that film: she had wanted it to have a room of its own in the private museum she'd imagined for them. Lorna lifted the magazine from its slot and felt it flop open in her hands. She turned over a few pages and saw a double-page advertisement that made her pause. It was a panoramic photograph of a room. A pristine room, white as a laboratory. Mirrored panels the size of large windows were propped around the walls, each one a different colour.

Text floated across the top of the image, to one side.

Thomas Haller: Mirror Paintings
Galerie Claude Berlins, Hong Kong

The room in the photograph was a workshop or factory. A small forklift truck was parked to one side of the shot. Close by was a piece of high-tech machinery that looked like an oversized flatbed printer, with a raised gantry running along one end. Lying on its top surface was another sheet of glass, coloured a brilliant mid-blue. Each of the panels around the walls was a distinct shade, pink or green or golden-yellow.

Thomas's new works were mirrors, not paintings. By some trick of surface contouring, their reflections swerved between accurate images (she could see the edge of the forklift truck in one of them) and swimming distortion. Sections of each panel had been depressed or domed just enough to throw the image into disorder.

It was horrifying, in a banal way: Thomas's art transformed into an image of itself, plasticated and rote. These were pastiches of his earlier paintings. Factory-made pastiches – the machine, she guessed, was a laser cutter – and this was the factory, some place in Zürich that specialised in fabrication. Thomas probably hadn't even set foot in it. He would see the objects for the first time in Hong Kong. It seemed like the final stage in Claude's takeover. She found herself breathing deeply. Was this an atone-

ment for Venice? A punishment? Either way, she knew – as she
held the magazine – that she wouldn't go to Hong Kong.

'I almost didn't recognise you,' said a voice she knew.

She turned. Fritz Schein was standing beside her. He wasn't
wearing his glasses. It made him look different – younger or
older. She wasn't sure which.

'What are you doing here?' she said.

'I work here, remember? I don't think I've ever seen you with
wet hair.'

'I went swimming.'

He looked down at the magazine in her hands. 'A new direction, no?'

'A dead end, more like. But they'll sell.'

'Oh, sure. It's art for narcissists – literally.' Fritz erupted in
his usual laughter, then stalled himself, as if remembering something.

'I've been wanting to ask you, Fritz—'

He nodded her on.

'Why were you so secretive about acquiring that painting for
Leo? The Haller painting from the London show. Why did you
let Leo think I'd negotiated the sale?'

He ran a finger inside the neck of his T-shirt, around the
velvet collar of his jacket. He seemed to be considering how to
answer.

'I was under instruction never to communicate with Berlins.
If Leo had ever found out, he would have cast me out – left me
with nothing. Leo hated Claude.' He glanced back and forth
along the ranks of magazines. 'The problem was, that painting
was like a talisman to him. It reminded him of Deborah. The
obsession was going to drive him mad – Bonita could tell. I had
to find a way of obtaining it for him, and I knew that Claude
would never sell via you, the way Leo hoped. So, I made out to
Claude that I was acting for a private client – that mad old film
star who was at the London opening, with the ropes of pearls.

She was happy to play along. And I set up a shell company to purchase the work—'

'Equitone.'

'Yes. That was a little reference to Deborah. She loved esoteric things . . . You see, I had a deeper loyalty – to Deborah, to the collection. I had to circumvent Leo's hatred.'

Lorna closed the magazine and placed it back on the shelf. 'Will there be a memorial?'

'There was talk of something at St Patrick's Cathedral. But who would go? He was entirely alone by the end. It was just him and Bonita and the art . . . and me.' He sighed through his teeth. 'You know what he always called me? *Fritzie*. He was the only person who called me that.'

'He told me that he and Deborah were like parents to you, when you first came to America.'

'It was Deborah, really.' His expression had changed, grown boyish. 'I have this vision of her from the night we first met. A small woman in a velvet jacket and matching dress. To look at her, you would have written her off as another rich socialite. But when she spoke, when she looked at you, she made you feel like you were her one object of fascination.'

'I can believe it. I saw an amazing old photo of her the other day.'

'I used to go round to the Goffmans' every few weeks, for their regular soirées. This was when they lived on the Upper East Side. I kept going until Deborah's death – 2003. The parties stopped after that.' He rocked himself gently on his heels, apparently lost in memory. 'Deborah used to call me her son. It was kind of a joke, except—'

'She meant it.'

He fixed her with the same enquiring look. 'She and I shared something that Leo wasn't part of, could never be part of. I guess I was like a messenger god, to her. She wanted to know all about my other life – you know, the discos, the sex, the *excess.*' He laughed to himself. 'It was all so different from her fundraising parties on Park Avenue. Deborah was the picture of elegance and restraint. Who could blame her for finding enchantment in the opposite? Once, when Leo was away, I took her to a costume party. She wore this incredible fur coat on the dance floor . . .' His words spun out.

They walked together into the lobby. Sunlight was falling through the entrance in a long triangle. Lorna could hear children playing outside.

'Did you know that the Goffmans had a daughter? A little girl who died in '84.'

Fritz turned to her, all trace of his smile gone. 'Bonita told you.'

'Yes.'

'It was in the papers at the time, but news could be made to disappear back then. Leo refused to talk about it with anyone, including Deborah. That's how he survived, I guess.'

'And Deborah – how did she survive?'

He breathed out at length. 'I don't believe she ever forgave him.'

'Who does that? Anything you don't like, or can't deal with, you just eradicate it from your mind.'

'Rich people do it a lot. I guess everyone does it to some degree. Leo was an extreme case.'

'A pathological case.'

She thought again of the smiling woman in *Vanity Fair*.

'I didn't like Leo early on,' Fritz said, after a while. 'I couldn't understand how he had come to be this towering success. I thought he was a bully and a blowhard. Then I saw that it's possible to make people – some people, anyway – think of you in a certain way. The trick is to think of yourself that way first.'

'And that's what you've done?'

She'd verbalised the question before she could stop herself, but Fritz just smiled.

'I'm sorry,' she said. 'For Leo, I mean. The way it all ended.'

'He had a long life. He was eighty-six. It had to happen.'

'What happens to the collection? I heard he'd been talking to Christie's and Sotheby's about a sale.'

'That was all talk. A way of spending his days. There were no instructions for the collection in his will. And I'm the sole executor – Deborah saw to that.'

'What will you do?'

'What I always wanted to. Create a museum. I've been at the Lucinda too long. This'll be like a new Guggenheim in Harlem. A place without budgets or committees or boards of trustees.' He held out his palms and looked to the ceiling. Then, with a tilt of his head, he indicated the door to the main gallery – a large rotunda space. 'Have you seen our latest show?'

'Not yet. I thought you were closed. What is it?'

He smiled oddly. 'People will say I'm an egomaniac. They're already saying it. *All surface, no depth*. But that's where I exist: on the hard, bright surface. It's where most of us exist. Except for you, Lorna. You're better than that.'

'I'm not better than anyone.'

He brushed her shoulder with his hand. 'You are, though.'

As he left, she had the strange sensation again of seeing a man she didn't know in the guise of one she did.

*

The lights inside the gallery were off. The large room seemed to be empty, but it was too dark to be sure. Projected across one wall at cinematic scale was a video of bodies cast in purple light. It was Fritz's iPhone video of the Serpentine summer party last year. The sound came in erratic waves, distorted beyond recognition. Lorna's vision synched with the veering camera. The scale of the projection made the bodies appear life-size, but the frame rate had been slowed very slightly so that they moved with a not-quite-real languor.

She saw Joel Blair at the heart of the crowd, tossing back his head and lifting a counselling finger. She saw Carter Daily – revealed by a parting of bodies – looking nervous and distracted. Everyone emitted the same violet radiance; it mingled with their perspiration and the wetness of their eyeballs. The thing was like a dream. An imitation of life, but luridly vivid. She took a few steps closer to the projection. The camera swung abruptly and Sylvia Rosso was in the centre of the shot, reacting to someone who stood out of view. Her laughter erupted as a heaving, screeching noise. Claude Berlins strode into view. His silver hair emitted an alien sheen. He and Sylvia began to dance, clasping hands. The crowd withdrew as people watched. The music refracted into a tuneless blare that made their jiving movements seem deranged.

Lorna felt as if she were underwater with her eyes wide open. The camera swung away. She half expected to see an image of herself in the video, amid the crowd, but instead she saw Thomas. He was in the corner of the shot. He seemed to be alone, absorbed in thought. Then the camera jolted and she saw that he was speaking – murmuring almost imperceptibly – to a young man. It took her a second or two to recognise Luca. He looked the same as in the photographs. He was listening to Thomas with an attuned expression. As Thomas spoke, Luca's face broke into a grin. His handsomeness, which was also a sort of prettiness, made her shiver. She kept watching the two of them, there at the leftmost edge of the frame, at the periphery of the party. The crowd was reshaping itself. Other figures began to obscure them, but for a second longer she could see their two faces coming close, almost touching, before the camera swerved.

Acknowledgements

I wish to thank my editors, Ansa Khan Khattak and Juliet Brooke, for their invaluable guidance and insights at every stage. I am grateful to the friends who read early versions of the novel: Ruth Allen, Samuel Hodder, Matthew Ingleby, Iain Ross, and Richard Shone. For their advice on specific aspects of the plot – whether medical, legal, or erotic – thank you to Tom Cahill and Charlotte Brierley, Mark Norbury, Hugh Monk, Meg Utterback, Aaron Wolfson, and Annette Yeo; and to Patrick and Frances Cahill for their help in countless ways. More than anyone, my husband Alexander has encouraged and suffered the writing of this book: without him, it couldn't have been written. I remain hugely grateful to Louise Court, Holly Knox, and the entire team at Sceptre. Above all, I want to thank my agent, Isobel Dixon, for her enduring support and her belief in my writing.